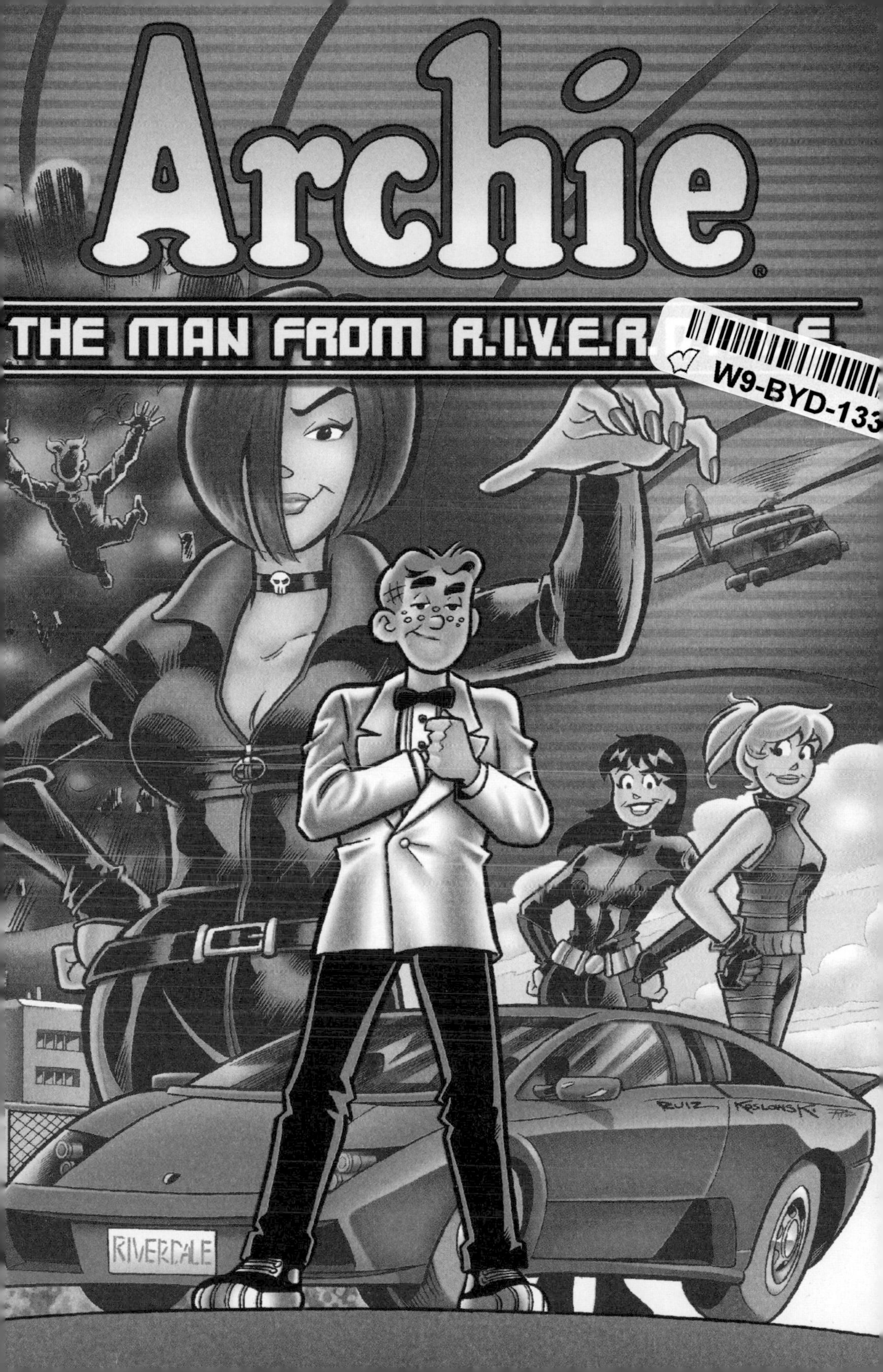
Archie®
THE MAN FROM R.I.V.E.R.
RIVERDALE
RUIZ KOSLOWSKI

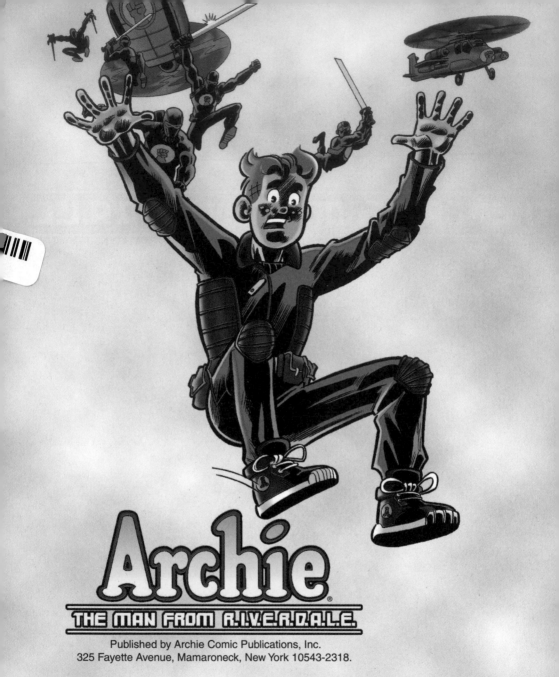

Archie

THE MAN FROM R.I.V.E.R.D.A.L.E.

Published by Archie Comic Publications, Inc.
325 Fayette Avenue, Mamaroneck, New York 10543-2318.

ArchieComics.com

ISBN-13: 978-1-879794-68-9

10 9 8 7 6 5 4 3 2 1
Printed in U.S.A.

Archie®

THE MAN FROM R.I.V.E.R.D.A.L.E.

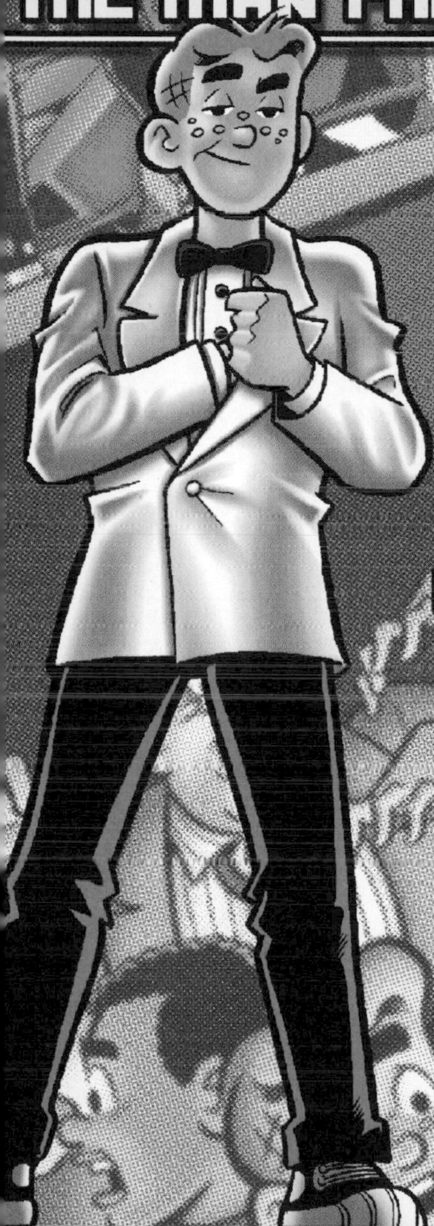

WRITTEN BY
TOM DEFALCO

PENCILED BY
FERNANDO RUIZ

INKED BY
RICH KOSLOWSKI

LETTERED BY
JACK MORELLI

COLORED BY
TOM CHU

Co-CEO: Jon Goldwater, Co-CEO: Nancy Silberkleit, President: Mike Pellerito, Co-President/Editor-In-Chief: Victor Gorelick, Director of Circulation: Bill Horan, Executive Director of Publishing/Operations: Harold Buchholz, Executive Director of Publicity & Marketing: Alex Segura, Project Coordinator: Joe Morciglio, Production Manager: Stephen Oswald, Production: Jon Gray & Duncan McLachlan

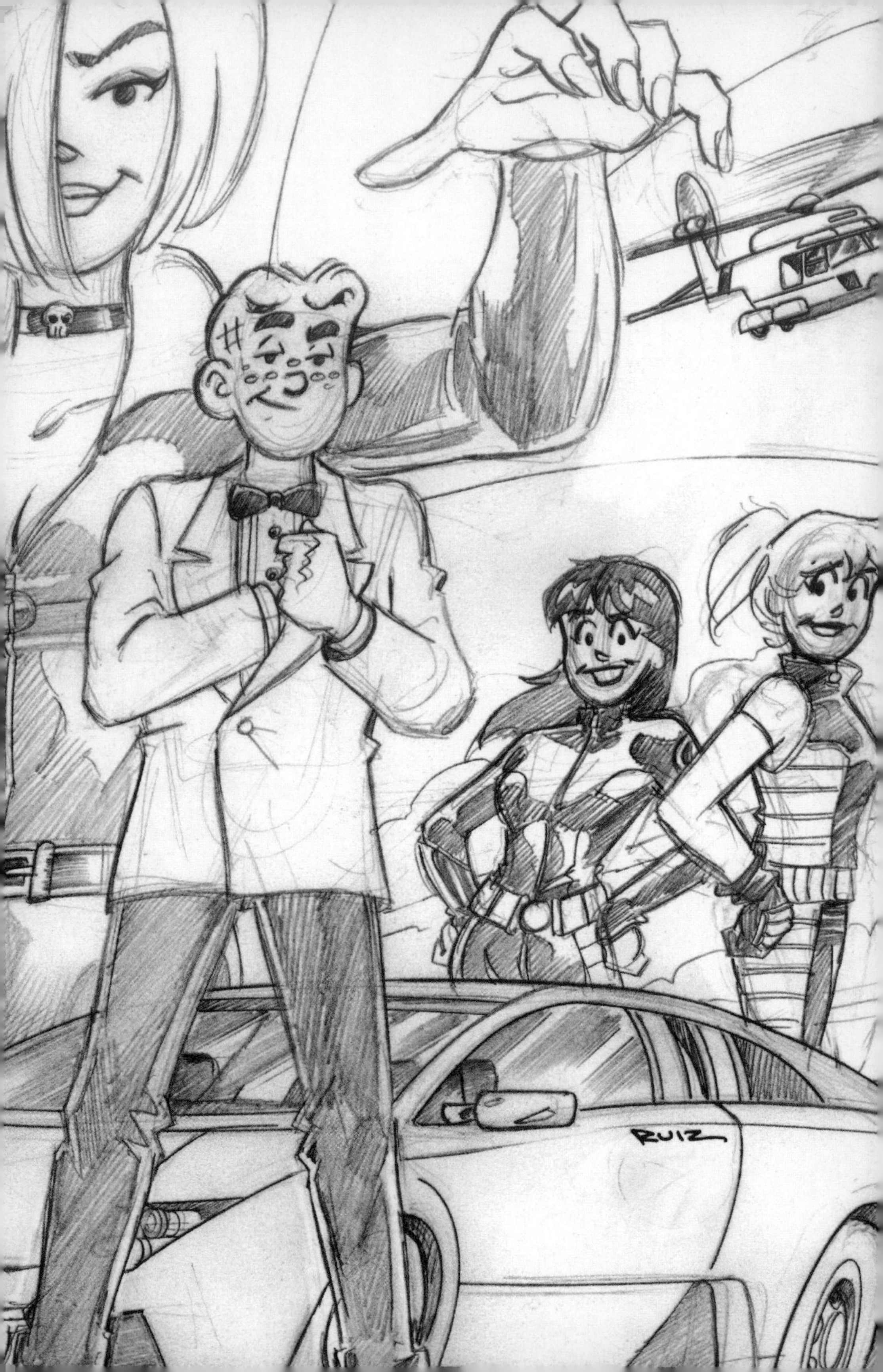
RUIZ

MISSION 1: THE BLACKEST (AND BLUEST) DAY

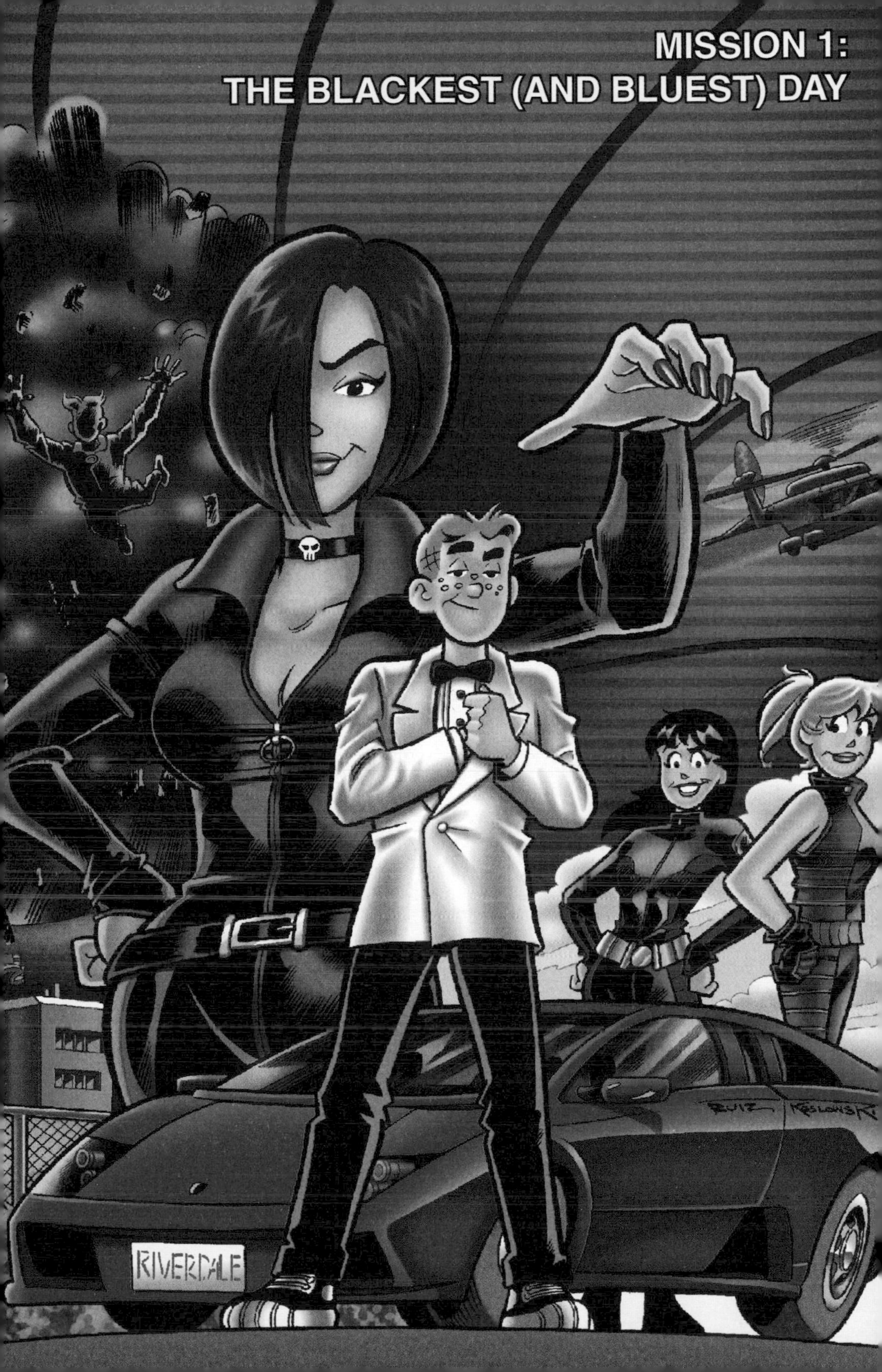

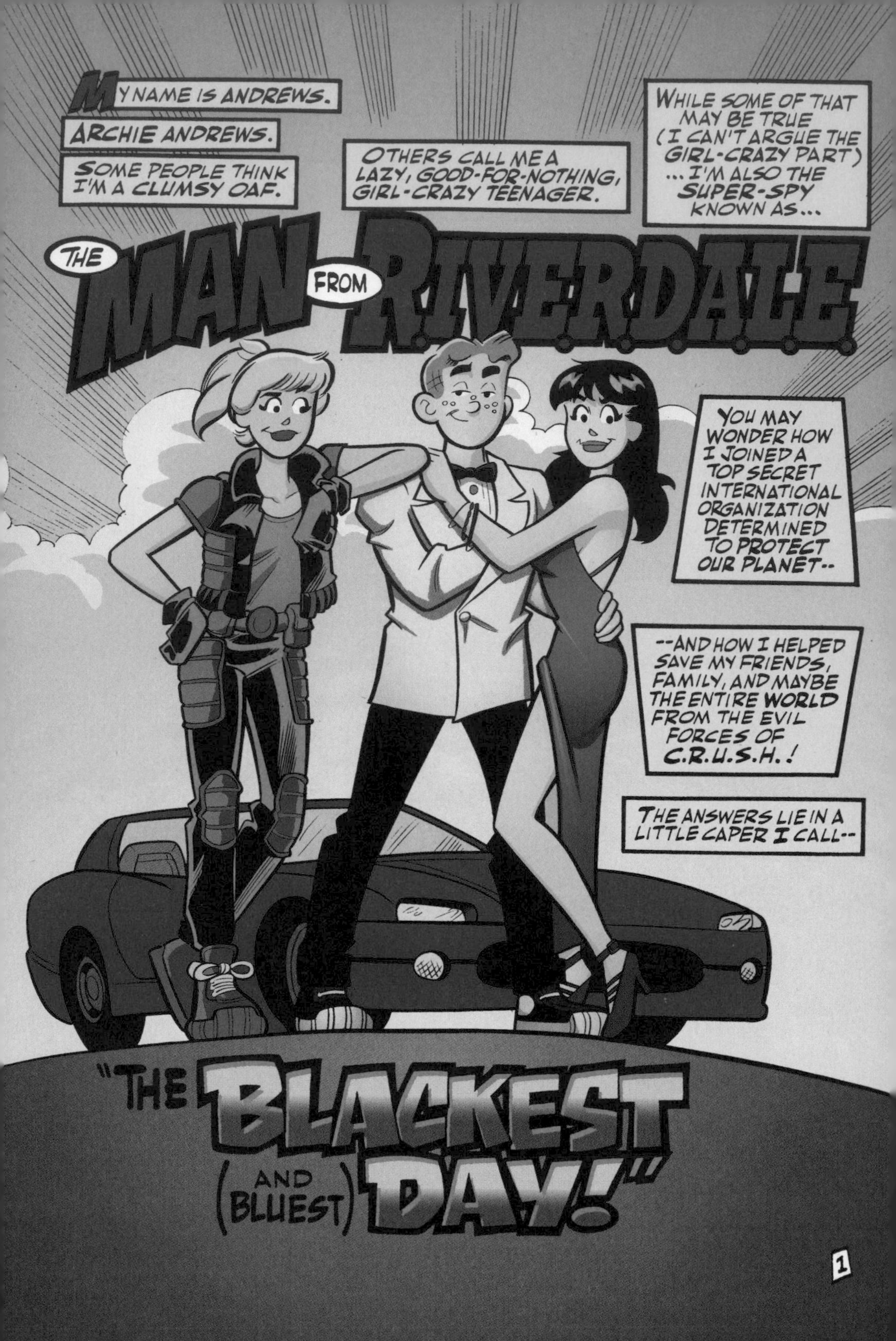
MY NAME IS ANDREWS.
ARCHIE ANDREWS.
SOME PEOPLE THINK I'M A CLUMSY OAF.
OTHERS CALL ME A LAZY, GOOD-FOR-NOTHING, GIRL-CRAZY TEENAGER.
WHILE SOME OF THAT MAY BE TRUE (I CAN'T ARGUE THE GIRL-CRAZY PART) ...I'M ALSO THE SUPER-SPY KNOWN AS...
THE MAN FROM R.I.V.E.R.D.A.L.E.
YOU MAY WONDER HOW I JOINED A TOP SECRET INTERNATIONAL ORGANIZATION DETERMINED TO PROTECT OUR PLANET--
--AND HOW I HELPED SAVE MY FRIENDS, FAMILY, AND MAYBE THE ENTIRE WORLD FROM THE EVIL FORCES OF C.R.U.S.H.!
THE ANSWERS LIE IN A LITTLE CAPER I CALL--
"THE BLACKEST (AND BLUEST) DAY!"

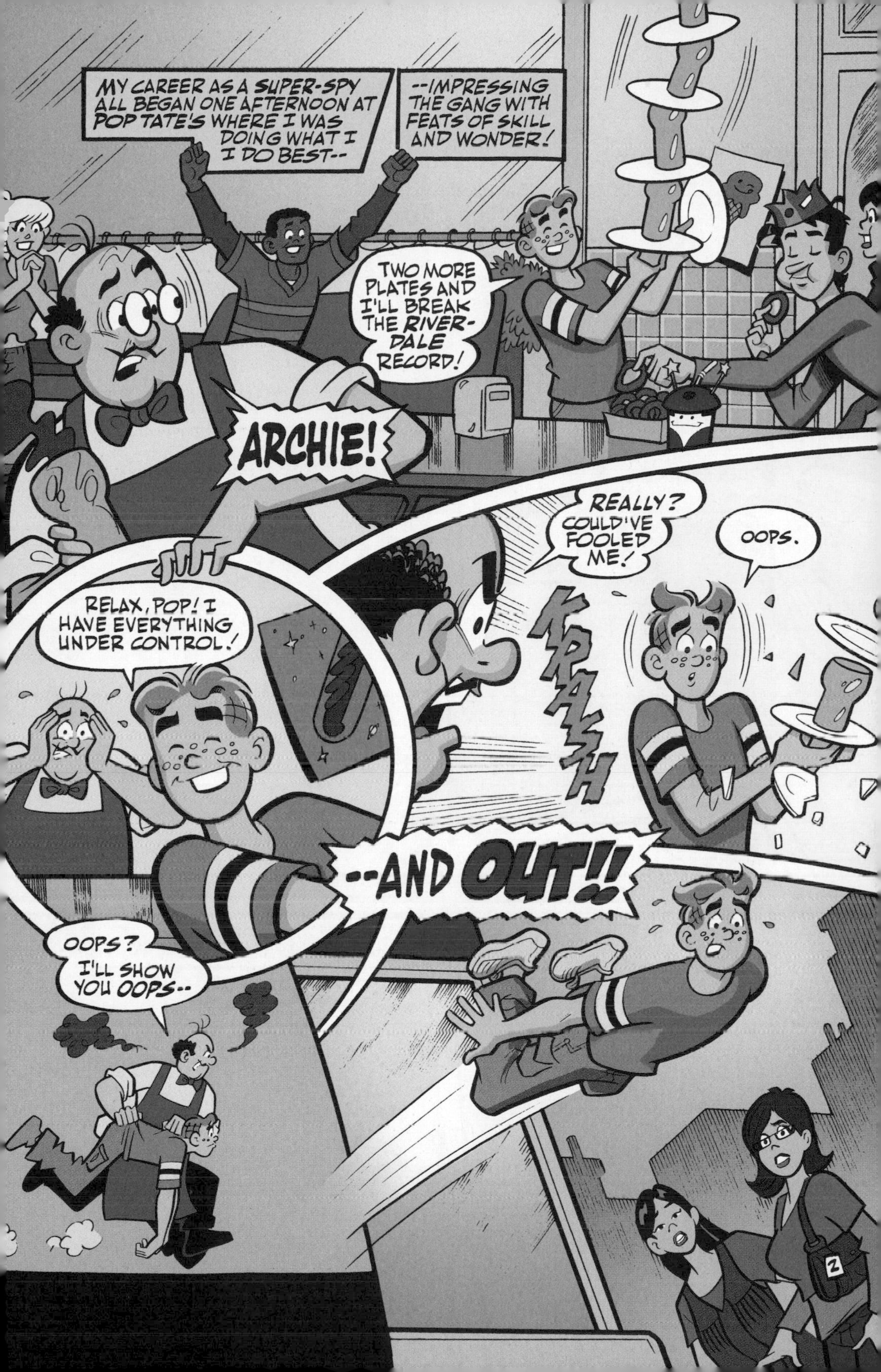
MY CAREER AS A SUPER-SPY ALL BEGAN ONE AFTERNOON AT POP TATE'S WHERE I WAS DOING WHAT I I DO BEST--
--IMPRESSING THE GANG WITH FEATS OF SKILL AND WONDER!
TWO MORE PLATES AND I'LL BREAK THE RIVERDALE RECORD!
ARCHIE!
RELAX, POP! I HAVE EVERYTHING UNDER CONTROL!
REALLY? COULD'VE FOOLED ME!
KRASH
OOPS.
OOPS? I'LL SHOW YOU OOPS--
--AND OUT!!

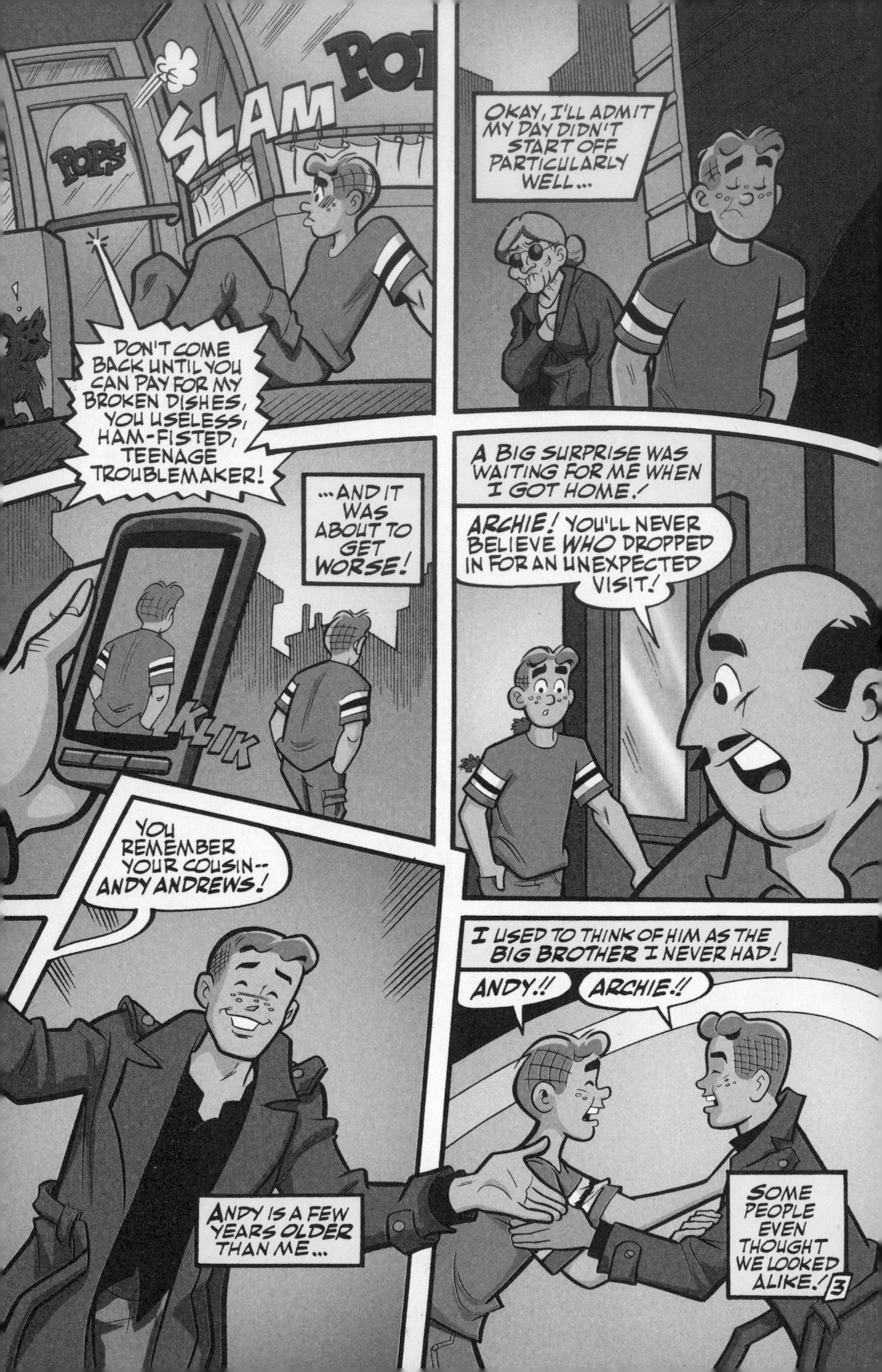
SLAM
POP'S
POP'S
DON'T COME BACK UNTIL YOU CAN PAY FOR MY BROKEN DISHES, YOU USELESS, HAM-FISTED, TEENAGE TROUBLEMAKER!
OKAY, I'LL ADMIT MY DAY DIDN'T START OFF PARTICULARLY WELL...
...AND IT WAS ABOUT TO GET WORSE!
KLIK
A BIG SURPRISE WAS WAITING FOR ME WHEN I GOT HOME.!
ARCHIE! YOU'LL NEVER BELIEVE WHO DROPPED IN FOR AN UNEXPECTED VISIT!
YOU REMEMBER YOUR COUSIN-- ANDY ANDREWS!
ANDY IS A FEW YEARS OLDER THAN ME...
I USED TO THINK OF HIM AS THE BIG BROTHER I NEVER HAD!
ANDY.!!
ARCHIE.!!
SOME PEOPLE EVEN THOUGHT WE LOOKED ALIKE.!
3

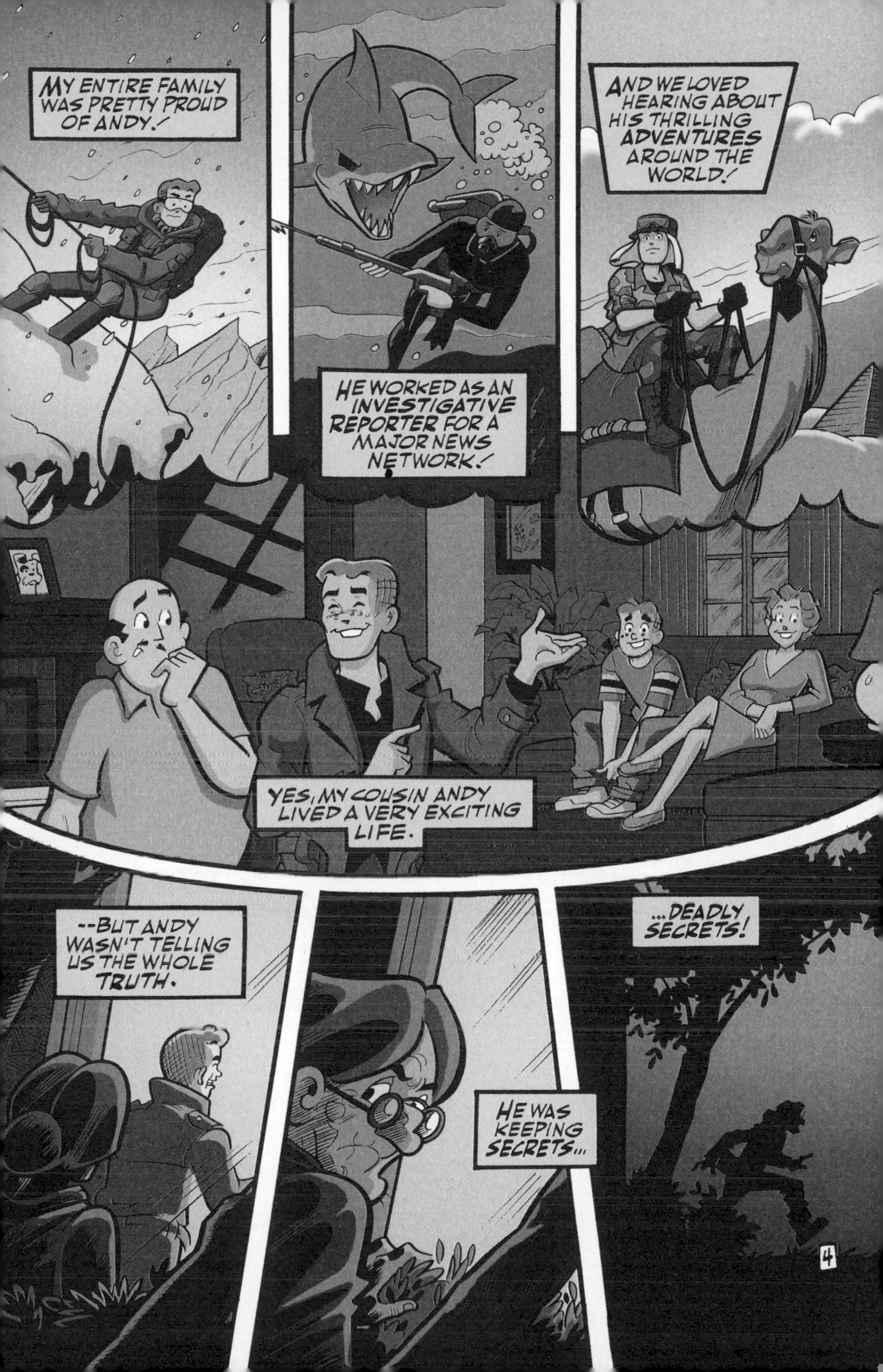
MY ENTIRE FAMILY WAS PRETTY PROUD OF ANDY!
HE WORKED AS AN INVESTIGATIVE REPORTER FOR A MAJOR NEWS NETWORK!
AND WE LOVED HEARING ABOUT HIS THRILLING ADVENTURES AROUND THE WORLD!
YES, MY COUSIN ANDY LIVED A VERY EXCITING LIFE.
--BUT ANDY WASN'T TELLING US THE WHOLE TRUTH.
HE WAS KEEPING SECRETS...
...DEADLY SECRETS!

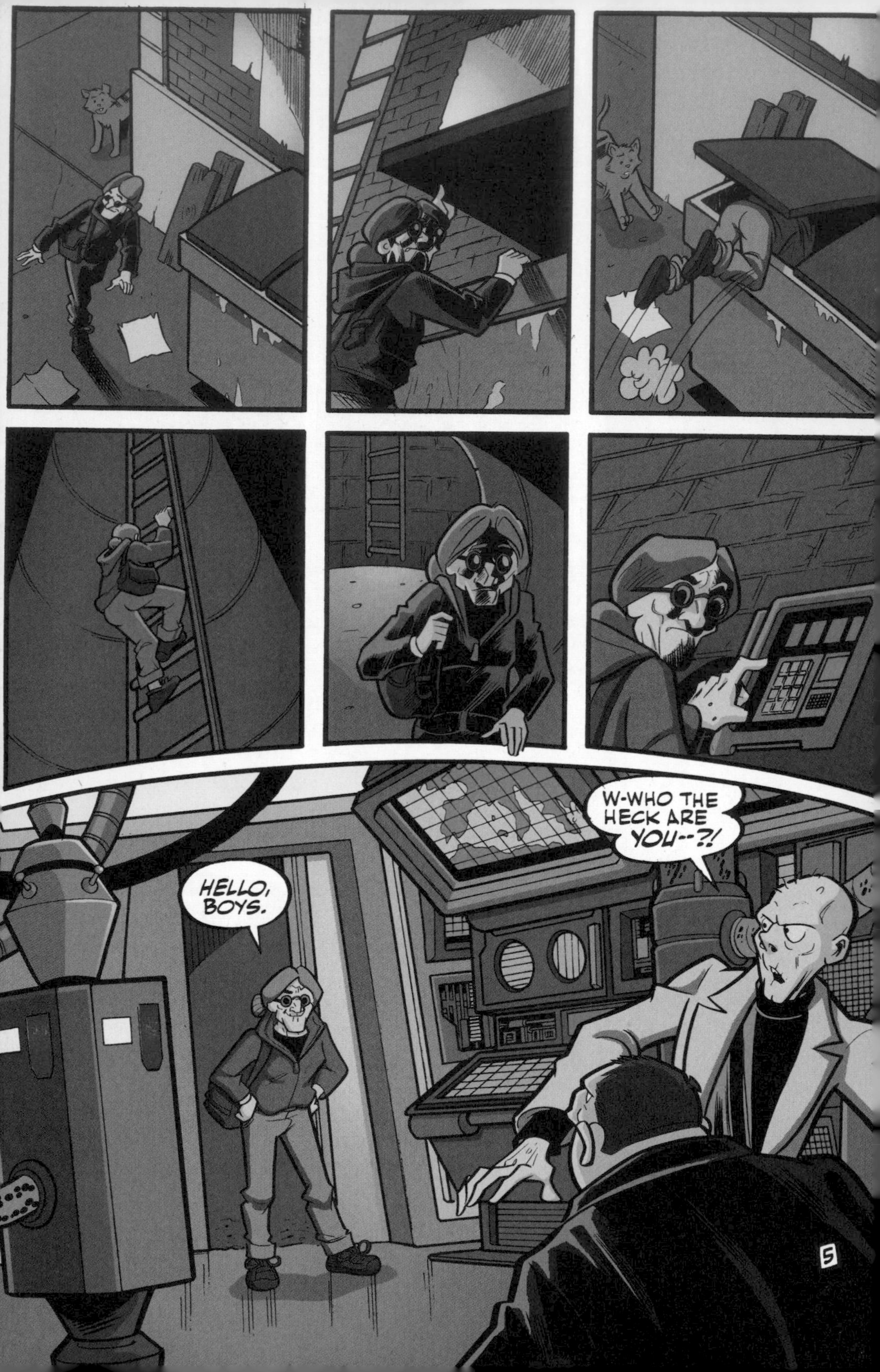
HELLO, BOYS.
W-WHO THE HECK ARE YOU--?!
5

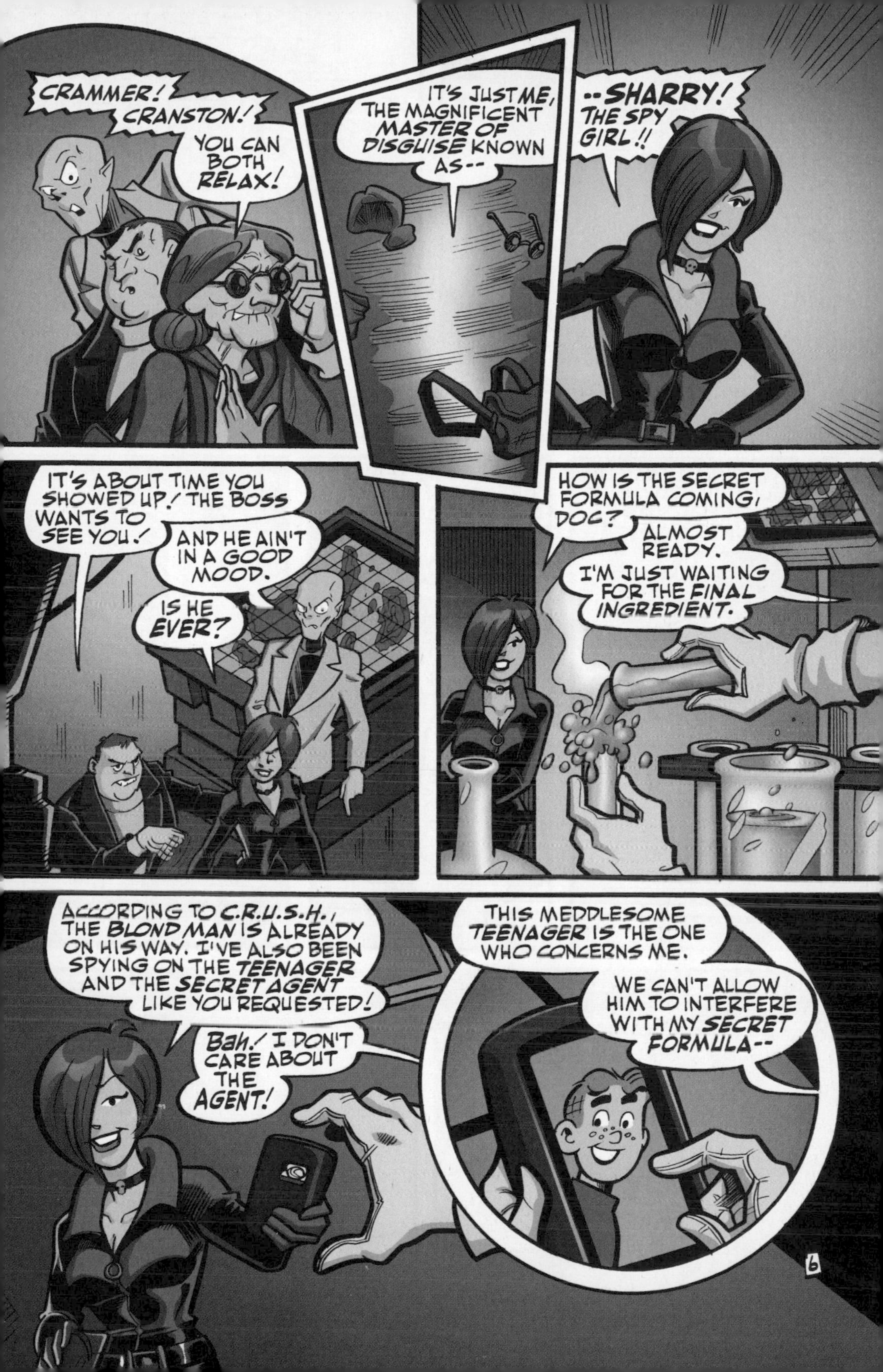
CRAMMER! CRANSTON!
YOU CAN BOTH RELAX!
IT'S JUST ME, THE MAGNIFICENT MASTER OF DISGUISE KNOWN AS--
--SHARRY! THE SPY GIRL!!
IT'S ABOUT TIME YOU SHOWED UP! THE BOSS WANTS TO SEE YOU!
AND HE AIN'T IN A GOOD MOOD.
IS HE EVER?
HOW IS THE SECRET FORMULA COMING, DOC?
ALMOST READY.
I'M JUST WAITING FOR THE FINAL INGREDIENT.
ACCORDING TO C.R.U.S.H., THE BLOND MAN IS ALREADY ON HIS WAY. I'VE ALSO BEEN SPYING ON THE TEENAGER AND THE SECRET AGENT LIKE YOU REQUESTED!
Bah! I DON'T CARE ABOUT THE AGENT!
THIS MEDDLESOME TEENAGER IS THE ONE WHO CONCERNS ME.
WE CAN'T ALLOW HIM TO INTERFERE WITH MY SECRET FORMULA--
6

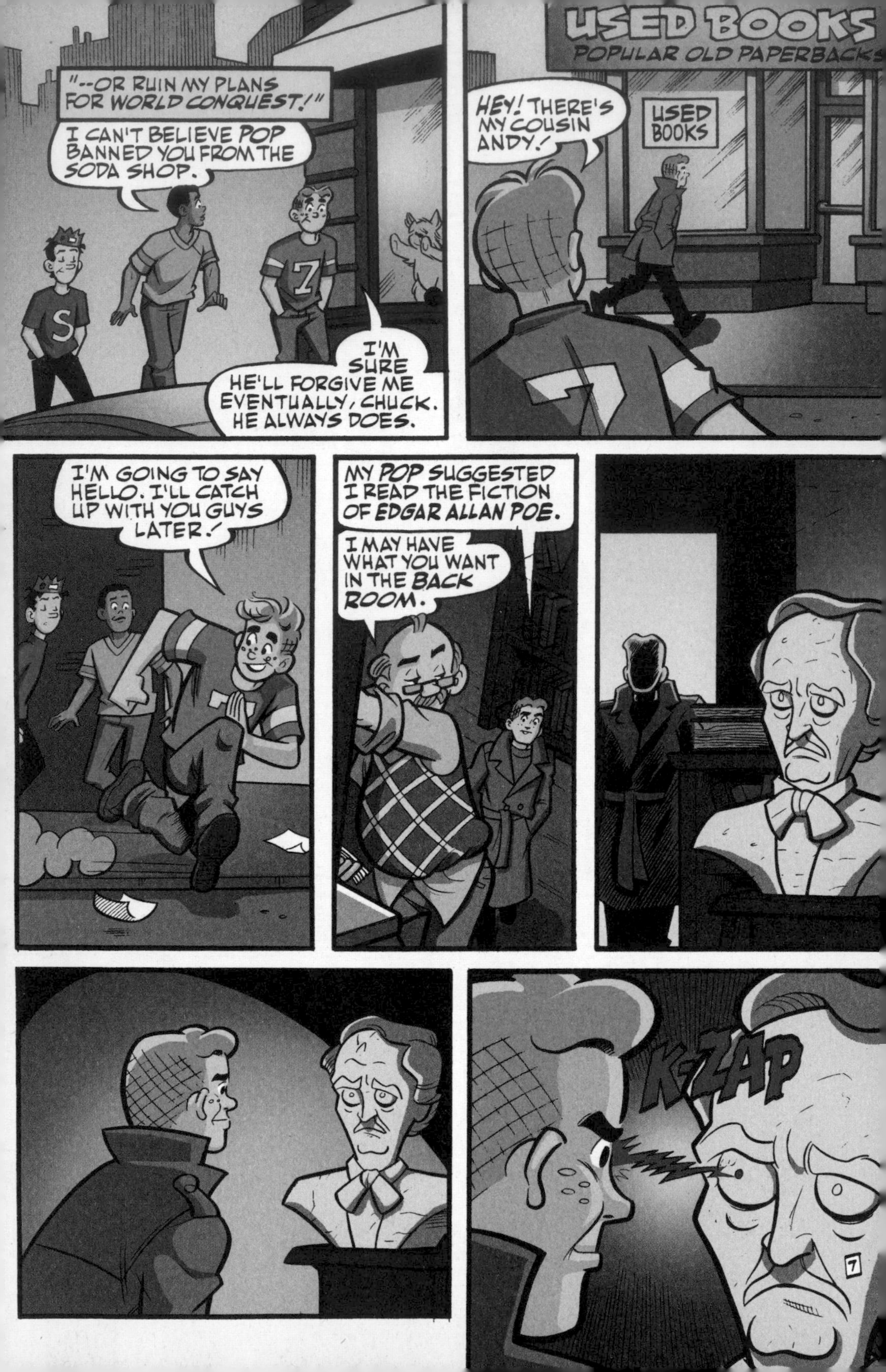
"--OR RUIN MY PLANS FOR WORLD CONQUEST!"
I CAN'T BELIEVE POP BANNED YOU FROM THE SODA SHOP.
I'M SURE HE'LL FORGIVE ME EVENTUALLY, CHUCK. HE ALWAYS DOES.
USED BOOKS
POPULAR OLD PAPERBACKS
HEY! THERE'S MY COUSIN ANDY!
USED BOOKS
I'M GOING TO SAY HELLO. I'LL CATCH UP WITH YOU GUYS LATER!
MY POP SUGGESTED I READ THE FICTION OF EDGAR ALLAN POE.
I MAY HAVE WHAT YOU WANT IN THE BACK ROOM.
K-ZAP
7

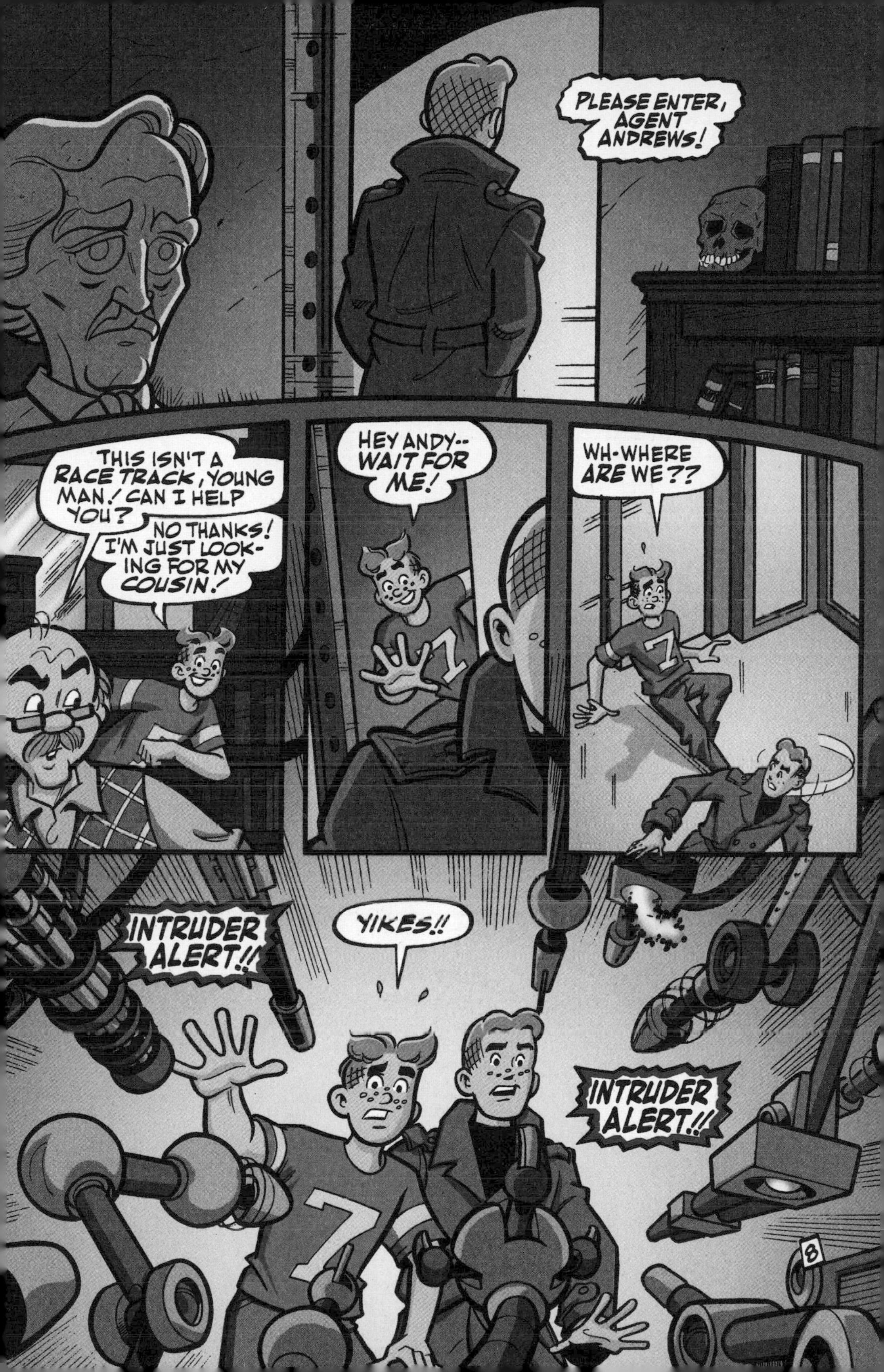
PLEASE ENTER, AGENT ANDREWS!
THIS ISN'T A RACE TRACK, YOUNG MAN.! CAN I HELP YOU?
NO THANKS! I'M JUST LOOKING FOR MY COUSIN.!
HEY ANDY.. WAIT FOR ME!
WH-WHERE ARE WE??
INTRUDER ALERT!!
YIKES!!
INTRUDER ALERT!!
8

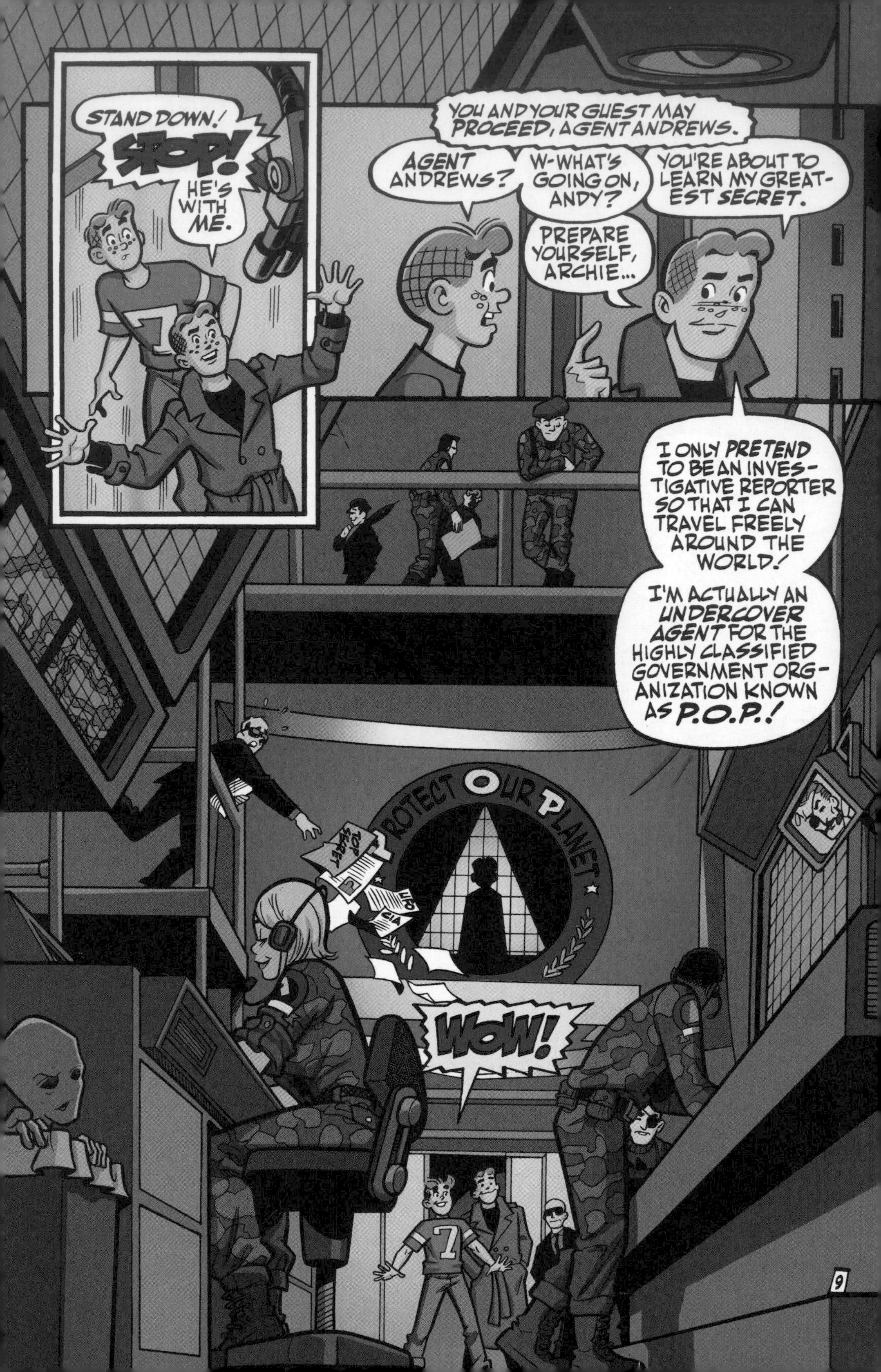
STAND DOWN!
STOP!
HE'S WITH ME.
YOU AND YOUR GUEST MAY PROCEED, AGENT ANDREWS.
AGENT ANDREWS?
W-WHAT'S GOING ON, ANDY?
PREPARE YOURSELF, ARCHIE...
YOU'RE ABOUT TO LEARN MY GREATEST SECRET.
I ONLY PRETEND TO BE AN INVESTIGATIVE REPORTER SO THAT I CAN TRAVEL FREELY AROUND THE WORLD!
I'M ACTUALLY AN UNDERCOVER AGENT FOR THE HIGHLY CLASSIFIED GOVERNMENT ORGANIZATION KNOWN AS P.O.P.!
PROTECT OUR PLANET
TOP SECRET
UFO
CIA
WOW!

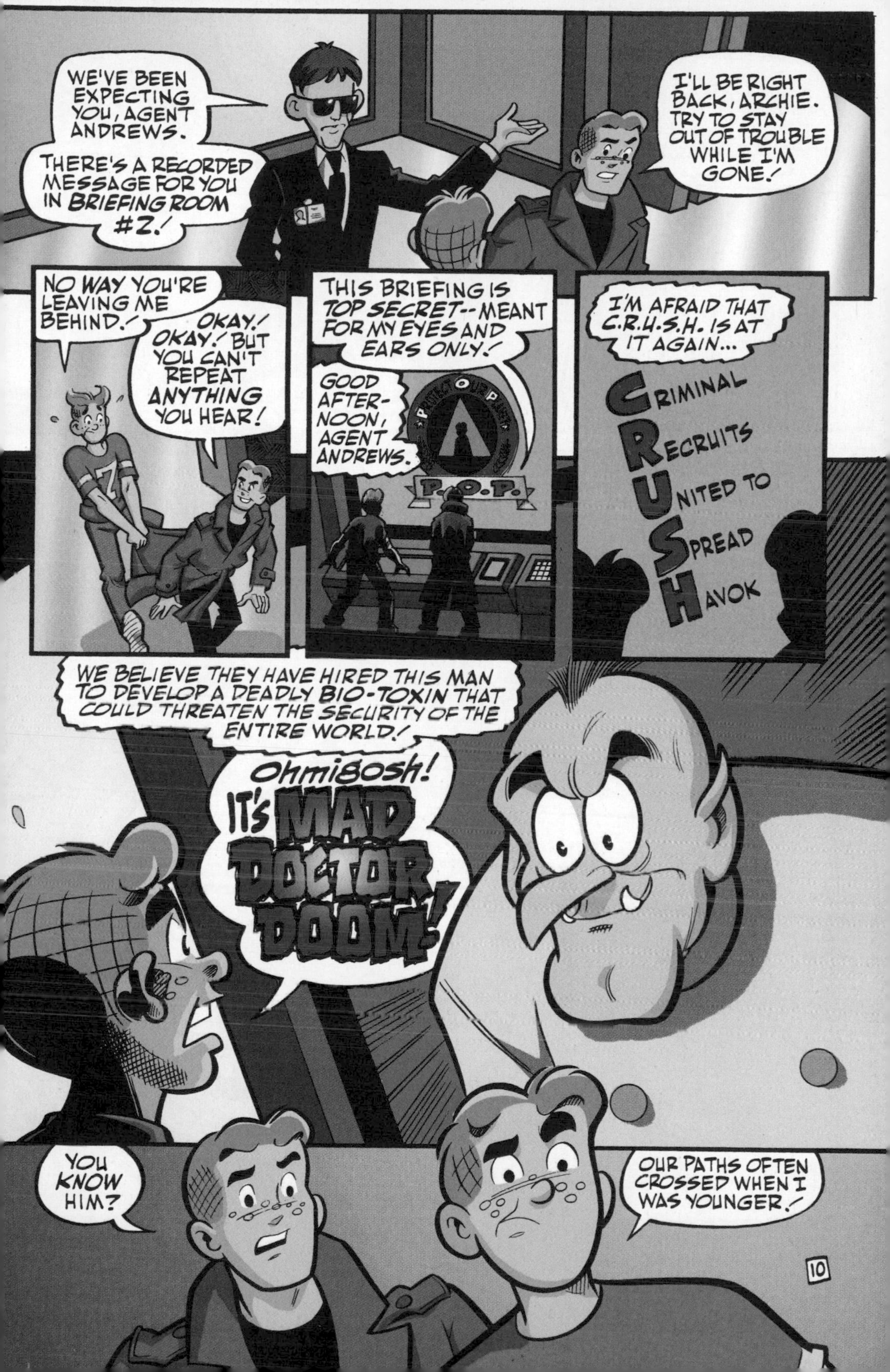
WE'VE BEEN EXPECTING YOU, AGENT ANDREWS.
THERE'S A RECORDED MESSAGE FOR YOU IN BRIEFING ROOM #2!
I'LL BE RIGHT BACK, ARCHIE. TRY TO STAY OUT OF TROUBLE WHILE I'M GONE!
NO WAY YOU'RE LEAVING ME BEHIND!
OKAY! OKAY! BUT YOU CAN'T REPEAT ANYTHING YOU HEAR!
THIS BRIEFING IS TOP SECRET--MEANT FOR MY EYES AND EARS ONLY!
GOOD AFTERNOON, AGENT ANDREWS.
P.O.P.
I'M AFRAID THAT C.R.U.S.H. IS AT IT AGAIN...
CRIMINAL
RECRUITS
UNITED TO
SPREAD
HAVOK
WE BELIEVE THEY HAVE HIRED THIS MAN TO DEVELOP A DEADLY BIO-TOXIN THAT COULD THREATEN THE SECURITY OF THE ENTIRE WORLD!
Ohmigosh! IT'S MAD DOCTOR DOOM!
YOU KNOW HIM?
OUR PATHS OFTEN CROSSED WHEN I WAS YOUNGER!
10

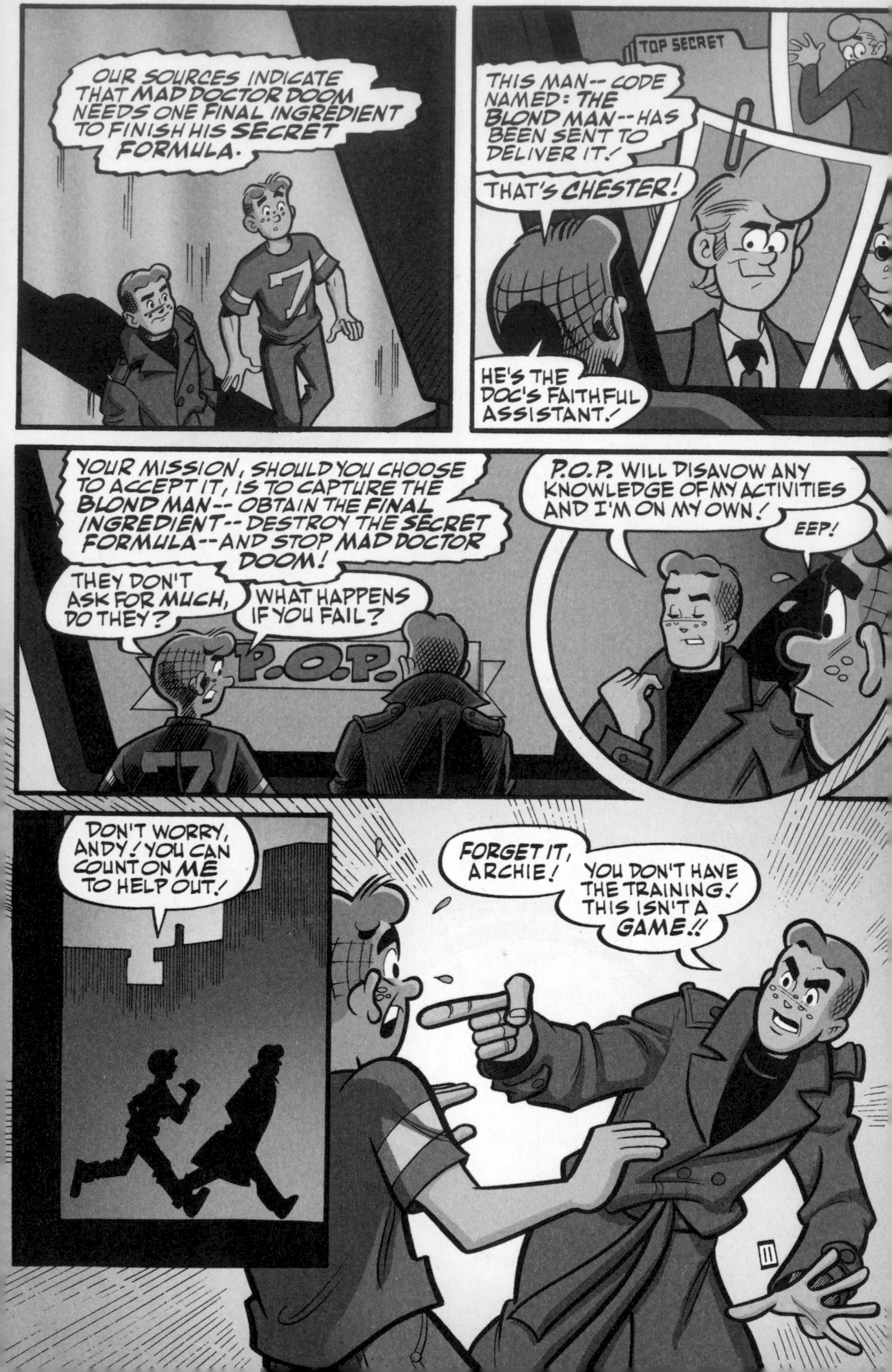
OUR SOURCES INDICATE THAT MAD DOCTOR DOOM NEEDS ONE FINAL INGREDIENT TO FINISH HIS SECRET FORMULA.
TOP SECRET
THIS MAN-- CODE NAMED: THE BLOND MAN--HAS BEEN SENT TO DELIVER IT!
THAT'S CHESTER!
HE'S THE DOC'S FAITHFUL ASSISTANT!
YOUR MISSION, SHOULD YOU CHOOSE TO ACCEPT IT, IS TO CAPTURE THE BLOND MAN-- OBTAIN THE FINAL INGREDIENT-- DESTROY THE SECRET FORMULA--AND STOP MAD DOCTOR DOOM!
THEY DON'T ASK FOR MUCH, DO THEY?
WHAT HAPPENS IF YOU FAIL?
P.O.P.
P.O.P. WILL DISAVOW ANY KNOWLEDGE OF MY ACTIVITIES AND I'M ON MY OWN!
EEP!
DON'T WORRY, ANDY! YOU CAN COUNT ON ME TO HELP OUT!
FORGET IT, ARCHIE!
YOU DON'T HAVE THE TRAINING! THIS ISN'T A GAME!!
11

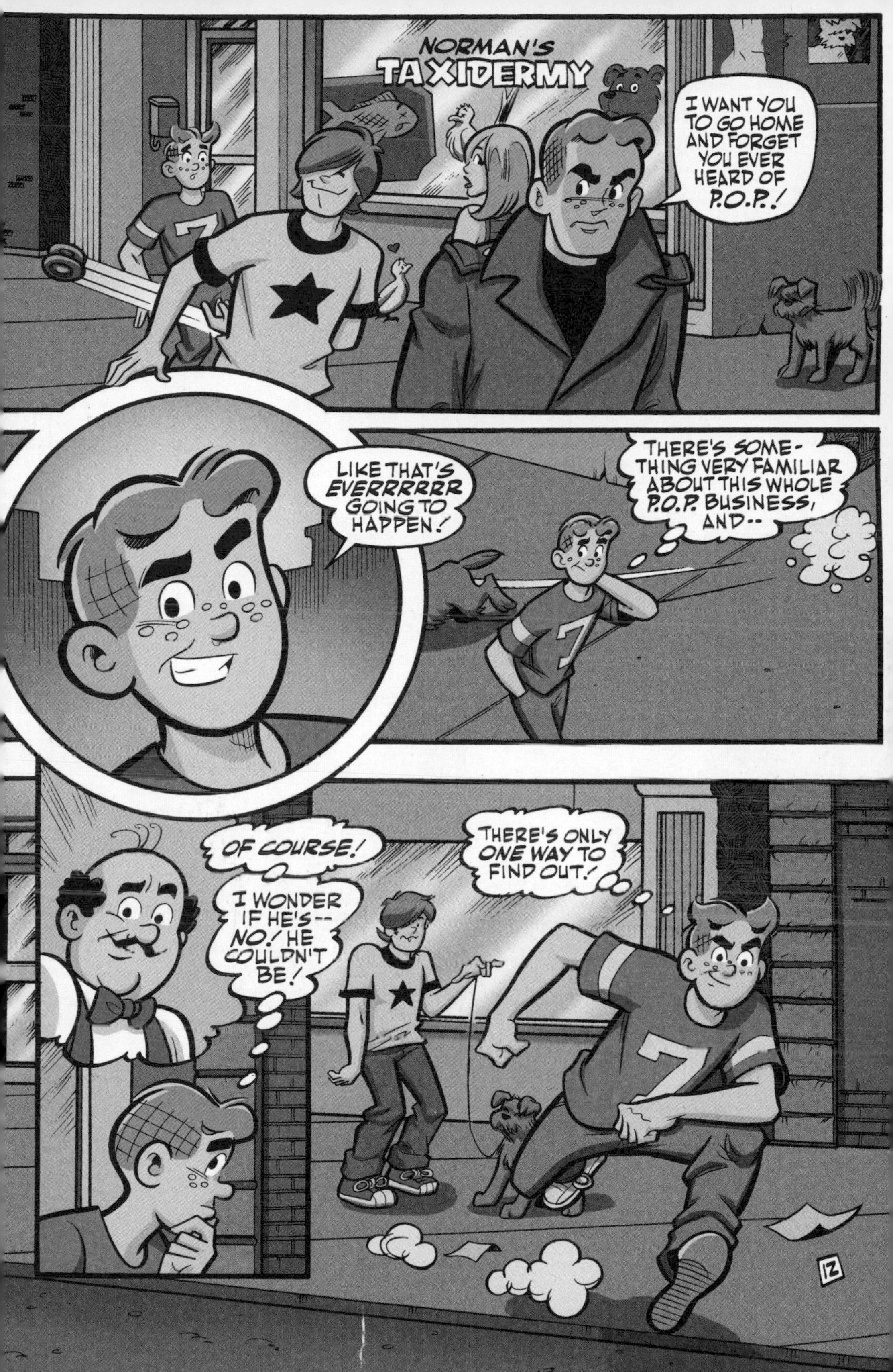
NORMAN'S TAXIDERMY
I WANT YOU TO GO HOME AND FORGET YOU EVER HEARD OF P.O.P.!
LIKE THAT'S EVERRRRRR GOING TO HAPPEN!
THERE'S SOME-THING VERY FAMILIAR ABOUT THIS WHOLE P.O.P. BUSINESS, AND--
OF COURSE!
I WONDER IF HE'S-- NO! HE COULDN'T BE!
THERE'S ONLY ONE WAY TO FIND OUT!
12

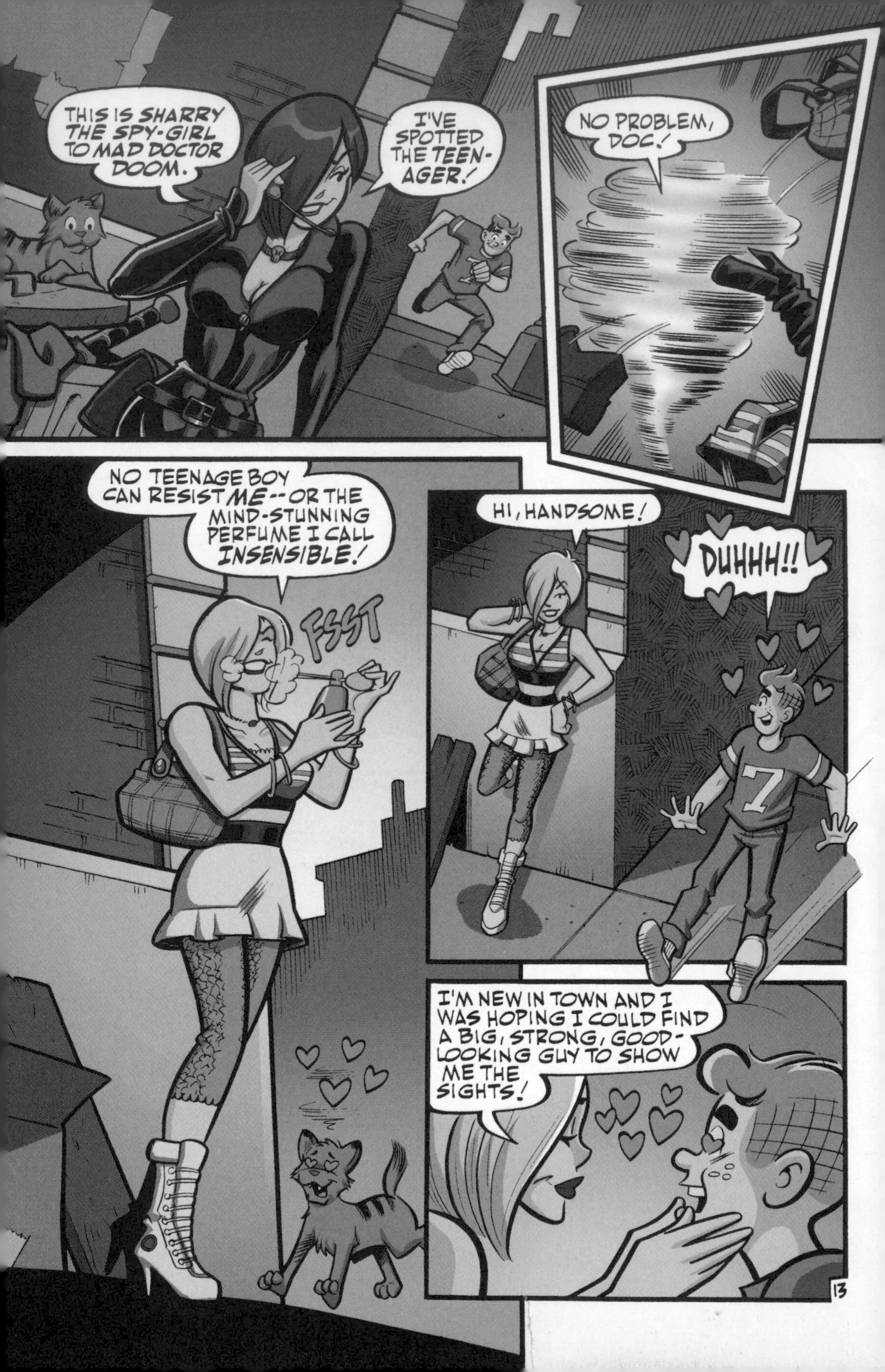
THIS IS SHARRY THE SPY-GIRL TO MAD DOCTOR DOOM.
I'VE SPOTTED THE TEEN-AGER!
NO PROBLEM, DOC!
NO TEENAGE BOY CAN RESIST ME--OR THE MIND-STUNNING PERFUME I CALL INSENSIBLE!
FSST
HI, HANDSOME!
DUHHH!!
I'M NEW IN TOWN AND I WAS HOPING I COULD FIND A BIG, STRONG, GOOD-LOOKING GUY TO SHOW ME THE SIGHTS!

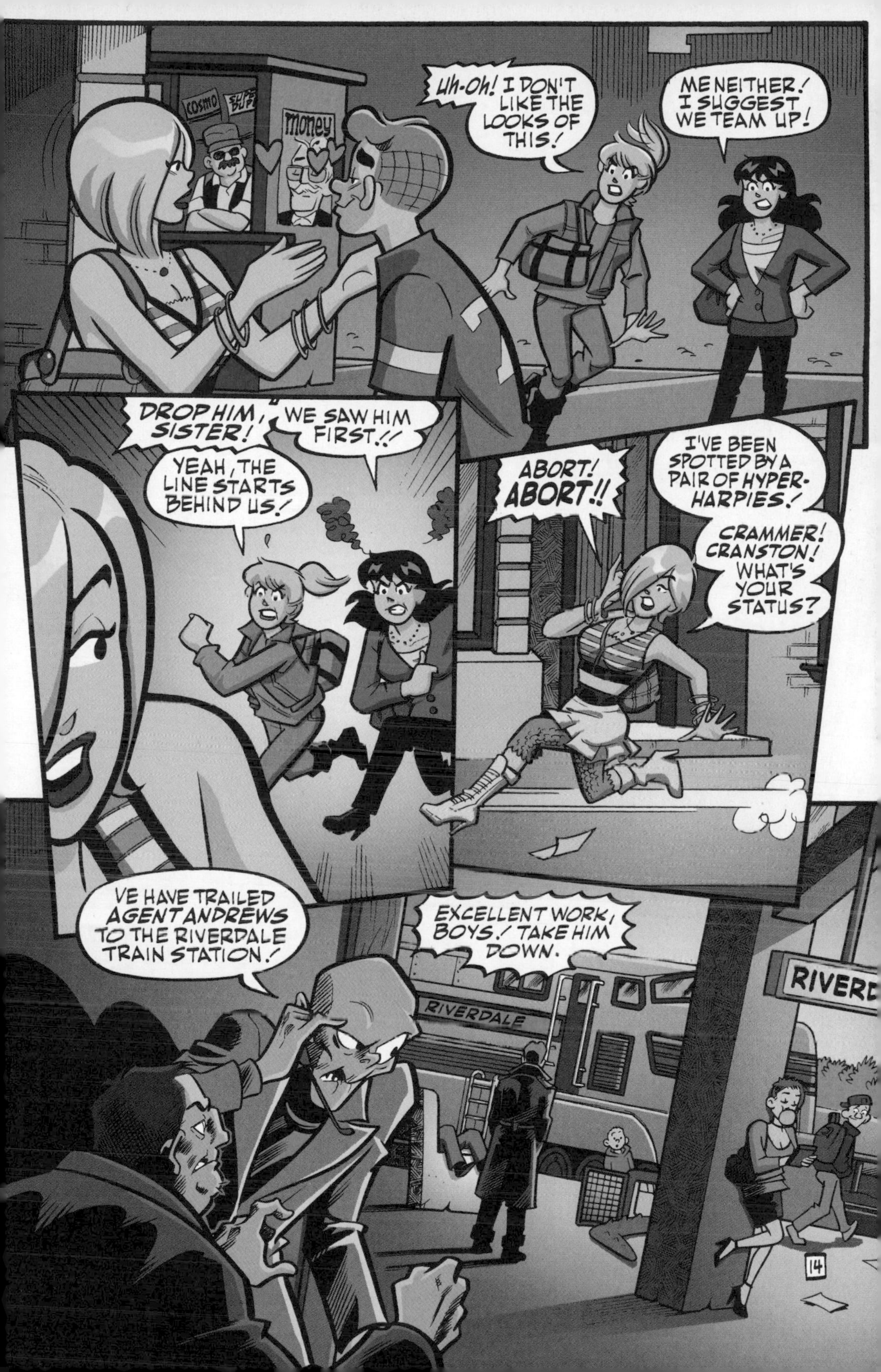

COSMO
MONEY
UH-OH! I DON'T LIKE THE LOOKS OF THIS!
ME NEITHER! I SUGGEST WE TEAM UP!
DROP HIM, SISTER!
WE SAW HIM FIRST!!
YEAH, THE LINE STARTS BEHIND US!
ABORT! ABORT!!
I'VE BEEN SPOTTED BY A PAIR OF HYPER-HARPIES!
CRAMMER! CRANSTON! WHAT'S YOUR STATUS?
VE HAVE TRAILED AGENT ANDREWS TO THE RIVERDALE TRAIN STATION!
EXCELLENT WORK, BOYS! TAKE HIM DOWN.
RIVERDALE
RIVERD
14

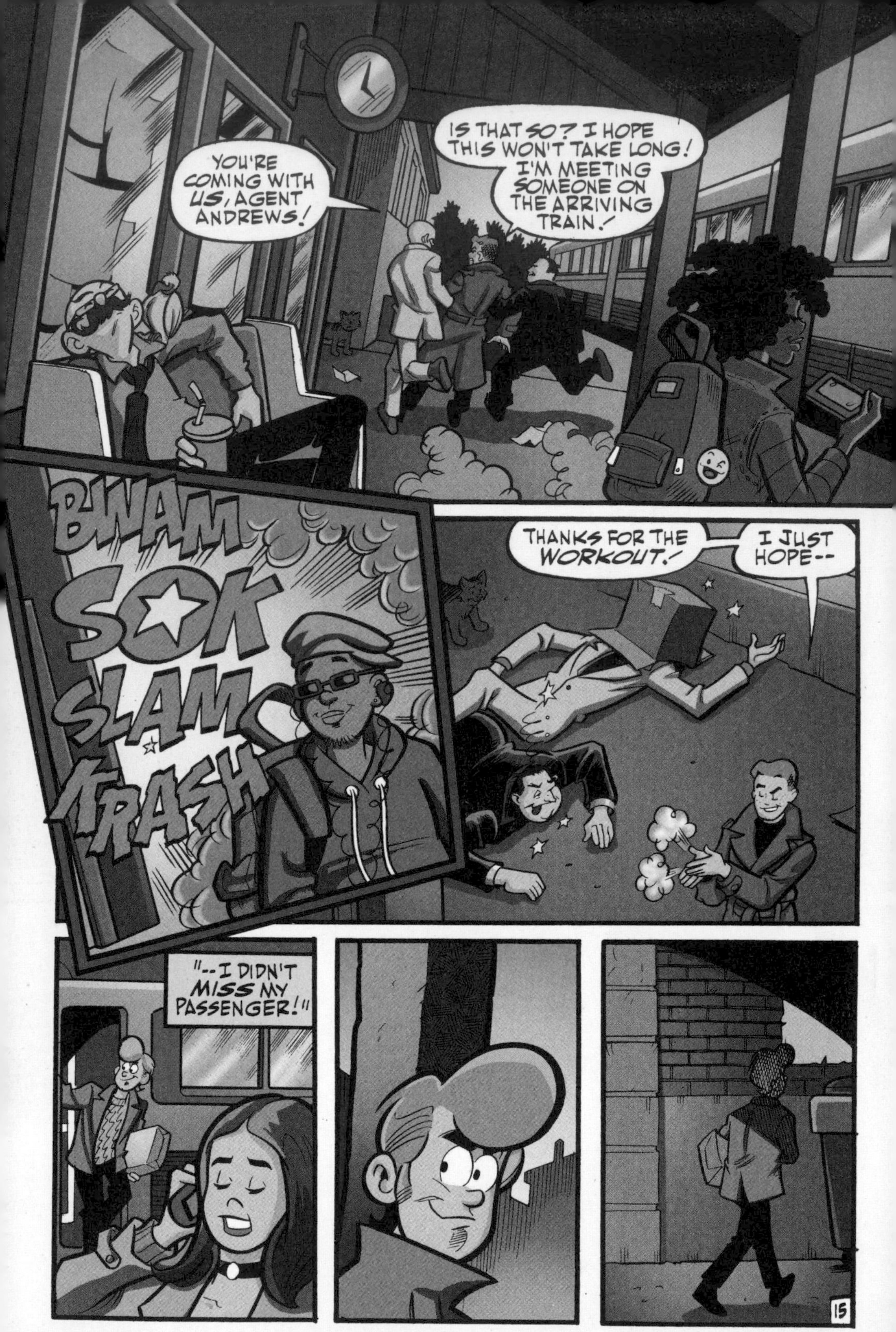
YOU'RE COMING WITH US, AGENT ANDREWS!
IS THAT SO? I HOPE THIS WON'T TAKE LONG! I'M MEETING SOMEONE ON THE ARRIVING TRAIN!
BWAM
SOK
SLAM
KRASH
THANKS FOR THE WORKOUT!
I JUST HOPE--
"--I DIDN'T MISS MY PASSENGER!"

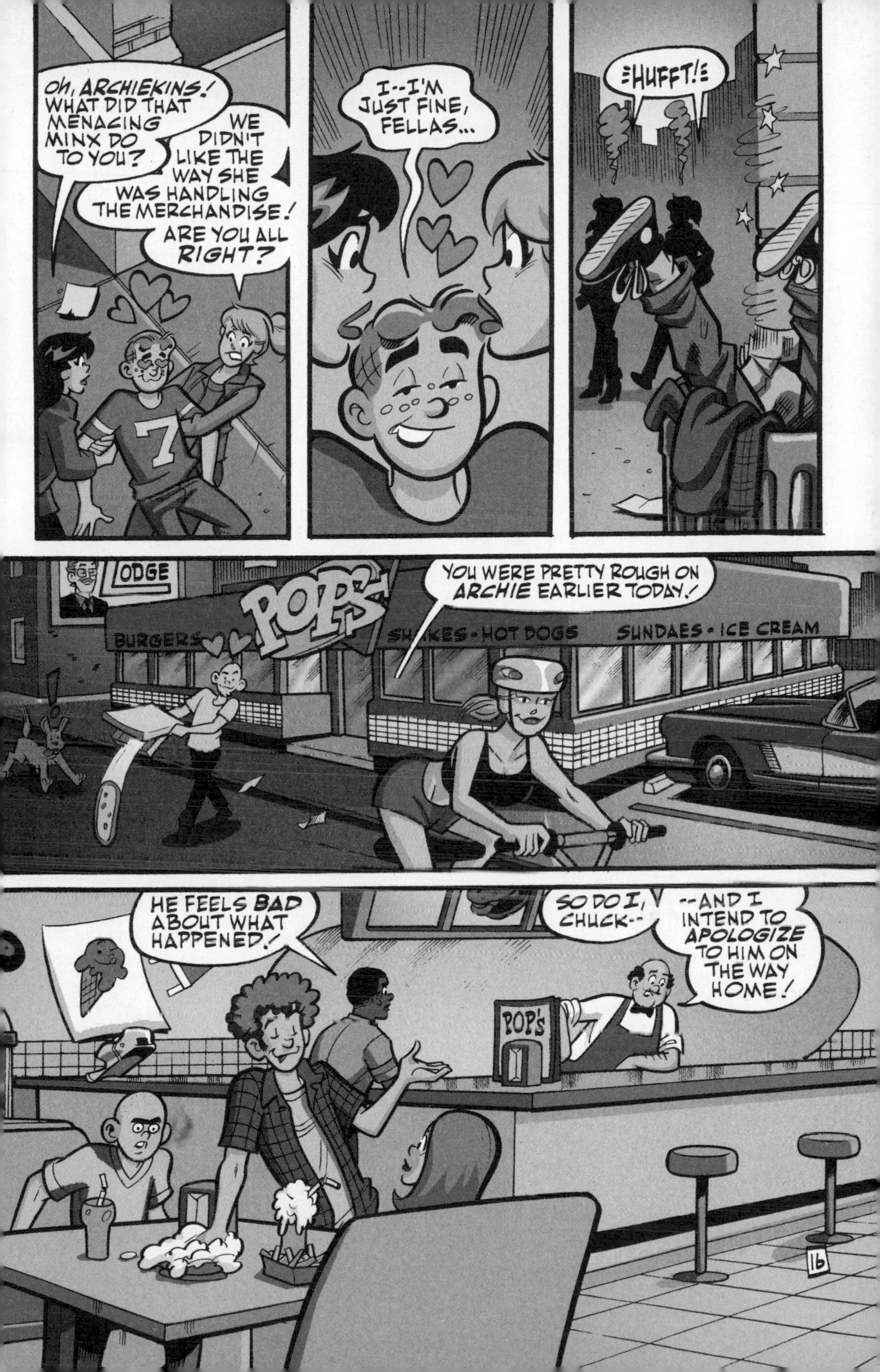
Oh, ARCHIEKINS! WHAT DID THAT MENACING MINX DO TO YOU?
WE DIDN'T LIKE THE WAY SHE WAS HANDLING THE MERCHANDISE! ARE YOU ALL RIGHT?
I--I'M JUST FINE, FELLAS...
HUFFT!
LODGE
POP'S
BURGERS
SHAKES • HOT DOGS
SUNDAES • ICE CREAM
YOU WERE PRETTY ROUGH ON ARCHIE EARLIER TODAY!
HE FEELS BAD ABOUT WHAT HAPPENED!
SO DO I, CHUCK--
--AND I INTEND TO APOLOGIZE TO HIM ON THE WAY HOME!
POP'S
16

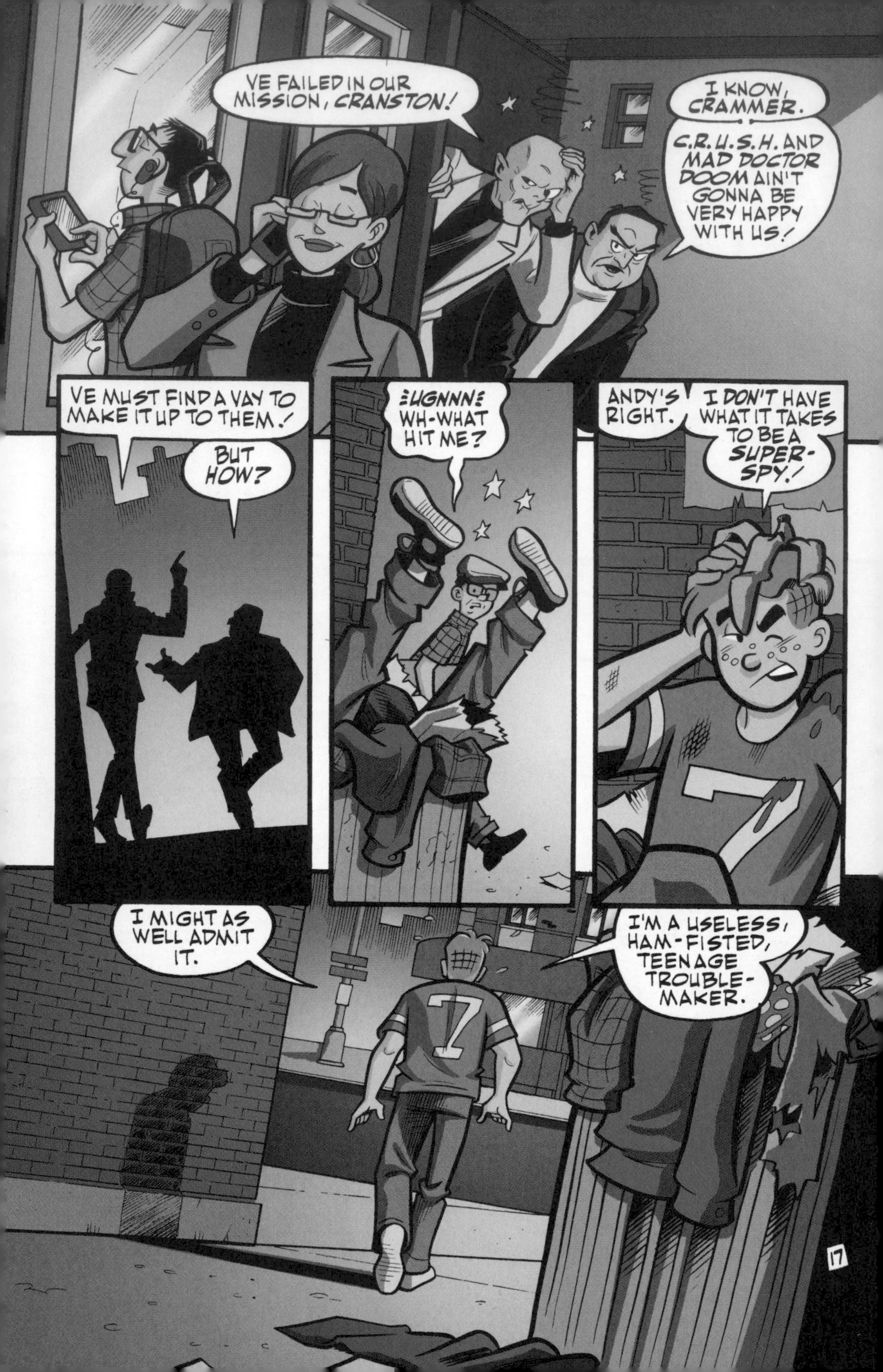
VE FAILED IN OUR MISSION, CRANSTON!
I KNOW, CRAMMER.
C.R.U.S.H. AND MAD DOCTOR DOOM AIN'T GONNA BE VERY HAPPY WITH US!
VE MUST FIND A VAY TO MAKE IT UP TO THEM!
BUT HOW?
UGNNN! WH-WHAT HIT ME?
ANDY'S RIGHT.
I DON'T HAVE WHAT IT TAKES TO BE A SUPER-SPY!
I MIGHT AS WELL ADMIT IT.
I'M A USELESS, HAM-FISTED, TEENAGE TROUBLE-MAKER.

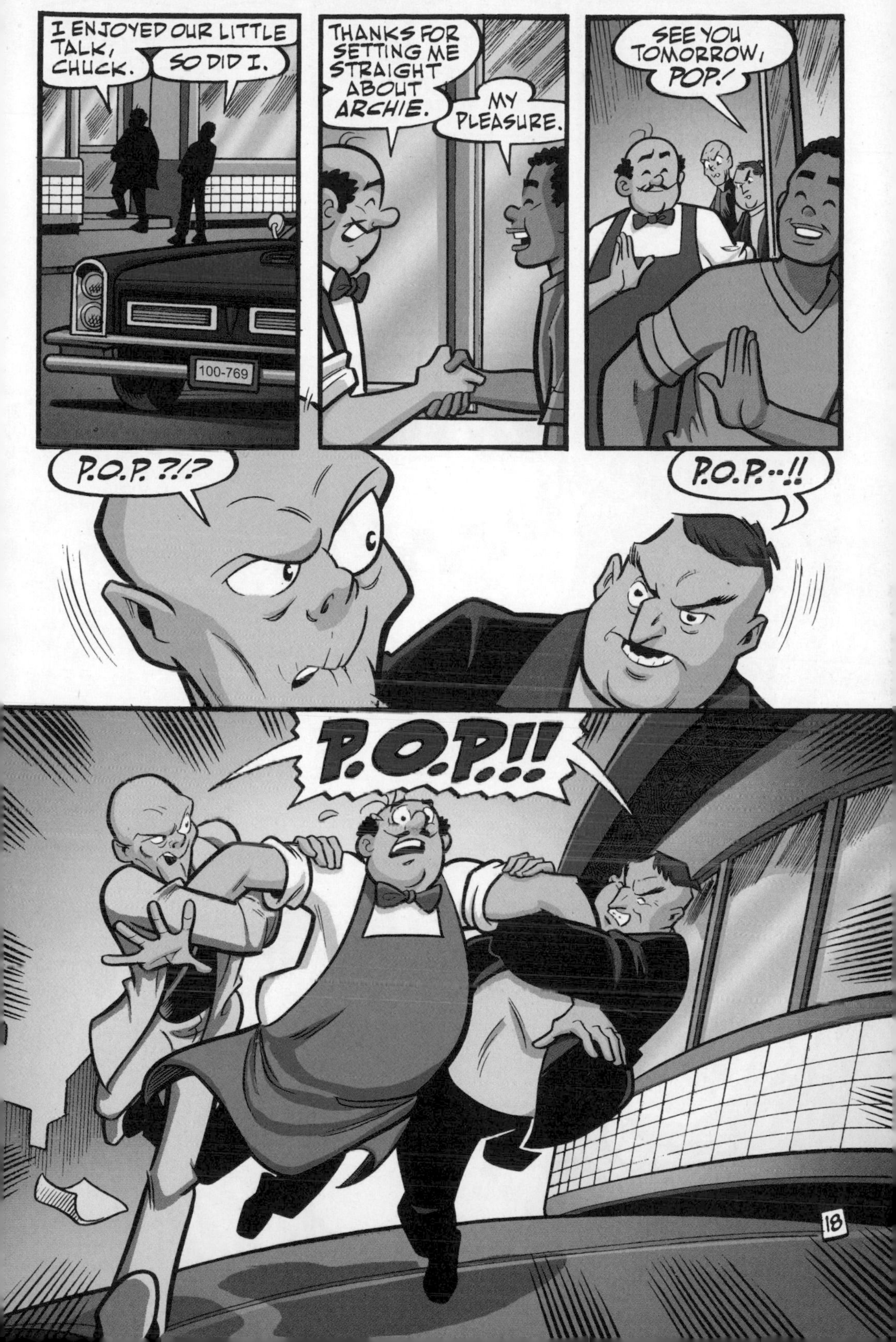
I ENJOYED OUR LITTLE TALK, CHUCK.
SO DID I.
100-769
THANKS FOR SETTING ME STRAIGHT ABOUT ARCHIE.
MY PLEASURE.
SEE YOU TOMORROW, POP!
P.O.P. ?!?
P.O.P.--!!
P.O.P.!!

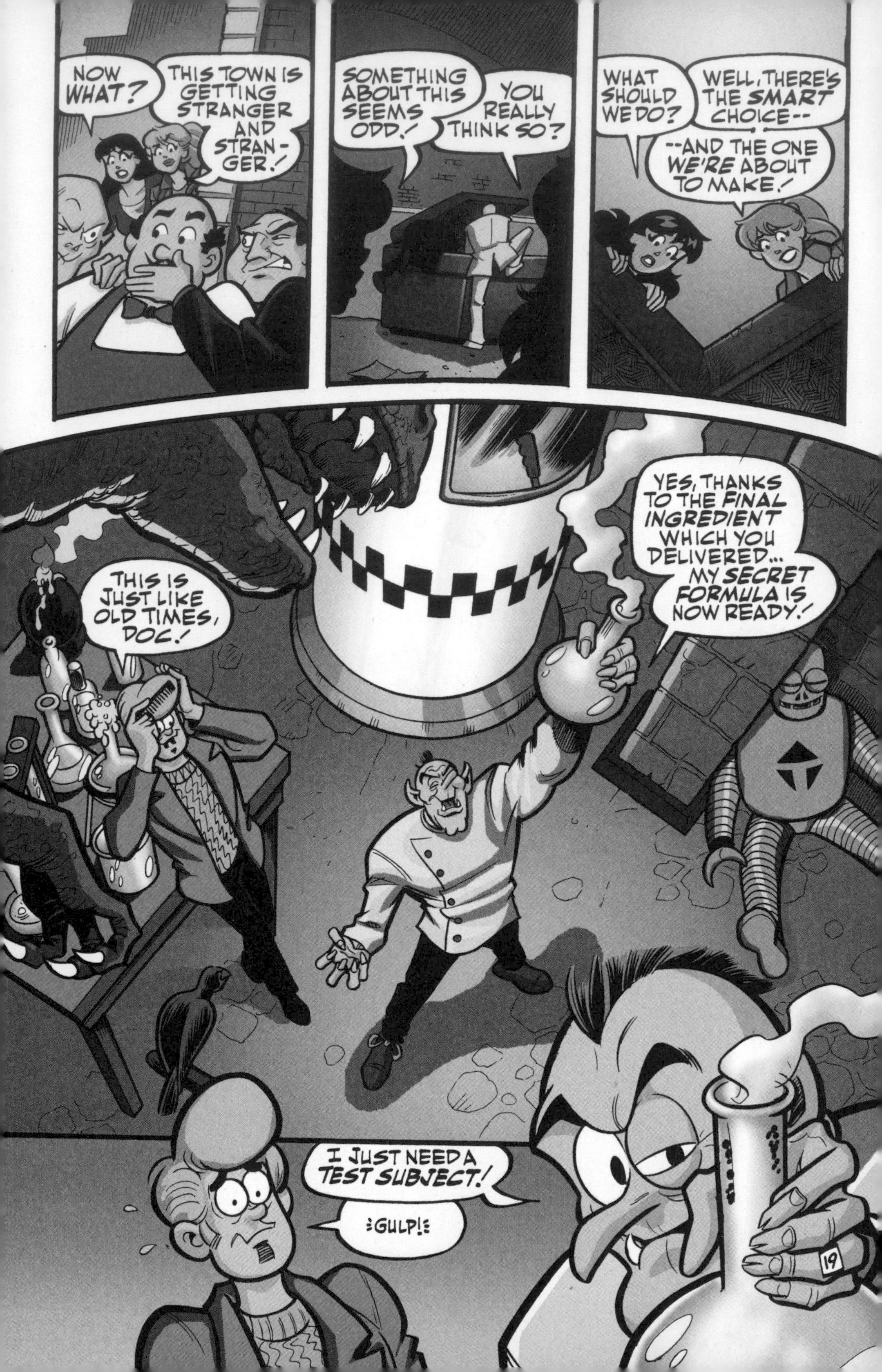
NOW WHAT?
THIS TOWN IS GETTING STRANGER AND STRANGER!
SOMETHING ABOUT THIS SEEMS ODD!
YOU REALLY THINK SO?
WHAT SHOULD WE DO?
WELL, THERE'S THE SMART CHOICE--
--AND THE ONE WE'RE ABOUT TO MAKE!
YES, THANKS TO THE FINAL INGREDIENT WHICH YOU DELIVERED... MY SECRET FORMULA IS NOW READY!
THIS IS JUST LIKE OLD TIMES, DOC!
I JUST NEED A TEST SUBJECT!
GULP!
19

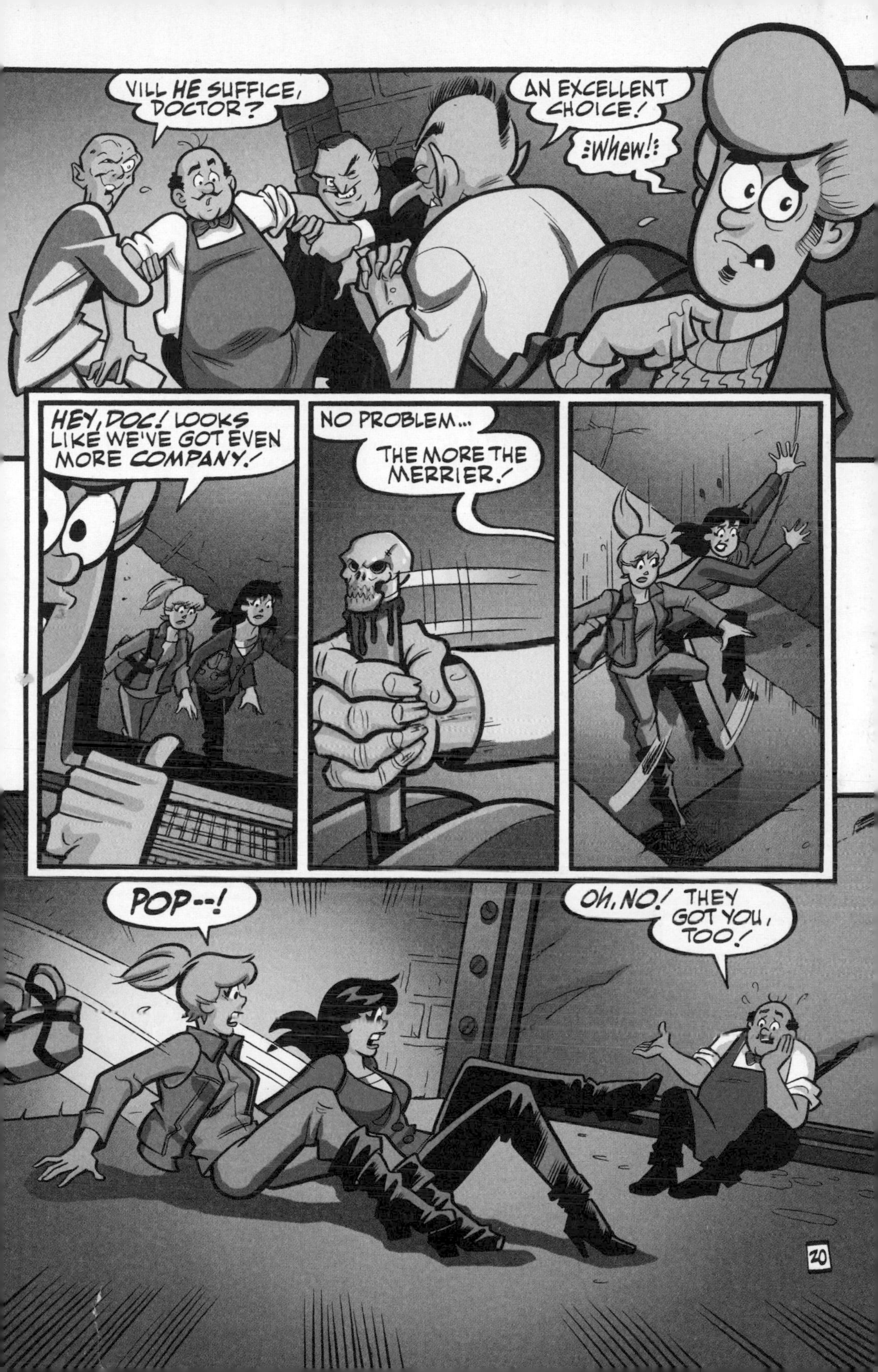
VILL HE SUFFICE, DOCTOR?
AN EXCELLENT CHOICE!
WHEW!
HEY, DOC! LOOKS LIKE WE'VE GOT EVEN MORE COMPANY!
NO PROBLEM...
THE MORE THE MERRIER!
POP--!
Oh, NO! THEY GOT YOU, TOO!

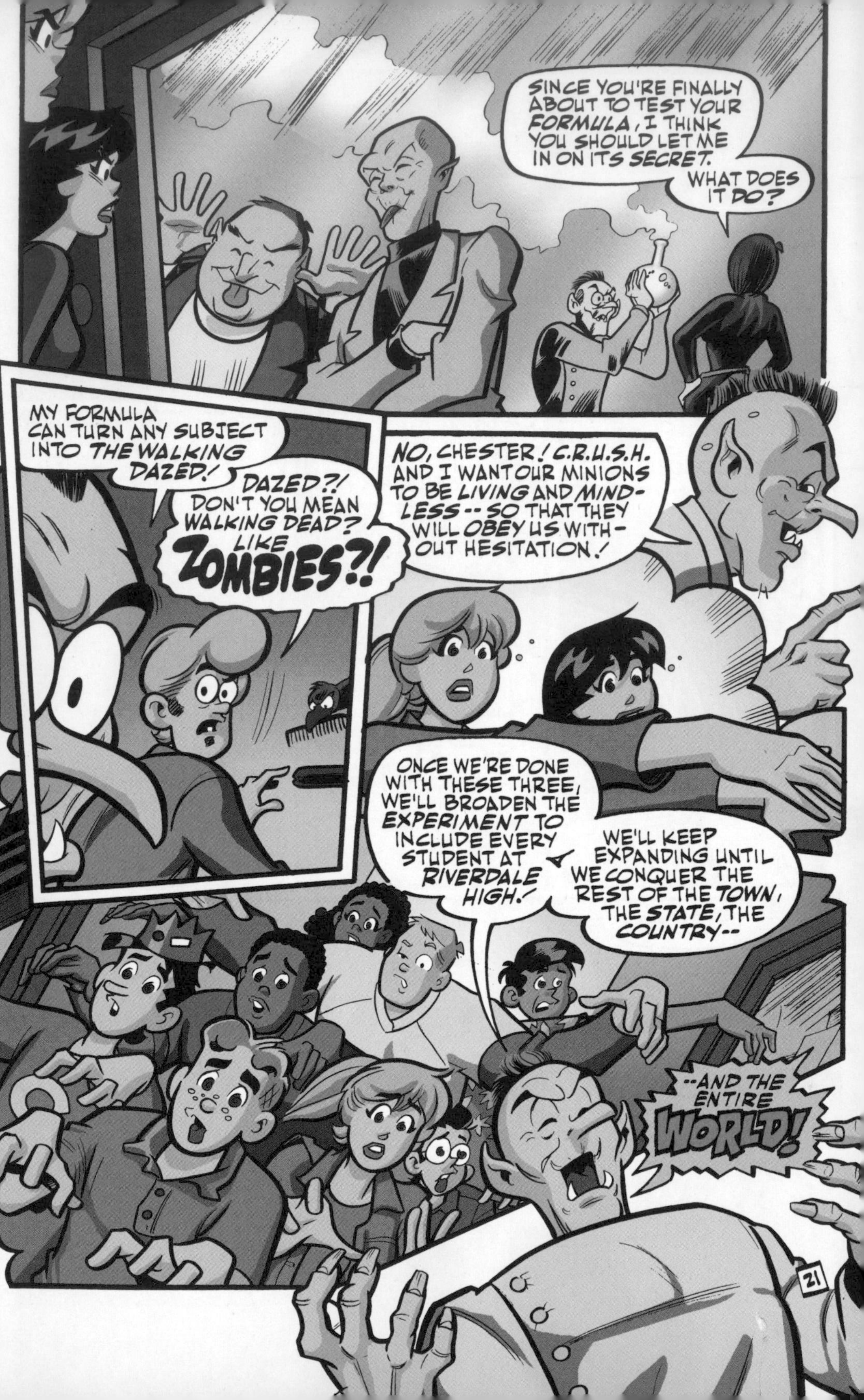

SINCE YOU'RE FINALLY ABOUT TO TEST YOUR FORMULA, I THINK YOU SHOULD LET ME IN ON ITS SECRET.
WHAT DOES IT DO?
MY FORMULA CAN TURN ANY SUBJECT INTO THE WALKING DAZED!
DAZED?! DON'T YOU MEAN WALKING DEAD? LIKE ZOMBIES?!
NO, CHESTER! C.R.U.S.H. AND I WANT OUR MINIONS TO BE LIVING AND MIND-LESS -- SO THAT THEY WILL OBEY US WITH-OUT HESITATION!
ONCE WE'RE DONE WITH THESE THREE, WE'LL BROADEN THE EXPERIMENT TO INCLUDE EVERY STUDENT AT RIVERDALE HIGH!
WE'LL KEEP EXPANDING UNTIL WE CONQUER THE REST OF THE TOWN, THE STATE, THE COUNTRY--
--AND THE ENTIRE WORLD!

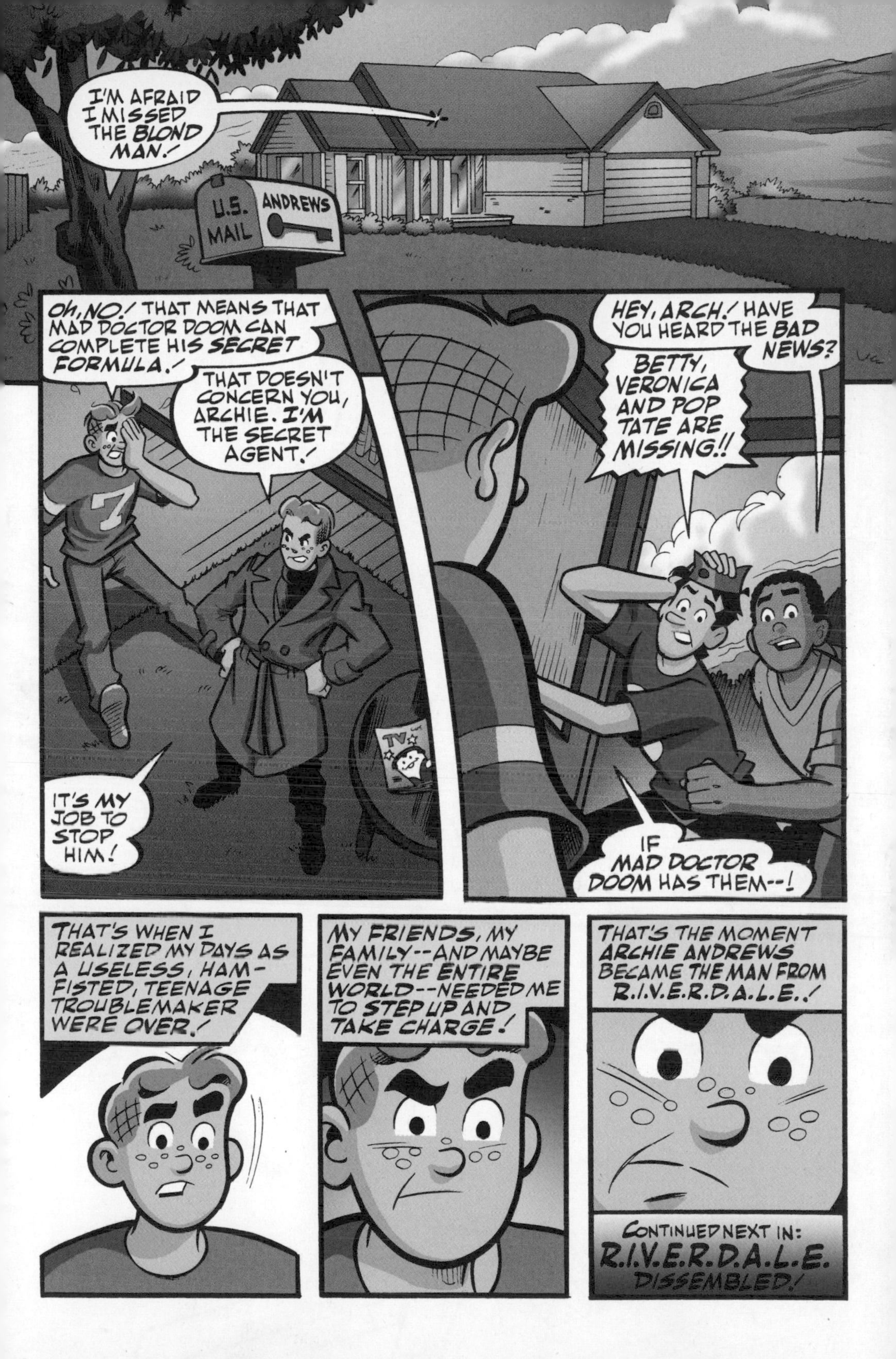

I'M AFRAID I MISSED THE BLOND MAN.!
U.S. MAIL
ANDREWS
OH, NO! THAT MEANS THAT MAD DOCTOR DOOM CAN COMPLETE HIS SECRET FORMULA.!
THAT DOESN'T CONCERN YOU, ARCHIE. I'M THE SECRET AGENT.!
IT'S MY JOB TO STOP HIM!
HEY, ARCH.! HAVE YOU HEARD THE BAD NEWS?
BETTY, VERONICA AND POP TATE ARE MISSING!!
IF MAD DOCTOR DOOM HAS THEM--!
THAT'S WHEN I REALIZED MY DAYS AS A USELESS, HAM-FISTED, TEENAGE TROUBLEMAKER WERE OVER.!
MY FRIENDS, MY FAMILY--AND MAYBE EVEN THE ENTIRE WORLD--NEEDED ME TO STEP UP AND TAKE CHARGE!
THAT'S THE MOMENT ARCHIE ANDREWS BECAME THE MAN FROM R.I.V.E.R.D.A.L.E.!
CONTINUED NEXT IN: R.I.V.E.R.D.A.L.E. DISSEMBLED!

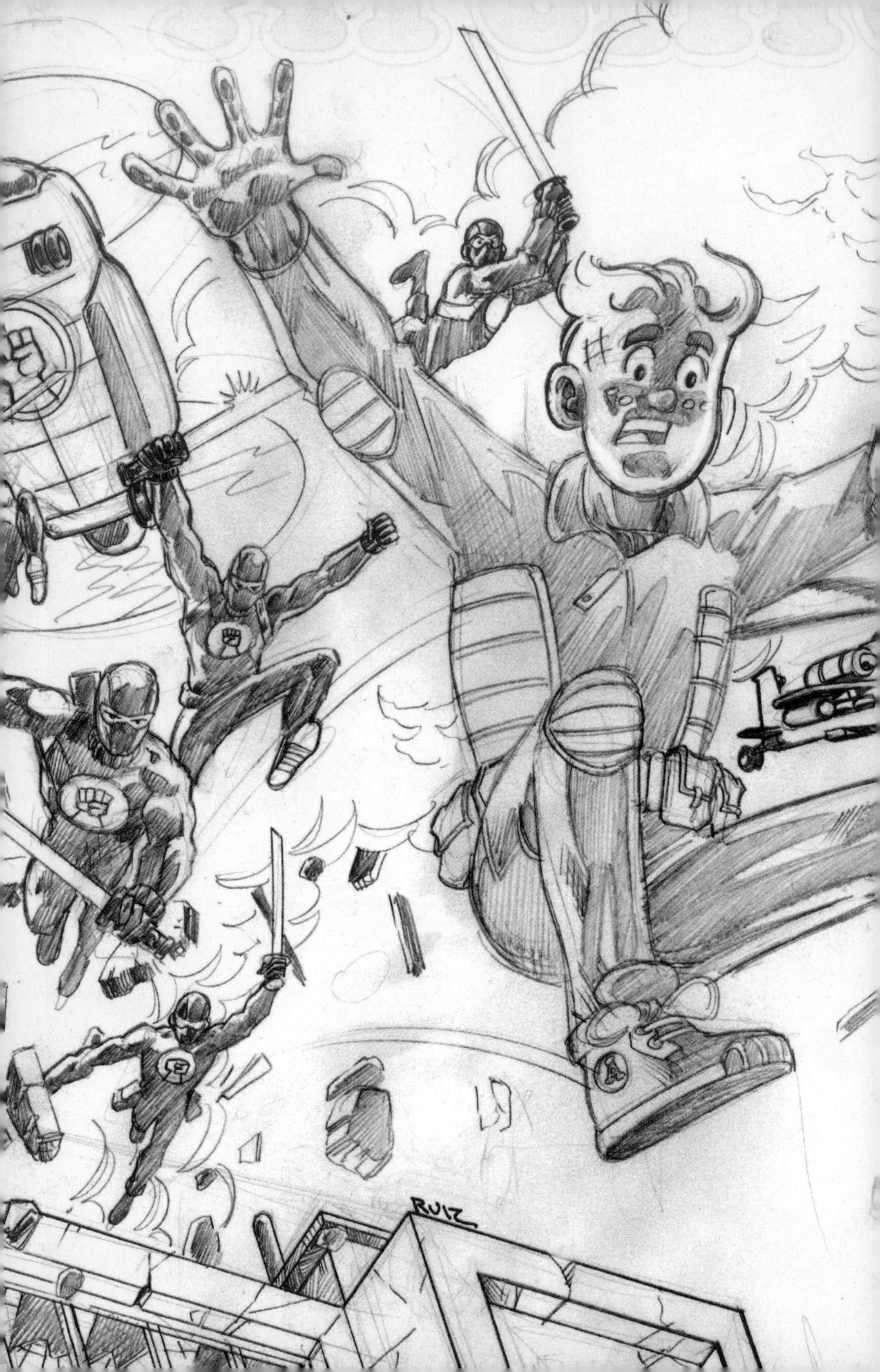
RUIZ

MISSION 2: R.I.V.E.R.D.A.L.E. DISSEMBLED

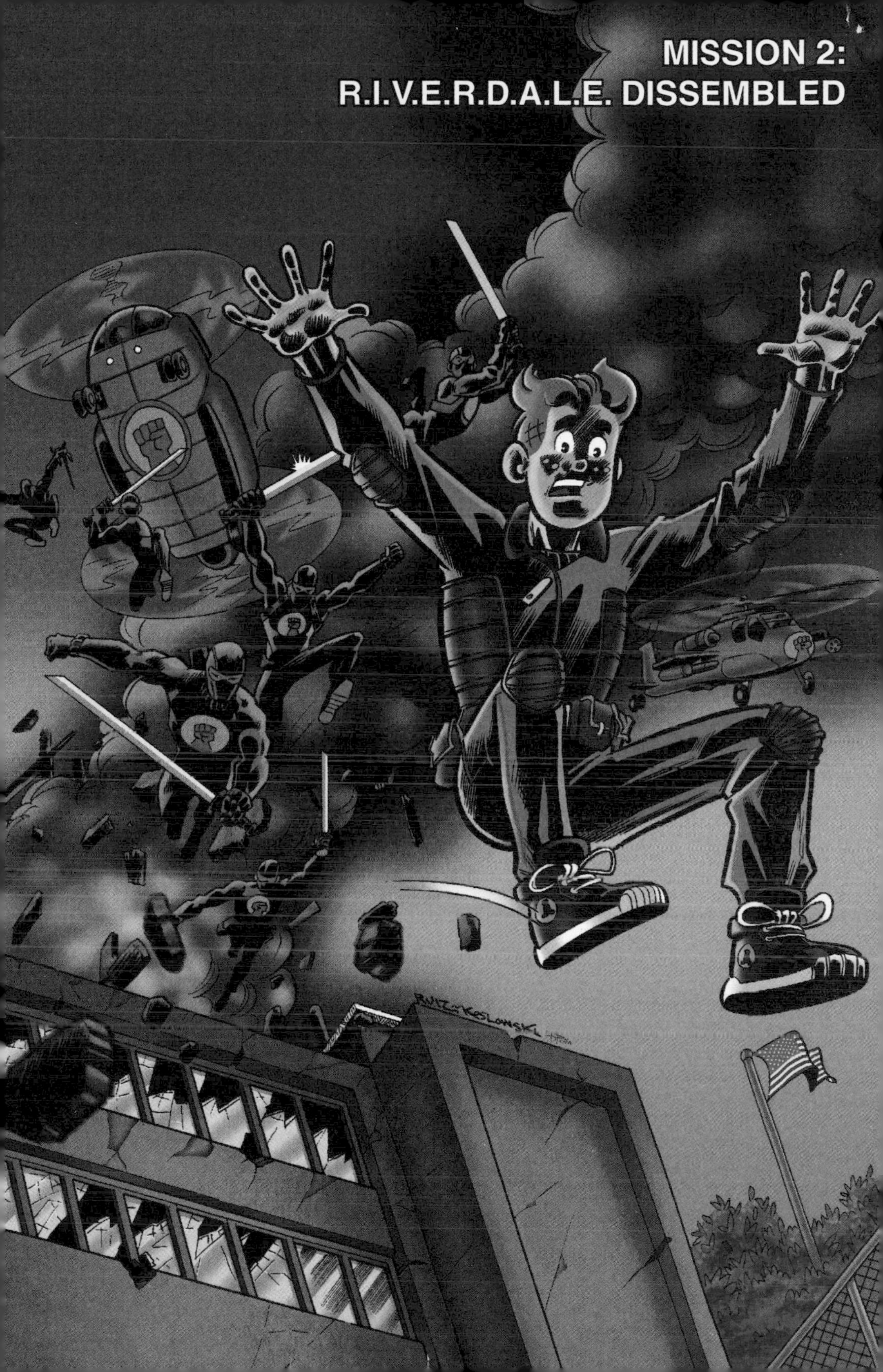

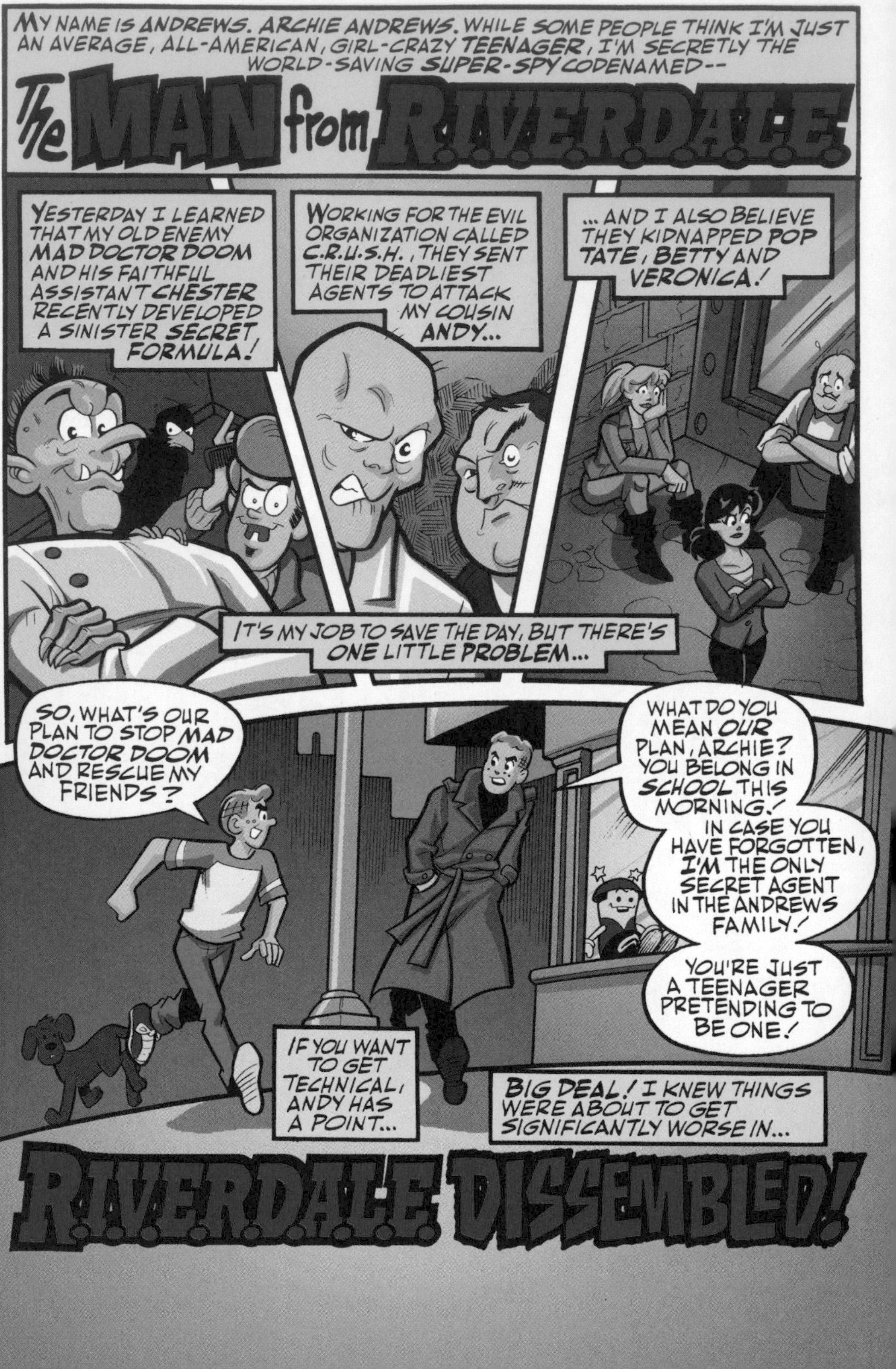
MY NAME IS ANDREWS. ARCHIE ANDREWS. WHILE SOME PEOPLE THINK I'M JUST AN AVERAGE, ALL-AMERICAN, GIRL-CRAZY TEENAGER, I'M SECRETLY THE WORLD-SAVING SUPER-SPY CODENAMED--
The MAN from R.I.V.E.R.D.A.L.E.!
YESTERDAY I LEARNED THAT MY OLD ENEMY MAD DOCTOR DOOM AND HIS FAITHFUL ASSISTANT CHESTER RECENTLY DEVELOPED A SINISTER SECRET FORMULA!
WORKING FOR THE EVIL ORGANIZATION CALLED C.R.U.S.H., THEY SENT THEIR DEADLIEST AGENTS TO ATTACK MY COUSIN ANDY...
...AND I ALSO BELIEVE THEY KIDNAPPED POP TATE, BETTY AND VERONICA!
IT'S MY JOB TO SAVE THE DAY, BUT THERE'S ONE LITTLE PROBLEM...
SO, WHAT'S OUR PLAN TO STOP MAD DOCTOR DOOM AND RESCUE MY FRIENDS?
WHAT DO YOU MEAN OUR PLAN, ARCHIE? YOU BELONG IN SCHOOL THIS MORNING!
IN CASE YOU HAVE FORGOTTEN, I'M THE ONLY SECRET AGENT IN THE ANDREWS FAMILY!
YOU'RE JUST A TEENAGER PRETENDING TO BE ONE!
IF YOU WANT TO GET TECHNICAL, ANDY HAS A POINT...
BIG DEAL! I KNEW THINGS WERE ABOUT TO GET SIGNIFICANTLY WORSE IN...
R.I.V.E.R.D.A.L.E. DISSEMBLED!

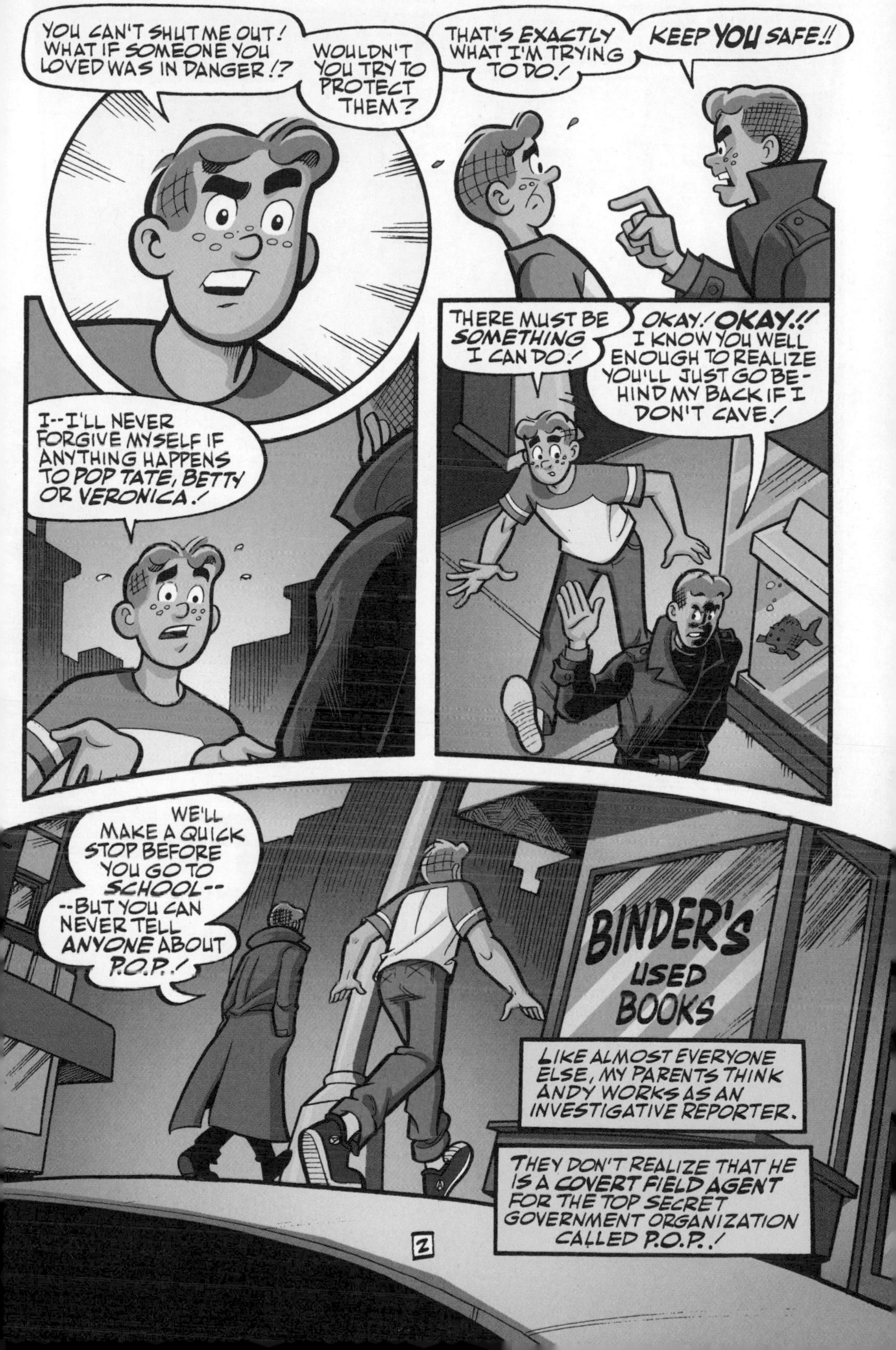

YOU CAN'T SHUT ME OUT! WHAT IF SOMEONE YOU LOVED WAS IN DANGER!?
WOULDN'T YOU TRY TO PROTECT THEM?
THAT'S EXACTLY WHAT I'M TRYING TO DO!
KEEP YOU SAFE!!
I--I'LL NEVER FORGIVE MYSELF IF ANYTHING HAPPENS TO POP TATE, BETTY OR VERONICA!
THERE MUST BE SOMETHING I CAN DO!
OKAY! OKAY!! I KNOW YOU WELL ENOUGH TO REALIZE YOU'LL JUST GO BE-HIND MY BACK IF I DON'T CAVE!
WE'LL MAKE A QUICK STOP BEFORE YOU GO TO SCHOOL--
--BUT YOU CAN NEVER TELL ANYONE ABOUT P.O.P.!
BINDER'S USED BOOKS
LIKE ALMOST EVERYONE ELSE, MY PARENTS THINK ANDY WORKS AS AN INVESTIGATIVE REPORTER.
THEY DON'T REALIZE THAT HE IS A COVERT FIELD AGENT FOR THE TOP SECRET GOVERNMENT ORGANIZATION CALLED P.O.P.!
2

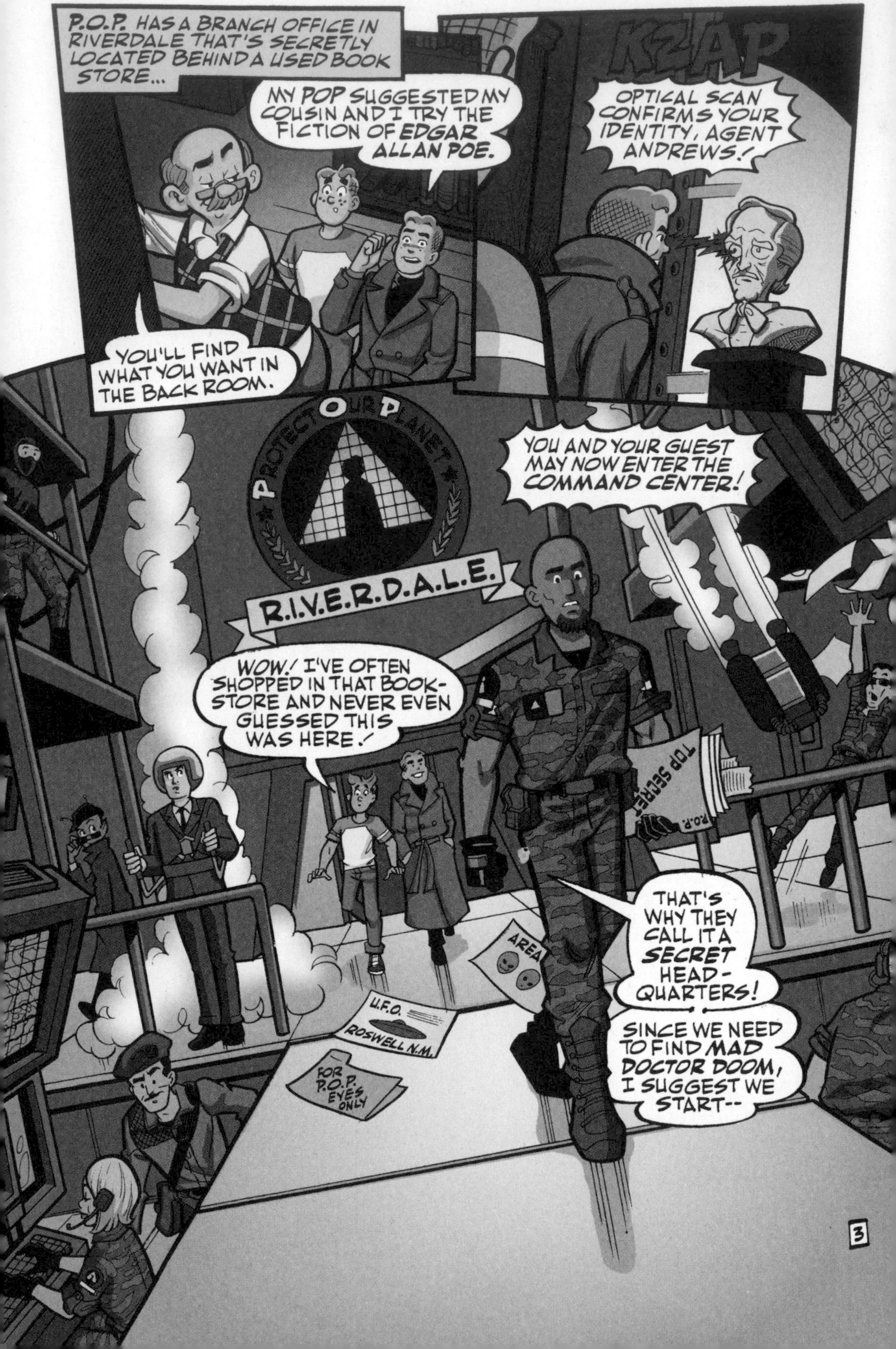
P.O.P. HAS A BRANCH OFFICE IN RIVERDALE THAT'S SECRETLY LOCATED BEHIND A USED BOOK STORE...
MY POP SUGGESTED MY COUSIN AND I TRY THE FICTION OF EDGAR ALLAN POE.
YOU'LL FIND WHAT YOU WANT IN THE BACK ROOM.
KZAP
OPTICAL SCAN CONFIRMS YOUR IDENTITY, AGENT ANDREWS!
PROTECT OUR PLANET
R.I.V.E.R.D.A.L.E.
YOU AND YOUR GUEST MAY NOW ENTER THE COMMAND CENTER!
WOW! I'VE OFTEN SHOPPED IN THAT BOOK-STORE AND NEVER EVEN GUESSED THIS WAS HERE!
TOP SECRET
P.O.P.
AREA
U.F.O.
ROSWELL N.M.
FOR P.O.P. EYES ONLY
THAT'S WHY THEY CALL IT A SECRET HEAD-QUARTERS!
SINCE WE NEED TO FIND MAD DOCTOR DOOM, I SUGGEST WE START--

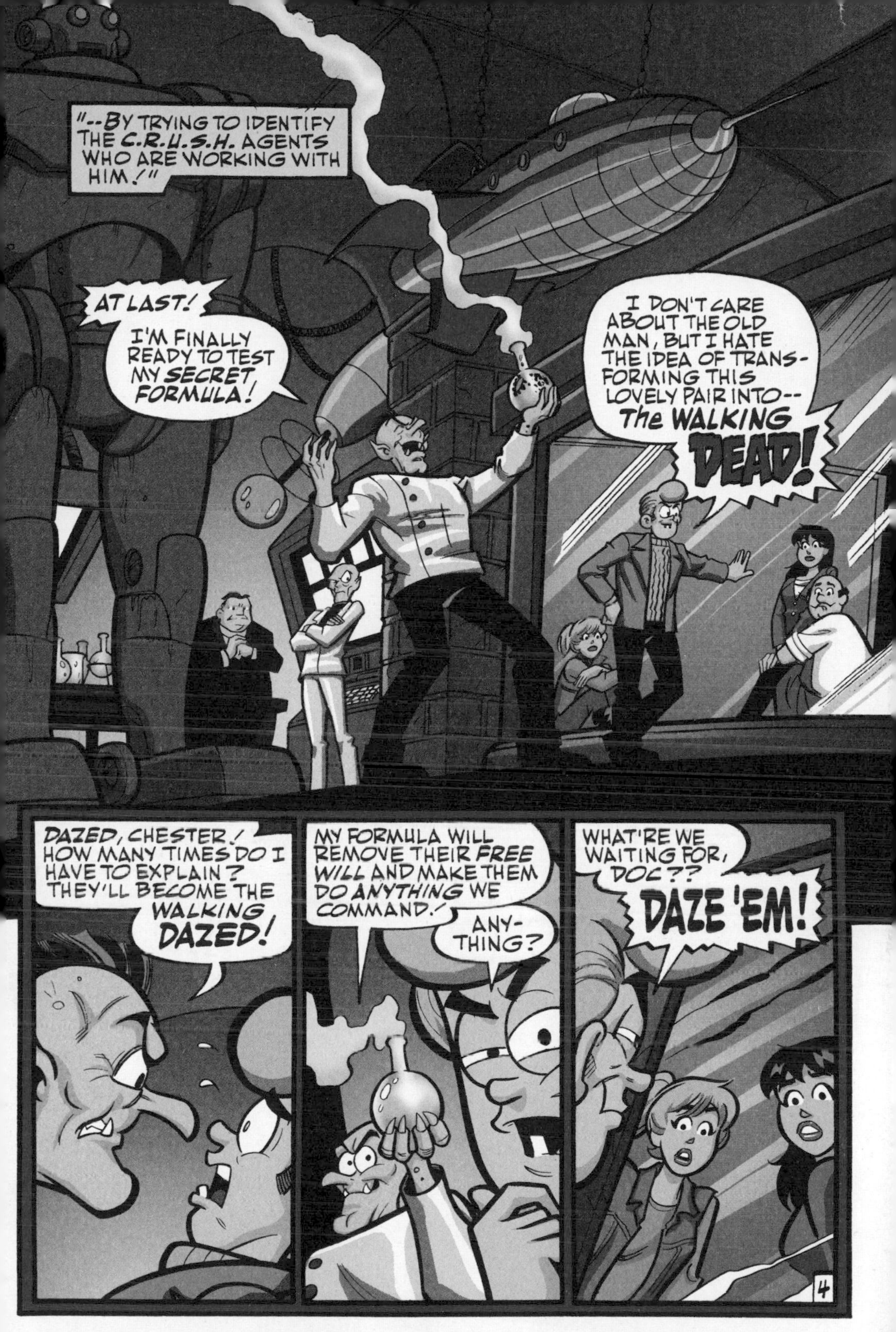
"--BY TRYING TO IDENTIFY THE C.R.U.S.H. AGENTS WHO ARE WORKING WITH HIM!"
AT LAST!
I'M FINALLY READY TO TEST MY SECRET FORMULA!
I DON'T CARE ABOUT THE OLD MAN, BUT I HATE THE IDEA OF TRANSFORMING THIS LOVELY PAIR INTO-- The WALKING DEAD!
DAZED, CHESTER! HOW MANY TIMES DO I HAVE TO EXPLAIN? THEY'LL BECOME THE WALKING DAZED!
MY FORMULA WILL REMOVE THEIR FREE WILL AND MAKE THEM DO ANYTHING WE COMMAND!
ANY-THING?
WHAT'RE WE WAITING FOR, DOC??
DAZE 'EM!
4

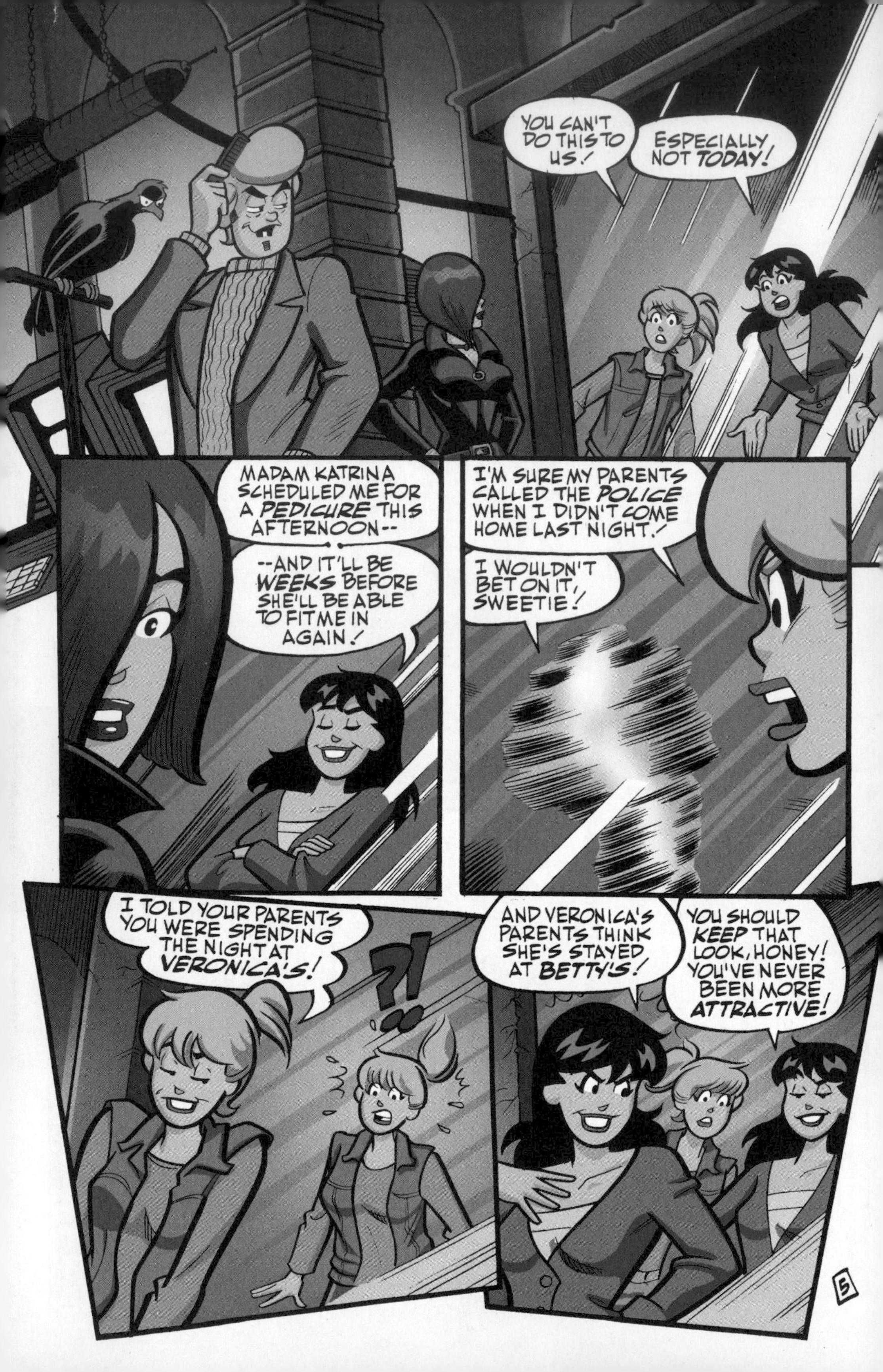
YOU CAN'T DO THIS TO US!
ESPECIALLY NOT TODAY!
MADAM KATRINA SCHEDULED ME FOR A PEDICURE THIS AFTERNOON--
--AND IT'LL BE WEEKS BEFORE SHE'LL BE ABLE TO FIT ME IN AGAIN!
I'M SURE MY PARENTS CALLED THE POLICE WHEN I DIDN'T COME HOME LAST NIGHT!
I WOULDN'T BET ON IT, SWEETIE!
I TOLD YOUR PARENTS YOU WERE SPENDING THE NIGHT AT VERONICA'S!
?!
AND VERONICA'S PARENTS THINK SHE'S STAYED AT BETTY'S!
YOU SHOULD KEEP THAT LOOK, HONEY! YOU'VE NEVER BEEN MORE ATTRACTIVE!
5

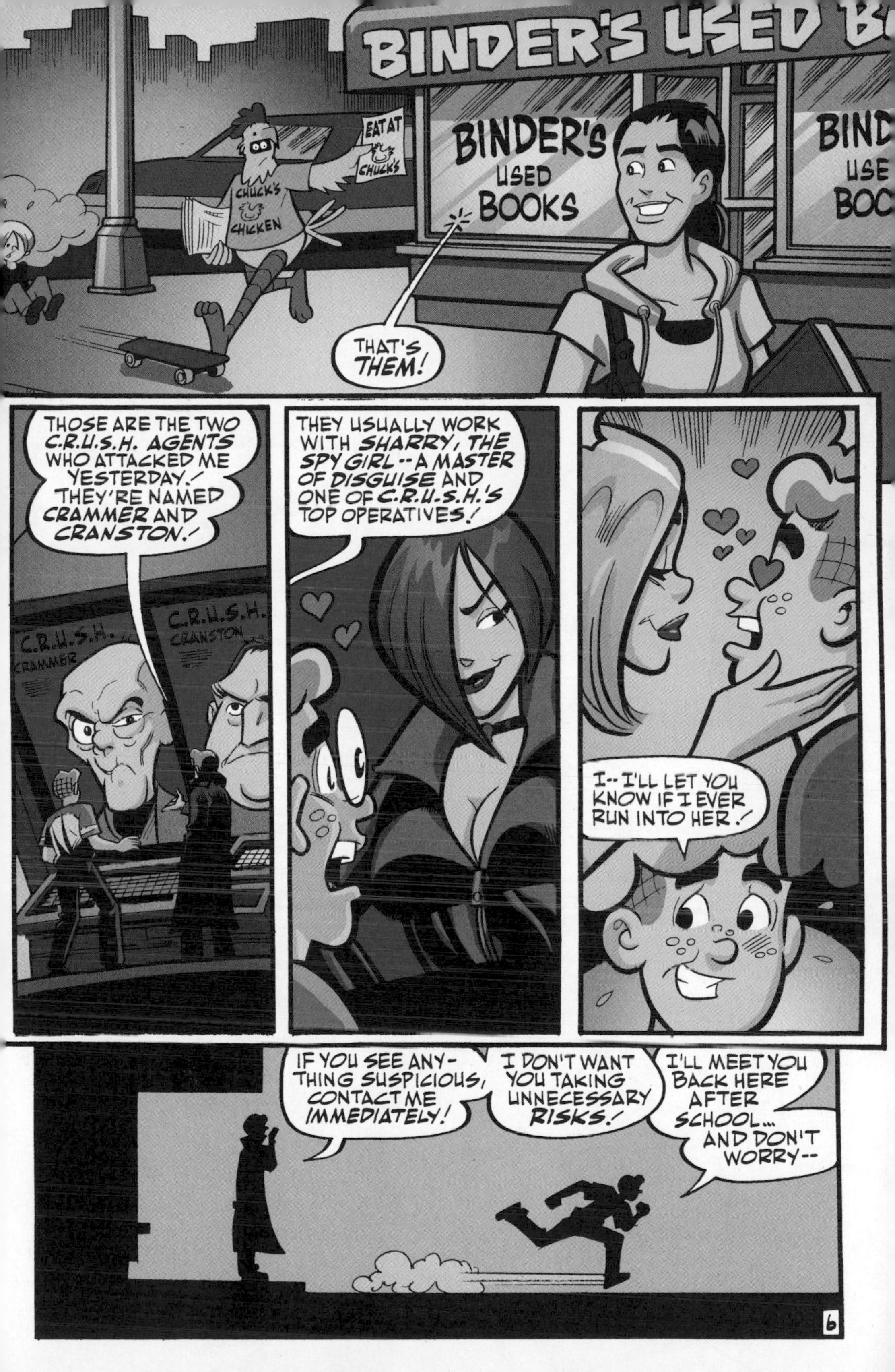

BINDER'S USED B
EAT AT CHUCK'S
CHUCK'S CHICKEN
BINDER'S USED BOOKS
BIND USE BOC
THAT'S THEM!
THOSE ARE THE TWO C.R.U.S.H. AGENTS WHO ATTACKED ME YESTERDAY.! THEY'RE NAMED CRAMMER AND CRANSTON.!
C.R.U.S.H. CRAMMER
C.R.U.S.H. CRANSTON
THEY USUALLY WORK WITH SHARRY, THE SPY GIRL -- A MASTER OF DISGUISE AND ONE OF C.R.U.S.H.'S TOP OPERATIVES!
I-- I'LL LET YOU KNOW IF I EVER RUN INTO HER.!
IF YOU SEE ANYTHING SUSPICIOUS, CONTACT ME IMMEDIATELY!
I DON'T WANT YOU TAKING UNNECESSARY RISKS.!
I'LL MEET YOU BACK HERE AFTER SCHOOL... AND DON'T WORRY--

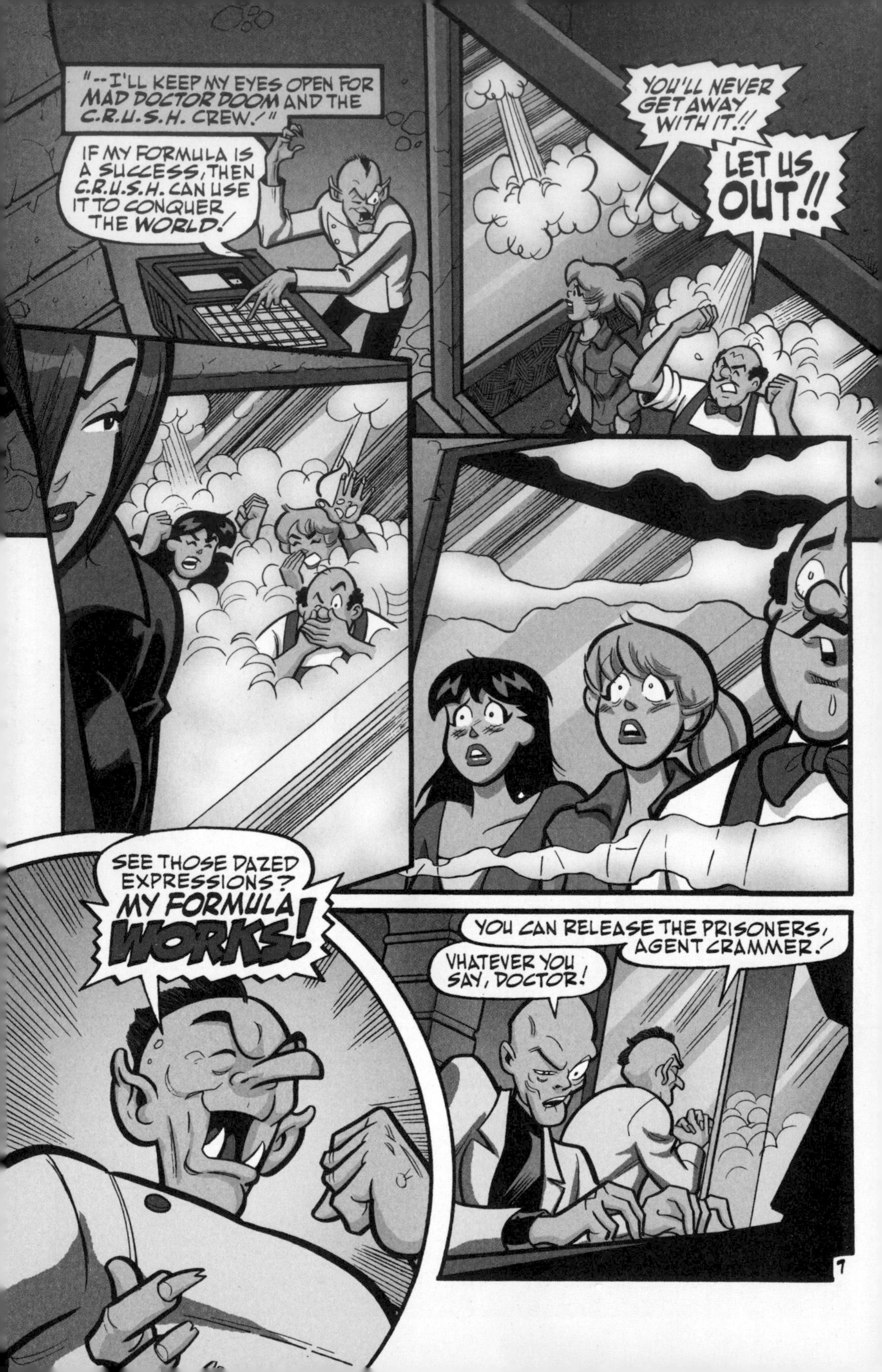
"--I'LL KEEP MY EYES OPEN FOR MAD DOCTOR DOOM AND THE C.R.U.S.H. CREW!"
IF MY FORMULA IS A SUCCESS, THEN C.R.U.S.H. CAN USE IT TO CONQUER THE WORLD!
YOU'LL NEVER GET AWAY WITH IT!!
LET US OUT!!
SEE THOSE DAZED EXPRESSIONS? MY FORMULA WORKS!
YOU CAN RELEASE THE PRISONERS, AGENT CRAMMER!
VHATEVER YOU SAY, DOCTOR!
7

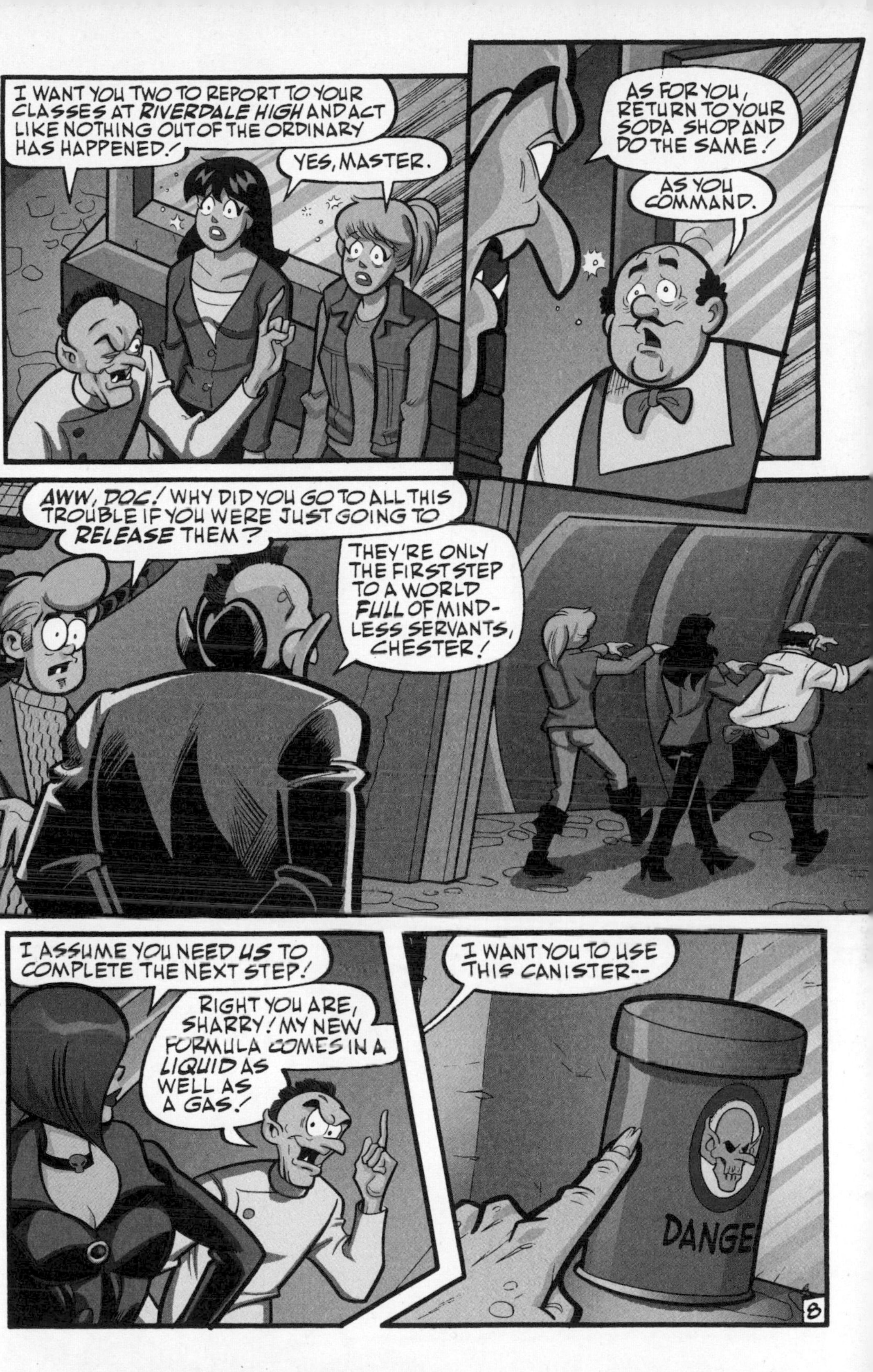
I WANT YOU TWO TO REPORT TO YOUR CLASSES AT RIVERDALE HIGH AND ACT LIKE NOTHING OUT OF THE ORDINARY HAS HAPPENED!
YES, MASTER.
AS FOR YOU, RETURN TO YOUR SODA SHOP AND DO THE SAME!
AS YOU COMMAND.
AWW, DOC! WHY DID YOU GO TO ALL THIS TROUBLE IF YOU WERE JUST GOING TO RELEASE THEM?
THEY'RE ONLY THE FIRST STEP TO A WORLD FULL OF MINDLESS SERVANTS, CHESTER!
I ASSUME YOU NEED US TO COMPLETE THE NEXT STEP!
RIGHT YOU ARE, SHARRY! MY NEW FORMULA COMES IN A LIQUID AS WELL AS A GAS!
I WANT YOU TO USE THIS CANISTER--
DANGE
8

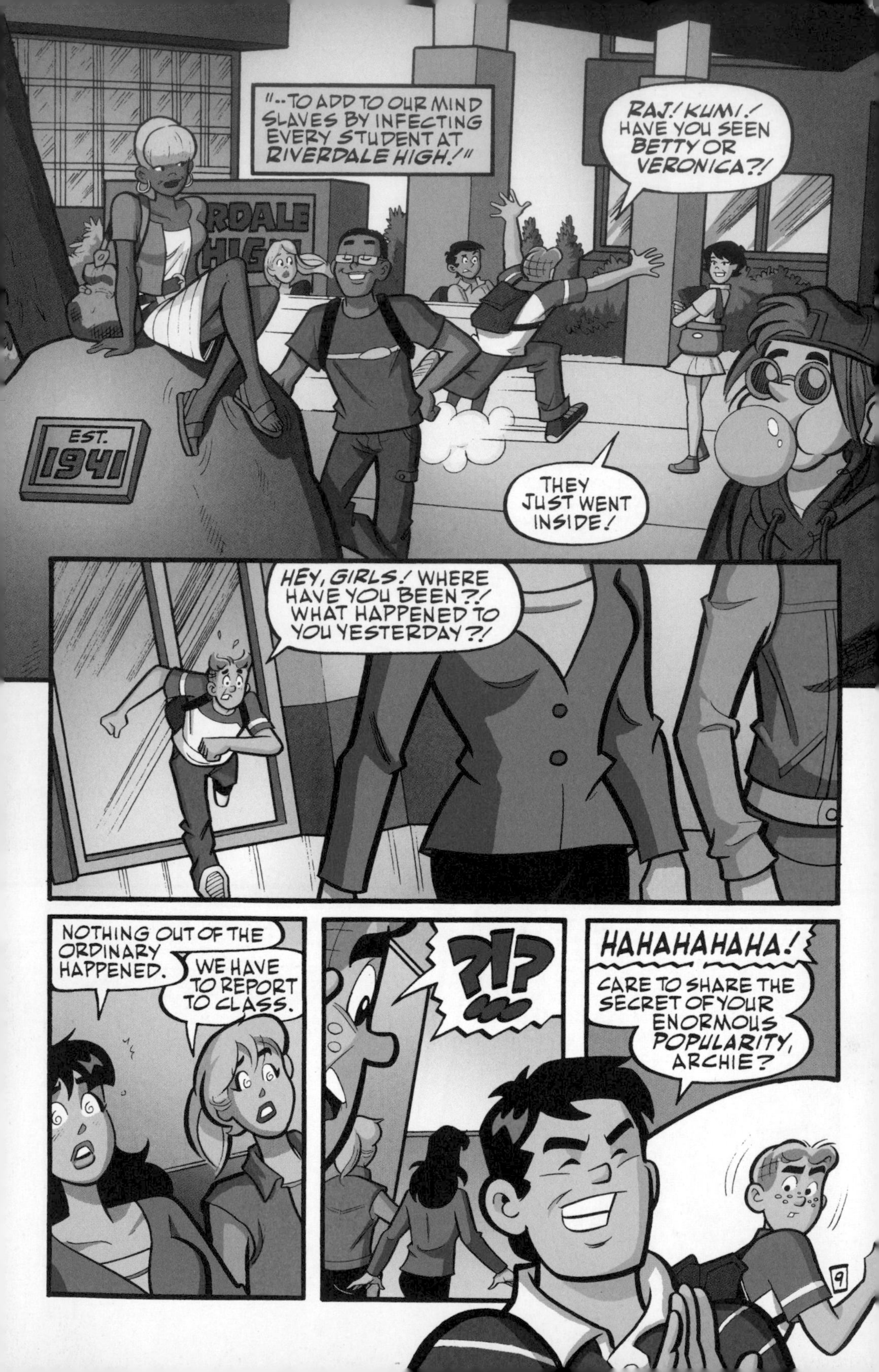
"..TO ADD TO OUR MIND SLAVES BY INFECTING EVERY STUDENT AT RIVERDALE HIGH!"
RAJ! KUMI! HAVE YOU SEEN BETTY OR VERONICA?!
RDALE HIGH
EST. 1941
THEY JUST WENT INSIDE!
HEY, GIRLS! WHERE HAVE YOU BEEN?! WHAT HAPPENED TO YOU YESTERDAY?!
NOTHING OUT OF THE ORDINARY HAPPENED.
WE HAVE TO REPORT TO CLASS.
?!?
HAHAHAHAHA!
CARE TO SHARE THE SECRET OF YOUR ENORMOUS POPULARITY, ARCHIE?
9

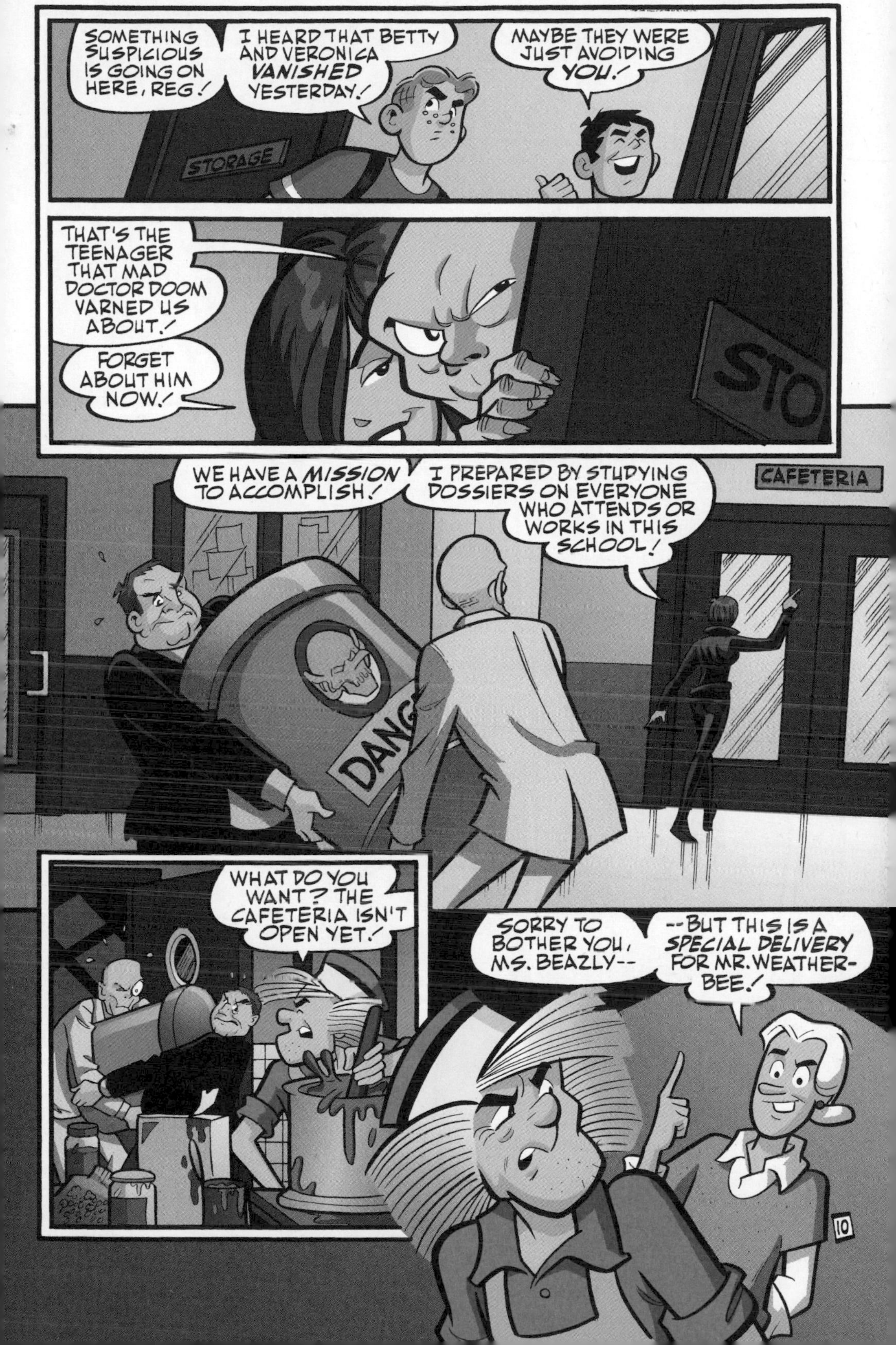
SOMETHING SUSPICIOUS IS GOING ON HERE, REG!
I HEARD THAT BETTY AND VERONICA VANISHED YESTERDAY!
MAYBE THEY WERE JUST AVOIDING YOU!
STORAGE
THAT'S THE TEENAGER THAT MAD DOCTOR DOOM VARNED US ABOUT!
FORGET ABOUT HIM NOW!
STO
WE HAVE A MISSION TO ACCOMPLISH!
I PREPARED BY STUDYING DOSSIERS ON EVERYONE WHO ATTENDS OR WORKS IN THIS SCHOOL!
CAFETERIA
DANG
WHAT DO YOU WANT? THE CAFETERIA ISN'T OPEN YET!
SORRY TO BOTHER YOU, MS. BEAZLY--
--BUT THIS IS A SPECIAL DELIVERY FOR MR. WEATHER-BEE!
10

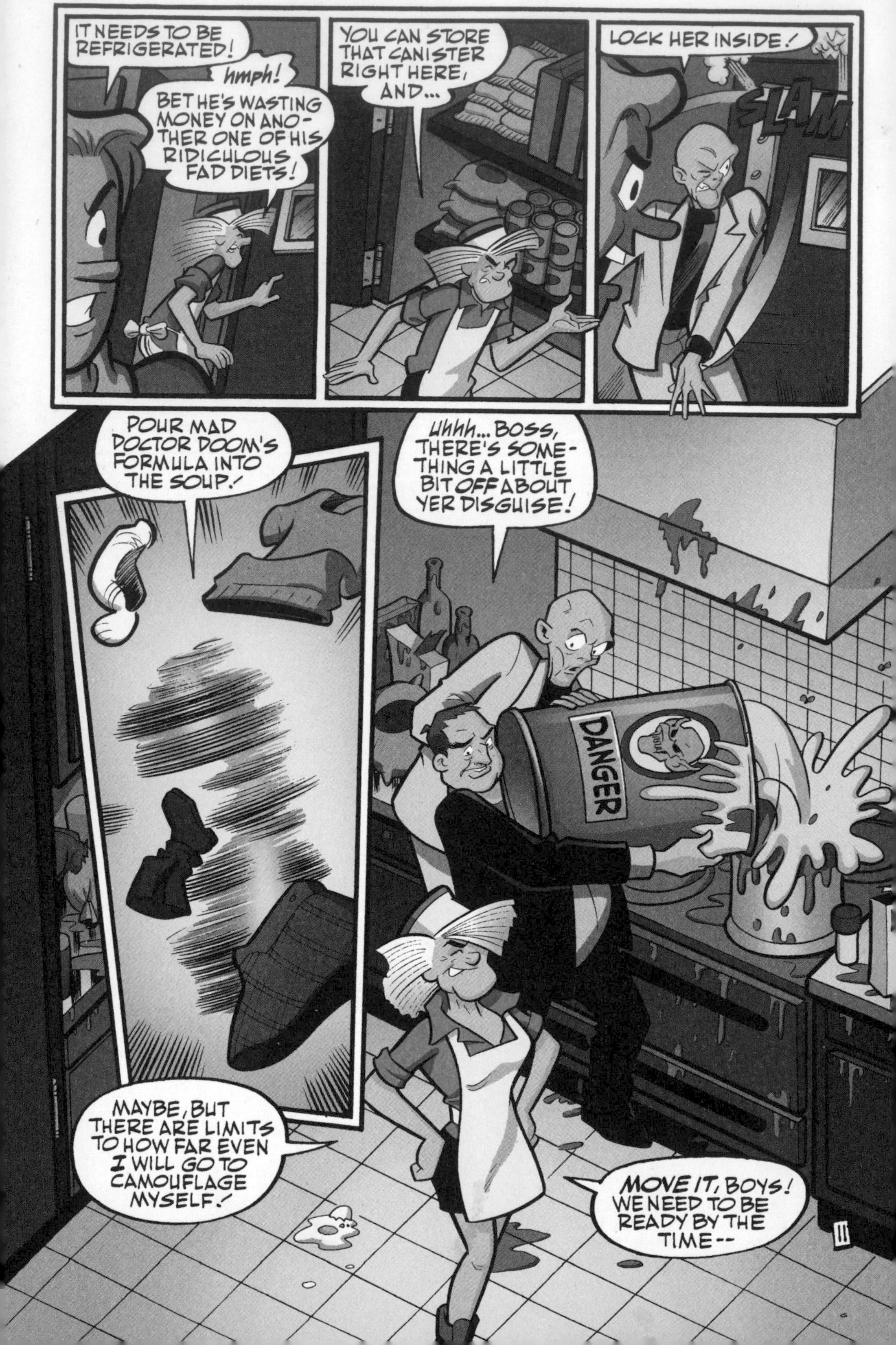
IT NEEDS TO BE REFRIGERATED!
hmph!
BET HE'S WASTING MONEY ON ANOTHER ONE OF HIS RIDICULOUS FAD DIETS!
YOU CAN STORE THAT CANISTER RIGHT HERE, AND...
LOCK HER INSIDE!
SLAM
POUR MAD DOCTOR DOOM'S FORMULA INTO THE SOUP!
uhhh... BOSS, THERE'S SOMETHING A LITTLE BIT OFF ABOUT YER DISGUISE!
DANGER
MAYBE, BUT THERE ARE LIMITS TO HOW FAR EVEN I WILL GO TO CAMOUFLAGE MYSELF!
MOVE IT, BOYS! WE NEED TO BE READY BY THE TIME--

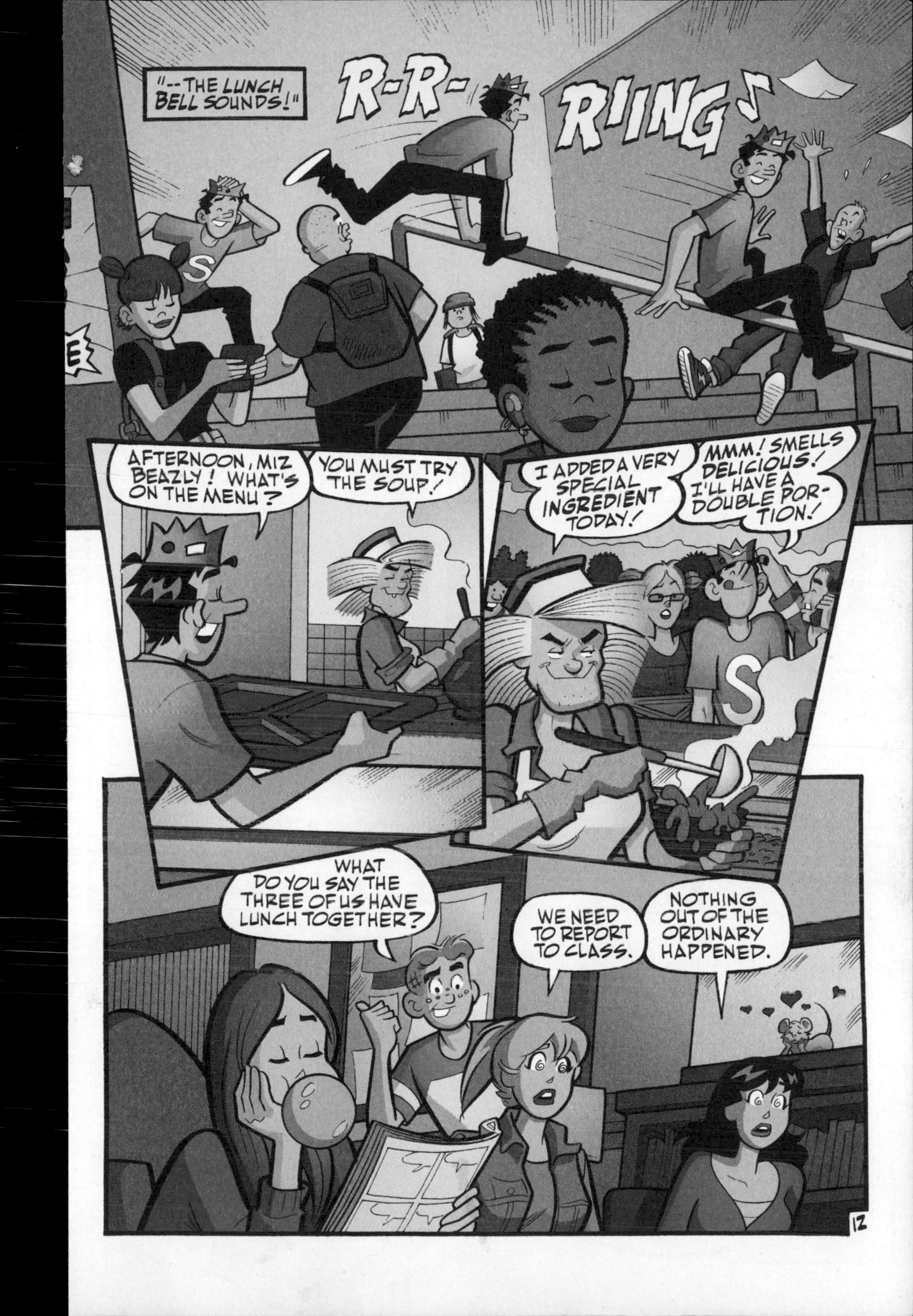
"--THE LUNCH BELL SOUNDS!"
R-R-RING
AFTERNOON, MIZ BEAZLY! WHAT'S ON THE MENU?
YOU MUST TRY THE SOUP!
I ADDED A VERY SPECIAL INGREDIENT TODAY!
MMM! SMELLS DELICIOUS! I'LL HAVE A DOUBLE POR-TION!
WHAT DO YOU SAY THE THREE OF US HAVE LUNCH TOGETHER?
WE NEED TO REPORT TO CLASS.
NOTHING OUT OF THE ORDINARY HAPPENED.

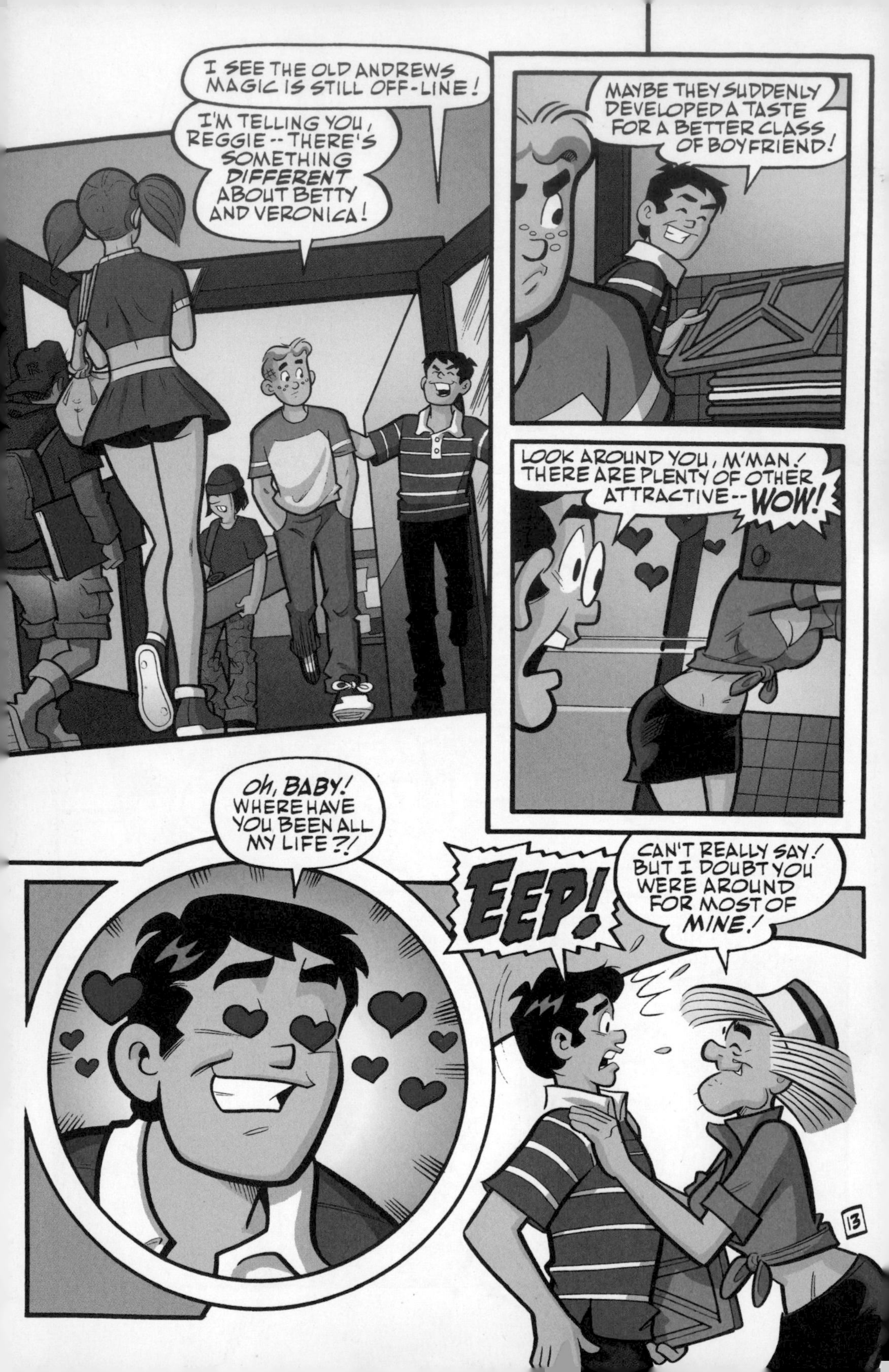

I SEE THE OLD ANDREWS MAGIC IS STILL OFF-LINE!
I'M TELLING YOU, REGGIE -- THERE'S SOMETHING DIFFERENT ABOUT BETTY AND VERONICA!
MAYBE THEY SUDDENLY DEVELOPED A TASTE FOR A BETTER CLASS OF BOYFRIEND!
LOOK AROUND YOU, M'MAN! THERE ARE PLENTY OF OTHER ATTRACTIVE-- WOW!
Oh, BABY! WHERE HAVE YOU BEEN ALL MY LIFE?!
EEP!
CAN'T REALLY SAY! BUT I DOUBT YOU WERE AROUND FOR MOST OF MINE!
13

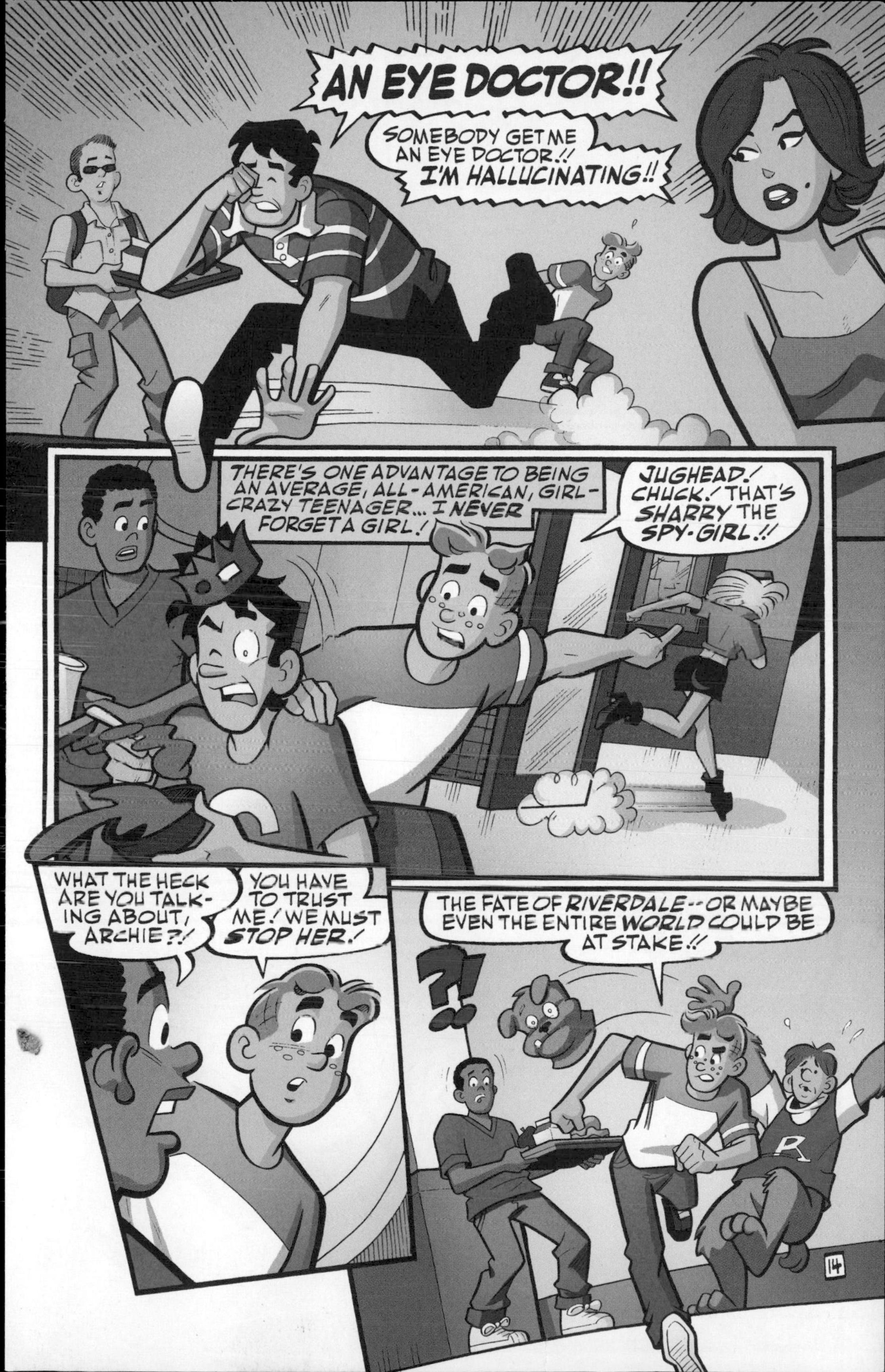
AN EYE DOCTOR!!
SOMEBODY GET ME AN EYE DOCTOR!! I'M HALLUCINATING!!
THERE'S ONE ADVANTAGE TO BEING AN AVERAGE, ALL-AMERICAN, GIRL-CRAZY TEENAGER... I NEVER FORGET A GIRL!
JUGHEAD! CHUCK! THAT'S SHARRY THE SPY-GIRL!!
WHAT THE HECK ARE YOU TALKING ABOUT, ARCHIE?!
YOU HAVE TO TRUST ME! WE MUST STOP HER!
THE FATE OF RIVERDALE--OR MAYBE EVEN THE ENTIRE WORLD COULD BE AT STAKE!!
?!
14

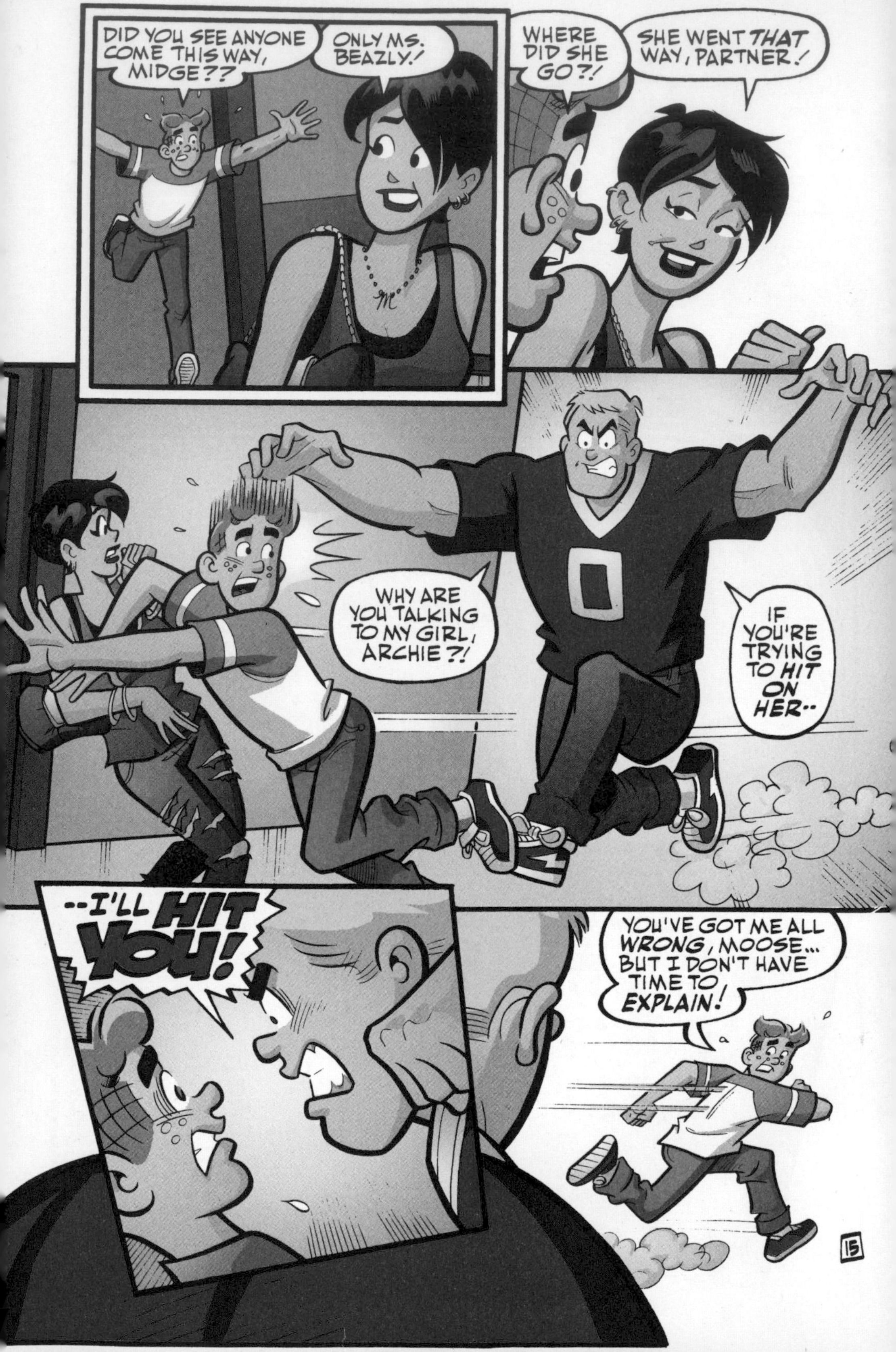
DID YOU SEE ANYONE COME THIS WAY, MIDGE??
ONLY MS. BEAZLY!
WHERE DID SHE GO?!
SHE WENT *THAT* WAY, PARTNER!
WHY ARE YOU TALKING TO MY GIRL, ARCHIE?!
IF YOU'RE TRYING TO *HIT ON HER*--
--I'LL *HIT YOU!*
YOU'VE GOT ME ALL *WRONG*, MOOSE... BUT I DON'T HAVE TIME TO *EXPLAIN*!

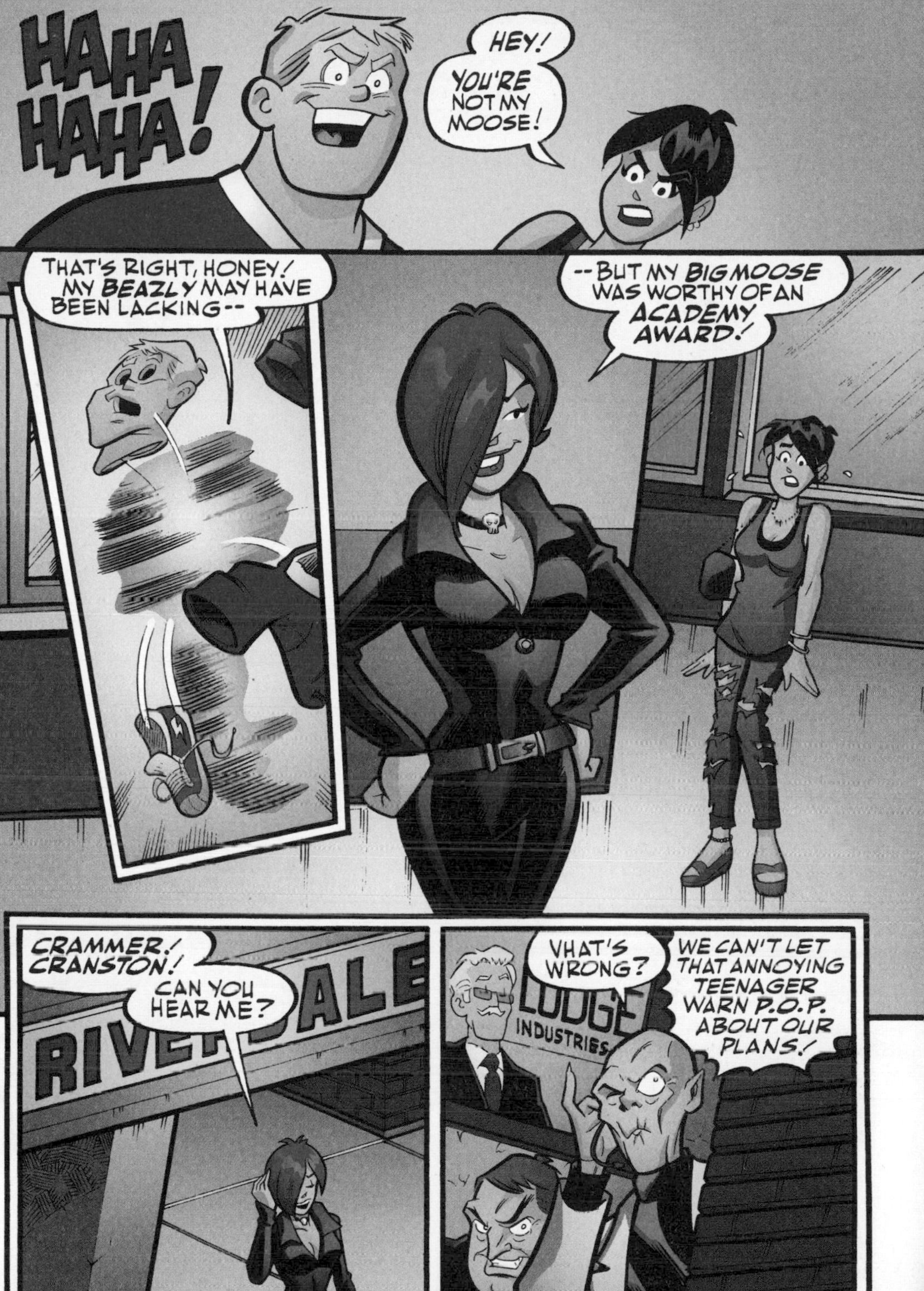
HAHA HAHA!
HEY! YOU'RE NOT MY MOOSE!
THAT'S RIGHT, HONEY! MY BEAZLY MAY HAVE BEEN LACKING--
--BUT MY BIG MOOSE WAS WORTHY OF AN ACADEMY AWARD!
CRAMMER! CRANSTON!
CAN YOU HEAR ME?
RIVERDALE
LODGE INDUSTRIES
VHAT'S WRONG?
WE CAN'T LET THAT ANNOYING TEENAGER WARN P.O.P. ABOUT OUR PLANS!
16

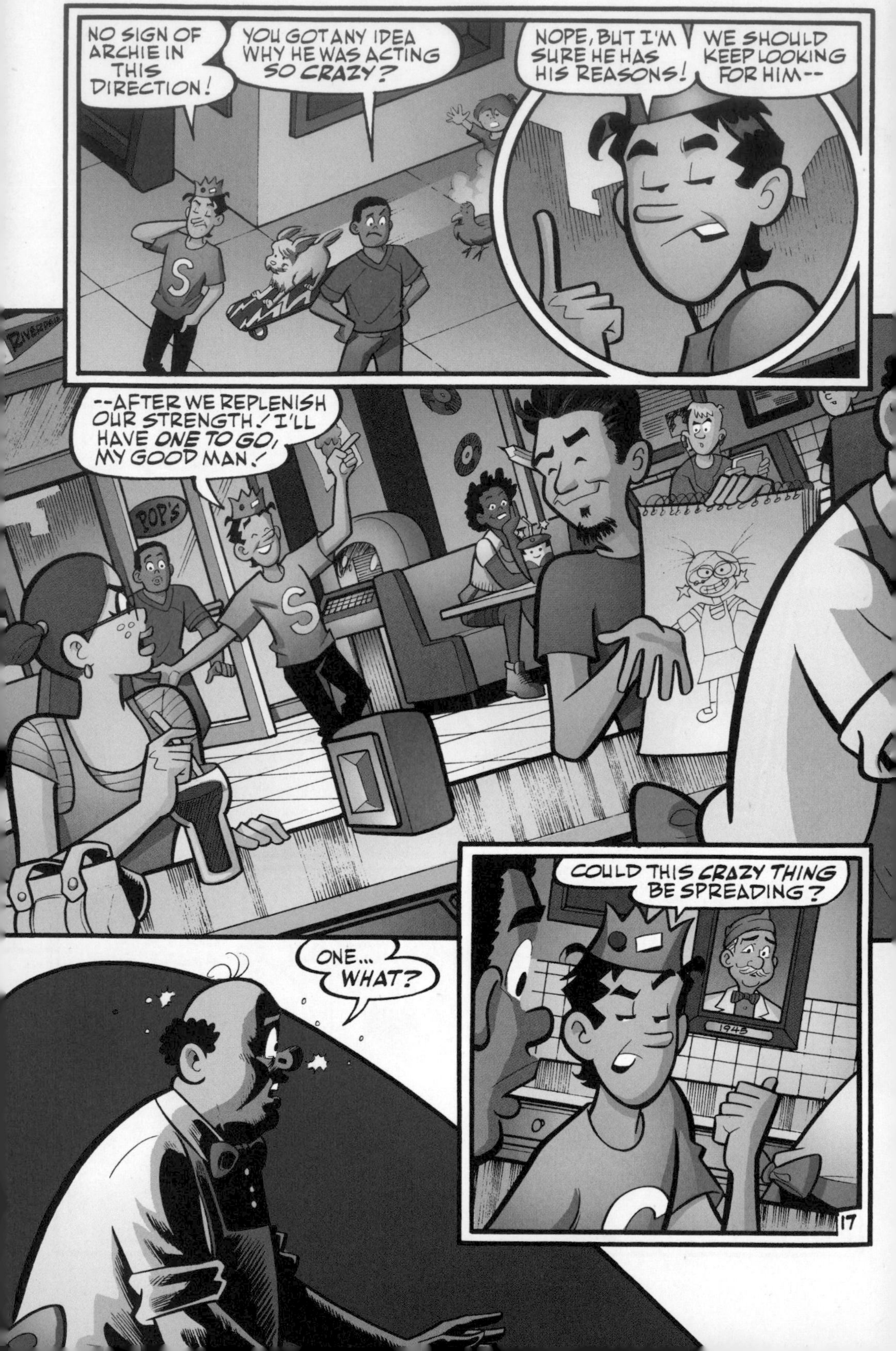

NO SIGN OF ARCHIE IN THIS DIRECTION!
YOU GOT ANY IDEA WHY HE WAS ACTING SO CRAZY?
NOPE, BUT I'M SURE HE HAS HIS REASONS!
WE SHOULD KEEP LOOKING FOR HIM--
--AFTER WE REPLENISH OUR STRENGTH! I'LL HAVE ONE TO GO, MY GOOD MAN!
POP'S
ONE... WHAT?
COULD THIS CRAZY THING BE SPREADING?
1943

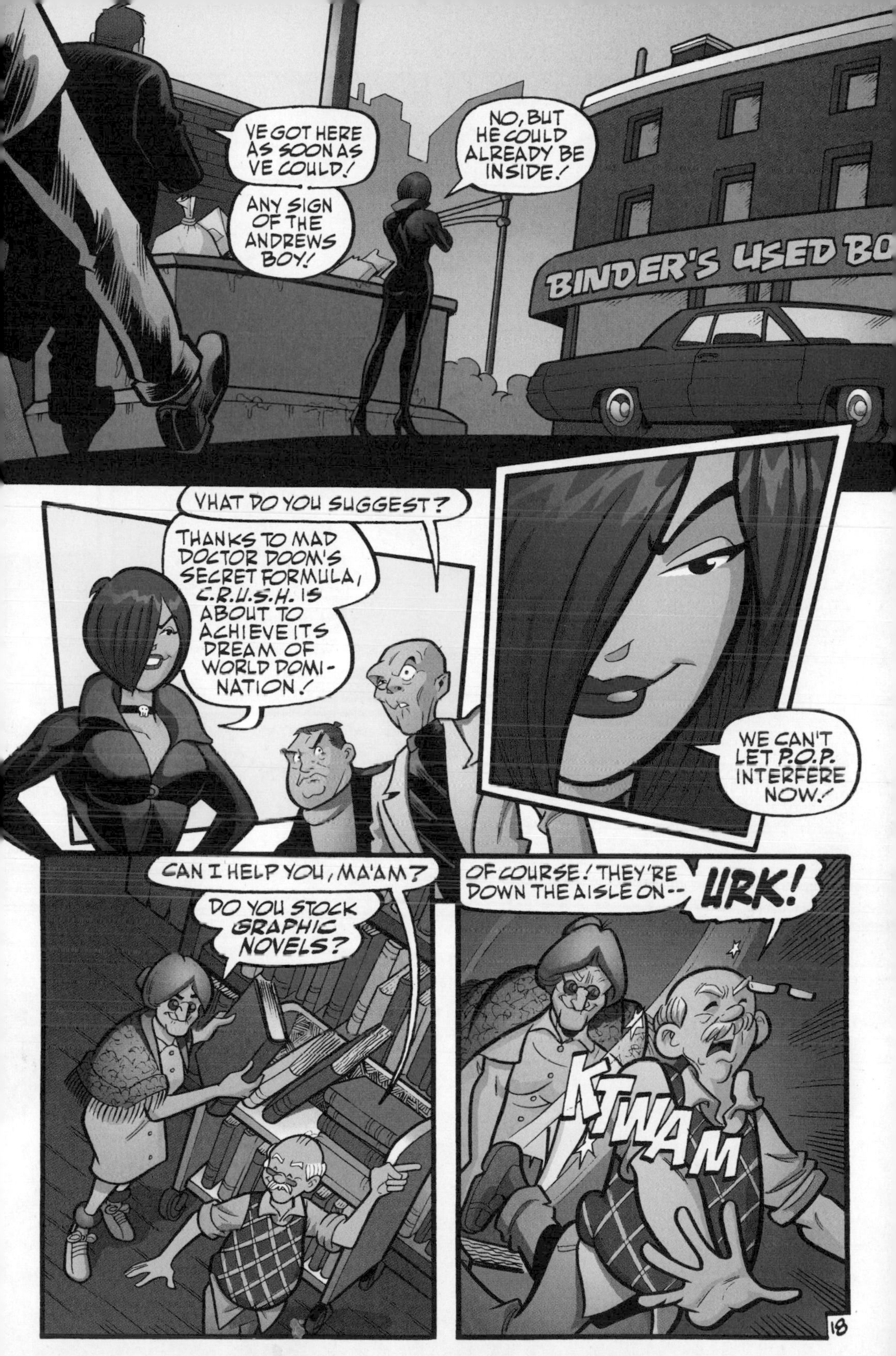
VE GOT HERE AS SOON AS VE COULD!
ANY SIGN OF THE ANDREWS BOY!
NO, BUT HE COULD ALREADY BE INSIDE!
BINDER'S USED BO
VHAT DO YOU SUGGEST?
THANKS TO MAD DOCTOR DOOM'S SECRET FORMULA, C.R.U.S.H. IS ABOUT TO ACHIEVE ITS DREAM OF WORLD DOMI-NATION!
WE CAN'T LET P.O.P. INTERFERE NOW!
CAN I HELP YOU, MA'AM?
DO YOU STOCK GRAPHIC NOVELS?
OF COURSE! THEY'RE DOWN THE AISLE ON--
URK!
KTWAM

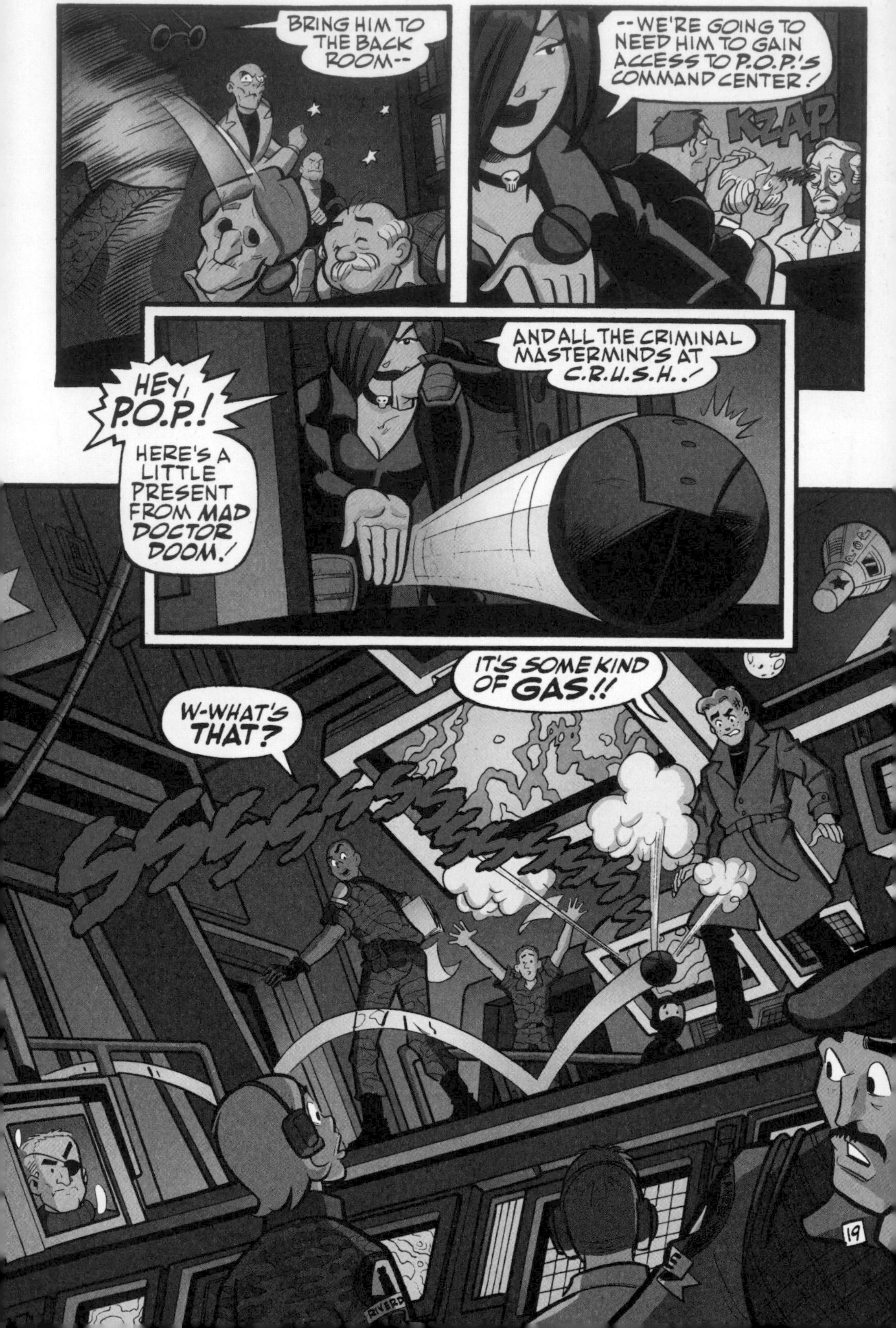
BRING HIM TO THE BACK ROOM--
--WE'RE GOING TO NEED HIM TO GAIN ACCESS TO P.O.P.'S COMMAND CENTER!
KZAP
AND ALL THE CRIMINAL MASTERMINDS AT C.R.U.S.H.!
HEY, P.O.P.!
HERE'S A LITTLE PRESENT FROM MAD DOCTOR DOOM!
IT'S SOME KIND OF GAS!!
W-WHAT'S THAT?
SSSHHHSSSSSSSSSS

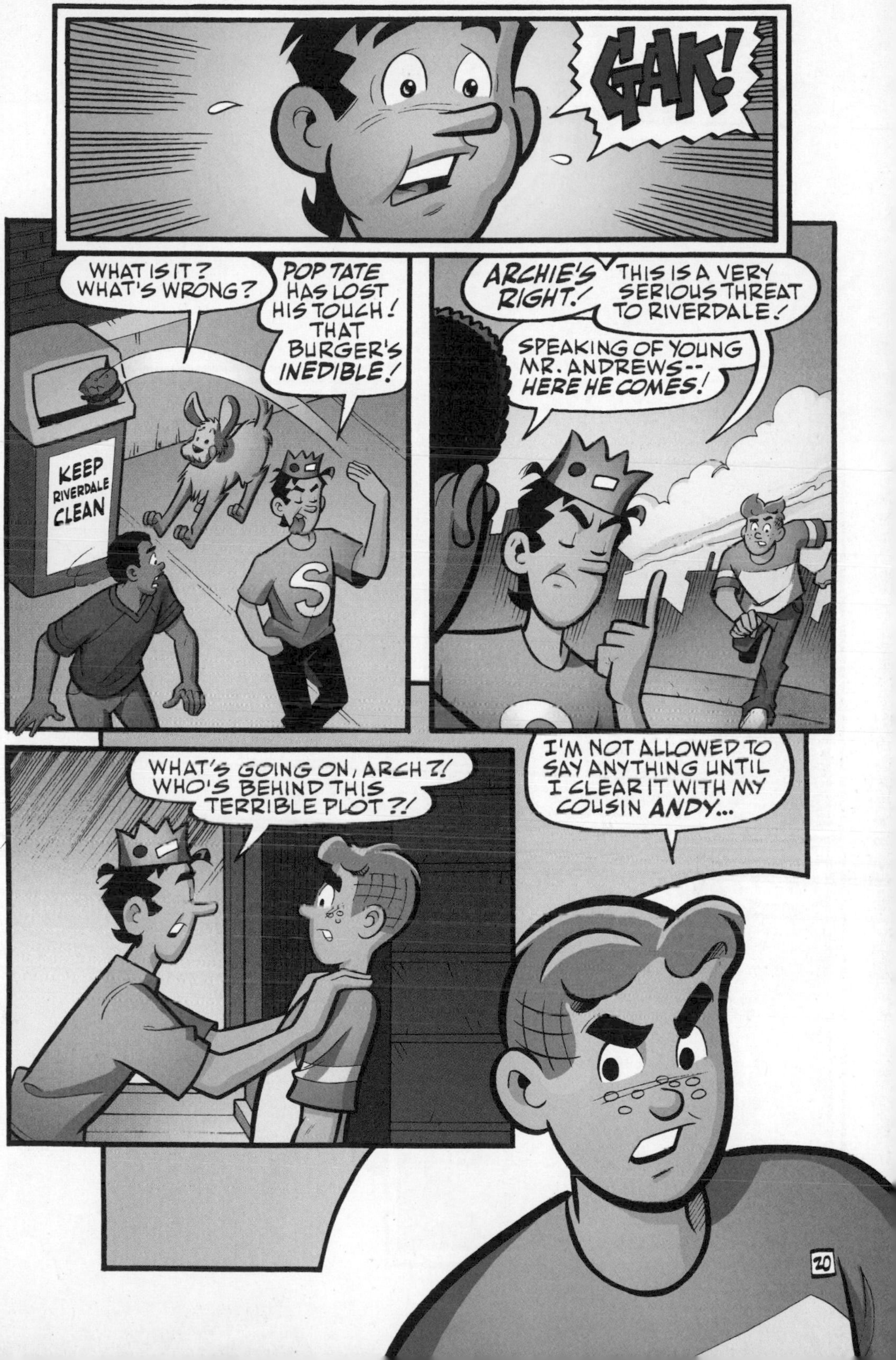
GAK!
WHAT IS IT? WHAT'S WRONG?
POP TATE HAS LOST HIS TOUCH! THAT BURGER'S INEDIBLE!
KEEP RIVERDALE CLEAN
ARCHIE'S RIGHT!
THIS IS A VERY SERIOUS THREAT TO RIVERDALE!
SPEAKING OF YOUNG MR. ANDREWS-- HERE HE COMES!
WHAT'S GOING ON, ARCH?! WHO'S BEHIND THIS TERRIBLE PLOT?!
I'M NOT ALLOWED TO SAY ANYTHING UNTIL I CLEAR IT WITH MY COUSIN ANDY...
20

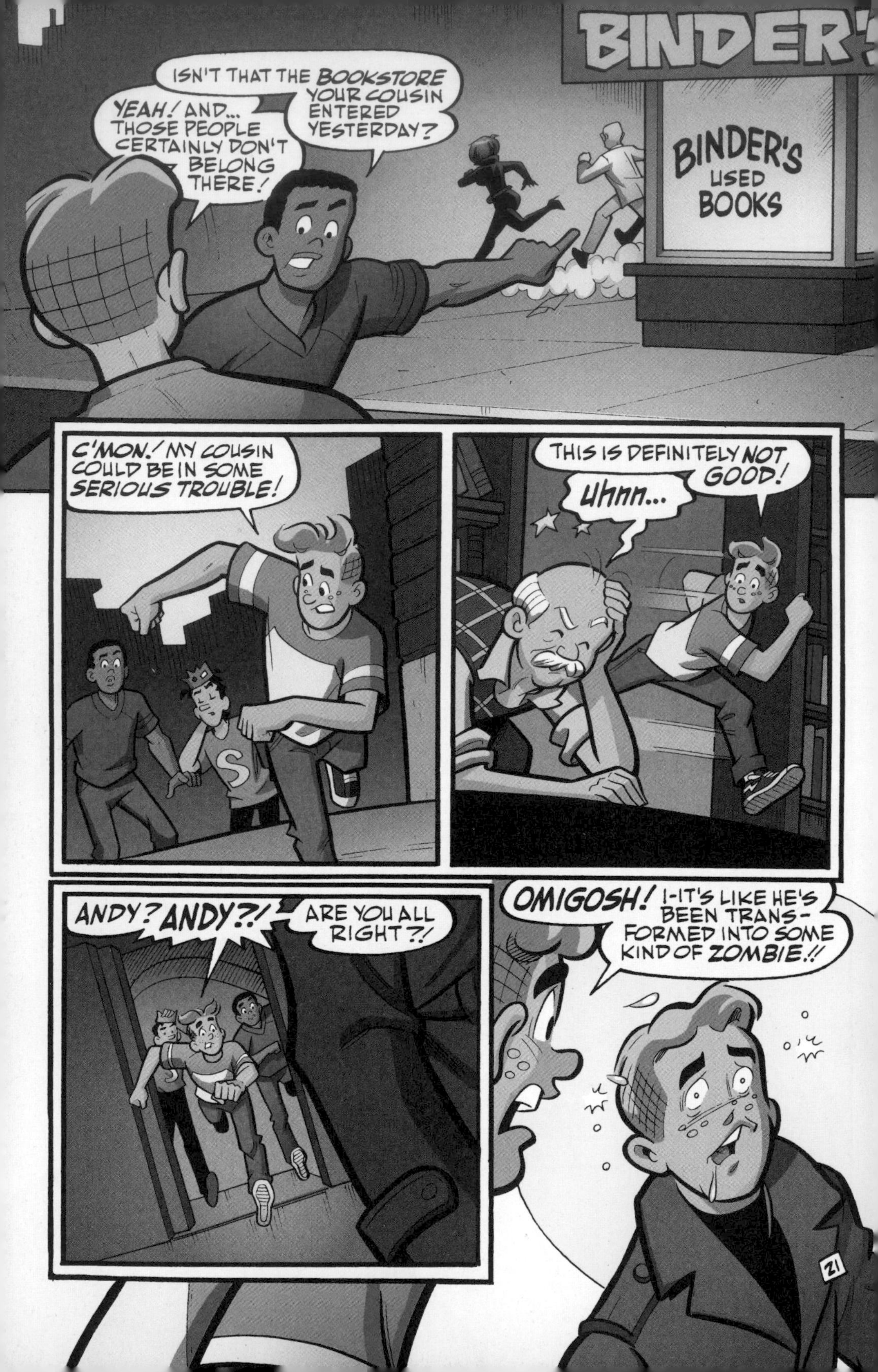
BINDER'S
ISN'T THAT THE BOOKSTORE YOUR COUSIN ENTERED YESTERDAY?
YEAH! AND... THOSE PEOPLE CERTAINLY DON'T BELONG THERE!
BINDER'S USED BOOKS
C'MON! MY COUSIN COULD BE IN SOME SERIOUS TROUBLE!
THIS IS DEFINITELY NOT GOOD!
uhnn...
ANDY? ANDY?!
ARE YOU ALL RIGHT?!
OMIGOSH! I-IT'S LIKE HE'S BEEN TRANS-FORMED INTO SOME KIND OF ZOMBIE!!
21

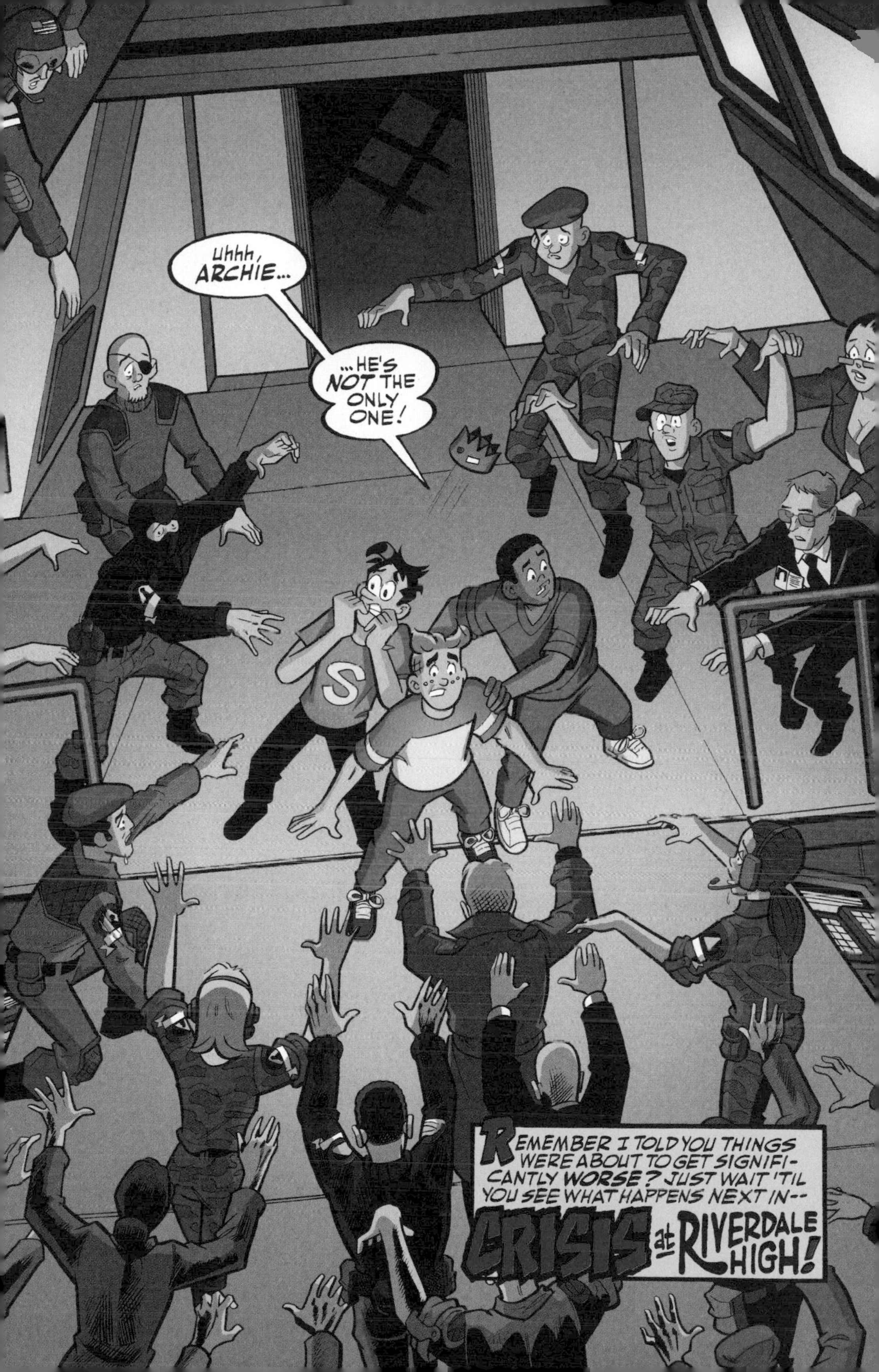
UHHH, ARCHIE...
...HE'S NOT THE ONLY ONE!
REMEMBER I TOLD YOU THINGS WERE ABOUT TO GET SIGNIFI-CANTLY WORSE? JUST WAIT 'TIL YOU SEE WHAT HAPPENS NEXT IN--
CRISIS at RIVERDALE HIGH!

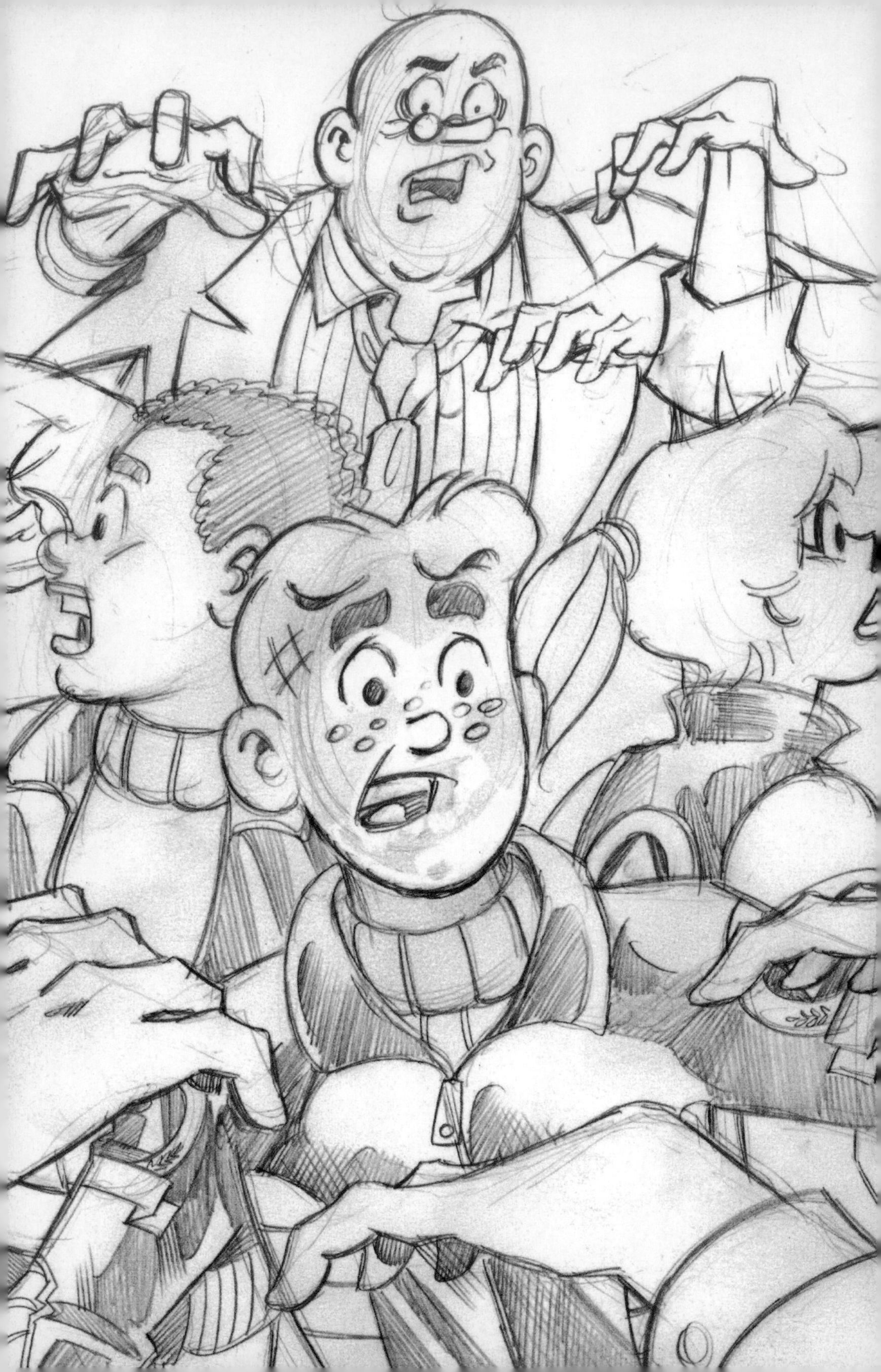

MISSION 3: CRISIS AT RIVERDALE HIGH

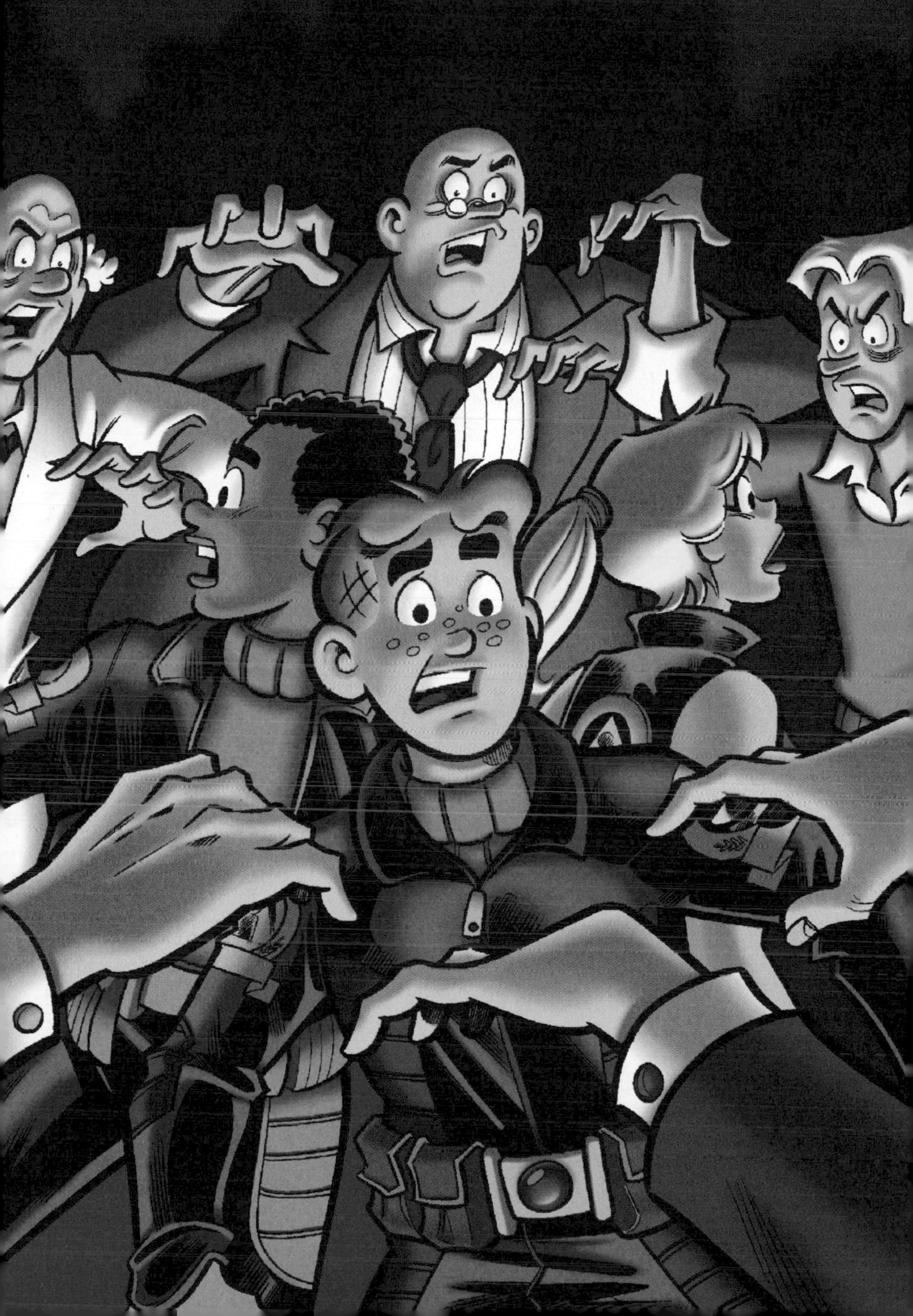

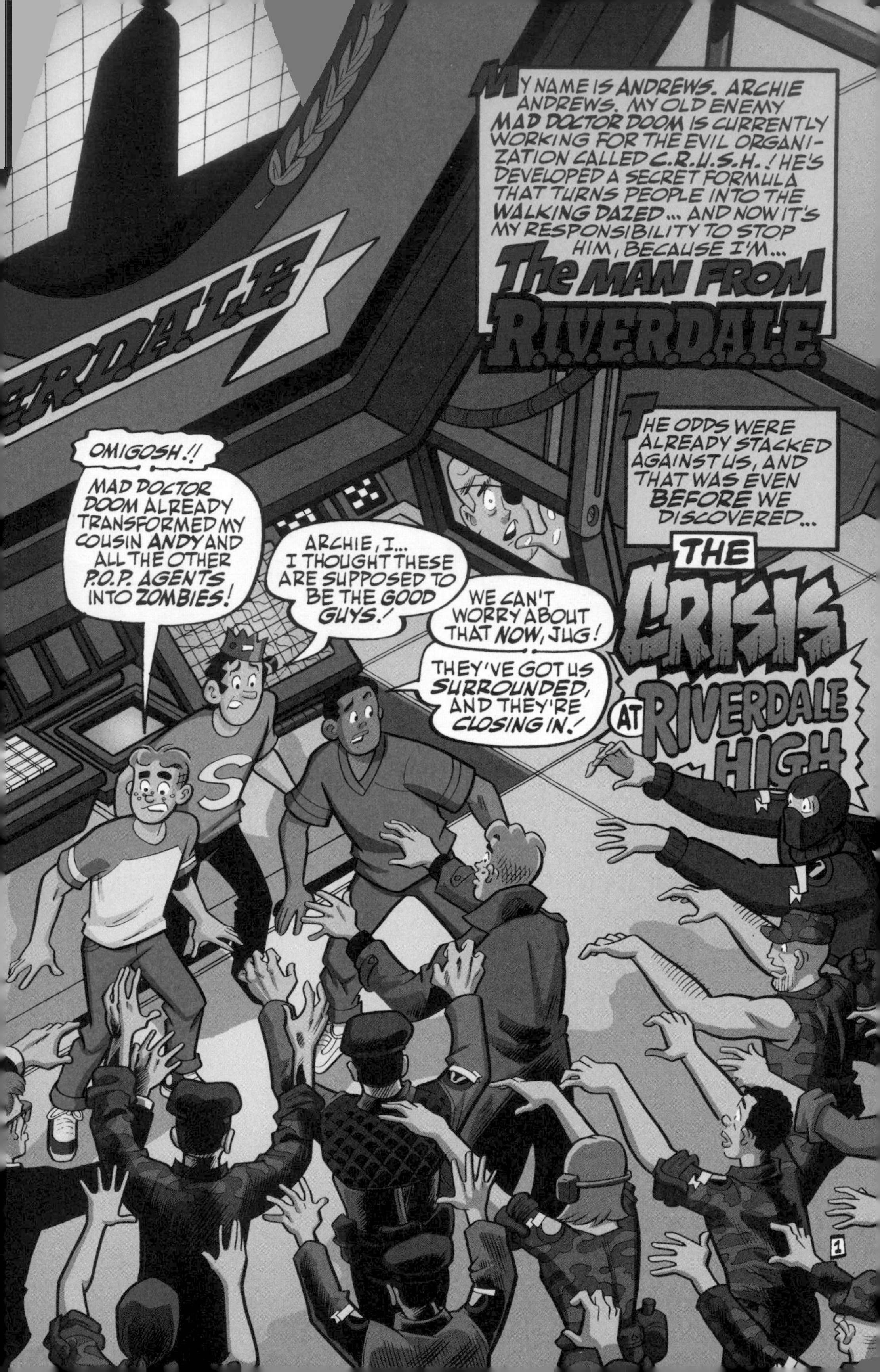

MY NAME IS ANDREWS. ARCHIE ANDREWS. MY OLD ENEMY MAD DOCTOR DOOM IS CURRENTLY WORKING FOR THE EVIL ORGANIZATION CALLED C.R.U.S.H.! HE'S DEVELOPED A SECRET FORMULA THAT TURNS PEOPLE INTO THE WALKING DAZED... AND NOW IT'S MY RESPONSIBILITY TO STOP HIM, BECAUSE I'M...
The MAN FROM R.I.V.E.R.D.A.L.E.
THE ODDS WERE ALREADY STACKED AGAINST US, AND THAT WAS EVEN BEFORE WE DISCOVERED...
THE CRISIS AT RIVERDALE HIGH
OMIGOSH!!
MAD DOCTOR DOOM ALREADY TRANSFORMED MY COUSIN ANDY AND ALL THE OTHER P.O.P. AGENTS INTO ZOMBIES!
ARCHIE, I... I THOUGHT THESE ARE SUPPOSED TO BE THE GOOD GUYS.!
WE CAN'T WORRY ABOUT THAT NOW, JUG!
THEY'VE GOT US SURROUNDED, AND THEY'RE CLOSING IN.!
1

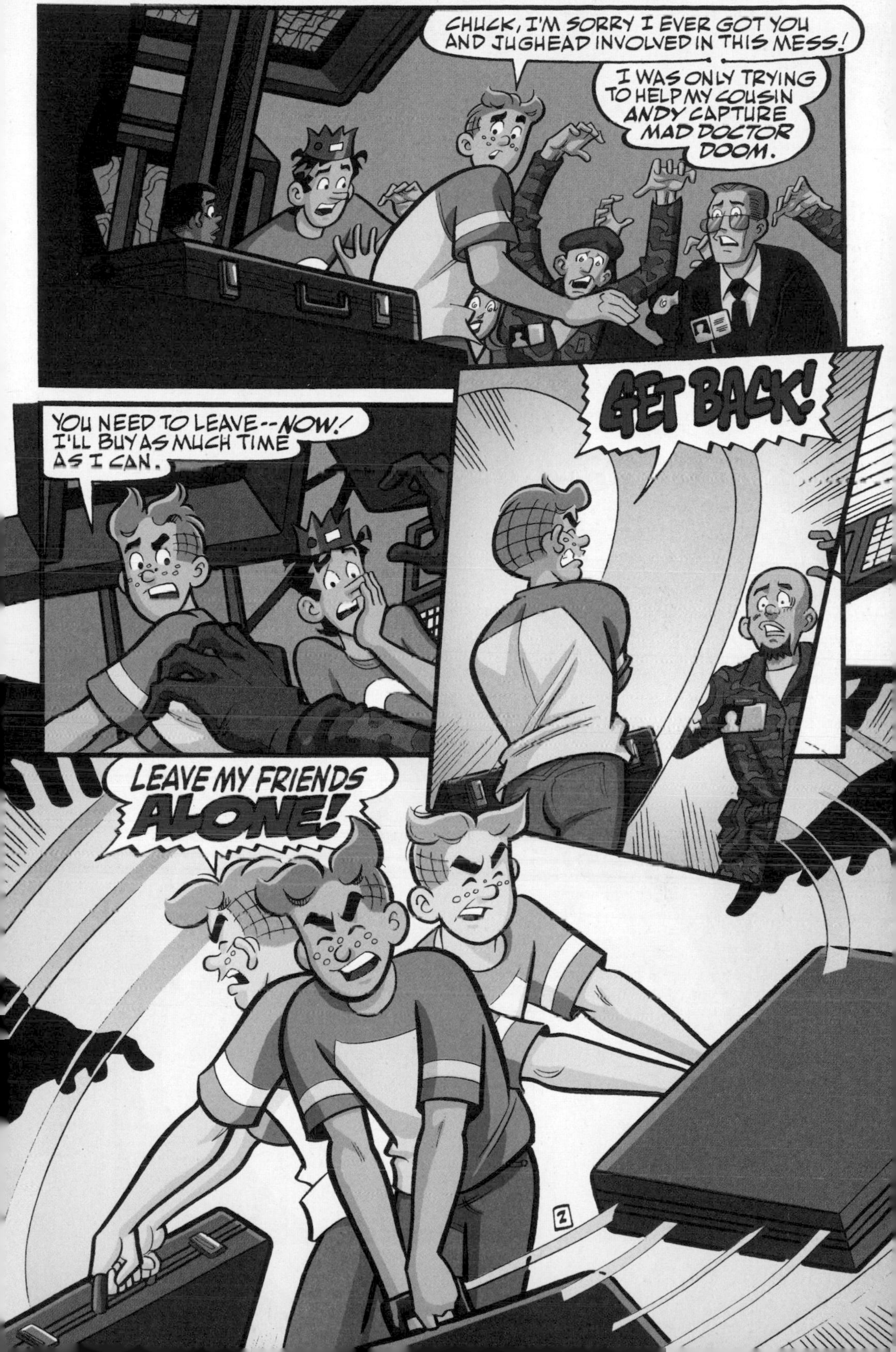

CHUCK, I'M SORRY I EVER GOT YOU AND JUGHEAD INVOLVED IN THIS MESS!
I WAS ONLY TRYING TO HELP MY COUSIN ANDY CAPTURE MAD DOCTOR DOOM.
YOU NEED TO LEAVE--NOW! I'LL BUY AS MUCH TIME AS I CAN.
GET BACK!
LEAVE MY FRIENDS ALONE!
2

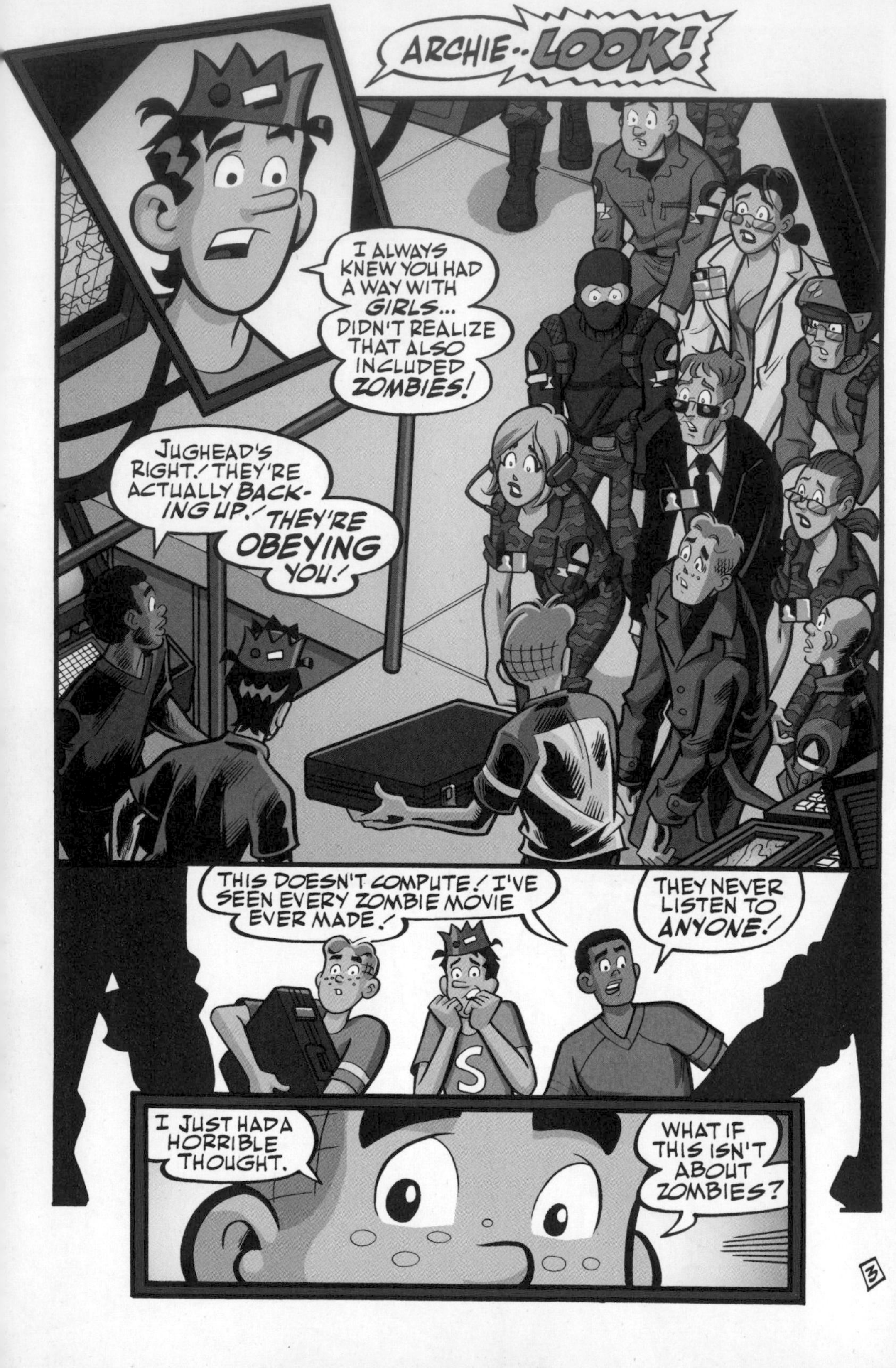

ARCHIE.. LOOK!
I ALWAYS KNEW YOU HAD A WAY WITH GIRLS... DIDN'T REALIZE THAT ALSO INCLUDED ZOMBIES!
JUGHEAD'S RIGHT! THEY'RE ACTUALLY BACKING UP!
THEY'RE OBEYING YOU!
THIS DOESN'T COMPUTE! I'VE SEEN EVERY ZOMBIE MOVIE EVER MADE!
THEY NEVER LISTEN TO ANYONE!
I JUST HAD A HORRIBLE THOUGHT.
WHAT IF THIS ISN'T ABOUT ZOMBIES?
3

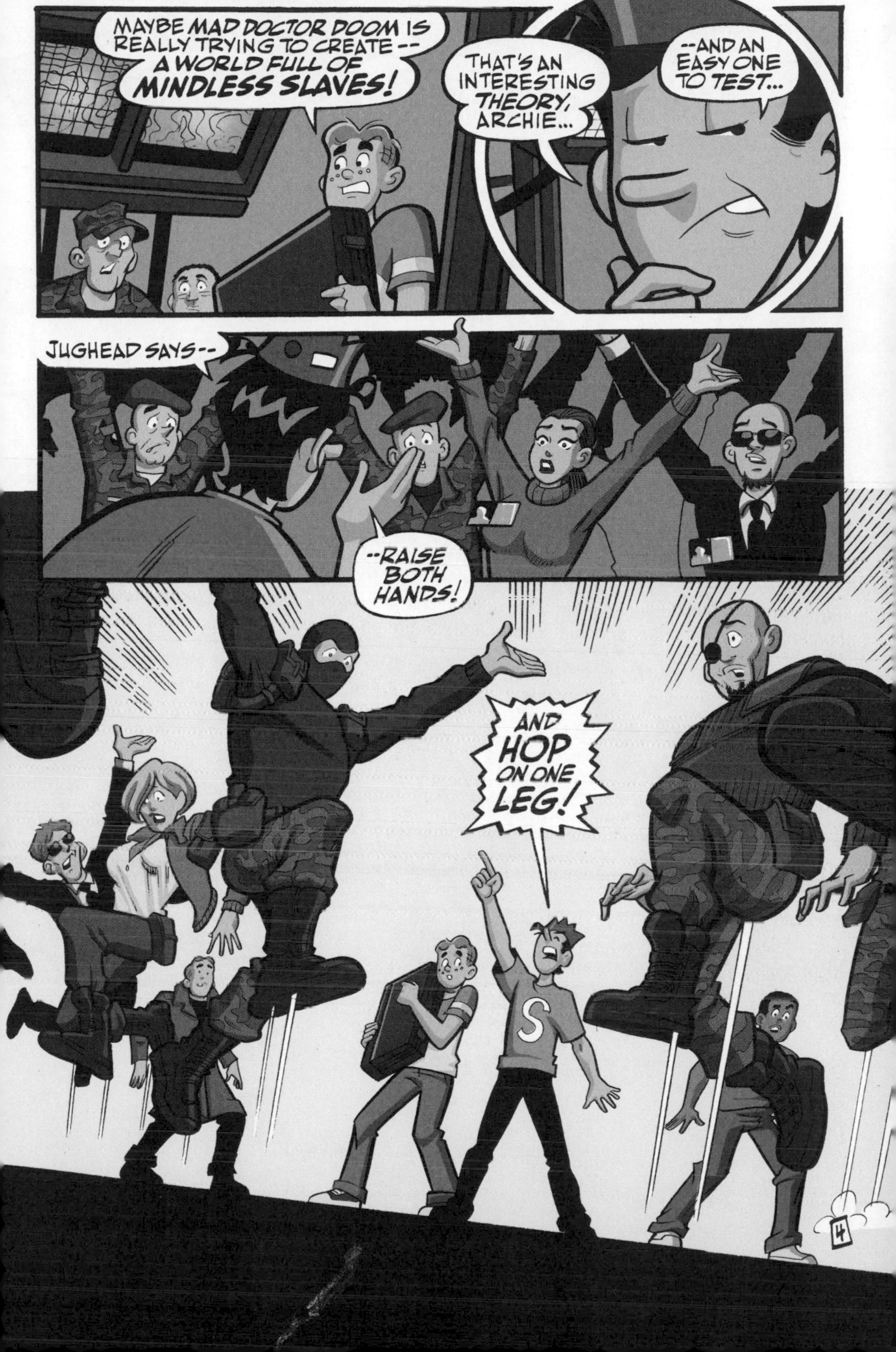
MAYBE MAD DOCTOR DOOM IS REALLY TRYING TO CREATE -- A WORLD FULL OF MINDLESS SLAVES!
THAT'S AN INTERESTING THEORY, ARCHIE...
--AND AN EASY ONE TO TEST...
JUGHEAD SAYS--
--RAISE BOTH HANDS!
AND HOP ON ONE LEG!
4

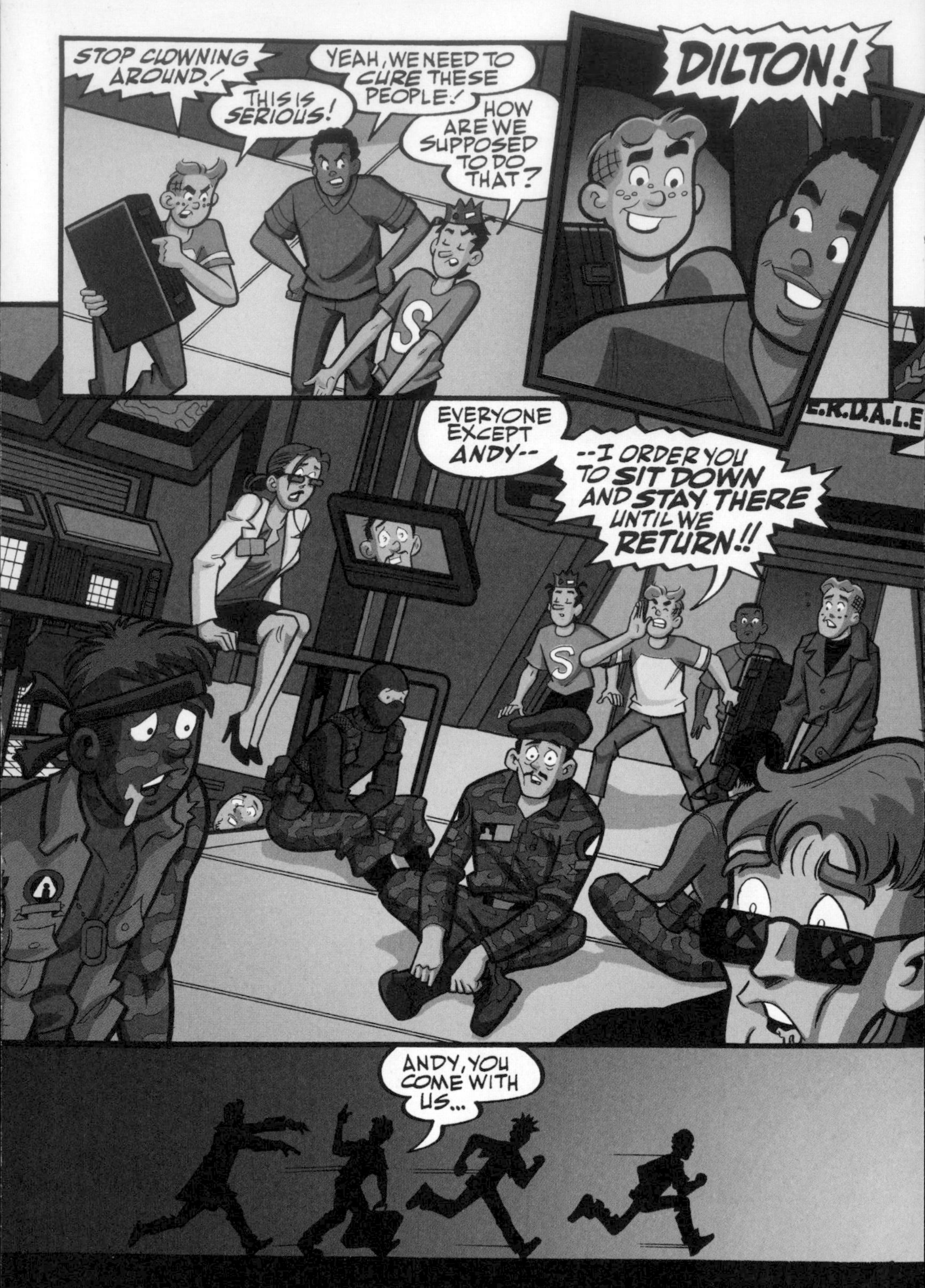

STOP CLOWNING AROUND!
THIS IS SERIOUS!
YEAH, WE NEED TO CURE THESE PEOPLE!
HOW ARE WE SUPPOSED TO DO THAT?
DILTON!
EVERYONE EXCEPT ANDY--
--I ORDER YOU TO SIT DOWN AND STAY THERE UNTIL WE RETURN!!
ANDY, YOU COME WITH US...

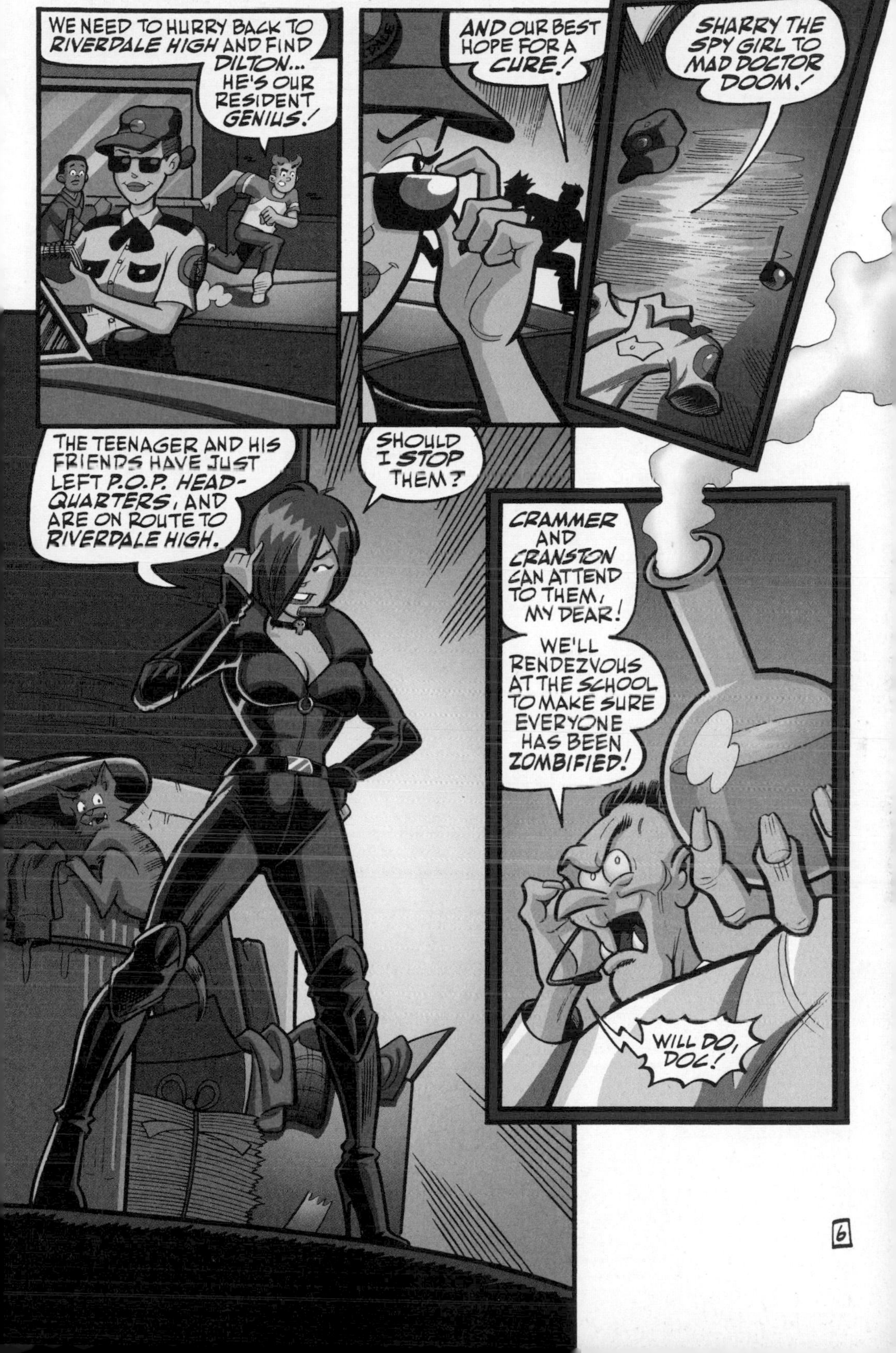
WE NEED TO HURRY BACK TO RIVERDALE HIGH AND FIND DILTON...
HE'S OUR RESIDENT GENIUS!
AND OUR BEST HOPE FOR A CURE!
SHARRY THE SPY GIRL TO MAD DOCTOR DOOM!
THE TEENAGER AND HIS FRIENDS HAVE JUST LEFT P.O.P. HEAD-QUARTERS, AND ARE ON ROUTE TO RIVERDALE HIGH.
SHOULD I STOP THEM?
CRAMMER AND CRANSTON CAN ATTEND TO THEM, MY DEAR!
WE'LL RENDEZVOUS AT THE SCHOOL TO MAKE SURE EVERYONE HAS BEEN ZOMBIFIED!
WILL DO, DOC!

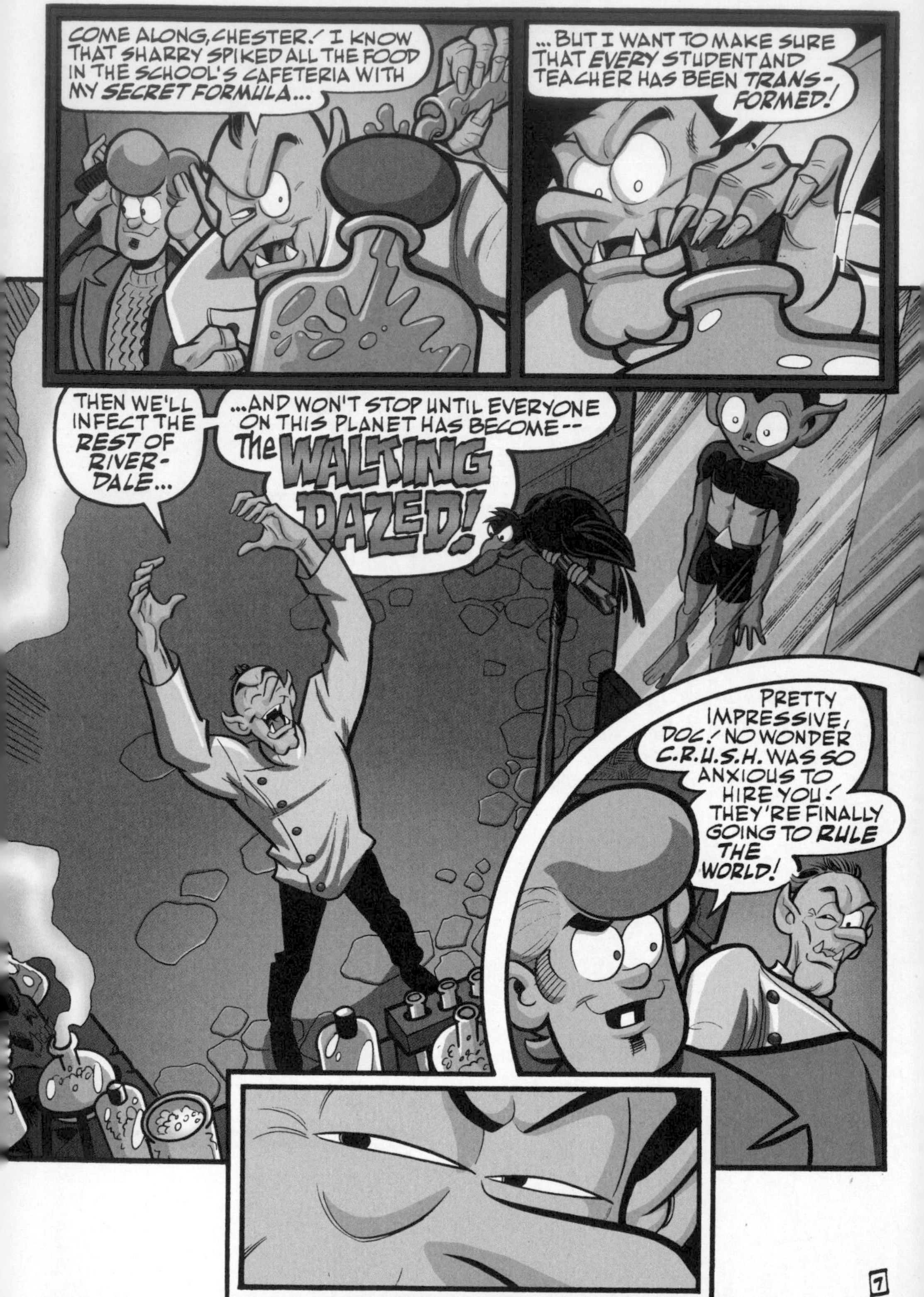
COME ALONG, CHESTER! I KNOW THAT SHARRY SPIKED ALL THE FOOD IN THE SCHOOL'S CAFETERIA WITH MY SECRET FORMULA...
... BUT I WANT TO MAKE SURE THAT EVERY STUDENT AND TEACHER HAS BEEN TRANS-FORMED!
THEN WE'LL INFECT THE REST OF RIVER-DALE...
...AND WON'T STOP UNTIL EVERYONE ON THIS PLANET HAS BECOME-- The WALKING DAZED!
PRETTY IMPRESSIVE, DOC! NO WONDER C.R.U.S.H. WAS SO ANXIOUS TO HIRE YOU! THEY'RE FINALLY GOING TO RULE THE WORLD!

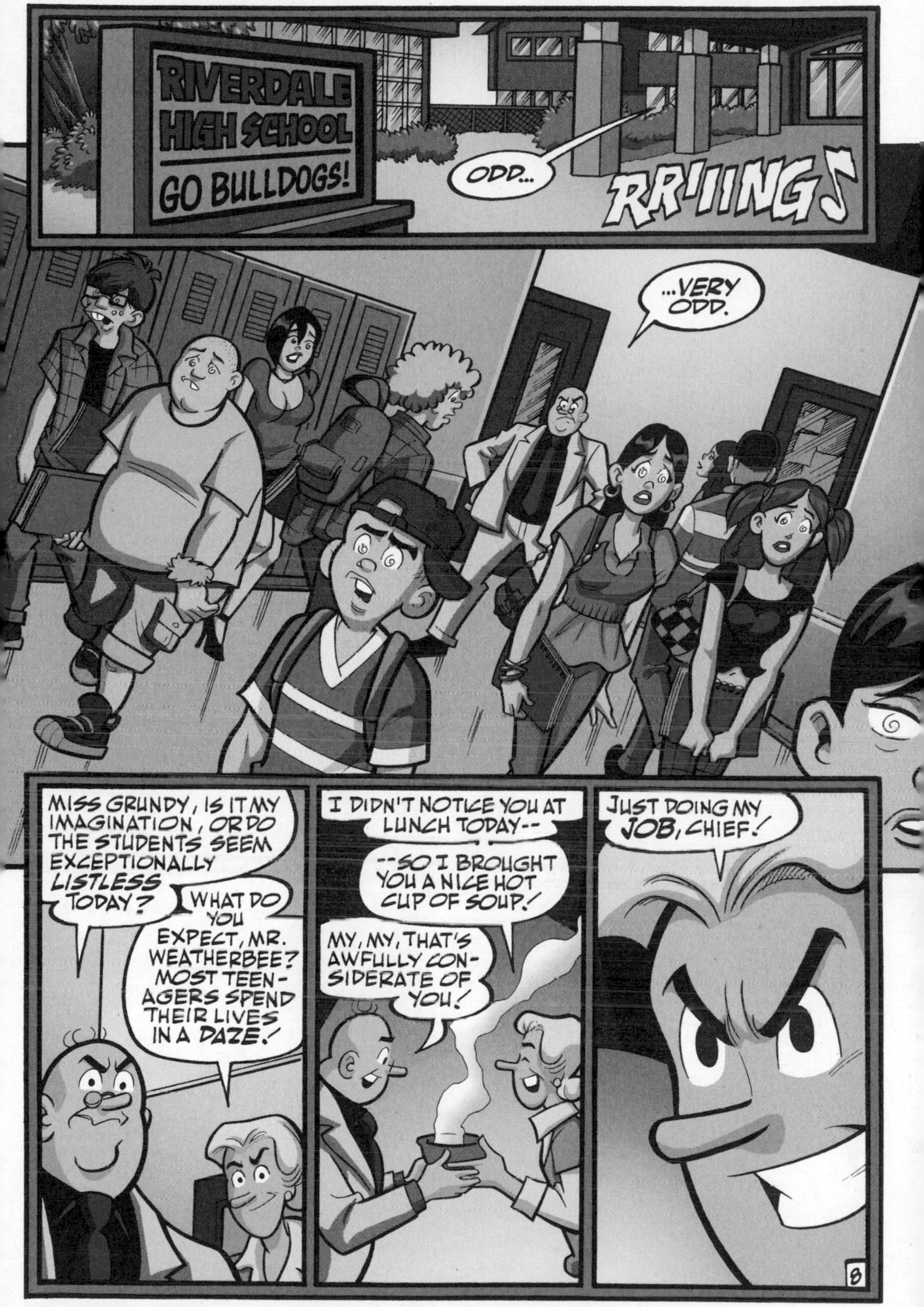
RIVERDALE HIGH SCHOOL
GO BULLDOGS!
ODD...
RRIIING
...VERY ODD.
MISS GRUNDY, IS IT MY IMAGINATION, OR DO THE STUDENTS SEEM EXCEPTIONALLY LISTLESS TODAY?
WHAT DO YOU EXPECT, MR. WEATHERBEE? MOST TEEN-AGERS SPEND THEIR LIVES IN A DAZE!
I DIDN'T NOTICE YOU AT LUNCH TODAY--
--SO I BROUGHT YOU A NICE HOT CUP OF SOUP!
MY, MY, THAT'S AWFULLY CON-SIDERATE OF YOU!
JUST DOING MY JOB, CHIEF!
8

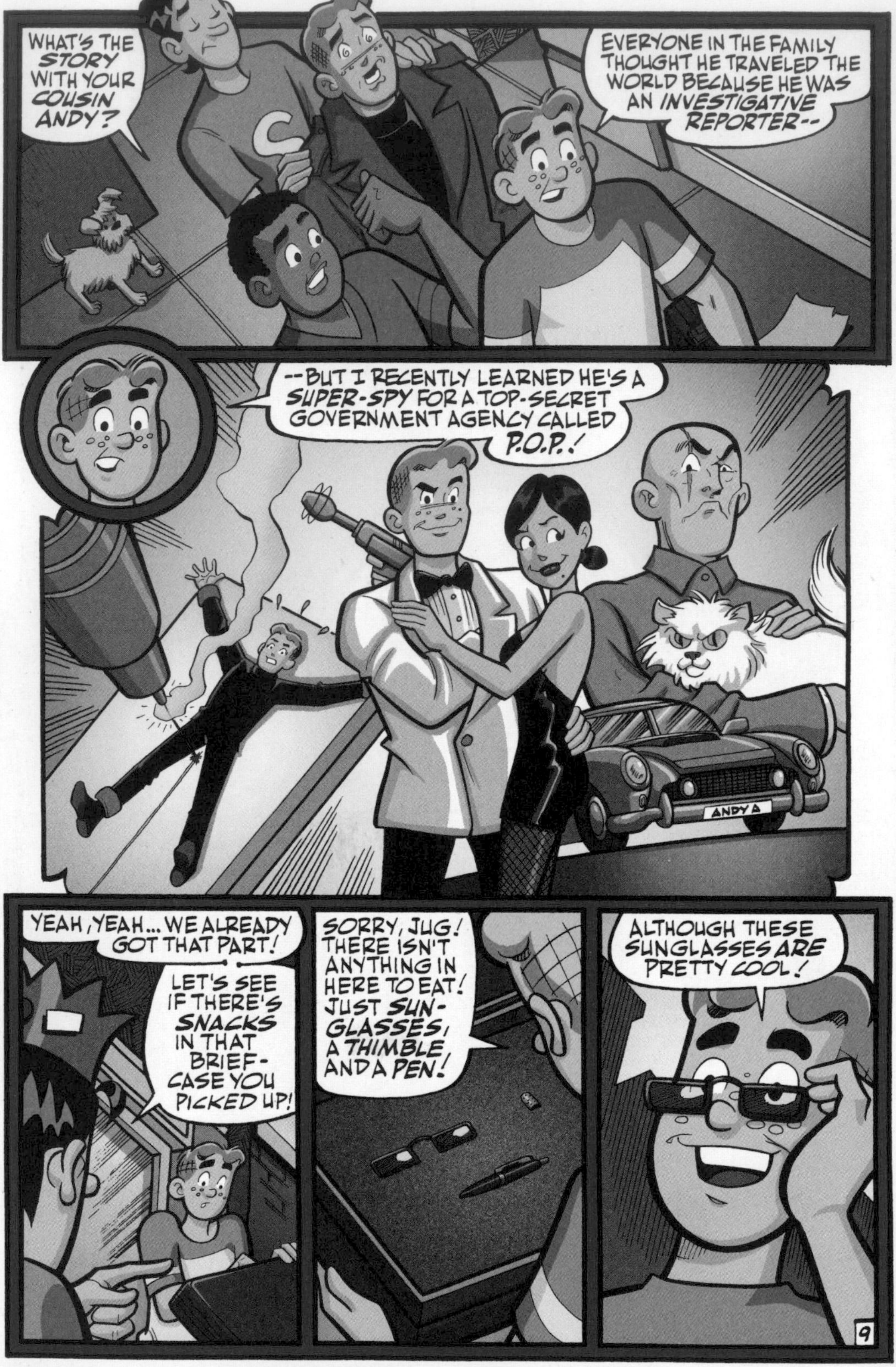
WHAT'S THE STORY WITH YOUR COUSIN ANDY?
EVERYONE IN THE FAMILY THOUGHT HE TRAVELED THE WORLD BECAUSE HE WAS AN INVESTIGATIVE REPORTER--
--BUT I RECENTLY LEARNED HE'S A SUPER-SPY FOR A TOP-SECRET GOVERNMENT AGENCY CALLED P.O.P.!
ANDY A
YEAH, YEAH... WE ALREADY GOT THAT PART!
LET'S SEE IF THERE'S SNACKS IN THAT BRIEF-CASE YOU PICKED UP!
SORRY, JUG! THERE ISN'T ANYTHING IN HERE TO EAT! JUST SUN-GLASSES, A THIMBLE AND A PEN!
ALTHOUGH THESE SUNGLASSES ARE PRETTY COOL!

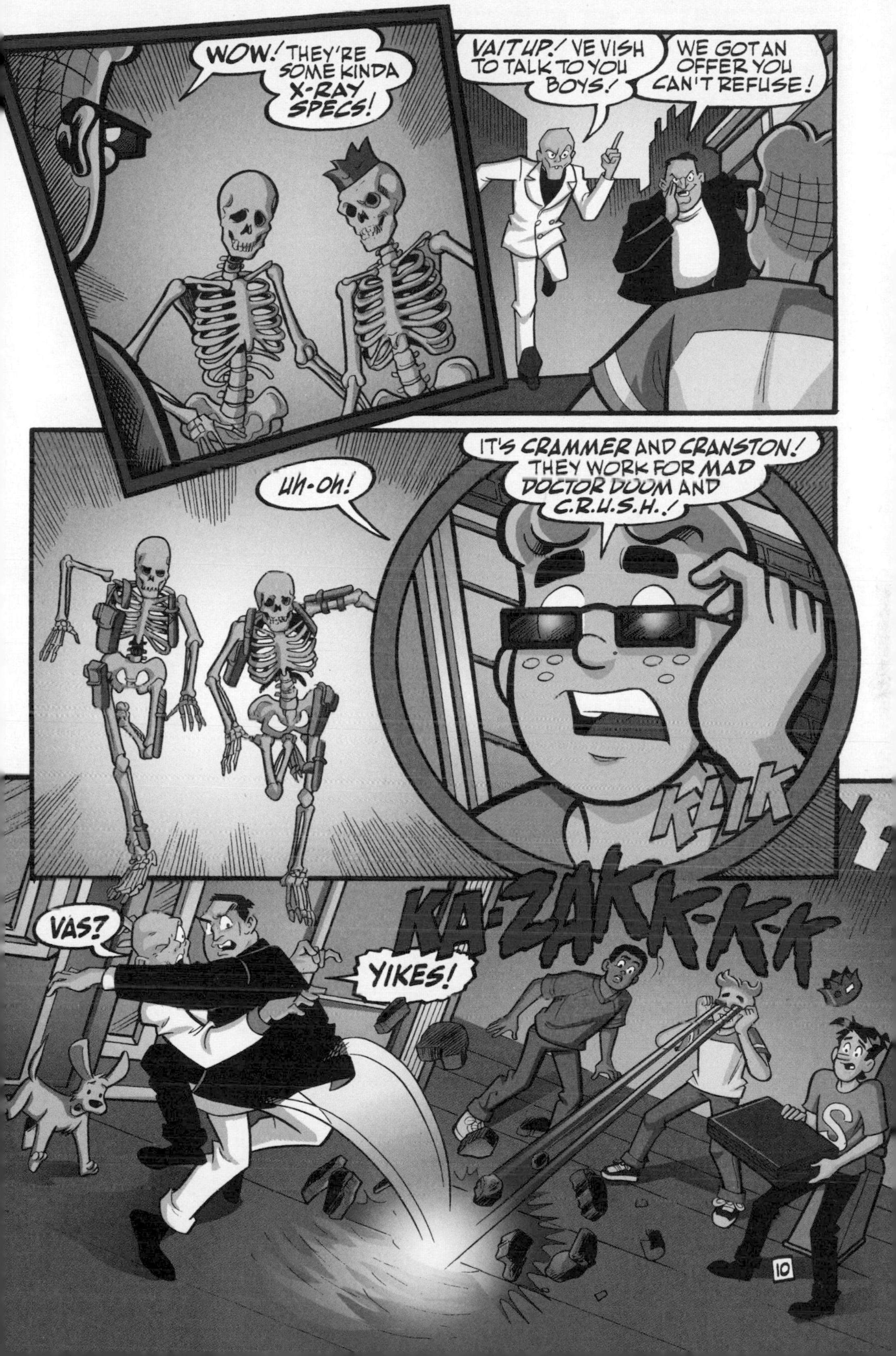
WOW! THEY'RE SOME KINDA X-RAY SPECS!
VAIT UP! VE VISH TO TALK TO YOU BOYS!
WE GOT AN OFFER YOU CAN'T REFUSE!
UH-OH!
IT'S CRAMMER AND CRANSTON! THEY WORK FOR MAD DOCTOR DOOM AND C.R.U.S.H.!
KLIK
KA-ZAKK-K-K
VAS?
YIKES!
10

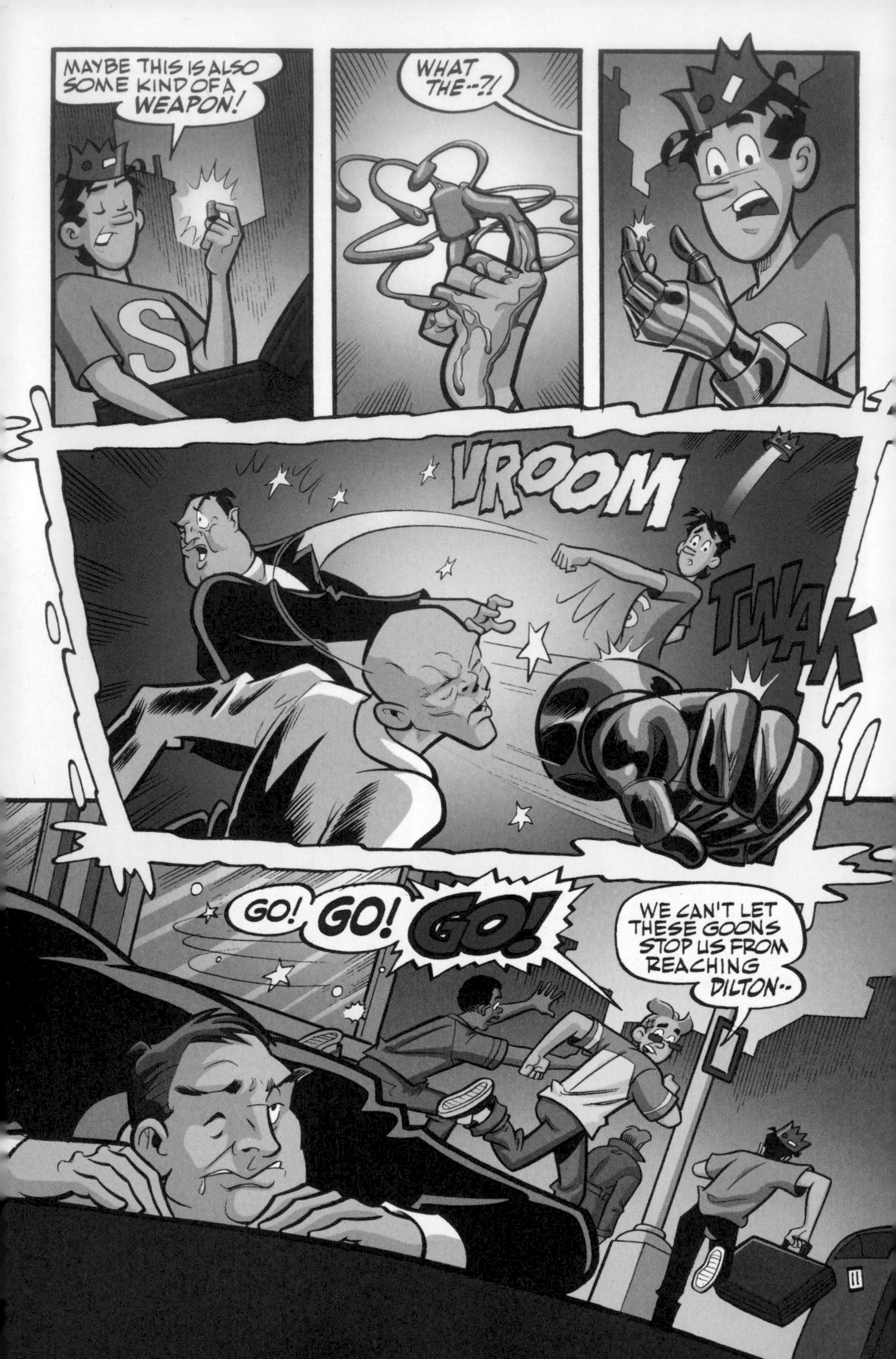

MAYBE THIS IS ALSO SOME KIND OF A WEAPON!
WHAT THE--?!
VROOM
TWAK
GO! GO! GO!
WE CAN'T LET THESE GOONS STOP US FROM REACHING DILTON..

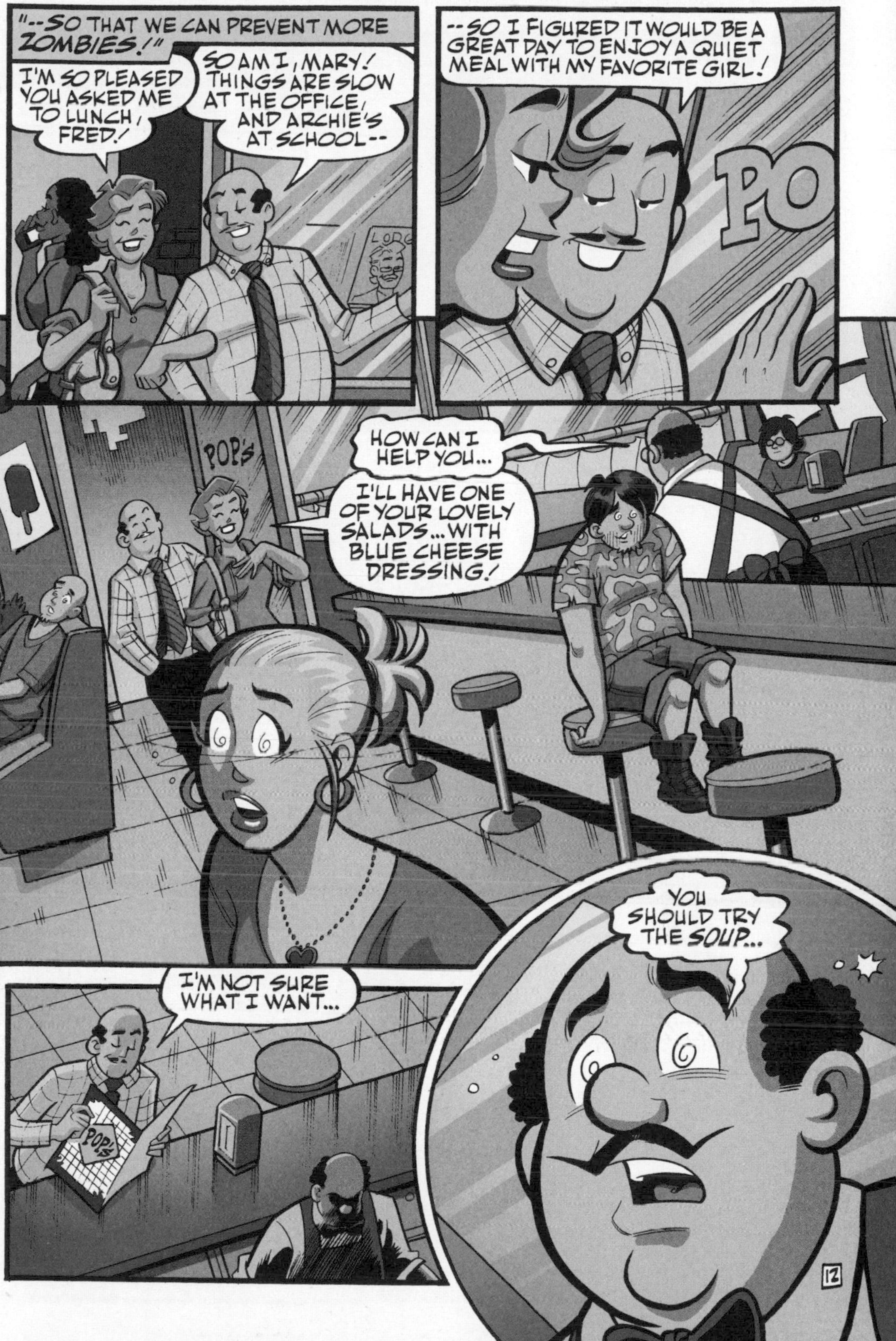
"--SO THAT WE CAN PREVENT MORE ZOMBIES!"
I'M SO PLEASED YOU ASKED ME TO LUNCH, FRED!
SO AM I, MARY! THINGS ARE SLOW AT THE OFFICE, AND ARCHIE'S AT SCHOOL--
--SO I FIGURED IT WOULD BE A GREAT DAY TO ENJOY A QUIET MEAL WITH MY FAVORITE GIRL!
PO
POP'S
HOW CAN I HELP YOU...
I'LL HAVE ONE OF YOUR LOVELY SALADS... WITH BLUE CHEESE DRESSING!
I'M NOT SURE WHAT I WANT...
POP'S
YOU SHOULD TRY THE SOUP...
12

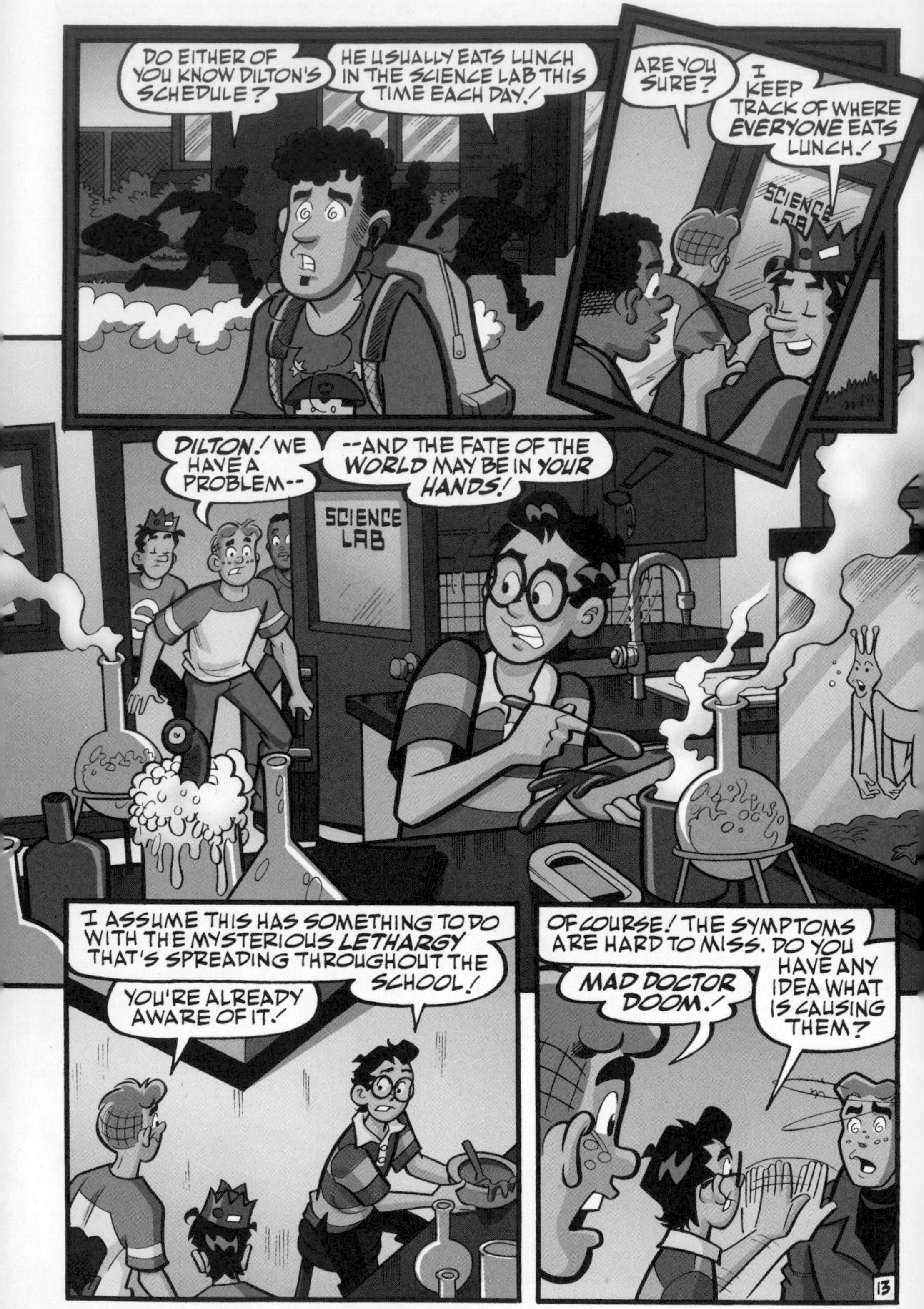
DO EITHER OF YOU KNOW DILTON'S SCHEDULE?
HE USUALLY EATS LUNCH IN THE SCIENCE LAB THIS TIME EACH DAY!
ARE YOU SURE?
I KEEP TRACK OF WHERE EVERYONE EATS LUNCH!
SCIENCE LAB
DILTON! WE HAVE A PROBLEM--
--AND THE FATE OF THE WORLD MAY BE IN YOUR HANDS!
SCIENCE LAB
I ASSUME THIS HAS SOMETHING TO DO WITH THE MYSTERIOUS LETHARGY THAT'S SPREADING THROUGHOUT THE SCHOOL!
YOU'RE ALREADY AWARE OF IT!
OF COURSE! THE SYMPTOMS ARE HARD TO MISS. DO YOU HAVE ANY IDEA WHAT IS CAUSING THEM?
MAD DOCTOR DOOM!

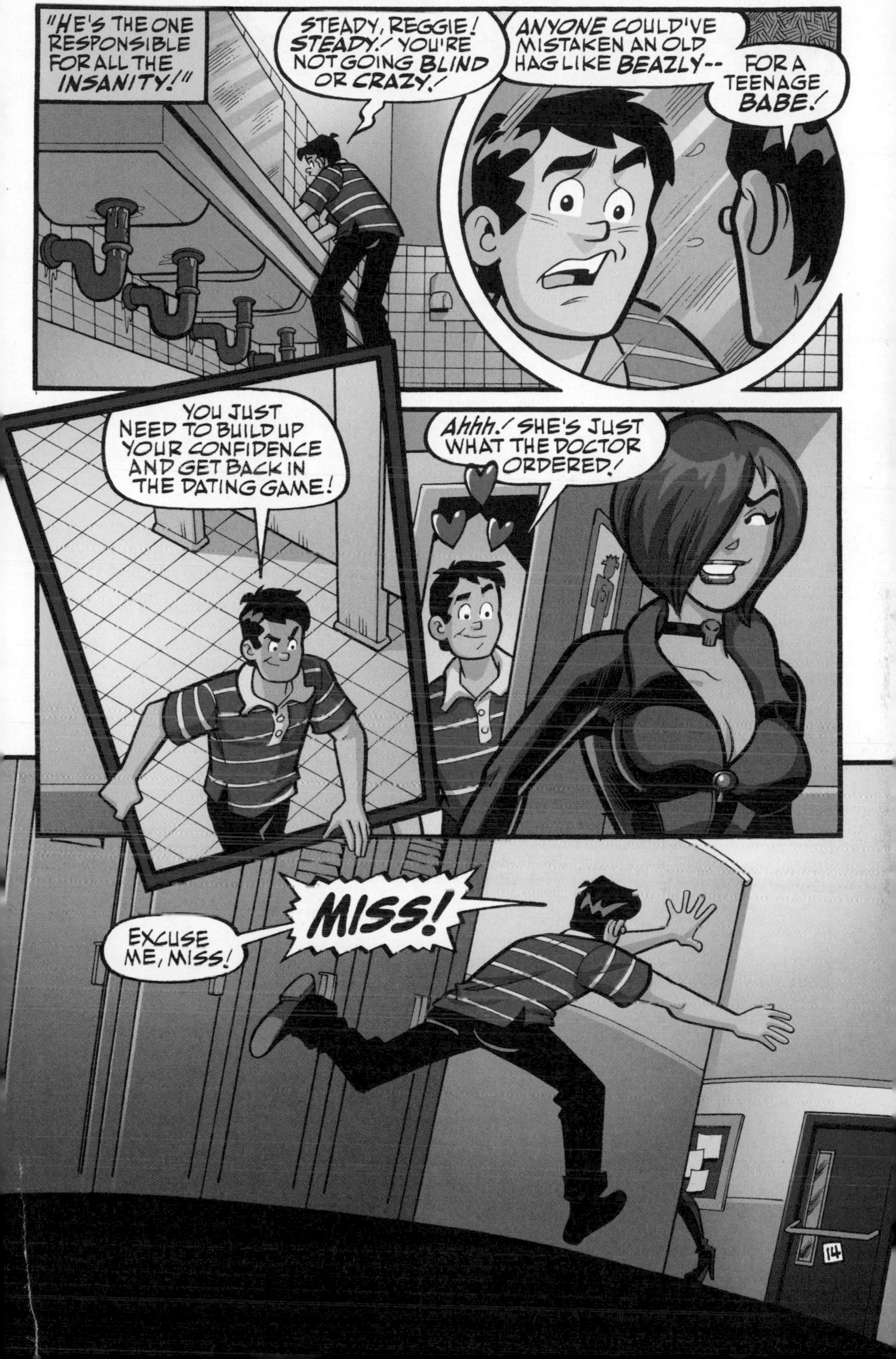
"HE'S THE ONE RESPONSIBLE FOR ALL THE INSANITY!"
STEADY, REGGIE! STEADY! YOU'RE NOT GOING BLIND OR CRAZY!
ANYONE COULD'VE MISTAKEN AN OLD HAG LIKE BEAZLY--
FOR A TEENAGE BABE!
YOU JUST NEED TO BUILD UP YOUR CONFIDENCE AND GET BACK IN THE DATING GAME!
Ahhh! SHE'S JUST WHAT THE DOCTOR ORDERED!
EXCUSE ME, MISS!
MISS!
14

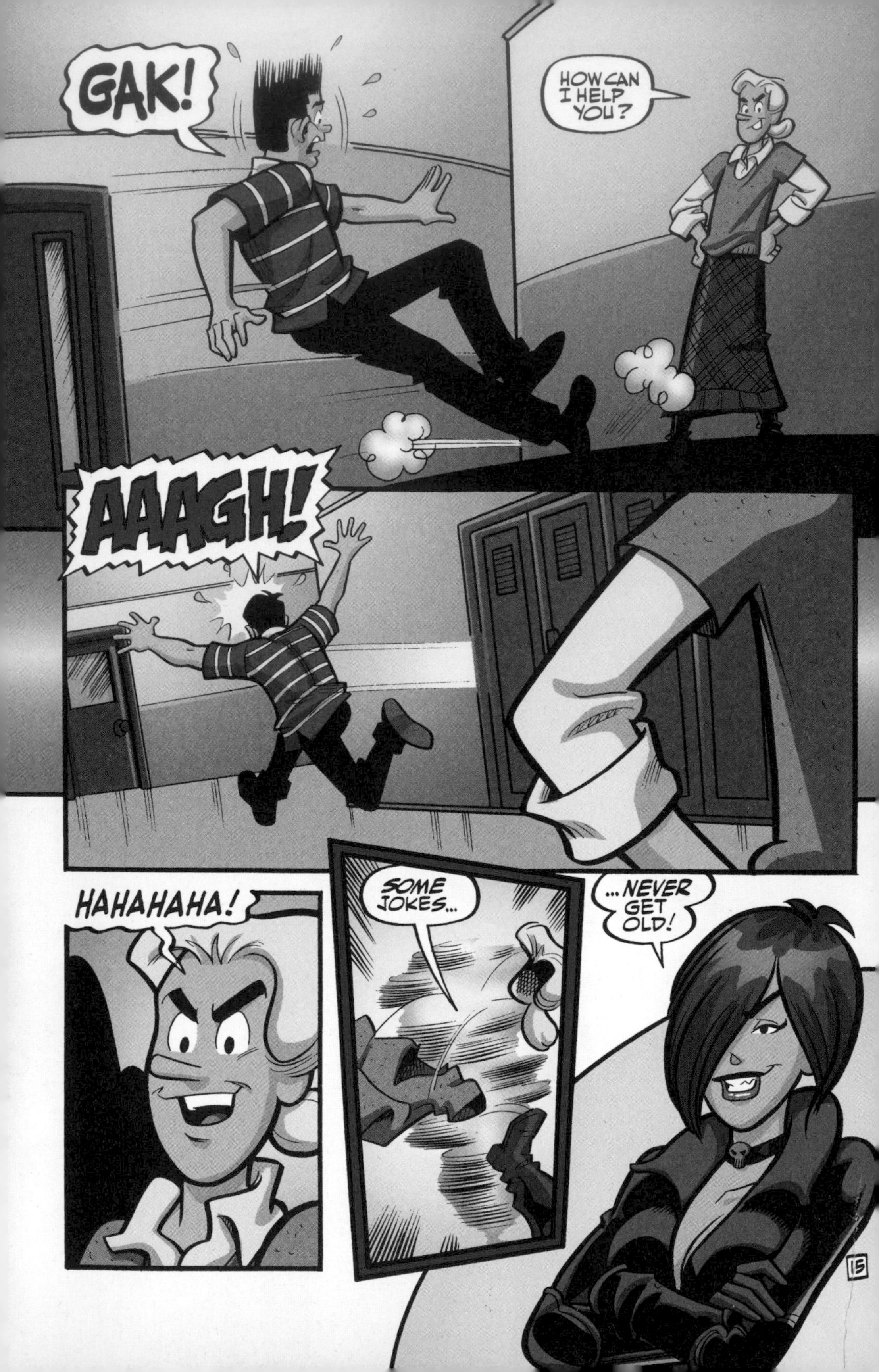
GAK!
HOW CAN I HELP YOU?
AAAGH!
HAHAHAHA!
SOME JOKES...
...NEVER GET OLD!
15

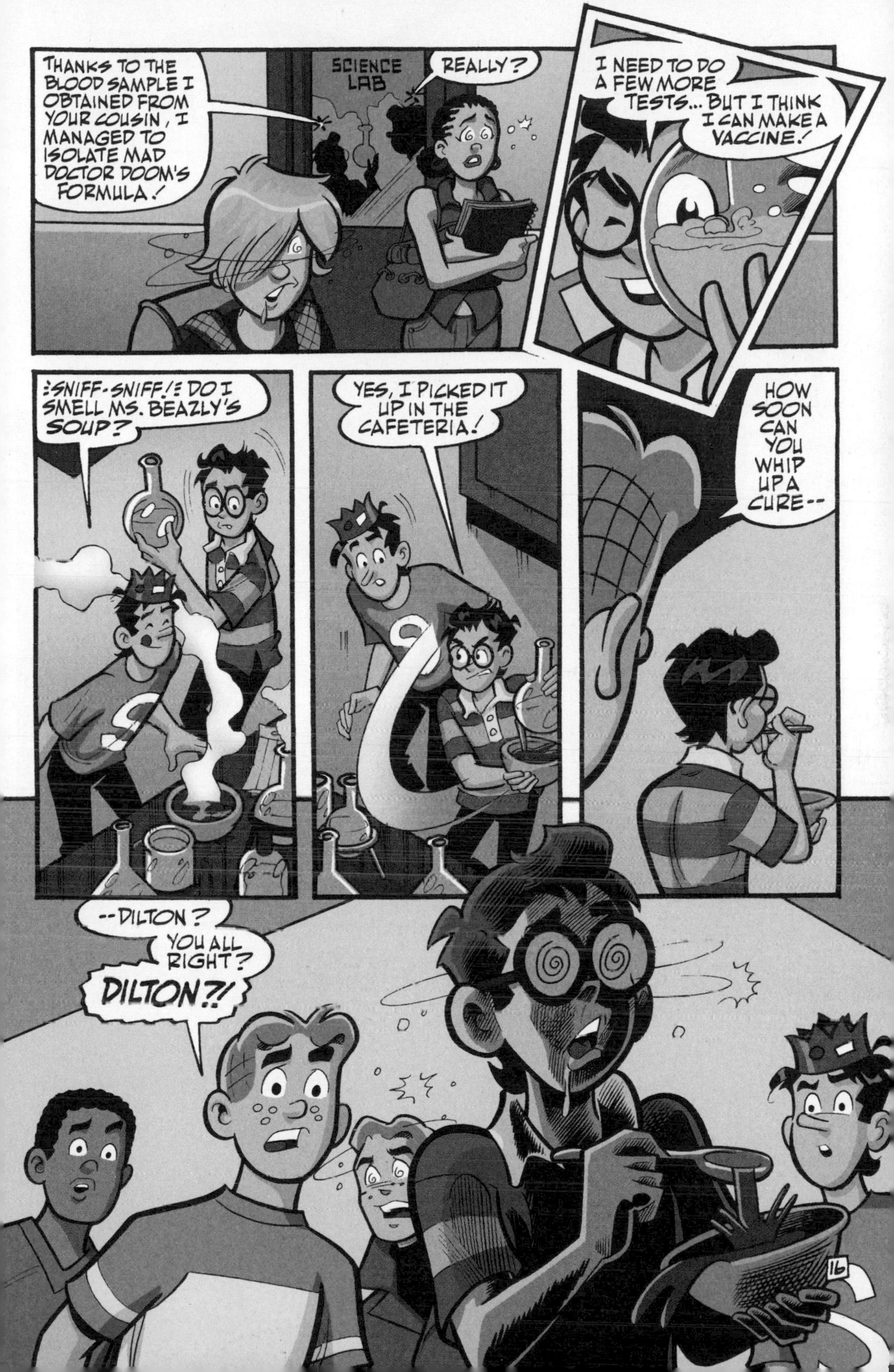
SCIENCE LAB
THANKS TO THE BLOOD SAMPLE I OBTAINED FROM YOUR COUSIN, I MANAGED TO ISOLATE MAD DOCTOR DOOM'S FORMULA!
REALLY?
I NEED TO DO A FEW MORE TESTS... BUT I THINK I CAN MAKE A VACCINE!
:SNIFF-SNIFF!: DO I SMELL MS. BEAZLY'S SOUP?
YES, I PICKED IT UP IN THE CAFETERIA!
HOW SOON CAN YOU WHIP UP A CURE--
--DILTON?
YOU ALL RIGHT?
DILTON?!
16

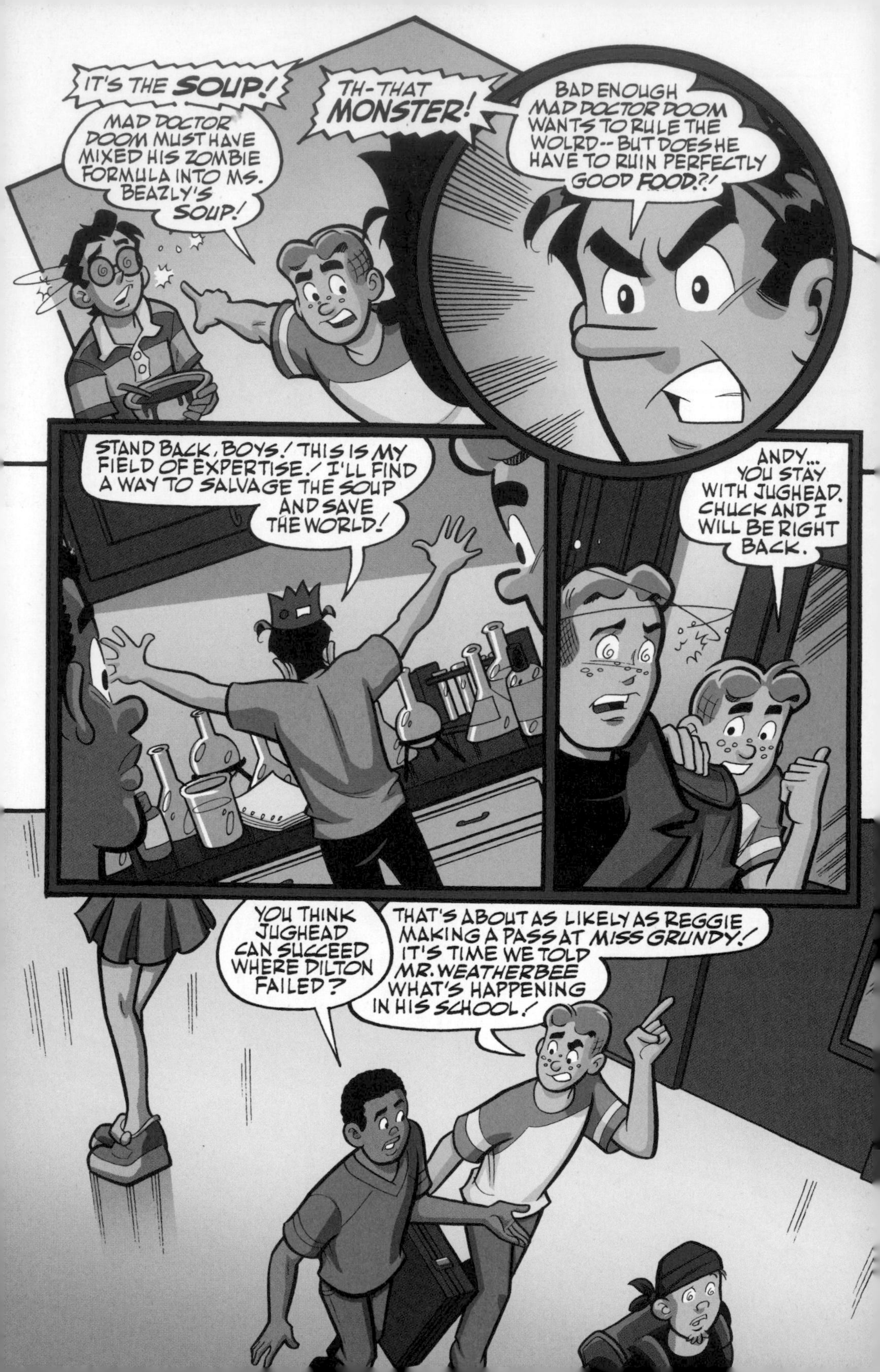

IT'S THE SOUP!
MAD DOCTOR DOOM MUST HAVE MIXED HIS ZOMBIE FORMULA INTO MS. BEAZLY'S SOUP!
TH-THAT MONSTER!
BAD ENOUGH MAD DOCTOR DOOM WANTS TO RULE THE WOLRD-- BUT DOES HE HAVE TO RUIN PERFECTLY GOOD FOOD?!
STAND BACK, BOYS! THIS IS MY FIELD OF EXPERTISE! I'LL FIND A WAY TO SALVAGE THE SOUP AND SAVE THE WORLD!
ANDY... YOU STAY WITH JUGHEAD. CHUCK AND I WILL BE RIGHT BACK.
YOU THINK JUGHEAD CAN SUCCEED WHERE DILTON FAILED?
THAT'S ABOUT AS LIKELY AS REGGIE MAKING A PASS AT MISS GRUNDY! IT'S TIME WE TOLD MR. WEATHERBEE WHAT'S HAPPENING IN HIS SCHOOL!

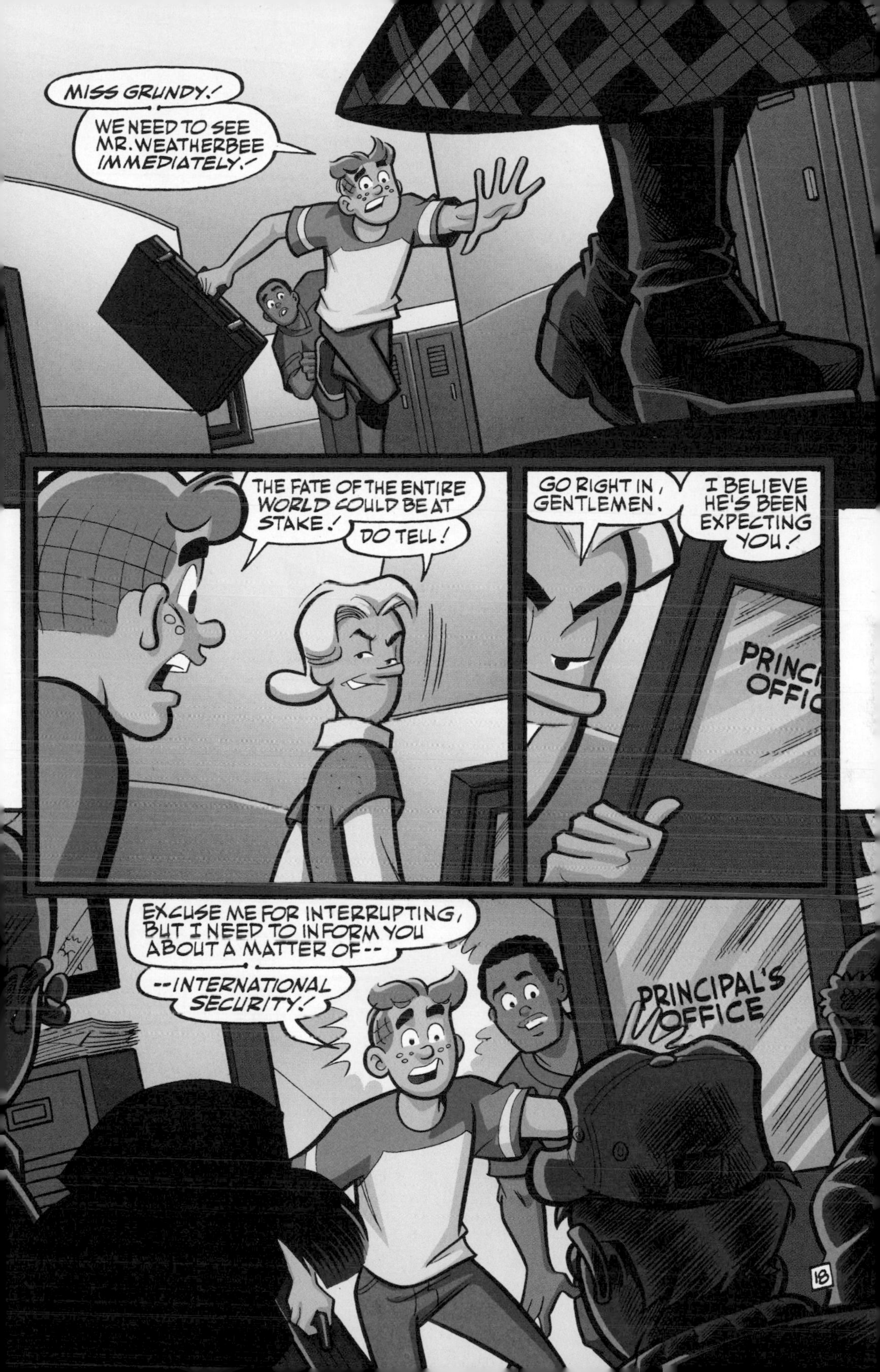
MISS GRUNDY!
WE NEED TO SEE MR. WEATHERBEE IMMEDIATELY!
THE FATE OF THE ENTIRE WORLD COULD BE AT STAKE!
DO TELL!
GO RIGHT IN, GENTLEMEN.
I BELIEVE HE'S BEEN EXPECTING YOU!
PRINCI
OFFIC
EXCUSE ME FOR INTERRUPTING, BUT I NEED TO INFORM YOU ABOUT A MATTER OF--
--INTERNATIONAL SECURITY!
PRINCIPAL'S OFFICE

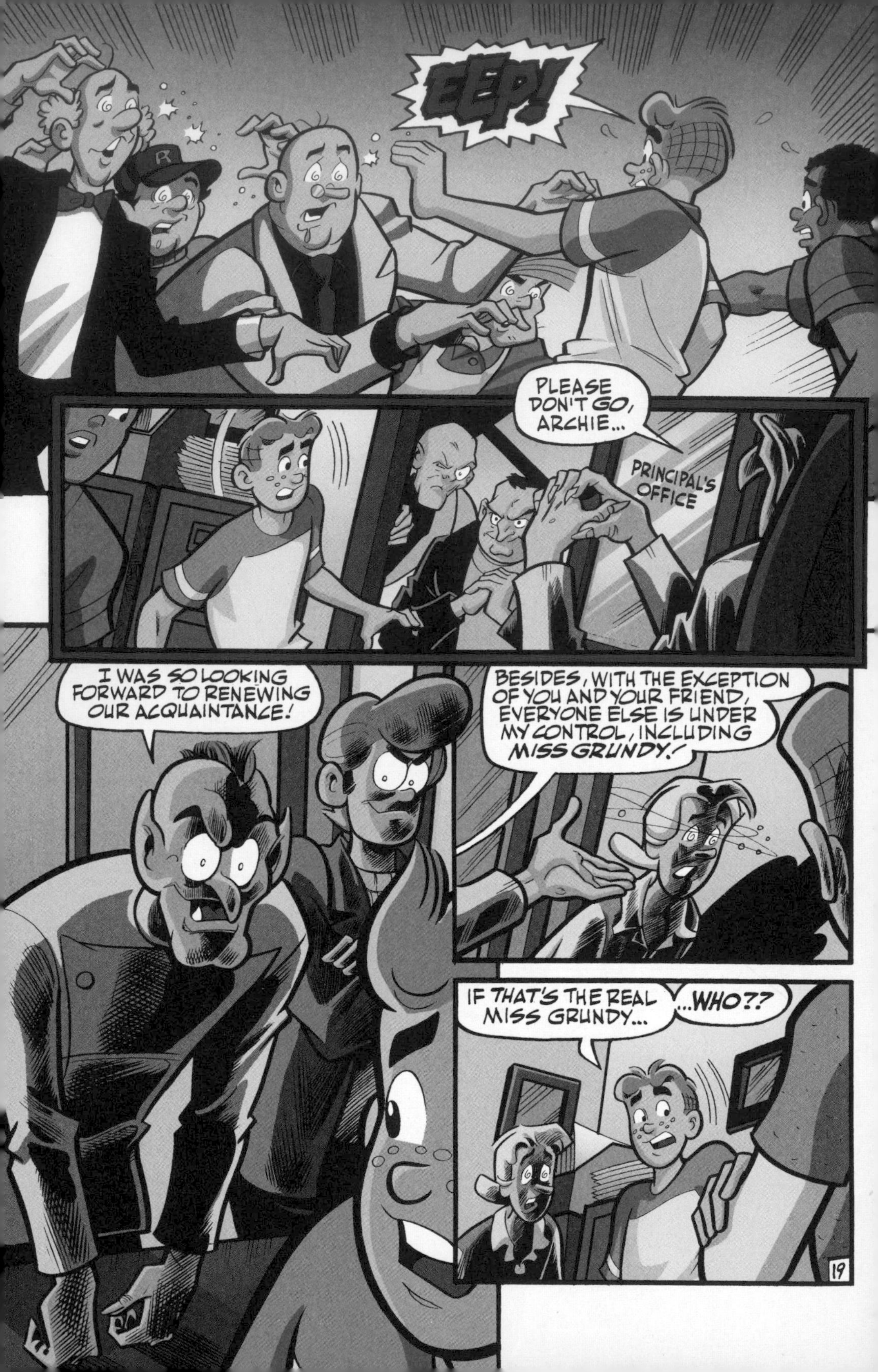
EEP!
PLEASE DON'T GO, ARCHIE...
PRINCIPAL'S OFFICE
I WAS SO LOOKING FORWARD TO RENEWING OUR ACQUAINTANCE!
BESIDES, WITH THE EXCEPTION OF YOU AND YOUR FRIEND, EVERYONE ELSE IS UNDER MY CONTROL, INCLUDING *MISS GRUNDY*!
IF *THAT'S* THE REAL MISS GRUNDY...
...WHO??
19

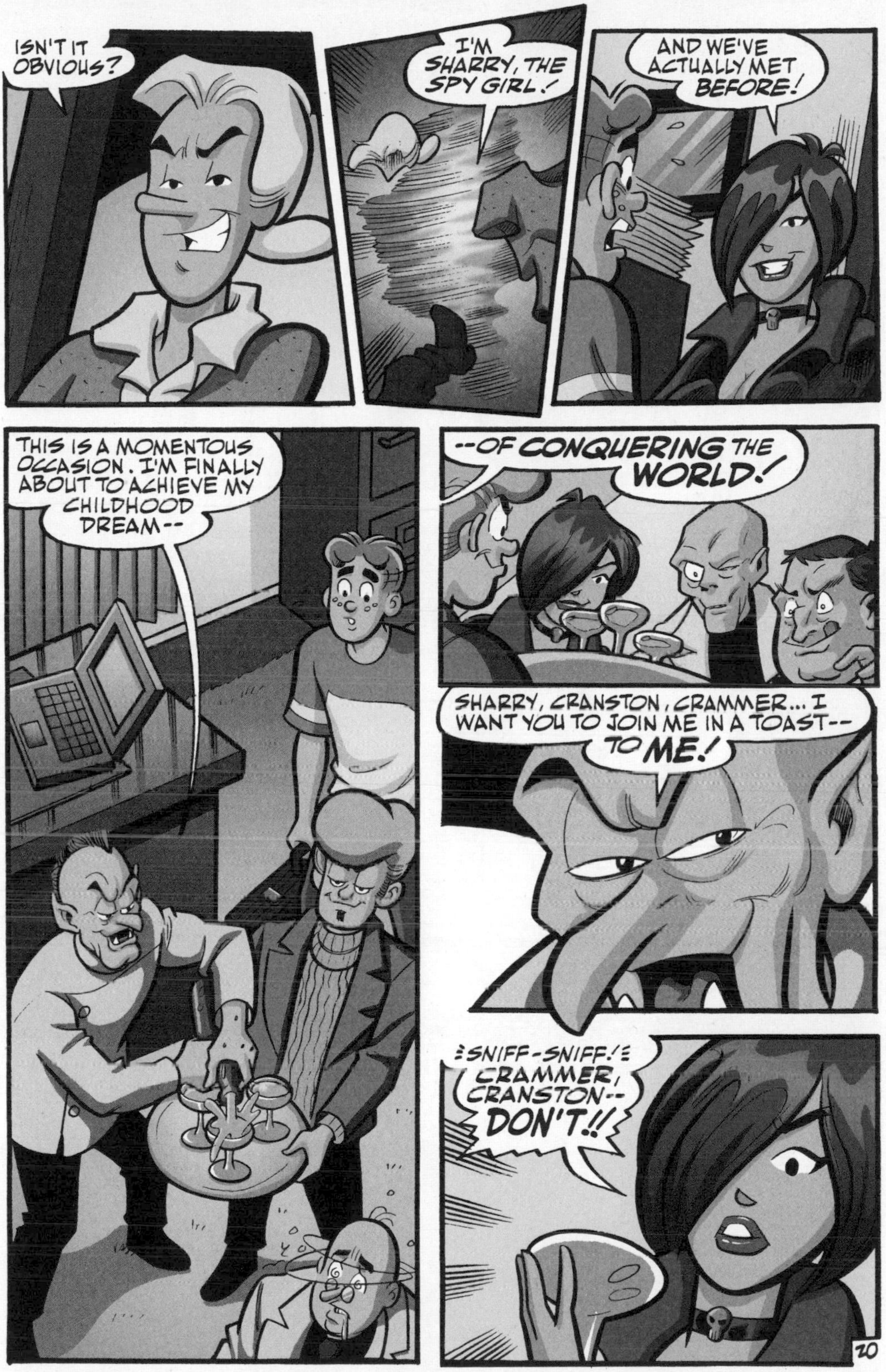
ISN'T IT OBVIOUS?
I'M SHARRY, THE SPY GIRL!
AND WE'VE ACTUALLY MET BEFORE!
THIS IS A MOMENTOUS OCCASION. I'M FINALLY ABOUT TO ACHIEVE MY CHILDHOOD DREAM--
--OF CONQUERING THE WORLD!
SHARRY, CRANSTON, CRAMMER... I WANT YOU TO JOIN ME IN A TOAST-- TO ME!
SNIFF-SNIFF! CRAMMER, CRANSTON-- DON'T!!
20

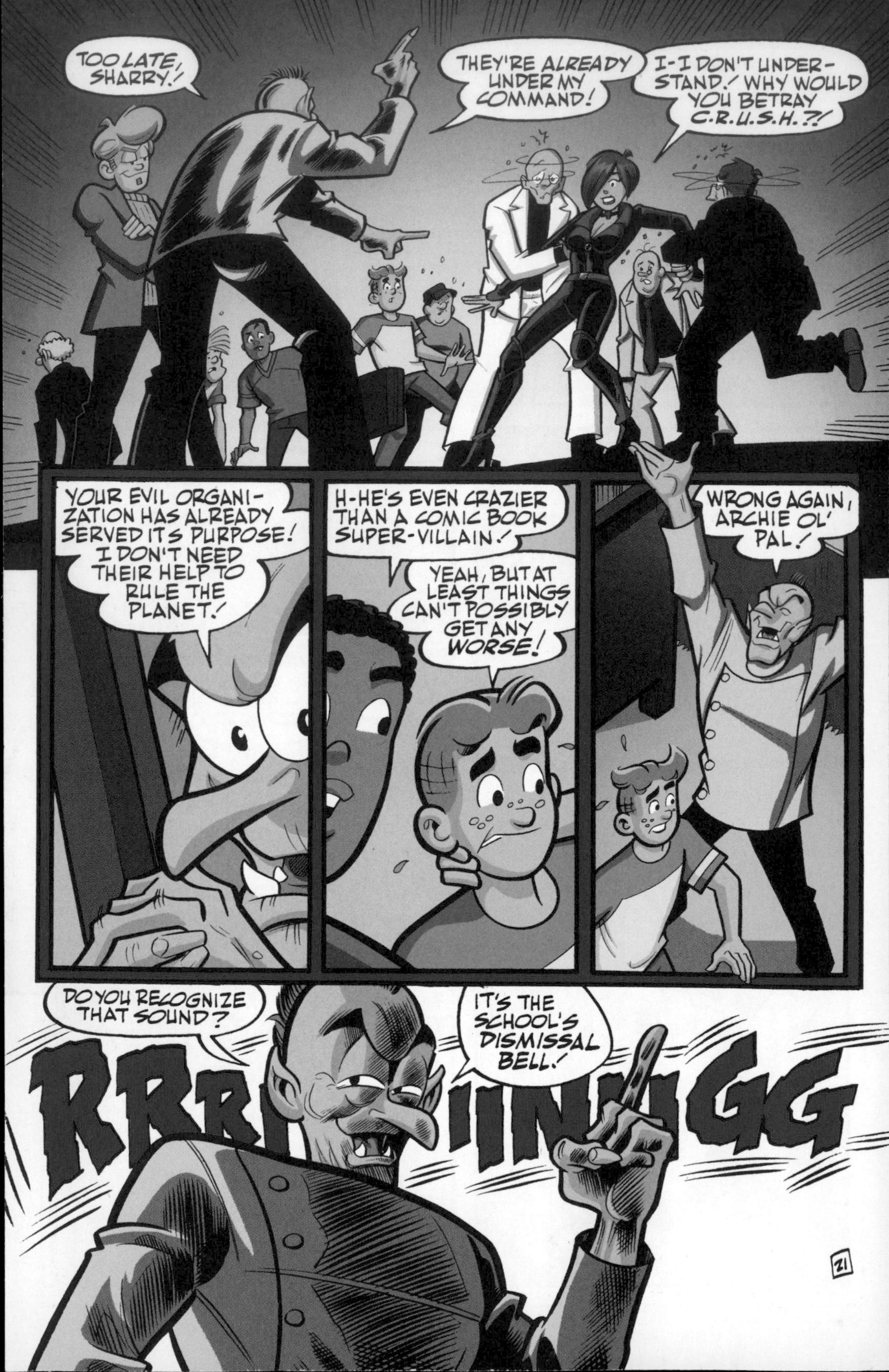
TOO LATE, SHARRY!
THEY'RE ALREADY UNDER MY COMMAND!
I-I DON'T UNDER-STAND! WHY WOULD YOU BETRAY C.R.U.S.H.?!
YOUR EVIL ORGANI-ZATION HAS ALREADY SERVED ITS PURPOSE! I DON'T NEED THEIR HELP TO RULE THE PLANET!
H-HE'S EVEN CRAZIER THAN A COMIC BOOK SUPER-VILLAIN!
YEAH, BUT AT LEAST THINGS CAN'T POSSIBLY GET ANY WORSE!
WRONG AGAIN, ARCHIE OL' PAL!
DO YOU RECOGNIZE THAT SOUND?
IT'S THE SCHOOL'S DISMISSAL BELL!
RRRIINNGG
21

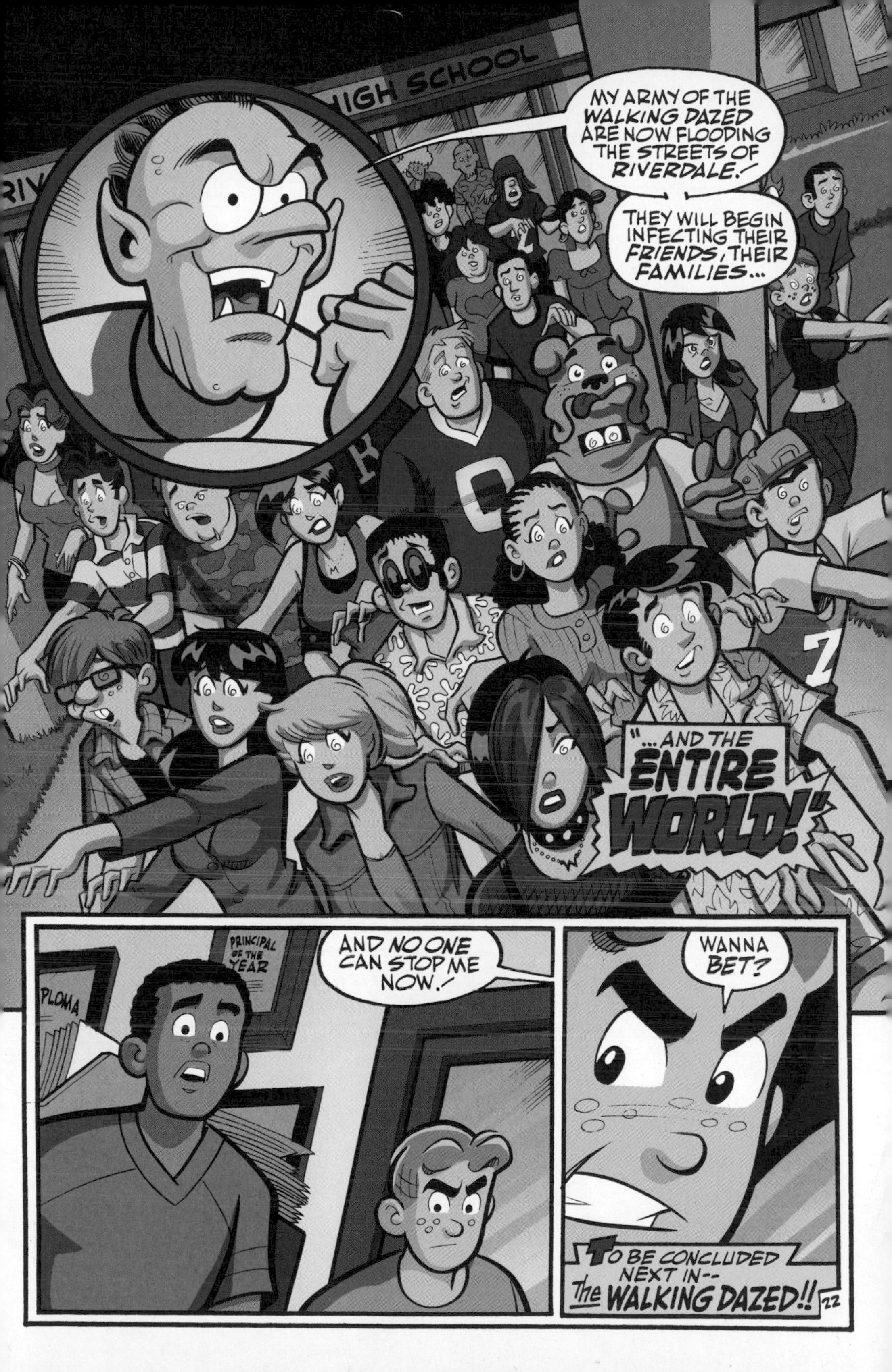
HIGH SCHOOL
MY ARMY OF THE WALKING DAZED ARE NOW FLOODING THE STREETS OF RIVERDALE!
THEY WILL BEGIN INFECTING THEIR FRIENDS, THEIR FAMILIES...
"...AND THE ENTIRE WORLD!"
PRINCIPAL OF THE YEAR
PLOMA
AND NO ONE CAN STOP ME NOW!
WANNA BET?
TO BE CONCLUDED NEXT IN-- The WALKING DAZED!!
22

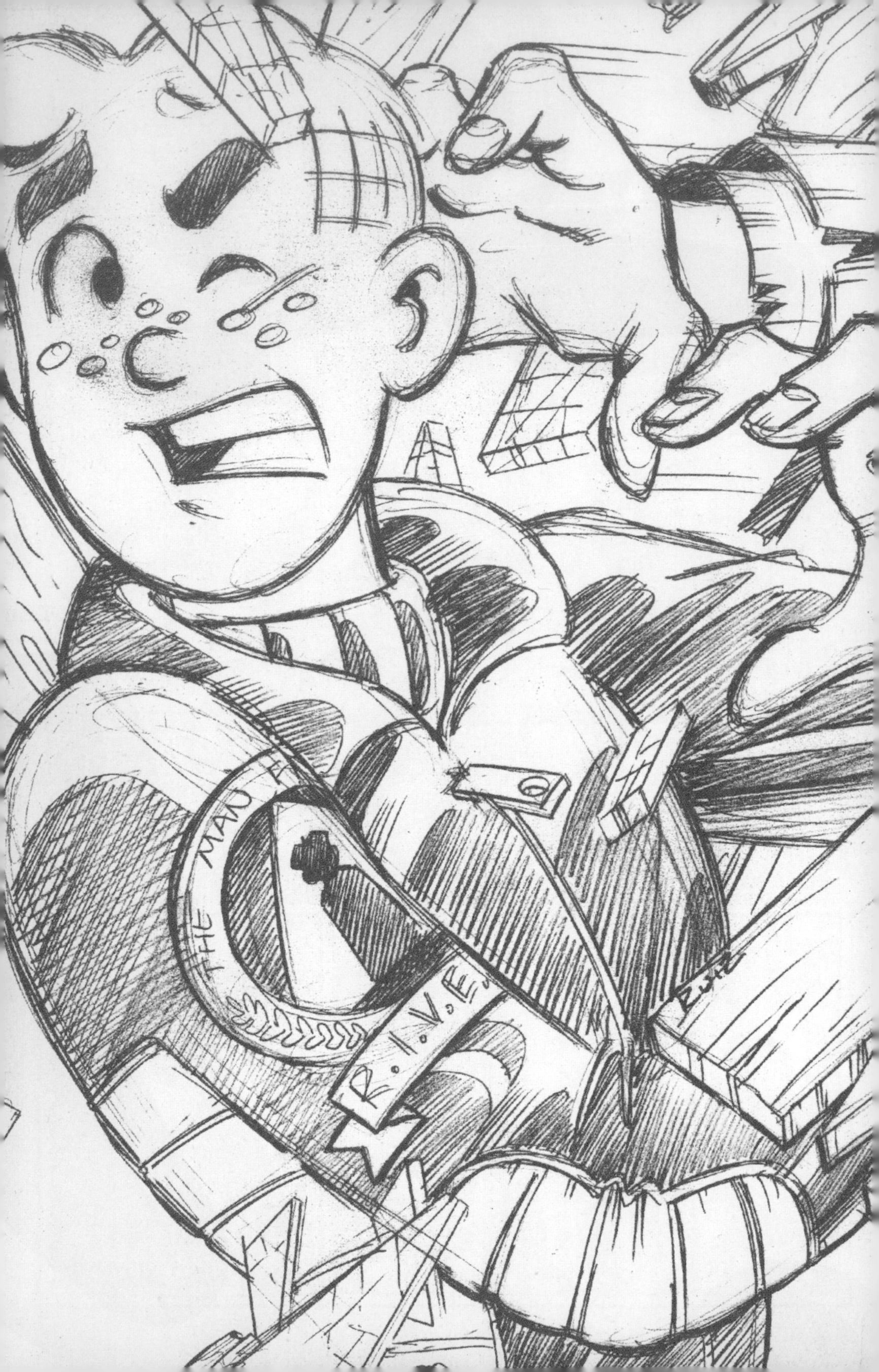
THE MAN
R.I.V.E.

MISSION 4: THE WALKING DAZED

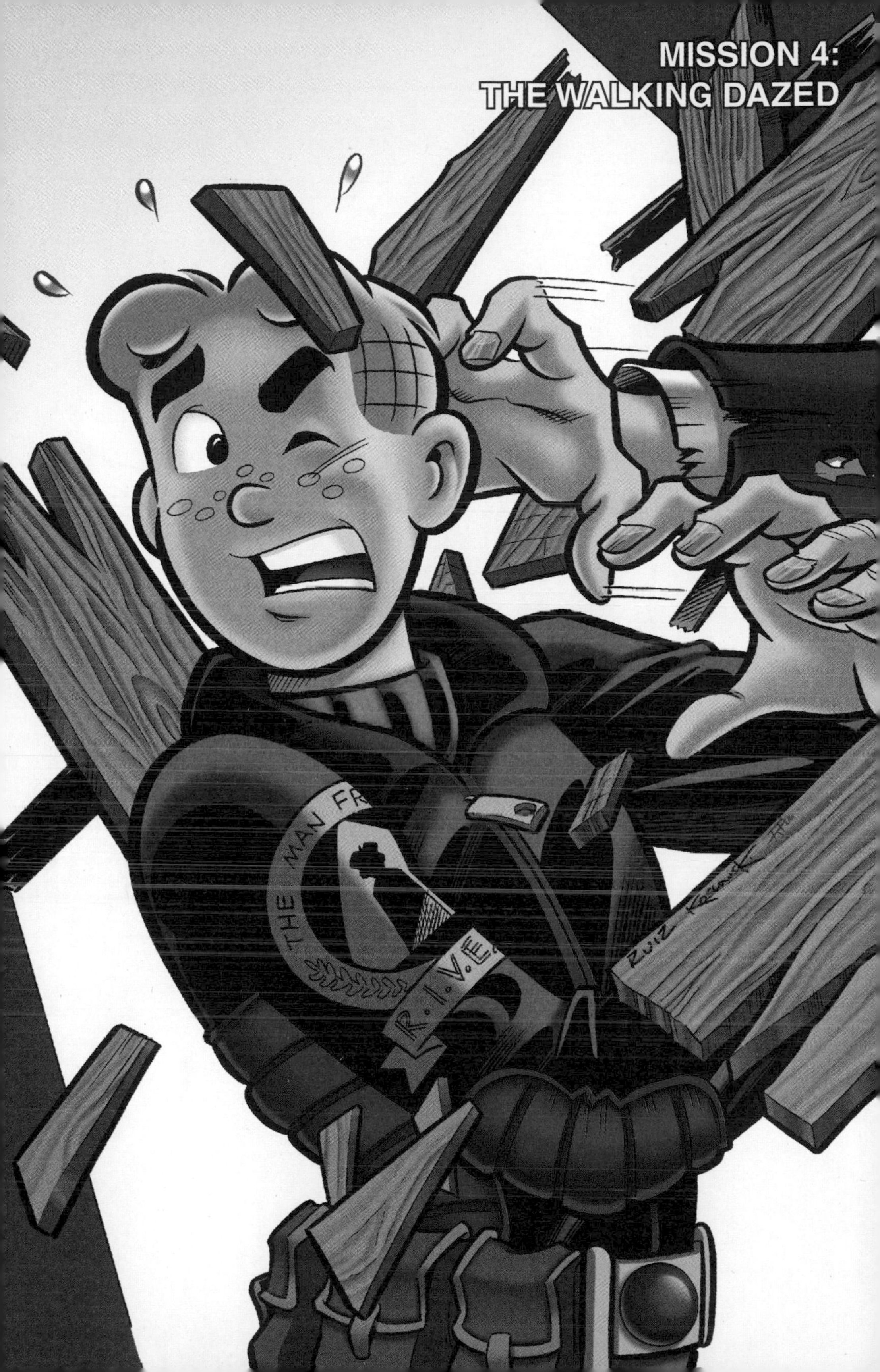

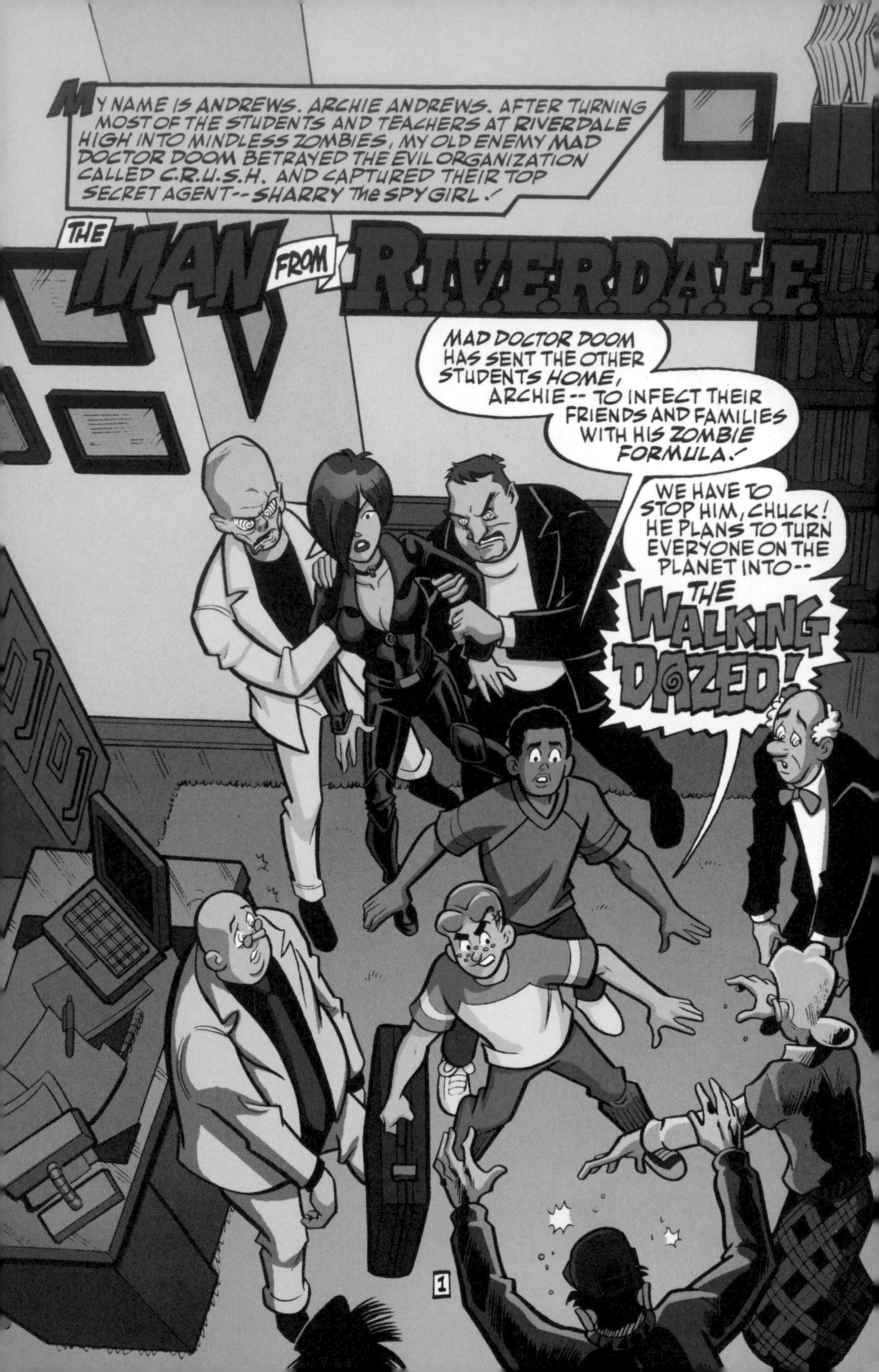
MY NAME IS ANDREWS. ARCHIE ANDREWS. AFTER TURNING MOST OF THE STUDENTS AND TEACHERS AT RIVERDALE HIGH INTO MINDLESS ZOMBIES, MY OLD ENEMY MAD DOCTOR DOOM BETRAYED THE EVIL ORGANIZATION CALLED C.R.U.S.H. AND CAPTURED THEIR TOP SECRET AGENT-- SHARRY The SPY GIRL!
THE MAN FROM R.I.V.E.R.D.A.L.E.
MAD DOCTOR DOOM HAS SENT THE OTHER STUDENTS HOME, ARCHIE-- TO INFECT THEIR FRIENDS AND FAMILIES WITH HIS ZOMBIE FORMULA!
WE HAVE TO STOP HIM, CHUCK! HE PLANS TO TURN EVERYONE ON THE PLANET INTO-- THE WALKING DAZED!
1

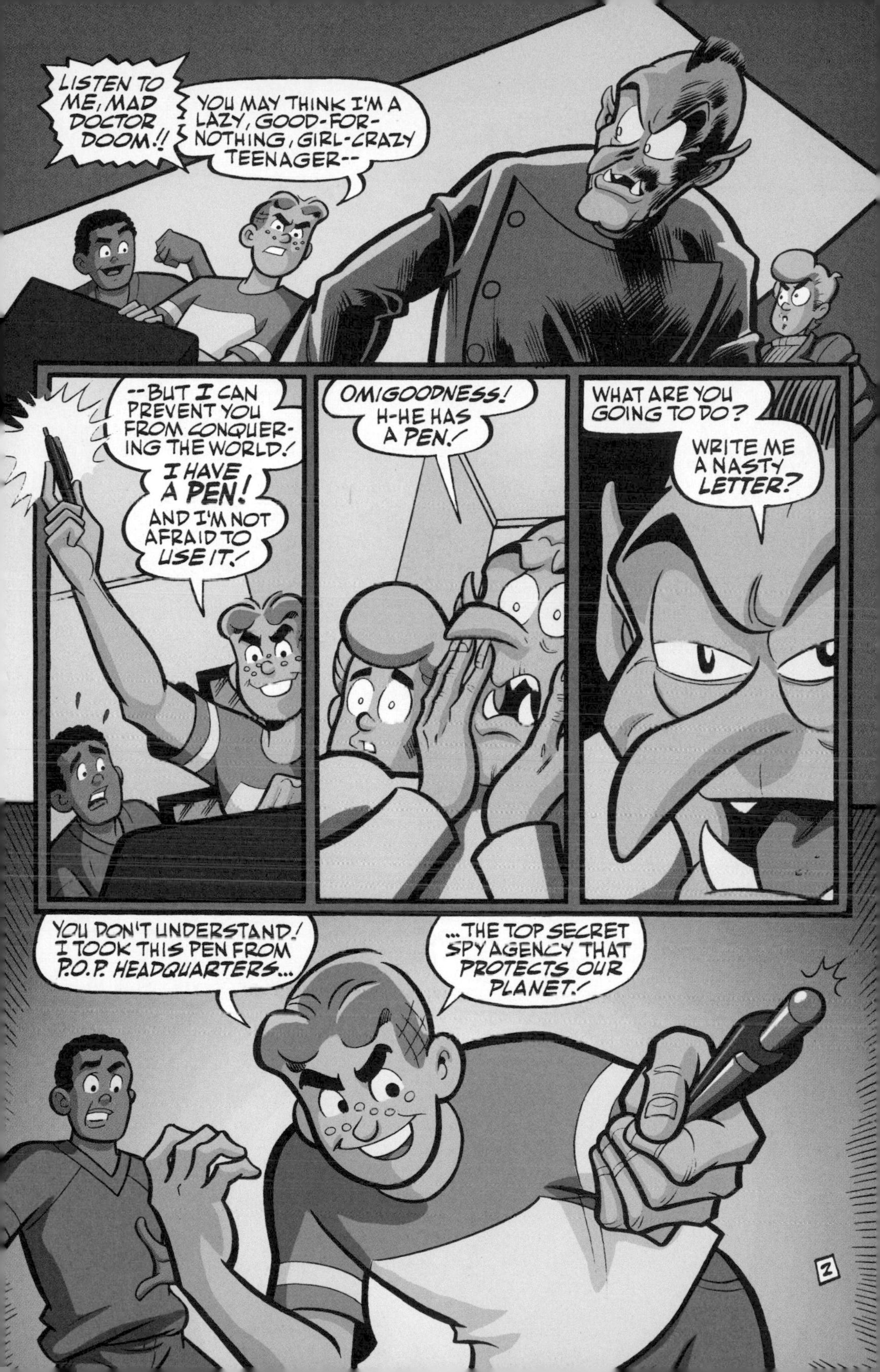
LISTEN TO ME, MAD DOCTOR DOOM!!
YOU MAY THINK I'M A LAZY, GOOD-FOR-NOTHING, GIRL-CRAZY TEENAGER--
--BUT I CAN PREVENT YOU FROM CONQUERING THE WORLD!
I HAVE A PEN!
AND I'M NOT AFRAID TO USE IT!
OMIGOODNESS! H-HE HAS A PEN!
WHAT ARE YOU GOING TO DO?
WRITE ME A NASTY LETTER?
YOU DON'T UNDERSTAND! I TOOK THIS PEN FROM P.O.P. HEADQUARTERS...
...THE TOP SECRET SPY AGENCY THAT PROTECTS OUR PLANET!
2

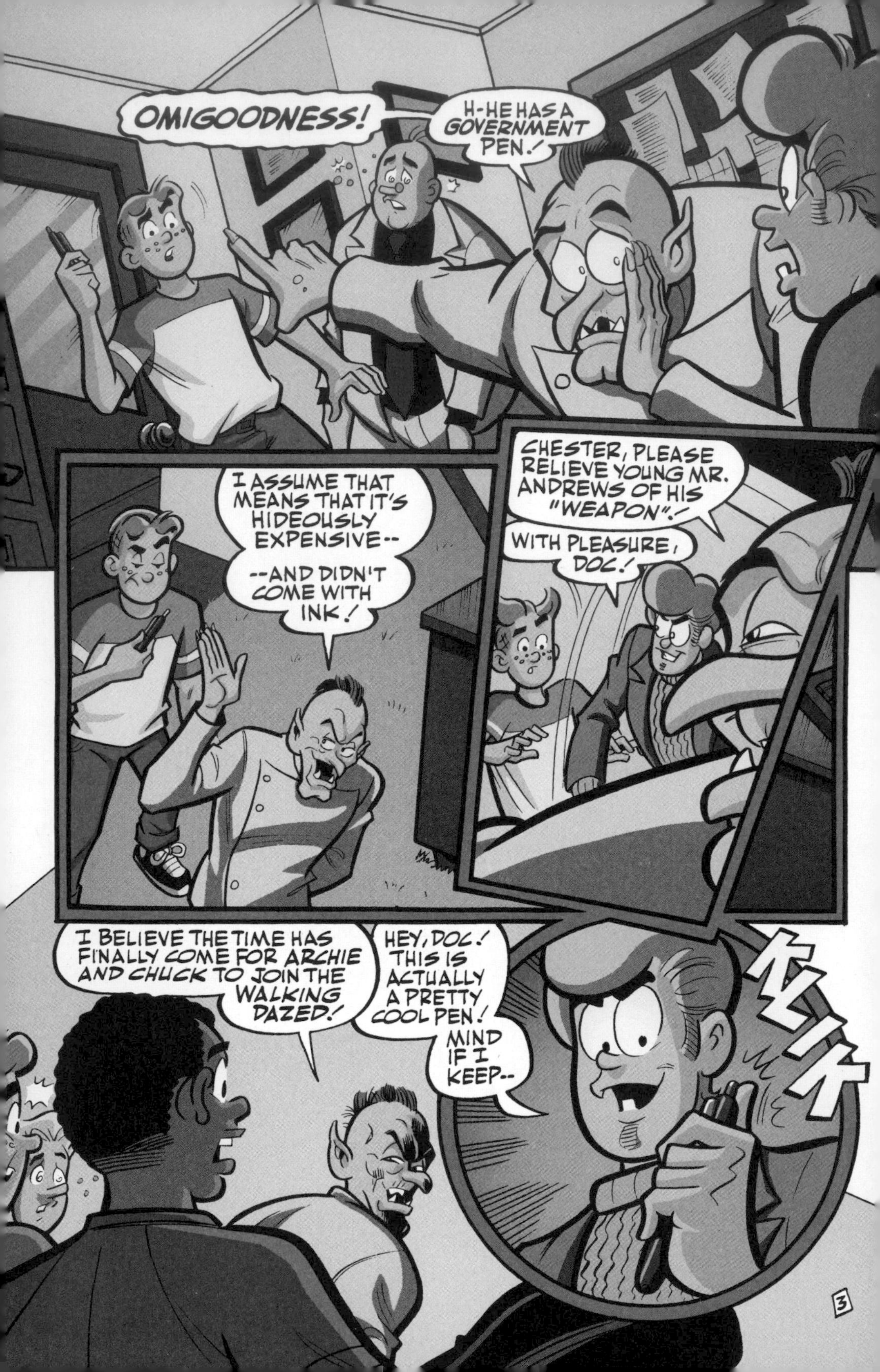
OMIGOODNESS!
H-HE HAS A GOVERNMENT PEN.!
I ASSUME THAT MEANS THAT IT'S HIDEOUSLY EXPENSIVE--
--AND DIDN'T COME WITH INK!
CHESTER, PLEASE RELIEVE YOUNG MR. ANDREWS OF HIS "WEAPON".!
WITH PLEASURE, DOC!
I BELIEVE THE TIME HAS FINALLY COME FOR ARCHIE AND CHUCK TO JOIN THE WALKING DAZED!
HEY, DOC! THIS IS ACTUALLY A PRETTY COOL PEN!
MIND IF I KEEP--
KLIK
3

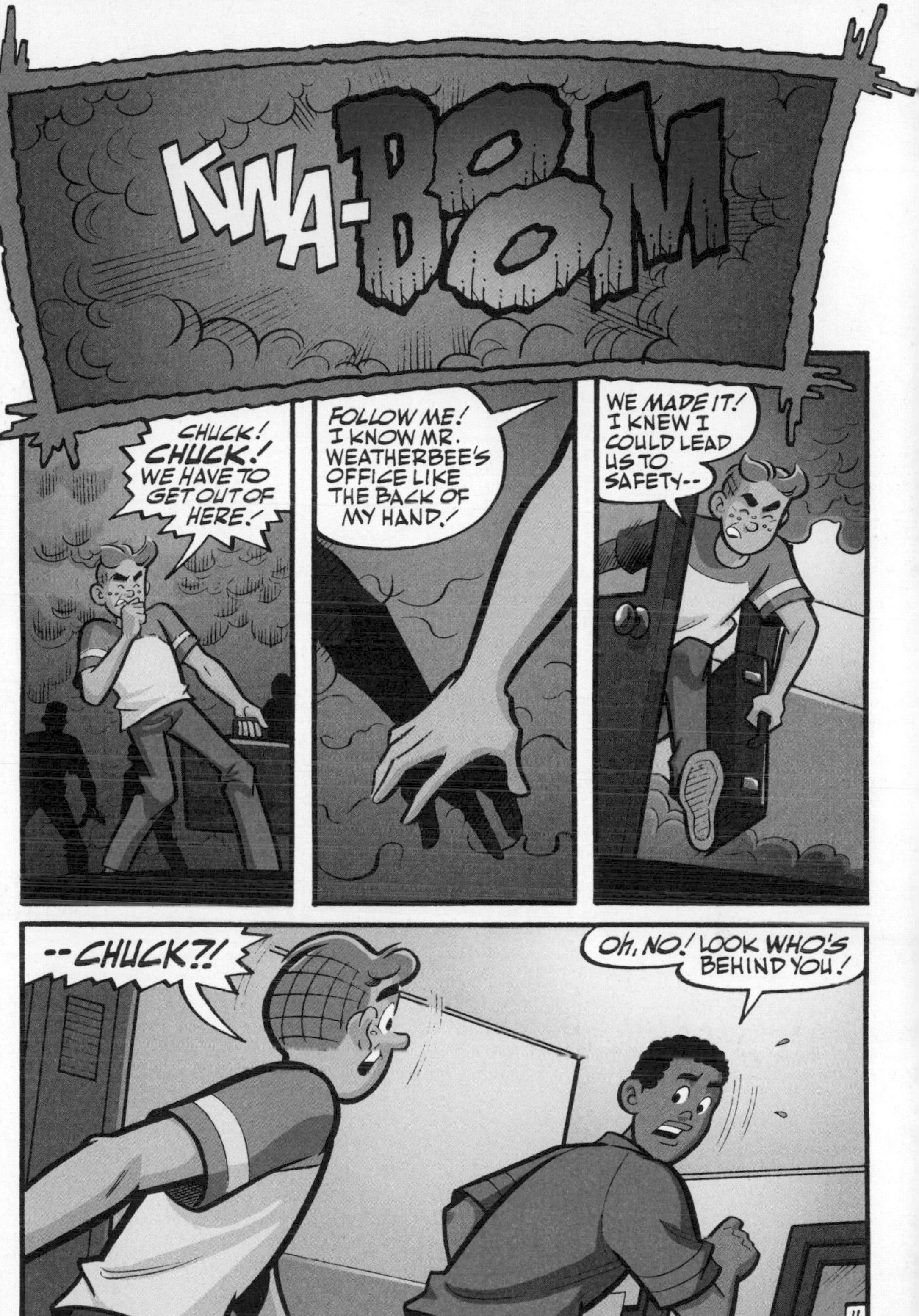
KWA-BOOM
CHUCK! CHUCK! WE HAVE TO GET OUT OF HERE!
FOLLOW ME! I KNOW MR. WEATHERBEE'S OFFICE LIKE THE BACK OF MY HAND!
WE MADE IT! I KNEW I COULD LEAD US TO SAFETY--
--CHUCK?!
Oh, NO! LOOK WHO'S BEHIND YOU!
4

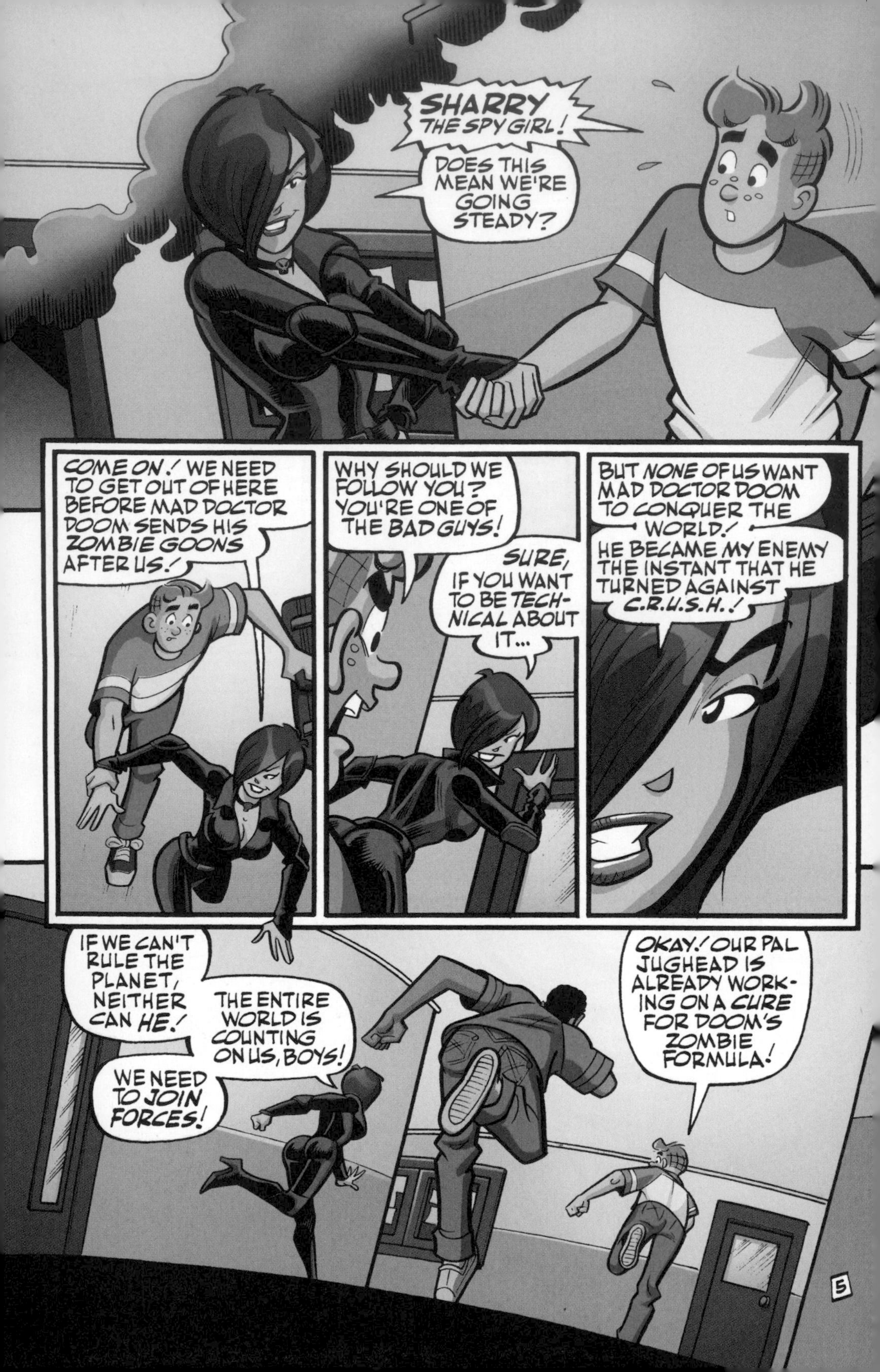
SHARRY THE SPY GIRL!
DOES THIS MEAN WE'RE GOING STEADY?
COME ON! WE NEED TO GET OUT OF HERE BEFORE MAD DOCTOR DOOM SENDS HIS ZOMBIE GOONS AFTER US!
WHY SHOULD WE FOLLOW YOU? YOU'RE ONE OF THE BAD GUYS!
SURE, IF YOU WANT TO BE TECHNICAL ABOUT IT...
BUT NONE OF US WANT MAD DOCTOR DOOM TO CONQUER THE WORLD!
HE BECAME MY ENEMY THE INSTANT THAT HE TURNED AGAINST C.R.U.S.H.!
IF WE CAN'T RULE THE PLANET, NEITHER CAN HE!
THE ENTIRE WORLD IS COUNTING ON US, BOYS!
WE NEED TO JOIN FORCES!
OKAY! OUR PAL JUGHEAD IS ALREADY WORKING ON A CURE FOR DOOM'S ZOMBIE FORMULA!

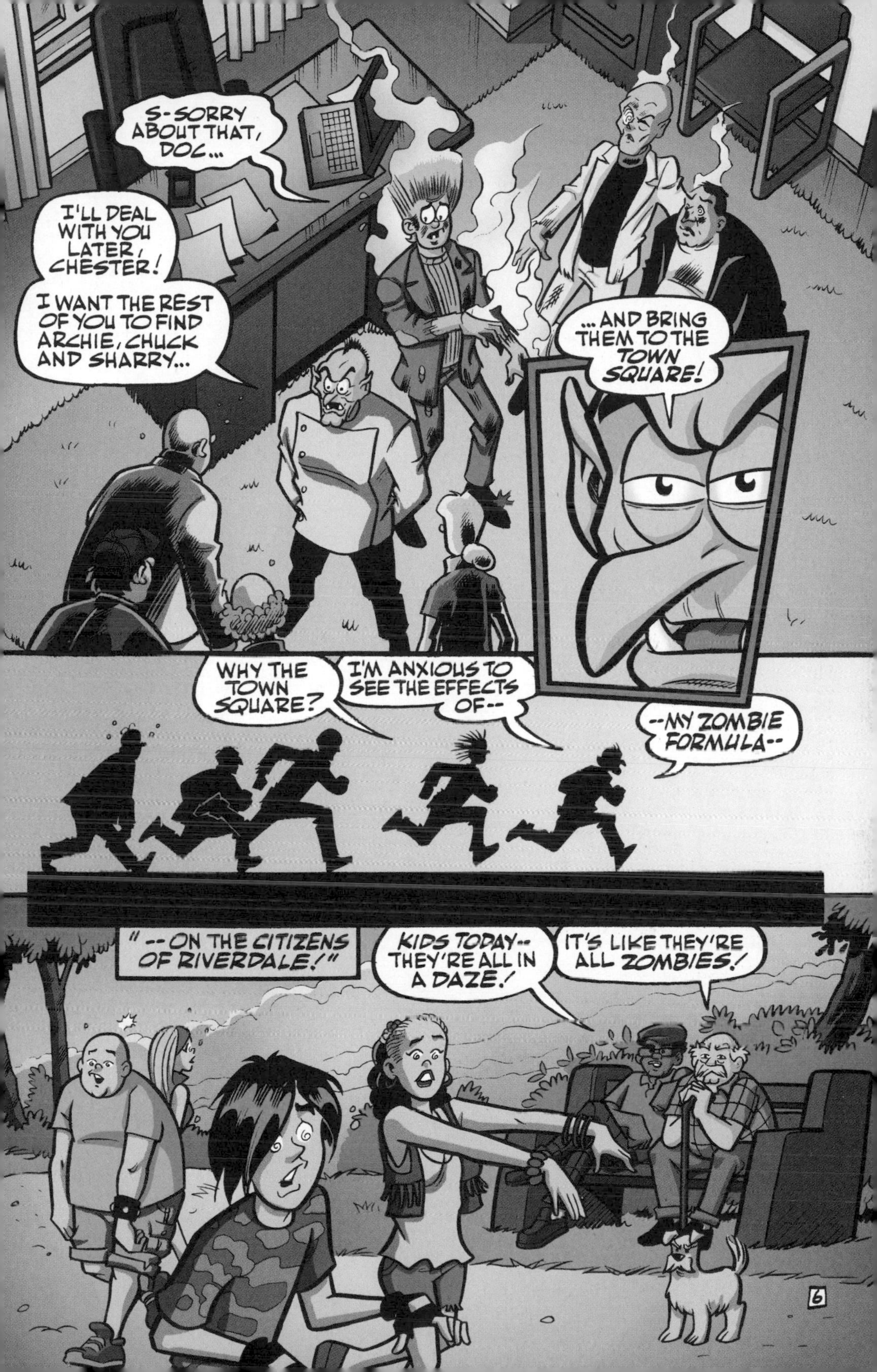

S-SORRY ABOUT THAT, DOC...
I'LL DEAL WITH YOU LATER, CHESTER!
I WANT THE REST OF YOU TO FIND ARCHIE, CHUCK AND SHARRY...
...AND BRING THEM TO THE TOWN SQUARE!
WHY THE TOWN SQUARE?
I'M ANXIOUS TO SEE THE EFFECTS OF--
--MY ZOMBIE FORMULA--
"--ON THE CITIZENS OF RIVERDALE!"
KIDS TODAY-- THEY'RE ALL IN A DAZE!
IT'S LIKE THEY'RE ALL ZOMBIES!
6

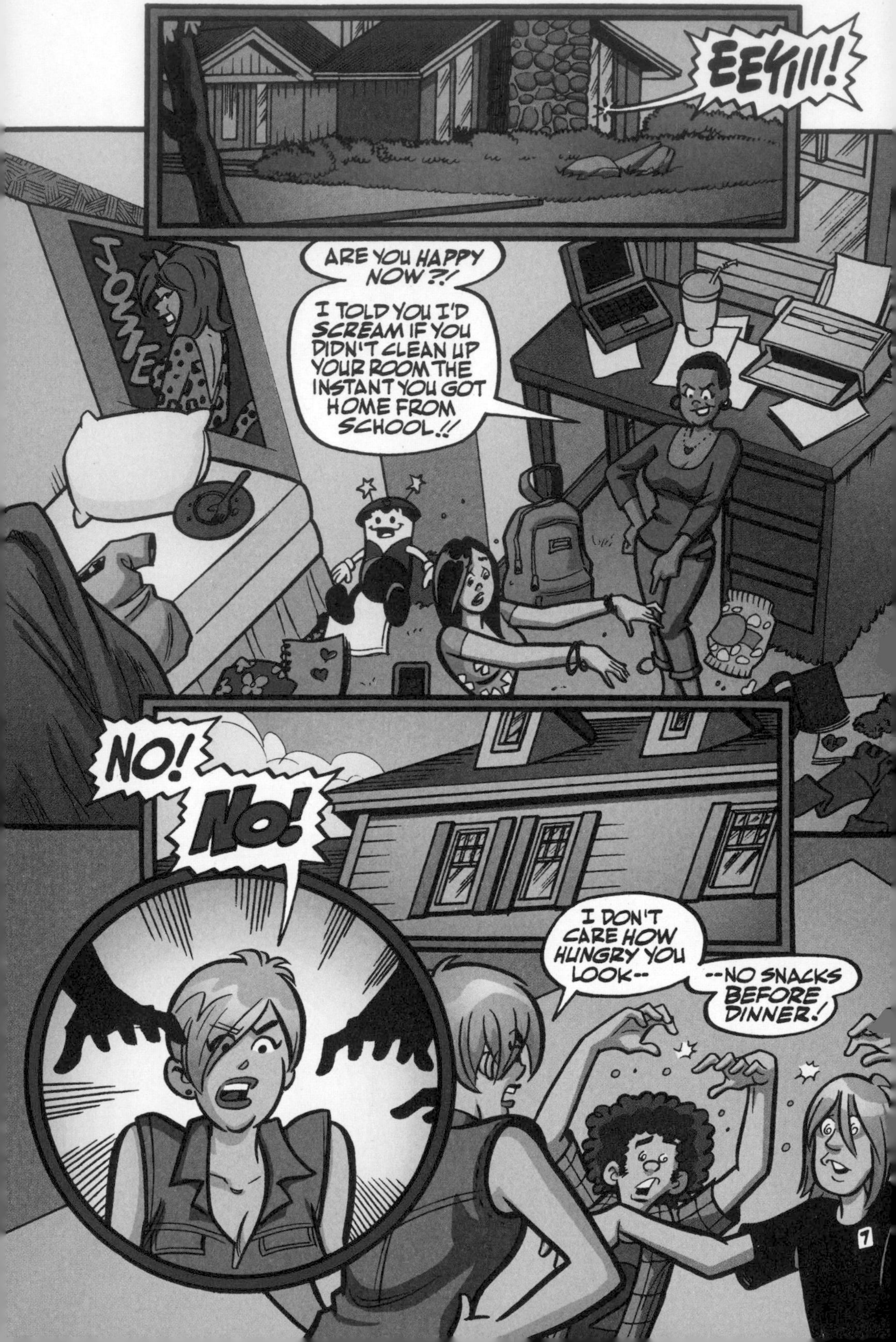
EEYIII!
ARE YOU HAPPY NOW?!
I TOLD YOU I'D SCREAM IF YOU DIDN'T CLEAN UP YOUR ROOM THE INSTANT YOU GOT HOME FROM SCHOOL!!
NO!
NO!
I DON'T CARE HOW HUNGRY YOU LOOK--
--NO SNACKS BEFORE DINNER!

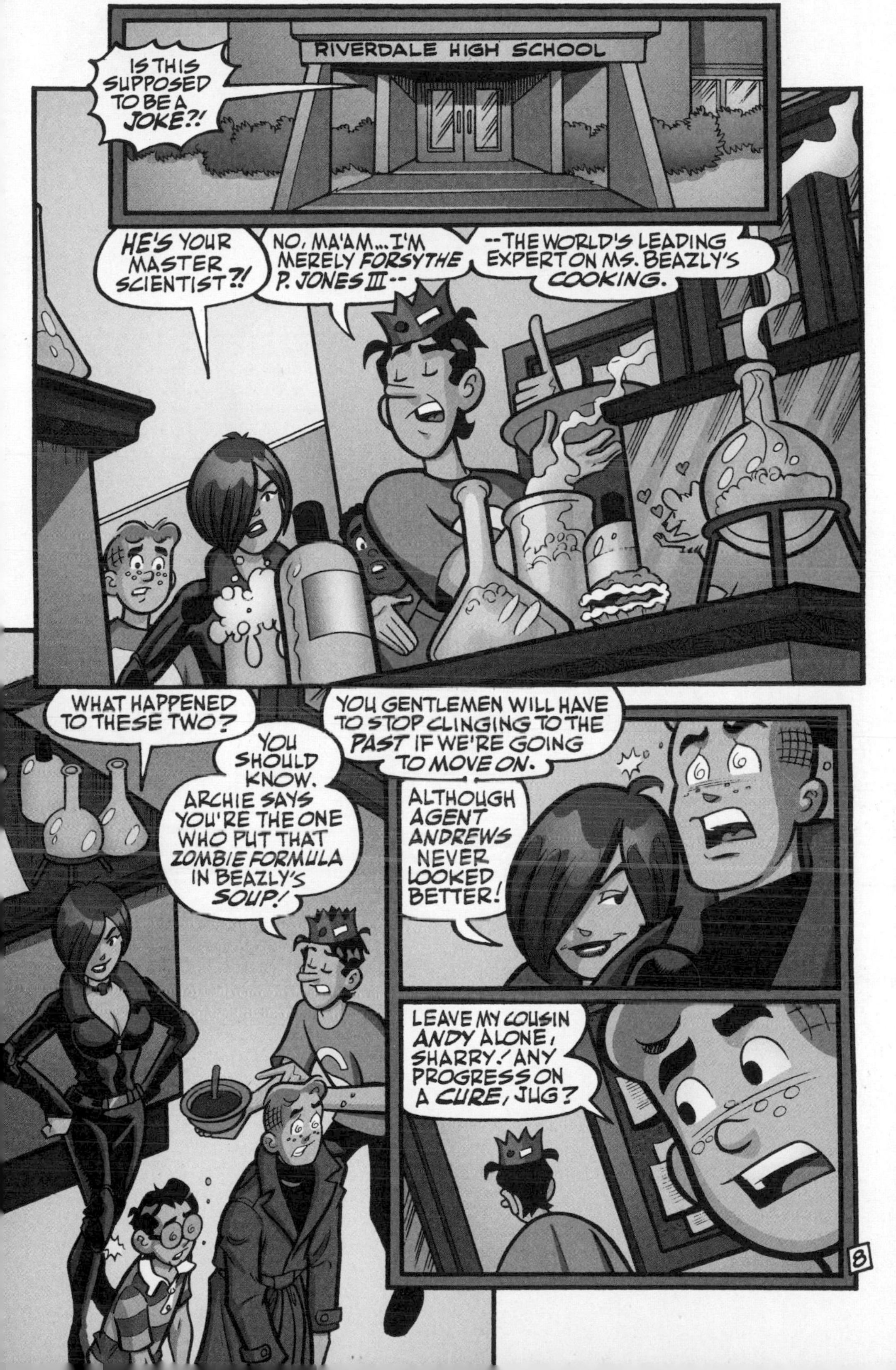
RIVERDALE HIGH SCHOOL
IS THIS SUPPOSED TO BE A JOKE?!
HE'S YOUR MASTER SCIENTIST?!
NO, MA'AM... I'M MERELY FORSYTHE P. JONES III --
-- THE WORLD'S LEADING EXPERT ON MS. BEAZLY'S COOKING.
WHAT HAPPENED TO THESE TWO?
YOU SHOULD KNOW. ARCHIE SAYS YOU'RE THE ONE WHO PUT THAT ZOMBIE FORMULA IN BEAZLY'S SOUP!
YOU GENTLEMEN WILL HAVE TO STOP CLINGING TO THE PAST IF WE'RE GOING TO MOVE ON.
ALTHOUGH AGENT ANDREWS NEVER LOOKED BETTER!
LEAVE MY COUSIN ANDY ALONE, SHARRY! ANY PROGRESS ON A CURE, JUG?
8

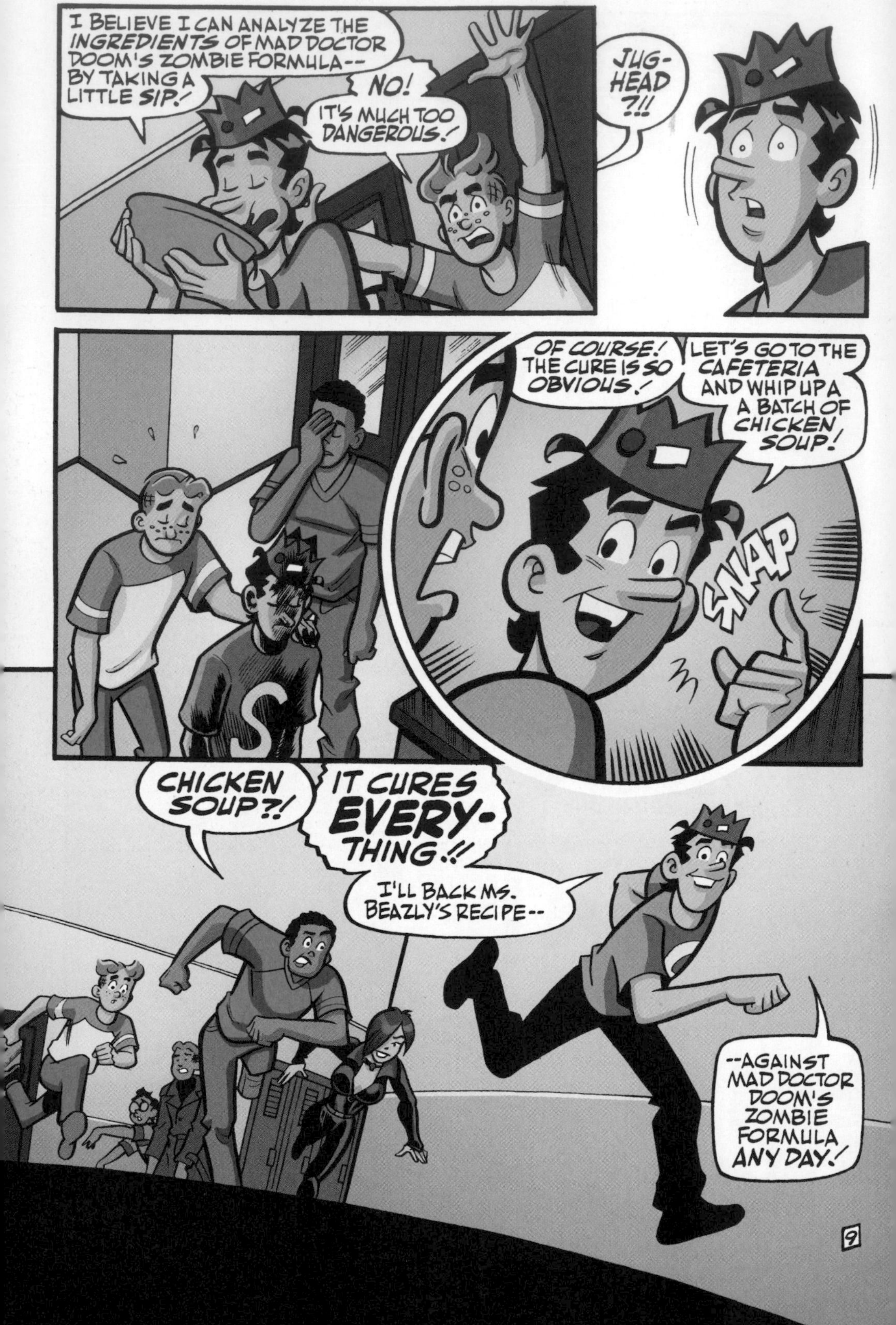
I BELIEVE I CAN ANALYZE THE INGREDIENTS OF MAD DOCTOR DOOM'S ZOMBIE FORMULA-- BY TAKING A LITTLE SIP!
NO!
IT'S MUCH TOO DANGEROUS!
JUG-HEAD ?!!
OF COURSE! THE CURE IS SO OBVIOUS!
LET'S GO TO THE CAFETERIA AND WHIP UP A A BATCH OF CHICKEN SOUP!
SNAP
CHICKEN SOUP?!
IT CURES EVERY-THING!!
I'LL BACK MS. BEAZLY'S RECIPE--
--AGAINST MAD DOCTOR DOOM'S ZOMBIE FORMULA ANY DAY!

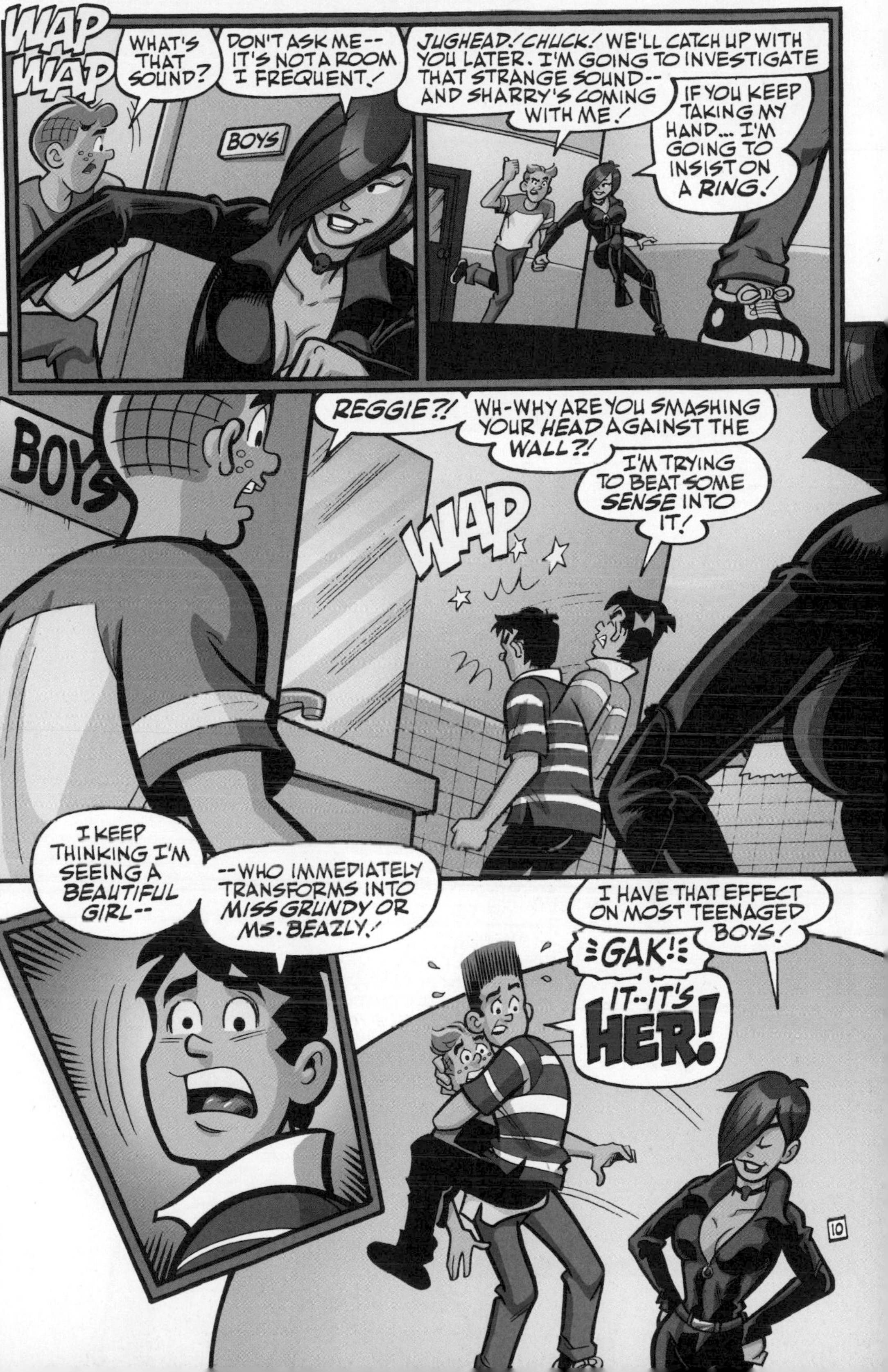
WAP WAP
WHAT'S THAT SOUND?
DON'T ASK ME-- IT'S NOT A ROOM I FREQUENT!
BOYS
JUGHEAD! CHUCK! WE'LL CATCH UP WITH YOU LATER. I'M GOING TO INVESTIGATE THAT STRANGE SOUND-- AND SHARRY'S COMING WITH ME!
IF YOU KEEP TAKING MY HAND... I'M GOING TO INSIST ON A RING!
BOYS
REGGIE?!
WH-WHY ARE YOU SMASHING YOUR HEAD AGAINST THE WALL?!
I'M TRYING TO BEAT SOME SENSE INTO IT!
WAP
I KEEP THINKING I'M SEEING A BEAUTIFUL GIRL--
--WHO IMMEDIATELY TRANSFORMS INTO MISS GRUNDY OR MS. BEAZLY!
I HAVE THAT EFFECT ON MOST TEENAGED BOYS!
GAK!
IT--IT'S HER!
10

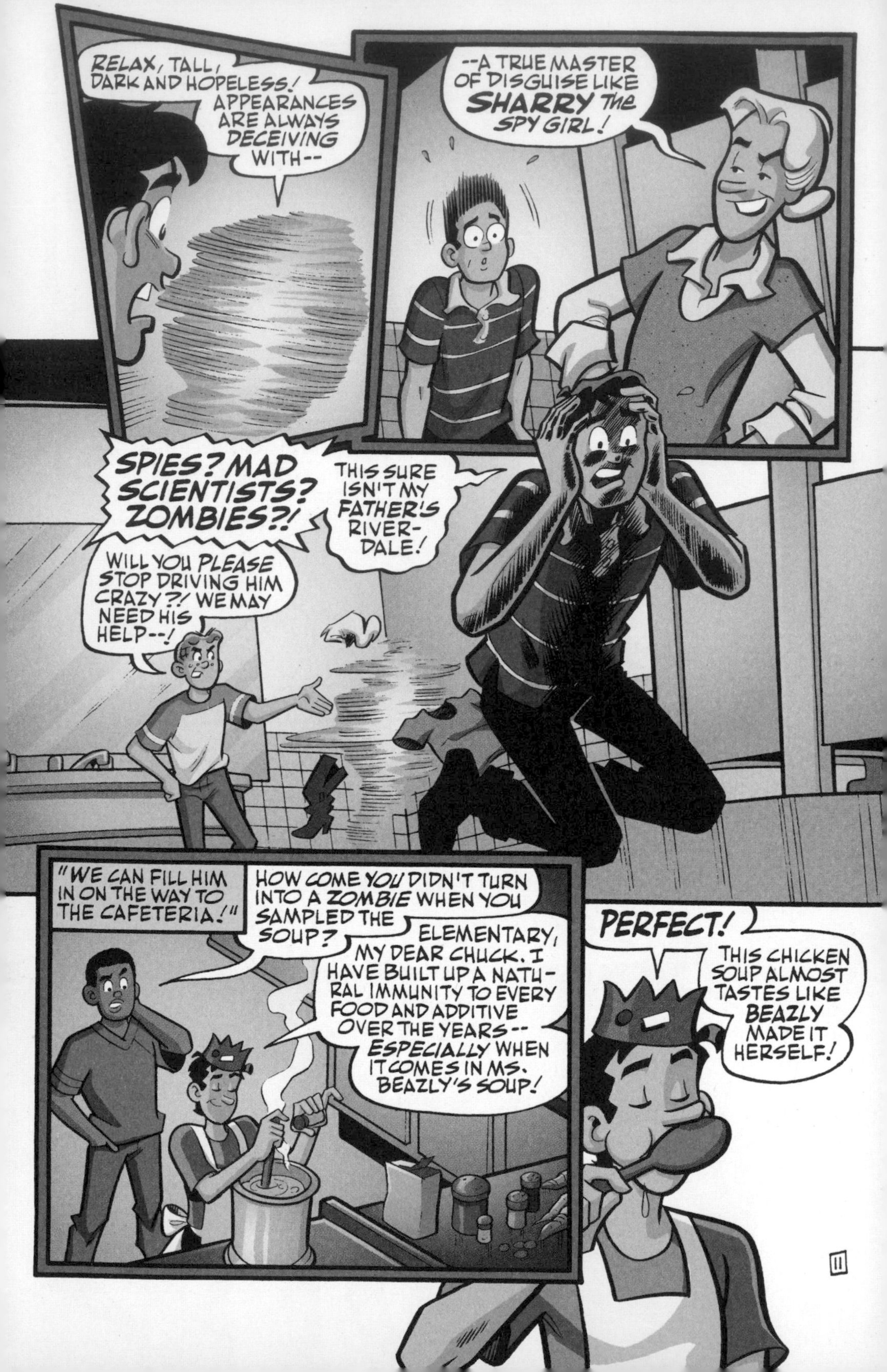

RELAX, TALL, DARK AND HOPELESS! APPEARANCES ARE ALWAYS DECEIVING WITH--
--A TRUE MASTER OF DISGUISE LIKE SHARRY THE SPY GIRL!
SPIES? MAD SCIENTISTS? ZOMBIES?!
THIS SURE ISN'T MY FATHER'S RIVER-DALE!
WILL YOU PLEASE STOP DRIVING HIM CRAZY?! WE MAY NEED HIS HELP--!
"WE CAN FILL HIM IN ON THE WAY TO THE CAFETERIA!"
HOW COME YOU DIDN'T TURN INTO A ZOMBIE WHEN YOU SAMPLED THE SOUP?
ELEMENTARY, MY DEAR CHUCK. I HAVE BUILT UP A NATU-RAL IMMUNITY TO EVERY FOOD AND ADDITIVE OVER THE YEARS-- ESPECIALLY WHEN IT COMES IN MS. BEAZLY'S SOUP!
PERFECT!
THIS CHICKEN SOUP ALMOST TASTES LIKE BEAZLY MADE IT HERSELF!

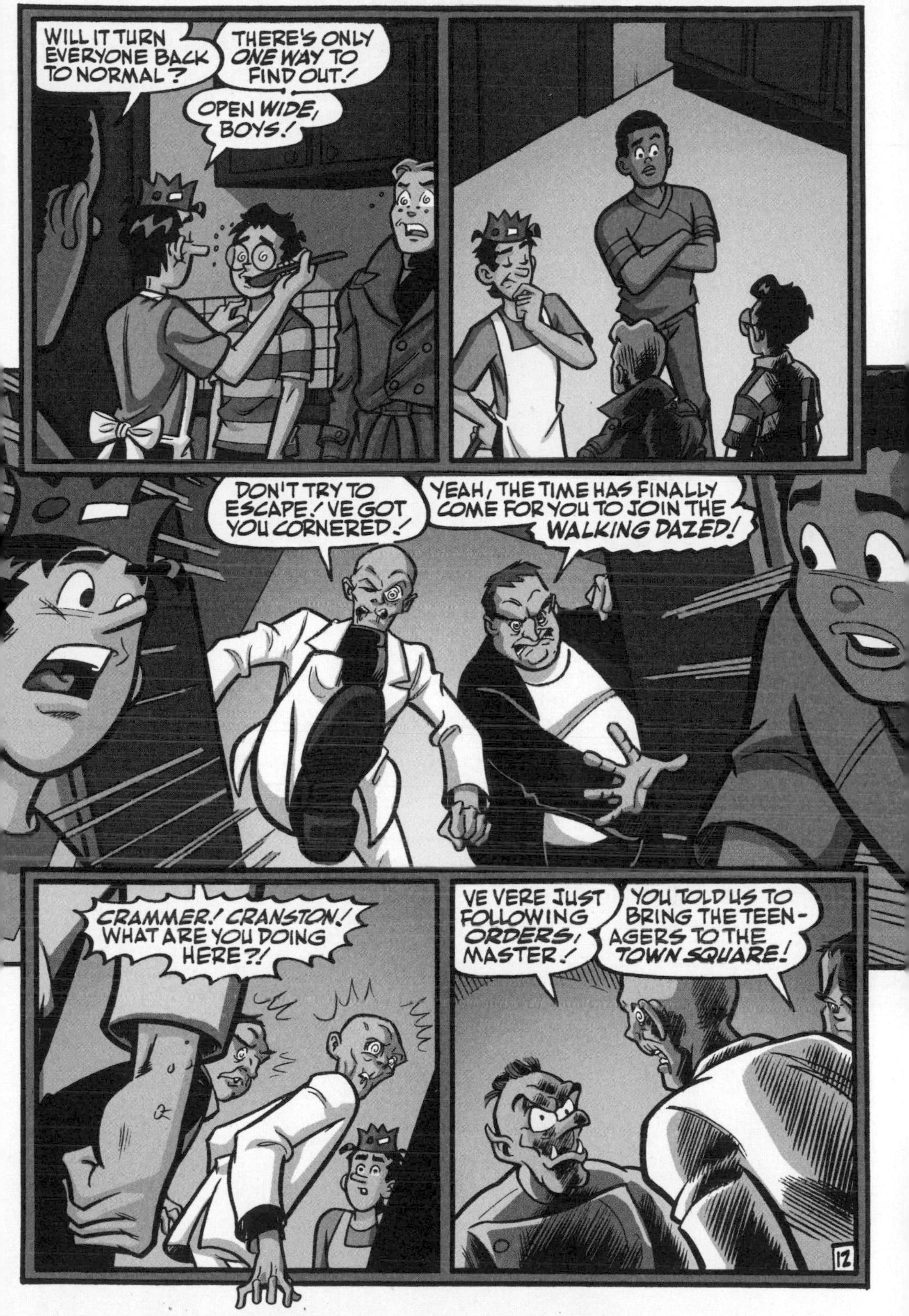
WILL IT TURN EVERYONE BACK TO NORMAL?
THERE'S ONLY ONE WAY TO FIND OUT!
OPEN WIDE, BOYS!
DON'T TRY TO ESCAPE! VE GOT YOU CORNERED!
YEAH, THE TIME HAS FINALLY COME FOR YOU TO JOIN THE WALKING DAZED!
CRAMMER! CRANSTON! WHAT ARE YOU DOING HERE?!
VE VERE JUST FOLLOWING ORDERS, MASTER!
YOU TOLD US TO BRING THE TEEN-AGERS TO THE TOWN SQUARE!
12

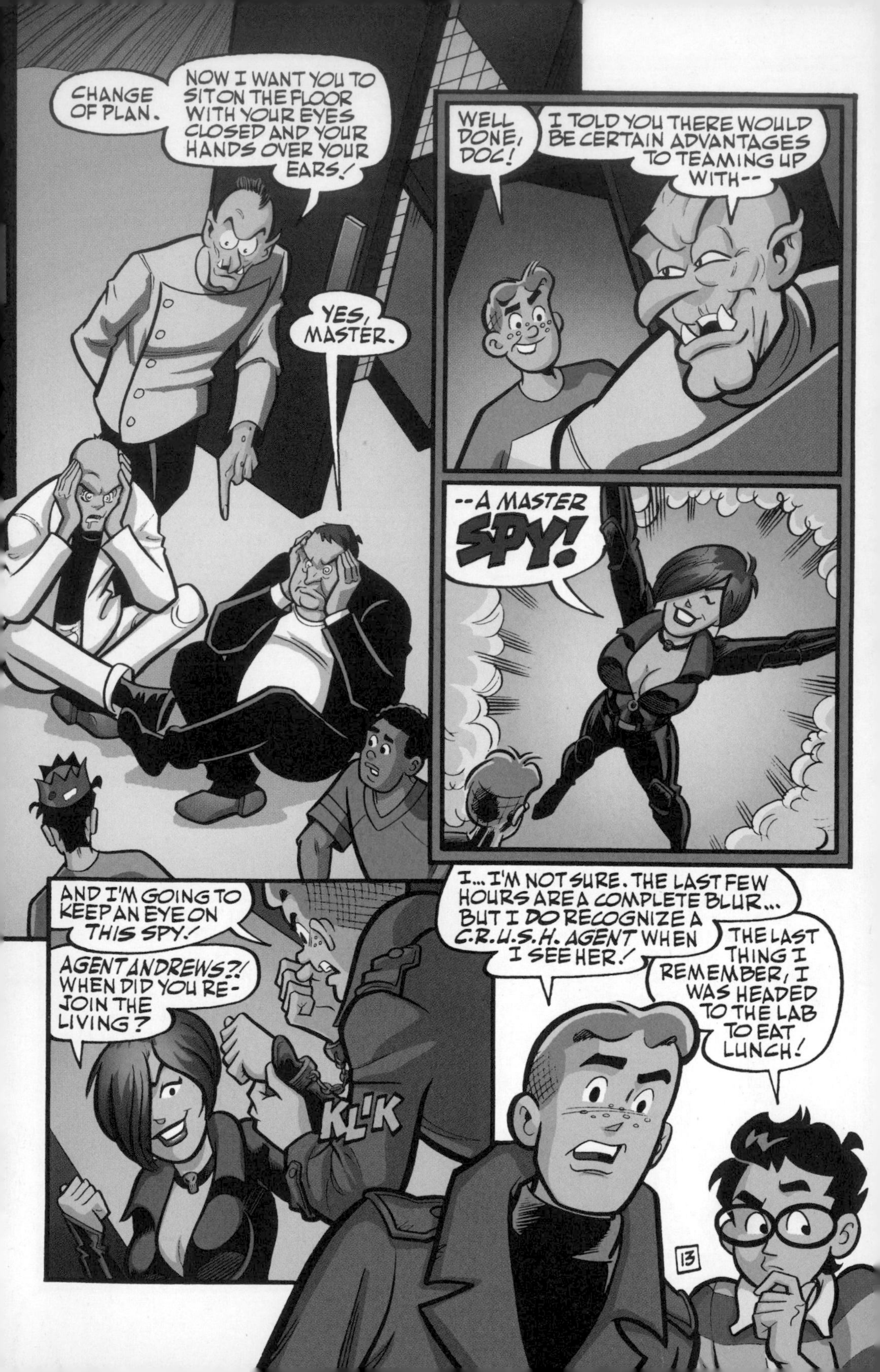
CHANGE OF PLAN.
NOW I WANT YOU TO SIT ON THE FLOOR WITH YOUR EYES CLOSED AND YOUR HANDS OVER YOUR EARS!
YES, MASTER.
WELL DONE, DOC!
I TOLD YOU THERE WOULD BE CERTAIN ADVANTAGES TO TEAMING UP WITH--
--A MASTER SPY!
AND I'M GOING TO KEEP AN EYE ON THIS SPY!
AGENT ANDREWS?! WHEN DID YOU RE-JOIN THE LIVING?
KLIK
I... I'M NOT SURE. THE LAST FEW HOURS ARE A COMPLETE BLUR... BUT I DO RECOGNIZE A C.R.U.S.H. AGENT WHEN I SEE HER!
THE LAST THING I REMEMBER, I WAS HEADED TO THE LAB TO EAT LUNCH!
13

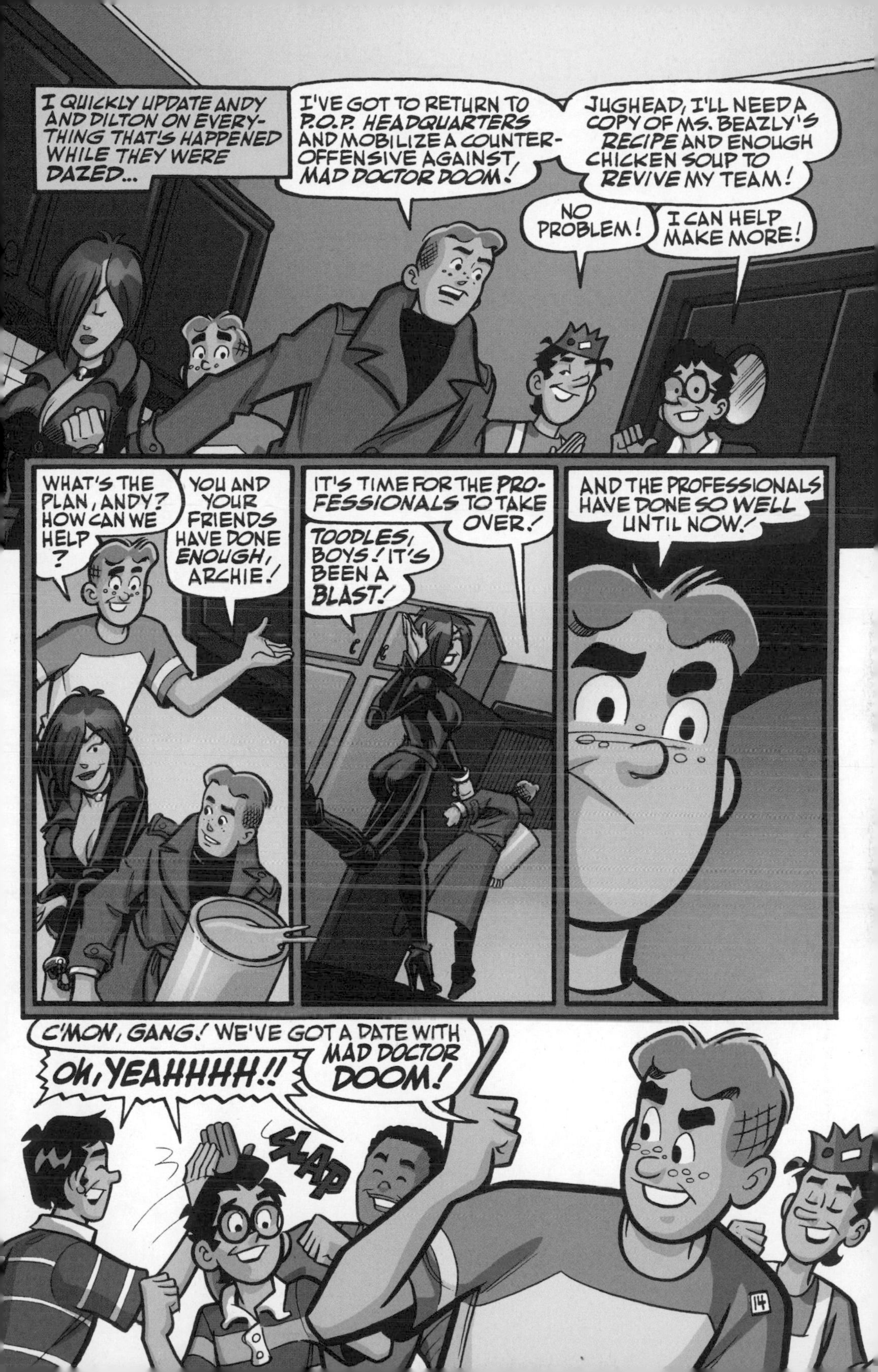

I QUICKLY UPDATE ANDY AND DILTON ON EVERYTHING THAT'S HAPPENED WHILE THEY WERE DAZED...
I'VE GOT TO RETURN TO P.O.P. HEADQUARTERS AND MOBILIZE A COUNTER-OFFENSIVE AGAINST MAD DOCTOR DOOM!
JUGHEAD, I'LL NEED A COPY OF MS. BEAZLY'S RECIPE AND ENOUGH CHICKEN SOUP TO REVIVE MY TEAM!
NO PROBLEM!
I CAN HELP MAKE MORE!
WHAT'S THE PLAN, ANDY? HOW CAN WE HELP?
YOU AND YOUR FRIENDS HAVE DONE ENOUGH, ARCHIE!
IT'S TIME FOR THE PROFESSIONALS TO TAKE OVER!
TOODLES, BOYS! IT'S BEEN A BLAST!
AND THE PROFESSIONALS HAVE DONE SO WELL UNTIL NOW!
C'MON, GANG! WE'VE GOT A DATE WITH MAD DOCTOR DOOM!
OH, YEAHHHHH!!
SLAP

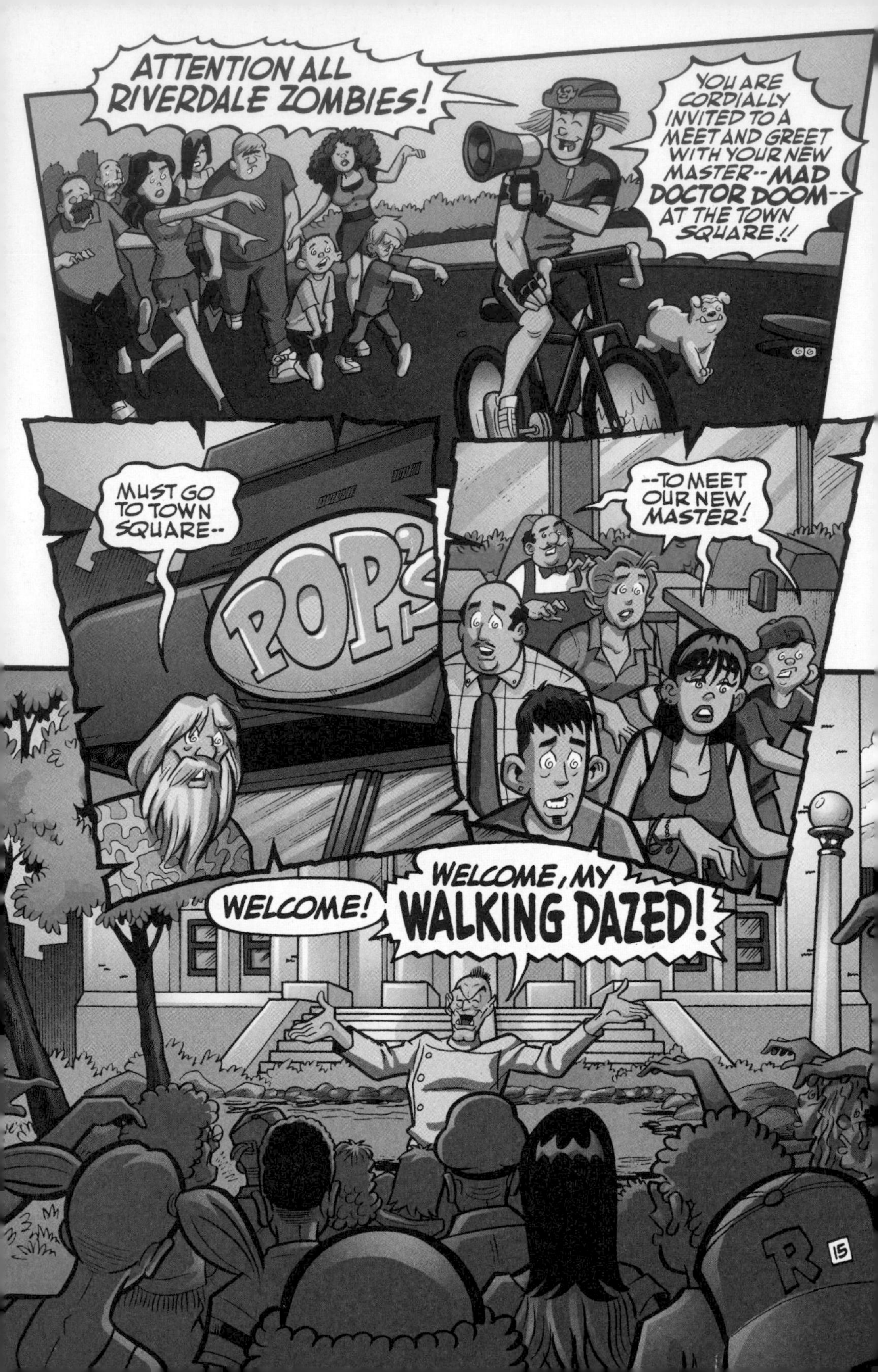
ATTENTION ALL RIVERDALE ZOMBIES!
YOU ARE CORDIALLY INVITED TO A MEET AND GREET WITH YOUR NEW MASTER-- MAD DOCTOR DOOM-- AT THE TOWN SQUARE!!
MUST GO TO TOWN SQUARE--
POP'S
--TO MEET OUR NEW MASTER!
WELCOME!
WELCOME, MY WALKING DAZED!
R
15

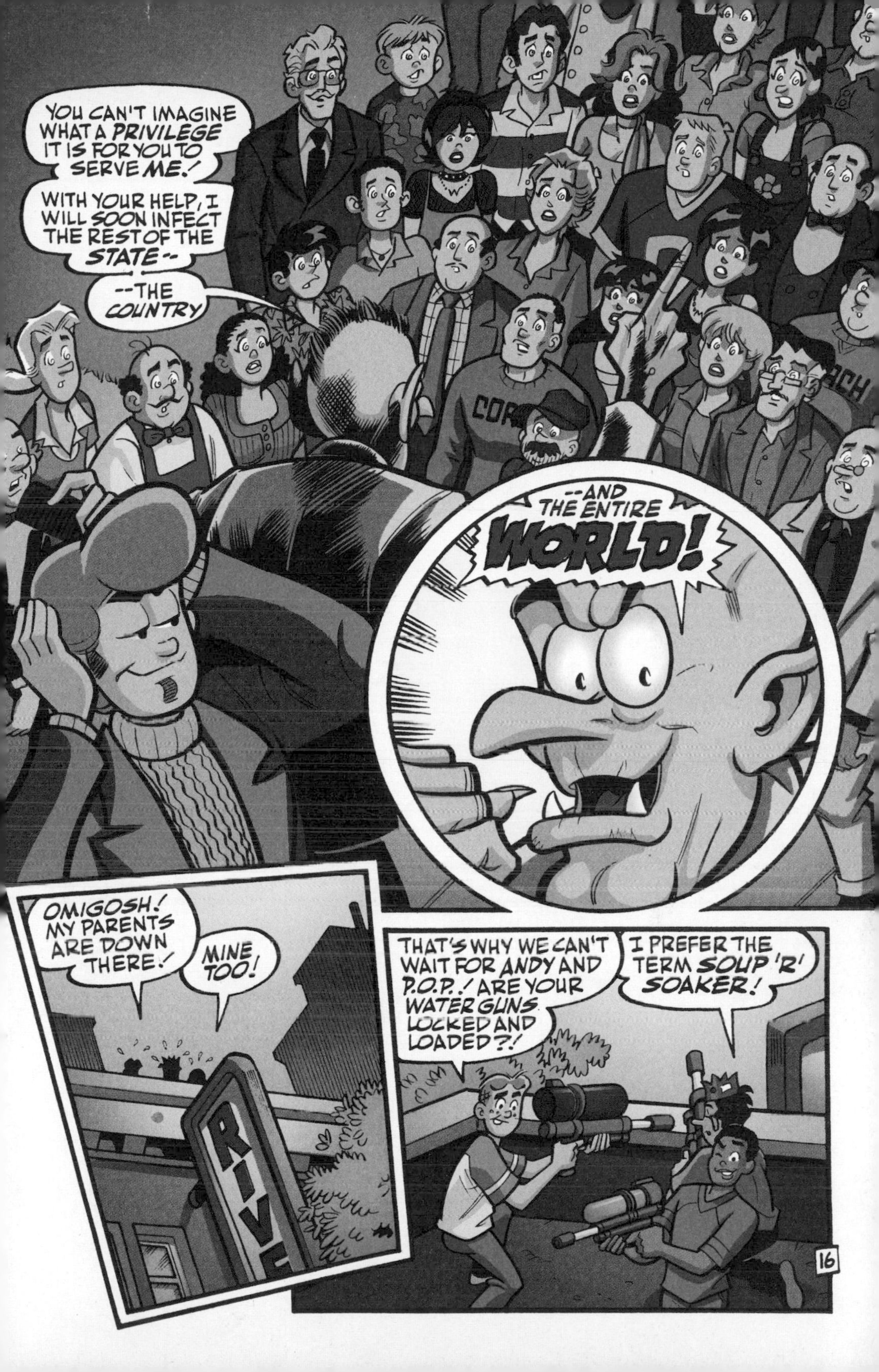
YOU CAN'T IMAGINE WHAT A PRIVILEGE IT IS FOR YOU TO SERVE ME!
WITH YOUR HELP, I WILL SOON INFECT THE REST OF THE STATE--
--THE COUNTRY
--AND THE ENTIRE WORLD!
OMIGOSH! MY PARENTS ARE DOWN THERE!
MINE TOO!
THAT'S WHY WE CAN'T WAIT FOR ANDY AND P.O.P.! ARE YOUR WATER GUNS LOCKED AND LOADED?!
I PREFER THE TERM SOUP 'R' SOAKER!
16

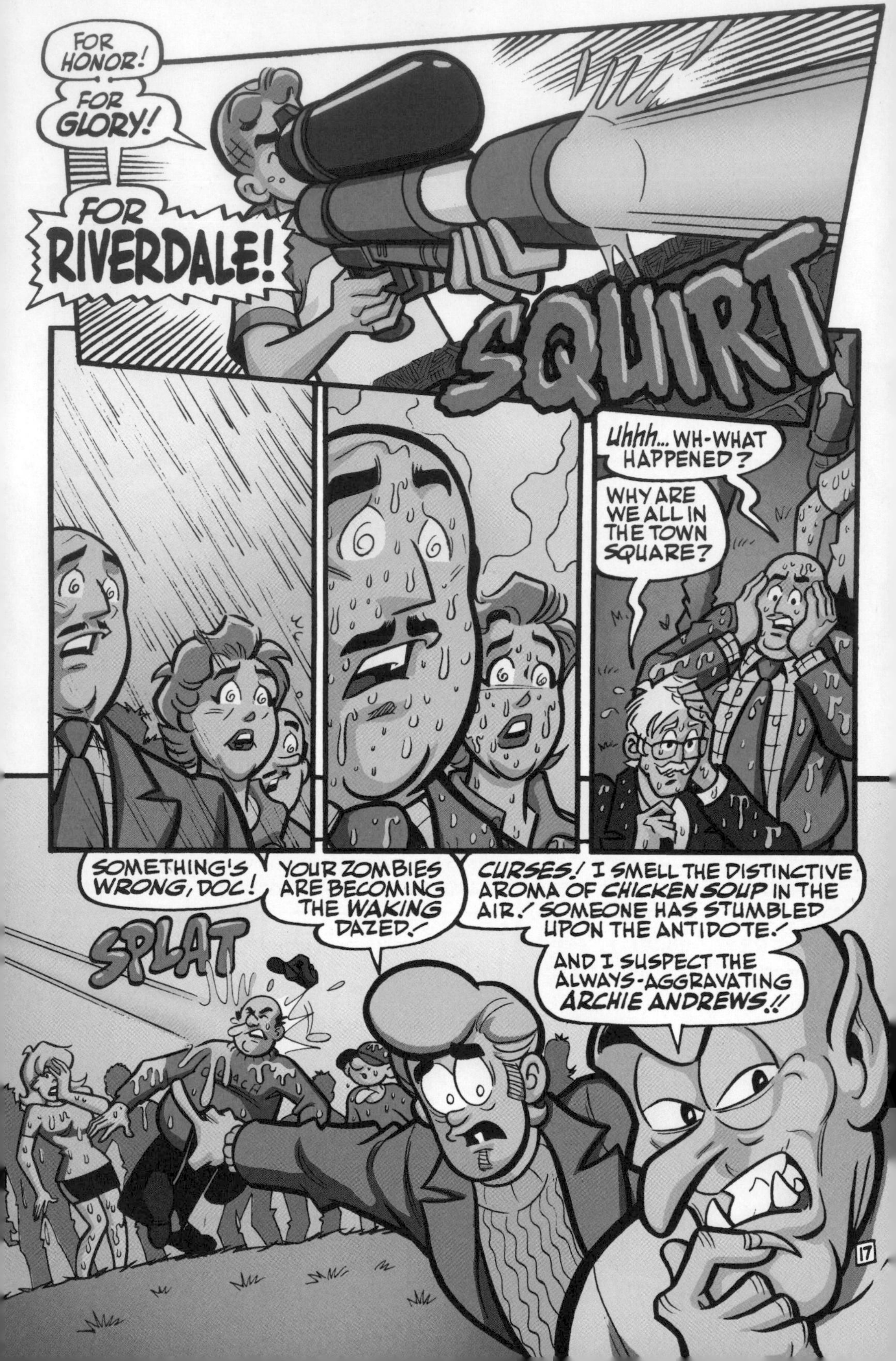

FOR HONOR!
FOR GLORY!
FOR RIVERDALE!
SQUIRT
UHHH... WH-WHAT HAPPENED?
WHY ARE WE ALL IN THE TOWN SQUARE?
SOMETHING'S WRONG, DOC!
YOUR ZOMBIES ARE BECOMING THE WAKING DAZED!
CURSES! I SMELL THE DISTINCTIVE AROMA OF CHICKEN SOUP IN THE AIR! SOMEONE HAS STUMBLED UPON THE ANTIDOTE!
AND I SUSPECT THE ALWAYS-AGGRAVATING ARCHIE ANDREWS!!
SPLAT

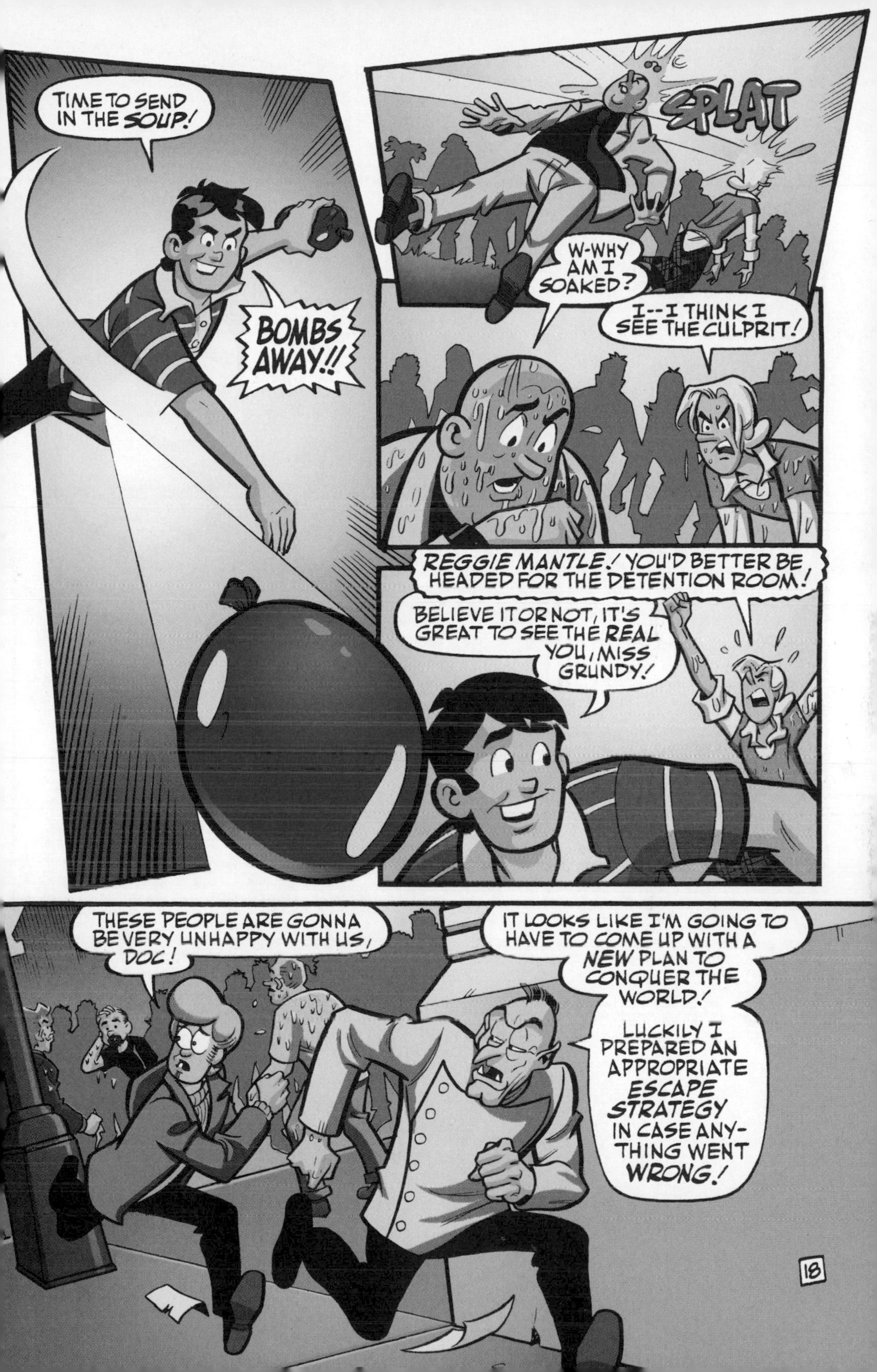

TIME TO SEND IN THE SOUP!
BOMBS AWAY!!
SPLAT
W-WHY AM I SOAKED?
I--I THINK I SEE THE CULPRIT!
REGGIE MANTLE! YOU'D BETTER BE HEADED FOR THE DETENTION ROOM!
BELIEVE IT OR NOT, IT'S GREAT TO SEE THE REAL YOU, MISS GRUNDY!
THESE PEOPLE ARE GONNA BE VERY UNHAPPY WITH US, DOC!
IT LOOKS LIKE I'M GOING TO HAVE TO COME UP WITH A NEW PLAN TO CONQUER THE WORLD!
LUCKILY I PREPARED AN APPROPRIATE ESCAPE STRATEGY IN CASE ANYTHING WENT WRONG!
18

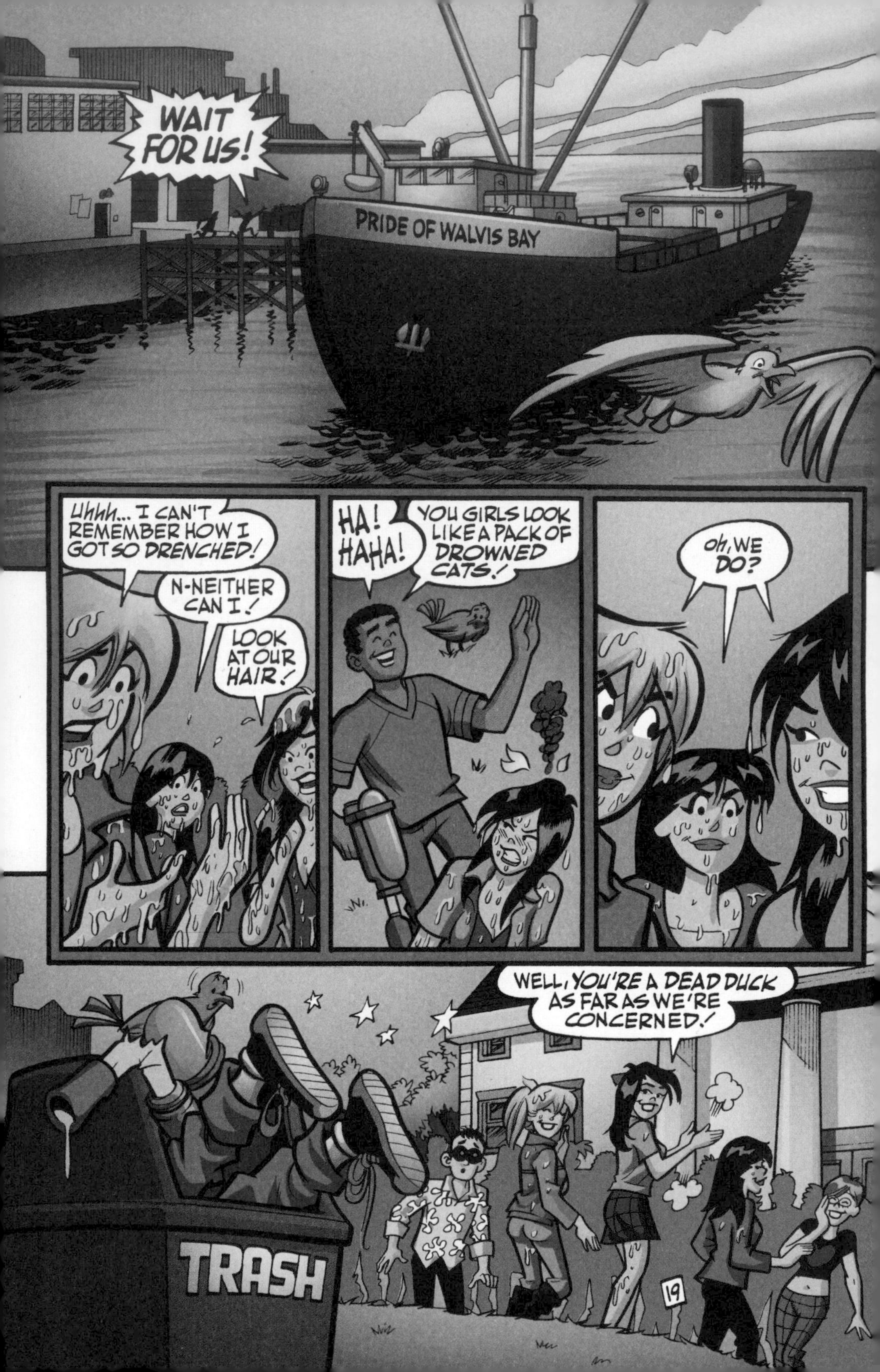
WAIT FOR US!
PRIDE OF WALVIS BAY
Uhhh... I CAN'T REMEMBER HOW I GOT SO DRENCHED!
N-NEITHER CAN I!
LOOK AT OUR HAIR!
HA! HAHA!
YOU GIRLS LOOK LIKE A PACK OF DROWNED CATS!
Oh, WE DO?
WELL, YOU'RE A DEAD DUCK AS FAR AS WE'RE CONCERNED!
TRASH
19

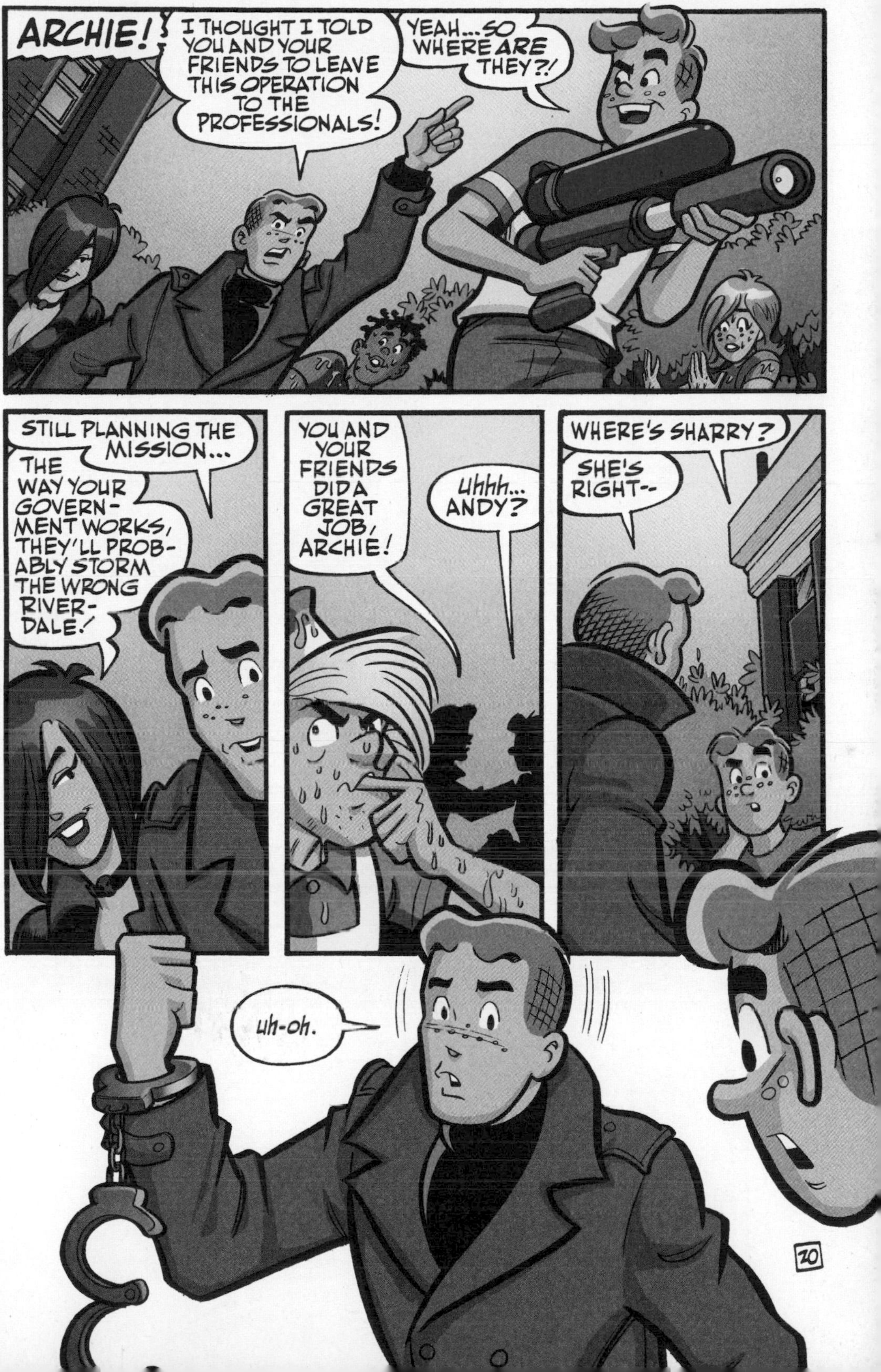
ARCHIE!
I THOUGHT I TOLD YOU AND YOUR FRIENDS TO LEAVE THIS OPERATION TO THE PROFESSIONALS!
YEAH...SO WHERE ARE THEY?!
STILL PLANNING THE MISSION...
THE WAY YOUR GOVERNMENT WORKS, THEY'LL PROBABLY STORM THE WRONG RIVERDALE!
YOU AND YOUR FRIENDS DID A GREAT JOB, ARCHIE!
uhhh... ANDY?
WHERE'S SHARRY?
SHE'S RIGHT--
uh-oh.

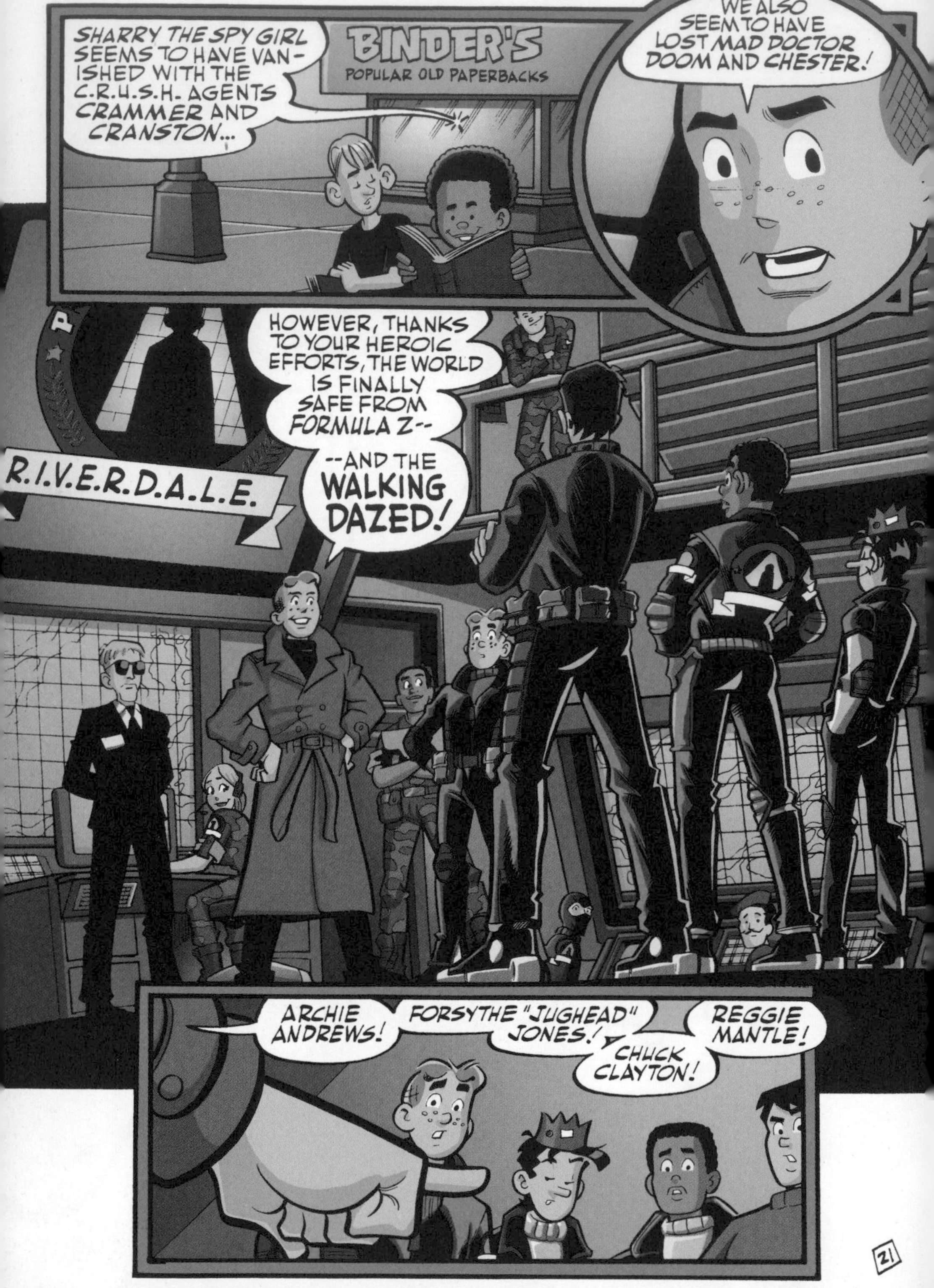
SHARRY THE SPY GIRL SEEMS TO HAVE VANISHED WITH THE C.R.U.S.H. AGENTS CRAMMER AND CRANSTON...
BINDER'S
POPULAR OLD PAPERBACKS
WE ALSO SEEM TO HAVE LOST MAD DOCTOR DOOM AND CHESTER!
HOWEVER, THANKS TO YOUR HEROIC EFFORTS, THE WORLD IS FINALLY SAFE FROM FORMULA Z--
--AND THE WALKING DAZED!
R.I.V.E.R.D.A.L.E.
ARCHIE ANDREWS!
FORSYTHE "JUGHEAD" JONES!
CHUCK CLAYTON!
REGGIE MANTLE!

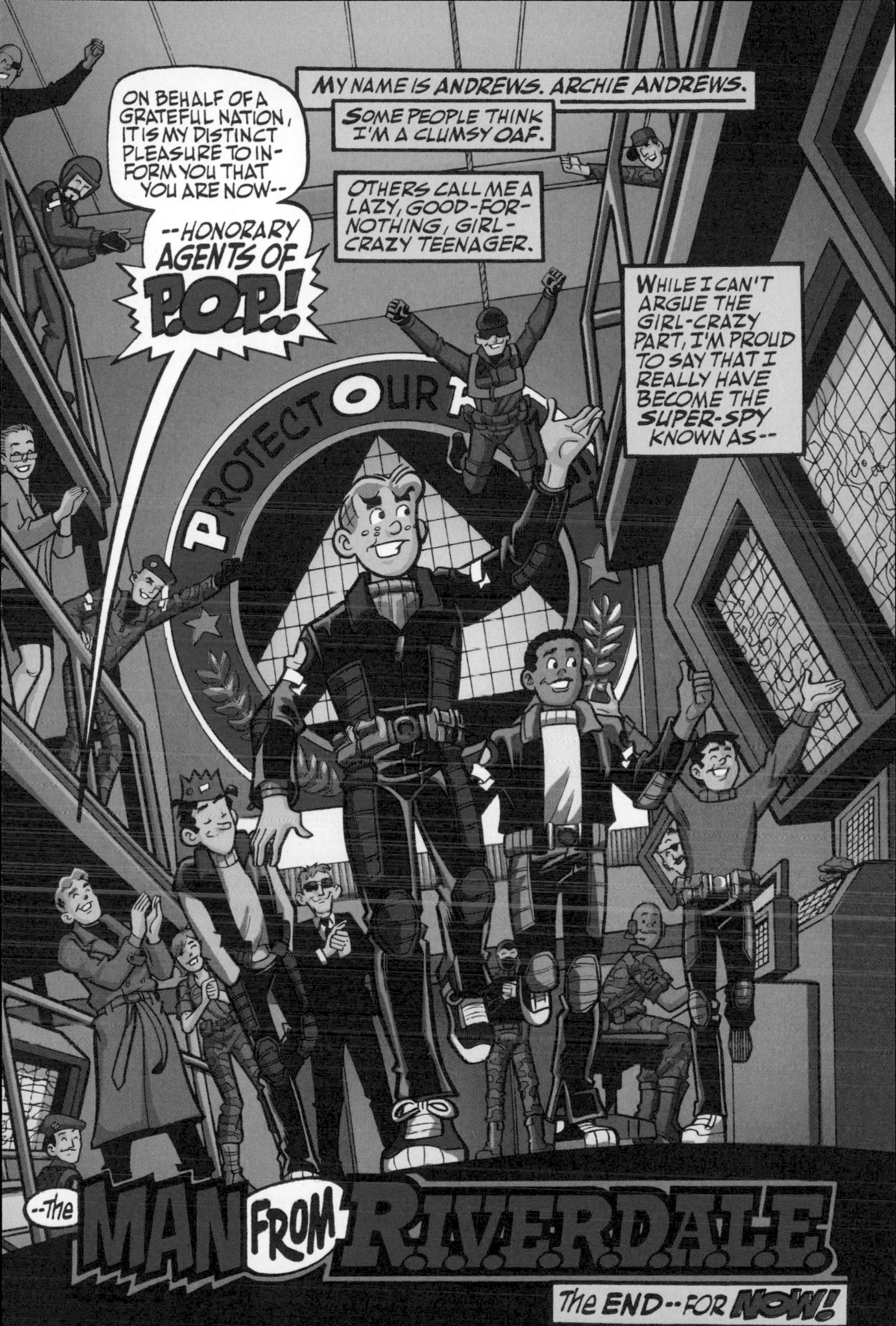

MY NAME IS ANDREWS. ARCHIE ANDREWS.
SOME PEOPLE THINK I'M A CLUMSY OAF.
OTHERS CALL ME A LAZY, GOOD-FOR-NOTHING, GIRL-CRAZY TEENAGER.
ON BEHALF OF A GRATEFUL NATION, IT IS MY DISTINCT PLEASURE TO INFORM YOU THAT YOU ARE NOW--
--HONORARY AGENTS OF P.O.P.!
WHILE I CAN'T ARGUE THE GIRL-CRAZY PART, I'M PROUD TO SAY THAT I REALLY HAVE BECOME THE SUPER-SPY KNOWN AS--
PROTECT OUR
--the MAN FROM R.I.V.E.R.D.A.L.E.
The END--FOR NOW!

TO: DIRECTOR OF P.O.P.
FROM: TOM DEFALCO
SUBJECT: PROJECT R.I.V.E.R.D.A.L.E.

You never know where a story will take you. When one works, it grabs you by the throat and drags you to some rather unexpected places. That's kind of what happened to me when Victor Gorelick--my all-powerful and all-knowing editor--asked me to bring back "The Man From R.I.V.E.R.D.A.L.E."

The original "The Man From R.I.V.E.R.D.A.L.E." first appeared in the 1960s, inspired by the first couple of James Bond movies and a television show called *The Man From U.N.C.L.E.* In the original series, Archie and the gang were all spies. I didn't think that would work today. I wasn't even sure Archie should start out as a spy. I needed someone else. That's when Victor reminded me of a heretofore unprinted Andy Andrews story that had been written and drawn by the legendary Harry Lucey. Since that story appears in this very book, you'll soon see why I decided to use Andy as my spy.

All I needed now was a villain. An obvious choice immediately leaped to mind. I have always been a fan of the Little Archie stories produced by Bob Bolling and Dexter Taylor. They often used a villain called Mad Doctor Doom and his assistant Chester. (Fantastic Fernando Ruiz got into the spirit by adding a picture of Little Archie's dog Spotty to the Andrews' mantle.) Fernando and I later created Sharry the spy girl, Crammer and Cranston, added Mad Doctor Doom's secret formula, mixed well and came up with the tale you've just read.

*Tom
DeFalco*

PROTECT OUR PLANET

R.I.V.E.R.D.A.L.E.

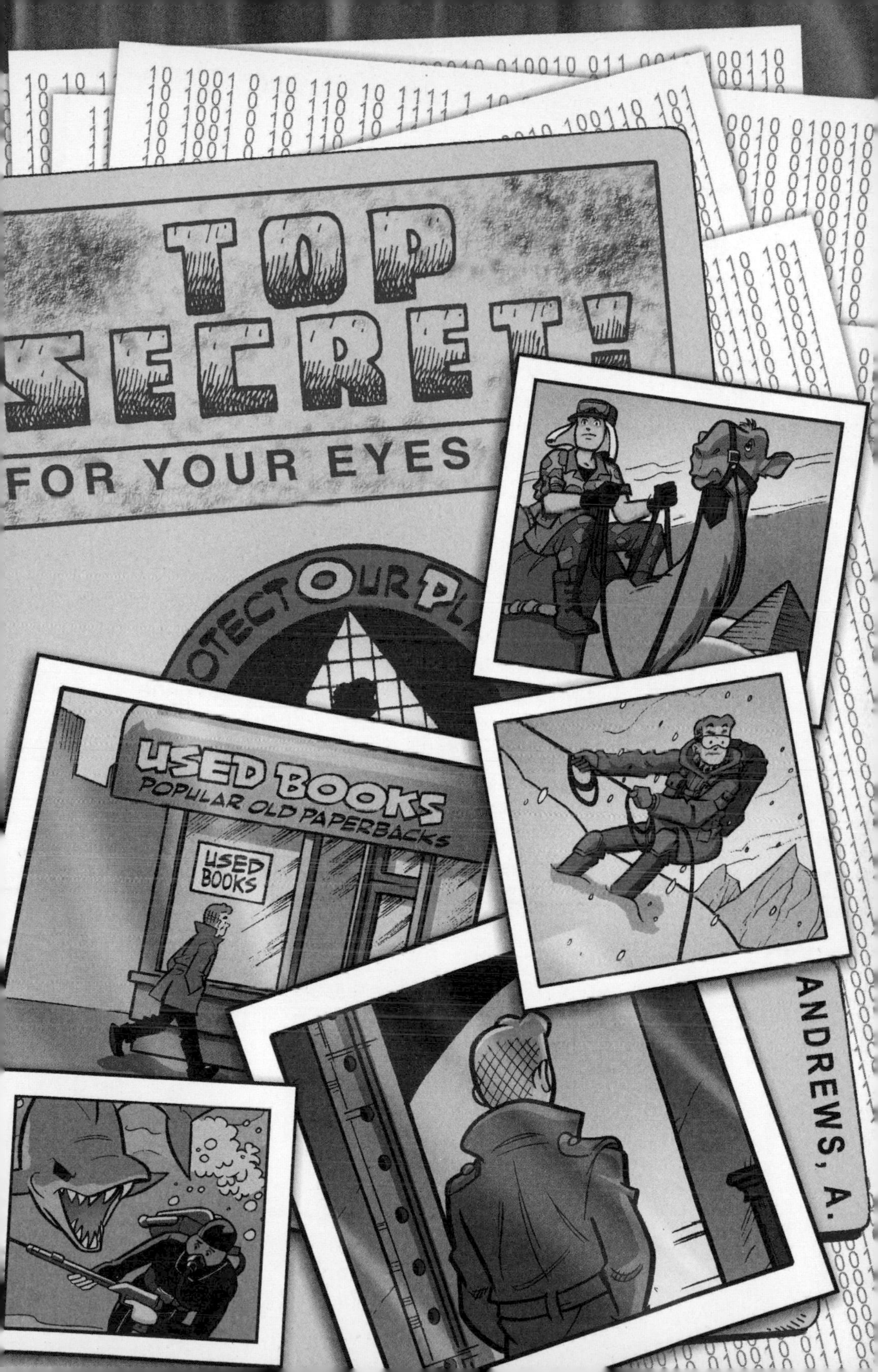
TOP SECRET!
FOR YOUR EYES
PROTECT OUR PL
USED BOOKS
POPULAR OLD PAPERBACKS
USED BOOKS
ANDREWS, A.

TO: ALL PERSONNEL
FROM: DIRECTOR OF P.O.P.
SUBJECT: SPECIAL AGENT ANDREWS

Due to the recent breach of security caused by the criminal activities perpetrated by Mad Doctor Doom and C.R.U.S.H. it is necessary to re-evaluate certain members of P.O.P. as well as individuals involved in Project R.I.V.E.R.D.A.L.E. With that stated, we present for review Special Agent Andy Andrews.

The following story has never before been released in any fashion. Discovered in a locked art cabinet hidden away in the offices of Archie Comic Publications since the mid-1950s, "The Iron Curtain Caper" introduces Andy Andrews and establishes his relationship with long-lost cousin Archie Andrews. Although there is not much information as to when the story was actually commissioned or why it had gone unpublished for so many years, we do know that it was written and illustrated by the legendary Harry Lucey.

Without further ado, we present to you the reader, in print for the first time ever, Andy Andrews in "The Iron Curtain Caper."

PROTECT OUR PLANET
R.I.V.E.R.D.A.L.E.

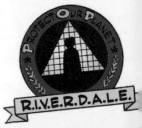

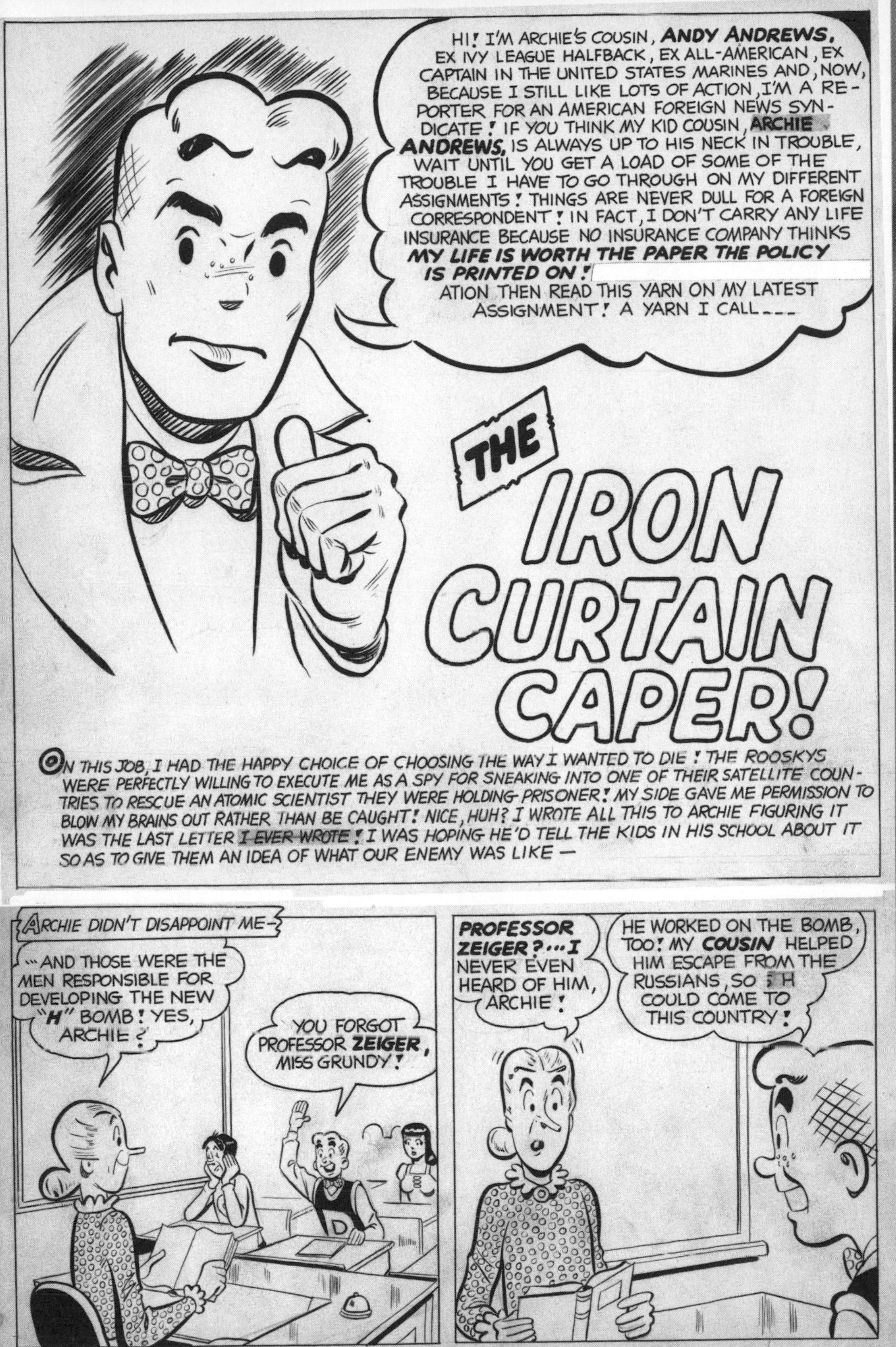
HI! I'M ARCHIE'S COUSIN, ANDY ANDREWS, EX IVY LEAGUE HALFBACK, EX ALL-AMERICAN, EX CAPTAIN IN THE UNITED STATES MARINES AND, NOW, BECAUSE I STILL LIKE LOTS OF ACTION, I'M A RE-PORTER FOR AN AMERICAN FOREIGN NEWS SYN-DICATE! IF YOU THINK MY KID COUSIN, ARCHIE ANDREWS, IS ALWAYS UP TO HIS NECK IN TROUBLE, WAIT UNTIL YOU GET A LOAD OF SOME OF THE TROUBLE I HAVE TO GO THROUGH ON MY DIFFERENT ASSIGNMENTS! THINGS ARE NEVER DULL FOR A FOREIGN CORRESPONDENT! IN FACT, I DON'T CARRY ANY LIFE INSURANCE BECAUSE NO INSURANCE COMPANY THINKS MY LIFE IS WORTH THE PAPER THE POLICY IS PRINTED ON!
ATION THEN READ THIS YARN ON MY LATEST ASSIGNMENT! A YARN I CALL---
THE IRON CURTAIN CAPER!
ON THIS JOB, I HAD THE HAPPY CHOICE OF CHOOSING THE WAY I WANTED TO DIE! THE ROOSKYS WERE PERFECTLY WILLING TO EXECUTE ME AS A SPY FOR SNEAKING INTO ONE OF THEIR SATELLITE COUN-TRIES TO RESCUE AN ATOMIC SCIENTIST THEY WERE HOLDING PRISONER! MY SIDE GAVE ME PERMISSION TO BLOW MY BRAINS OUT RATHER THAN BE CAUGHT! NICE, HUH? I WROTE ALL THIS TO ARCHIE FIGURING IT WAS THE LAST LETTER I EVER WROTE! I WAS HOPING HE'D TELL THE KIDS IN HIS SCHOOL ABOUT IT SO AS TO GIVE THEM AN IDEA OF WHAT OUR ENEMY WAS LIKE —
ARCHIE DIDN'T DISAPPOINT ME-
...AND THOSE WERE THE MEN RESPONSIBLE FOR DEVELOPING THE NEW "H" BOMB! YES, ARCHIE?
YOU FORGOT PROFESSOR ZEIGER, MISS GRUNDY!
PROFESSOR ZEIGER?...I NEVER EVEN HEARD OF HIM, ARCHIE!
HE WORKED ON THE BOMB, TOO! MY COUSIN HELPED HIM ESCAPE FROM THE RUSSIANS, SO H COULD COME TO THIS COUNTRY!
1

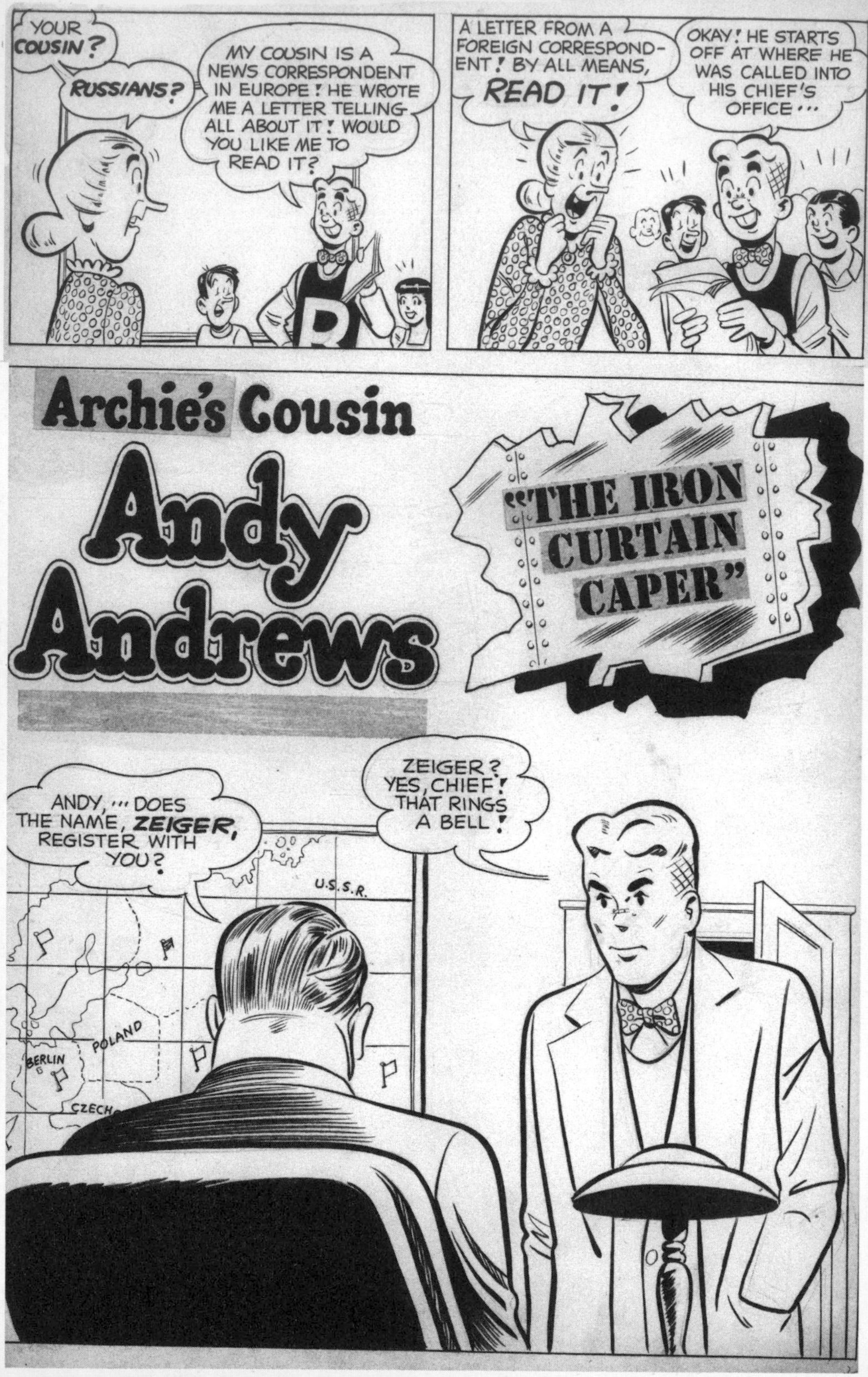
YOUR COUSIN?
RUSSIANS?
MY COUSIN IS A NEWS CORRESPONDENT IN EUROPE! HE WROTE ME A LETTER TELLING ALL ABOUT IT! WOULD YOU LIKE ME TO READ IT?
A LETTER FROM A FOREIGN CORRESPONDENT! BY ALL MEANS, READ IT!
OKAY! HE STARTS OFF AT WHERE HE WAS CALLED INTO HIS CHIEF'S OFFICE...
Archie's Cousin
Andy Andrews
"THE IRON CURTAIN CAPER"
ANDY, ... DOES THE NAME, ZEIGER, REGISTER WITH YOU?
ZEIGER? YES, CHIEF! THAT RINGS A BELL!
U.S.S.R.
POLAND
BERLIN
CZECH

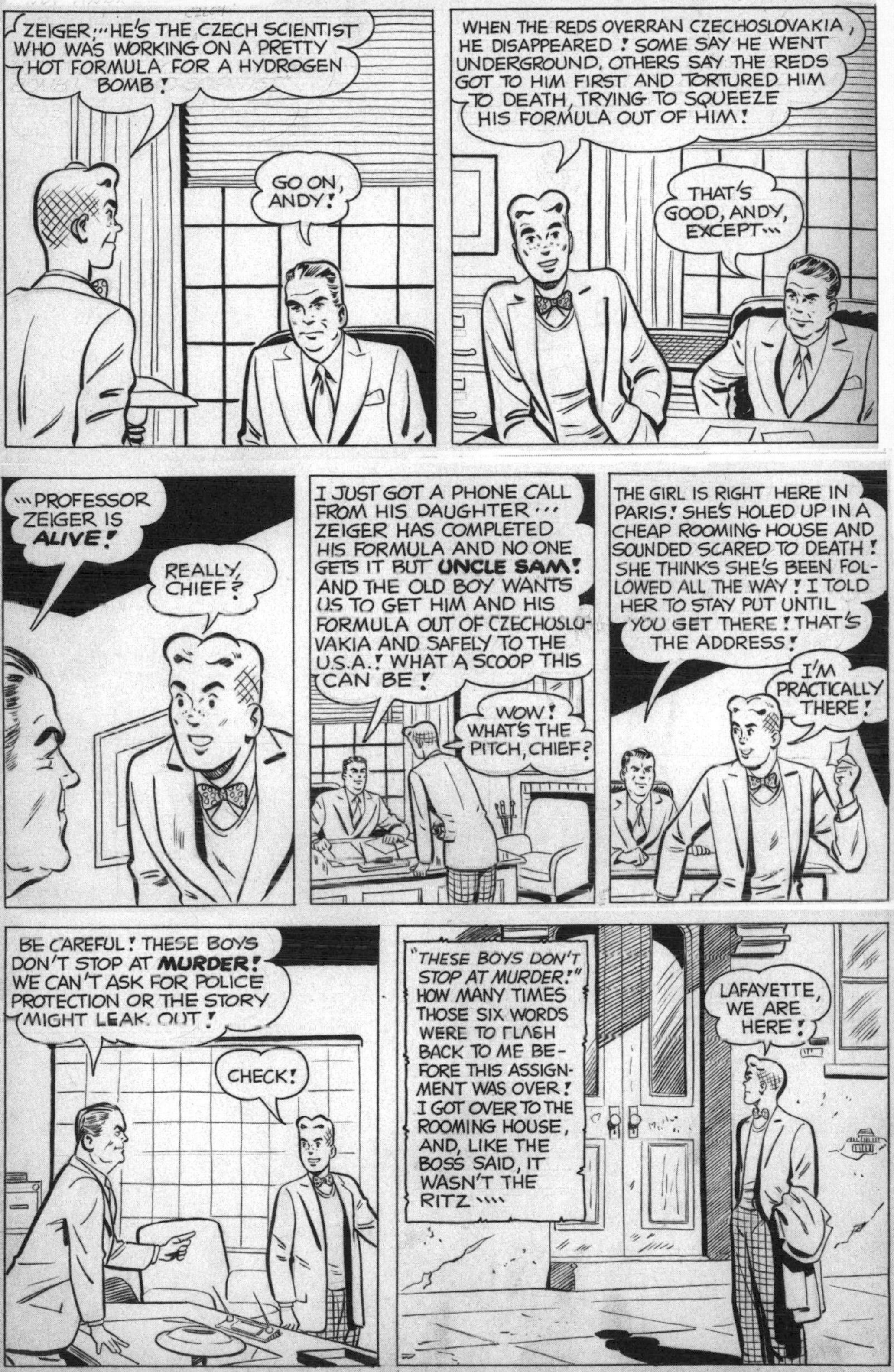

ZEIGER... HE'S THE CZECH SCIENTIST WHO WAS WORKING ON A PRETTY HOT FORMULA FOR A HYDROGEN BOMB!
GO ON, ANDY!
WHEN THE REDS OVERRAN CZECHOSLOVAKIA, HE DISAPPEARED! SOME SAY HE WENT UNDERGROUND, OTHERS SAY THE REDS GOT TO HIM FIRST AND TORTURED HIM TO DEATH, TRYING TO SQUEEZE HIS FORMULA OUT OF HIM!
THAT'S GOOD, ANDY, EXCEPT...
...PROFESSOR ZEIGER IS **ALIVE!**
REALLY, CHIEF?
I JUST GOT A PHONE CALL FROM HIS DAUGHTER... ZEIGER HAS COMPLETED HIS FORMULA AND NO ONE GETS IT BUT **UNCLE SAM!** AND THE OLD BOY WANTS US TO GET HIM AND HIS FORMULA OUT OF CZECHOSLOVAKIA AND SAFELY TO THE U.S.A.! WHAT A SCOOP THIS CAN BE!
WOW! WHAT'S THE PITCH, CHIEF?
THE GIRL IS RIGHT HERE IN PARIS! SHE'S HOLED UP IN A CHEAP ROOMING HOUSE AND SOUNDED SCARED TO DEATH! SHE THINKS SHE'S BEEN FOLLOWED ALL THE WAY! I TOLD HER TO STAY PUT UNTIL *YOU* GET THERE! THAT'S THE ADDRESS!
I'M PRACTICALLY THERE!
BE CAREFUL! THESE BOYS DON'T STOP AT **MURDER!** WE CAN'T ASK FOR POLICE PROTECTION OR THE STORY MIGHT LEAK OUT!
CHECK!
"THESE BOYS DON'T STOP AT MURDER!" HOW MANY TIMES THOSE SIX WORDS WERE TO FLASH BACK TO ME BEFORE THIS ASSIGNMENT WAS OVER! I GOT OVER TO THE ROOMING HOUSE, AND, LIKE THE BOSS SAID, IT WASN'T THE RITZ....
LAFAYETTE, WE ARE HERE!

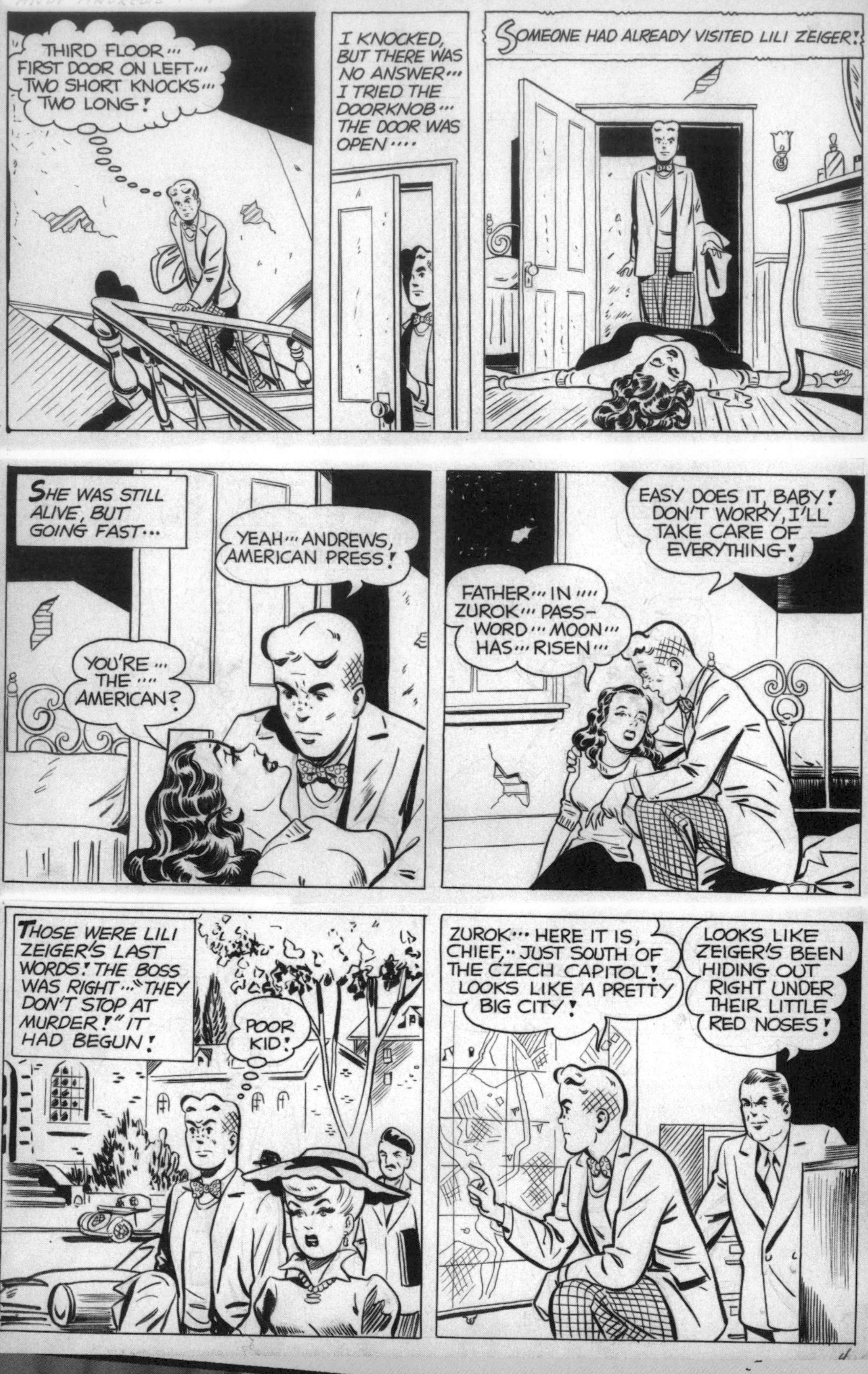

THIRD FLOOR... FIRST DOOR ON LEFT... TWO SHORT KNOCKS... TWO LONG!
I KNOCKED, BUT THERE WAS NO ANSWER... I TRIED THE DOORKNOB... THE DOOR WAS OPEN....
SOMEONE HAD ALREADY VISITED LILI ZEIGER!
SHE WAS STILL ALIVE, BUT GOING FAST...
YOU'RE... THE.... AMERICAN?
YEAH... ANDREWS, AMERICAN PRESS!
FATHER... IN... ZUROK... PASS-WORD... MOON... HAS... RISEN...
EASY DOES IT, BABY! DON'T WORRY, I'LL TAKE CARE OF EVERYTHING!
THOSE WERE LILI ZEIGER'S LAST WORDS! THE BOSS WAS RIGHT... "THEY DON'T STOP AT MURDER!" IT HAD BEGUN!
POOR KID!
ZUROK... HERE IT IS, CHIEF,.. JUST SOUTH OF THE CZECH CAPITOL! LOOKS LIKE A PRETTY BIG CITY!
LOOKS LIKE ZEIGER'S BEEN HIDING OUT RIGHT UNDER THEIR LITTLE RED NOSES!

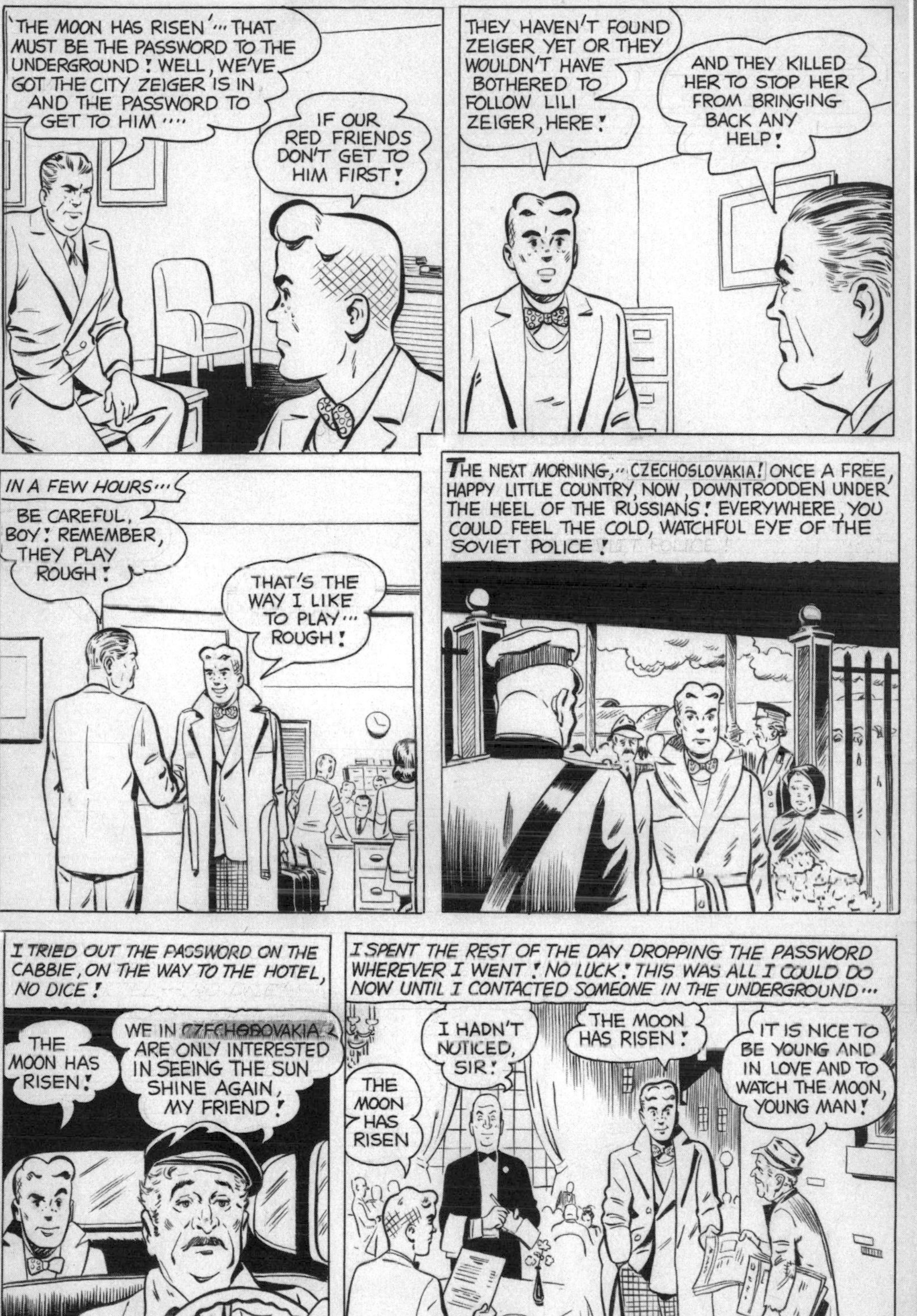

'THE MOON HAS RISEN'... THAT MUST BE THE PASSWORD TO THE UNDERGROUND! WELL, WE'VE GOT THE CITY ZEIGER IS IN AND THE PASSWORD TO GET TO HIM....
IF OUR RED FRIENDS DON'T GET TO HIM FIRST!
THEY HAVEN'T FOUND ZEIGER YET OR THEY WOULDN'T HAVE BOTHERED TO FOLLOW LILI ZEIGER, HERE!
AND THEY KILLED HER TO STOP HER FROM BRINGING BACK ANY HELP!
IN A FEW HOURS...
BE CAREFUL, BOY! REMEMBER, THEY PLAY ROUGH!
THAT'S THE WAY I LIKE TO PLAY... ROUGH!
THE NEXT MORNING... CZECHOSLOVAKIA! ONCE A FREE, HAPPY LITTLE COUNTRY, NOW, DOWNTRODDEN UNDER THE HEEL OF THE RUSSIANS! EVERYWHERE, YOU COULD FEEL THE COLD, WATCHFUL EYE OF THE SOVIET POLICE!
I TRIED OUT THE PASSWORD ON THE CABBIE, ON THE WAY TO THE HOTEL, NO DICE!
THE MOON HAS RISEN!
WE IN CZECHOSLOVAKIA ARE ONLY INTERESTED IN SEEING THE SUN SHINE AGAIN, MY FRIEND!
I SPENT THE REST OF THE DAY DROPPING THE PASSWORD WHEREVER I WENT! NO LUCK! THIS WAS ALL I COULD DO NOW UNTIL I CONTACTED SOMEONE IN THE UNDERGROUND...
THE MOON HAS RISEN
I HADN'T NOTICED, SIR!
THE MOON HAS RISEN!
IT IS NICE TO BE YOUNG AND IN LOVE AND TO WATCH THE MOON, YOUNG MAN!

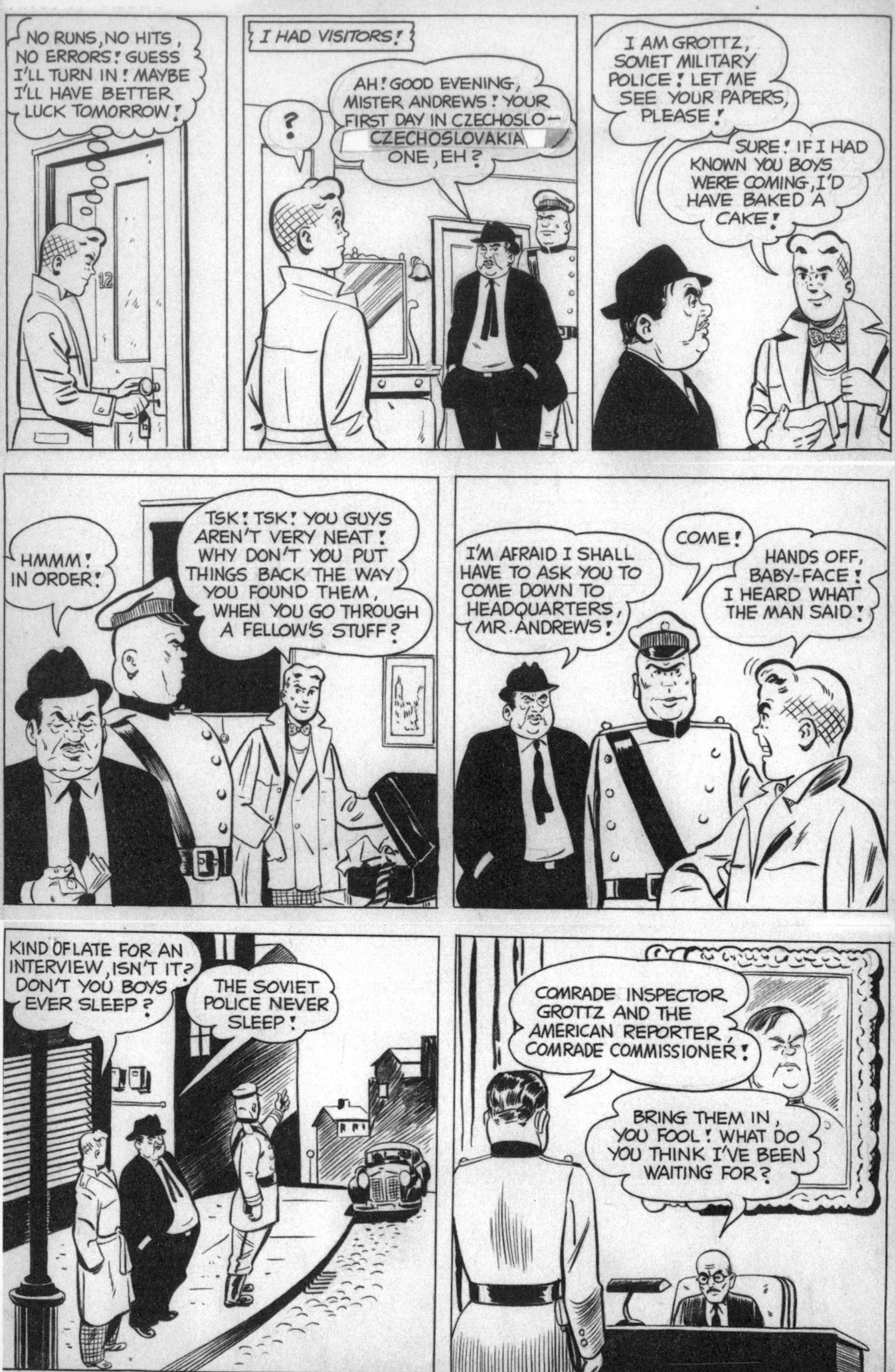
NO RUNS, NO HITS, NO ERRORS! GUESS I'LL TURN IN! MAYBE I'LL HAVE BETTER LUCK TOMORROW!
I HAD VISITORS!
?
AH! GOOD EVENING, MISTER ANDREWS! YOUR FIRST DAY IN CZECHOSLO- CZECHOSLOVAKIA ONE, EH?
I AM GROTTZ, SOVIET MILITARY POLICE! LET ME SEE YOUR PAPERS, PLEASE!
SURE! IF I HAD KNOWN YOU BOYS WERE COMING, I'D HAVE BAKED A CAKE!
HMMM! IN ORDER!
TSK! TSK! YOU GUYS AREN'T VERY NEAT! WHY DON'T YOU PUT THINGS BACK THE WAY YOU FOUND THEM, WHEN YOU GO THROUGH A FELLOW'S STUFF?
I'M AFRAID I SHALL HAVE TO ASK YOU TO COME DOWN TO HEADQUARTERS, MR. ANDREWS!
COME!
HANDS OFF, BABY-FACE! I HEARD WHAT THE MAN SAID!
KIND OF LATE FOR AN INTERVIEW, ISN'T IT? DON'T YOU BOYS EVER SLEEP?
THE SOVIET POLICE NEVER SLEEP!
COMRADE INSPECTOR GROTTZ AND THE AMERICAN REPORTER, COMRADE COMMISSIONER!
BRING THEM IN, YOU FOOL! WHAT DO YOU THINK I'VE BEEN WAITING FOR?

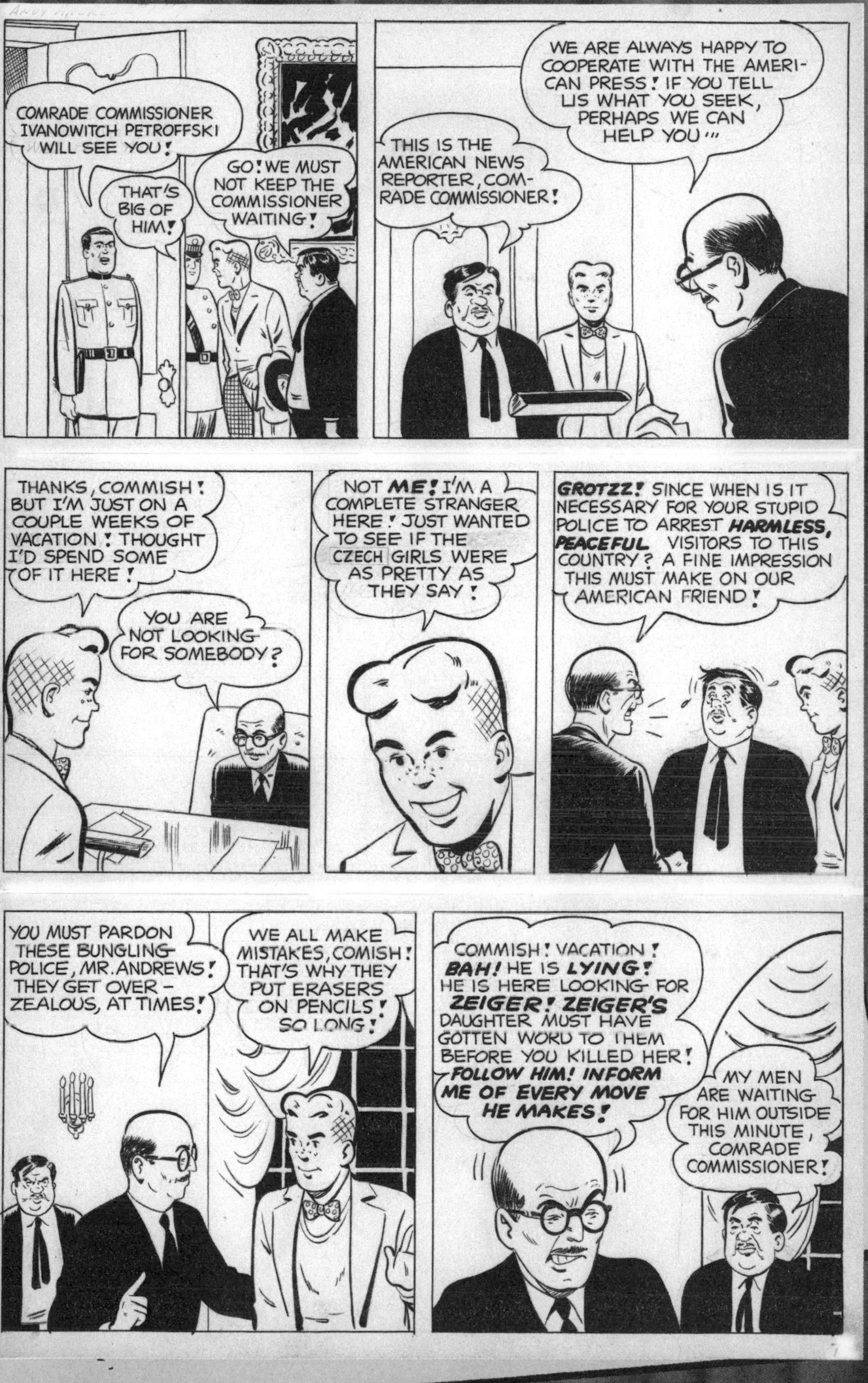

COMRADE COMMISSIONER IVANOWITCH PETROFFSKI WILL SEE YOU!
THAT'S BIG OF HIM!
GO! WE MUST NOT KEEP THE COMMISSIONER WAITING!
THIS IS THE AMERICAN NEWS REPORTER, COMRADE COMMISSIONER!
WE ARE ALWAYS HAPPY TO COOPERATE WITH THE AMERICAN PRESS! IF YOU TELL US WHAT YOU SEEK, PERHAPS WE CAN HELP YOU...
THANKS, COMMISH! BUT I'M JUST ON A COUPLE WEEKS OF VACATION! THOUGHT I'D SPEND SOME OF IT HERE!
YOU ARE NOT LOOKING FOR SOMEBODY?
NOT ME! I'M A COMPLETE STRANGER HERE! JUST WANTED TO SEE IF THE CZECH GIRLS WERE AS PRETTY AS THEY SAY!
GROTZZ! SINCE WHEN IS IT NECESSARY FOR YOUR STUPID POLICE TO ARREST HARMLESS, PEACEFUL VISITORS TO THIS COUNTRY? A FINE IMPRESSION THIS MUST MAKE ON OUR AMERICAN FRIEND!
YOU MUST PARDON THESE BUNGLING POLICE, MR. ANDREWS! THEY GET OVER-ZEALOUS, AT TIMES!
WE ALL MAKE MISTAKES, COMISH! THAT'S WHY THEY PUT ERASERS ON PENCILS! SO LONG!
COMMISH! VACATION! BAH! HE IS LYING! HE IS HERE LOOKING FOR ZEIGER! ZEIGER'S DAUGHTER MUST HAVE GOTTEN WORD TO THEM BEFORE YOU KILLED HER! FOLLOW HIM! INFORM ME OF EVERY MOVE HE MAKES!
MY MEN ARE WAITING FOR HIM OUTSIDE THIS MINUTE, COMRADE COMMISSIONER!

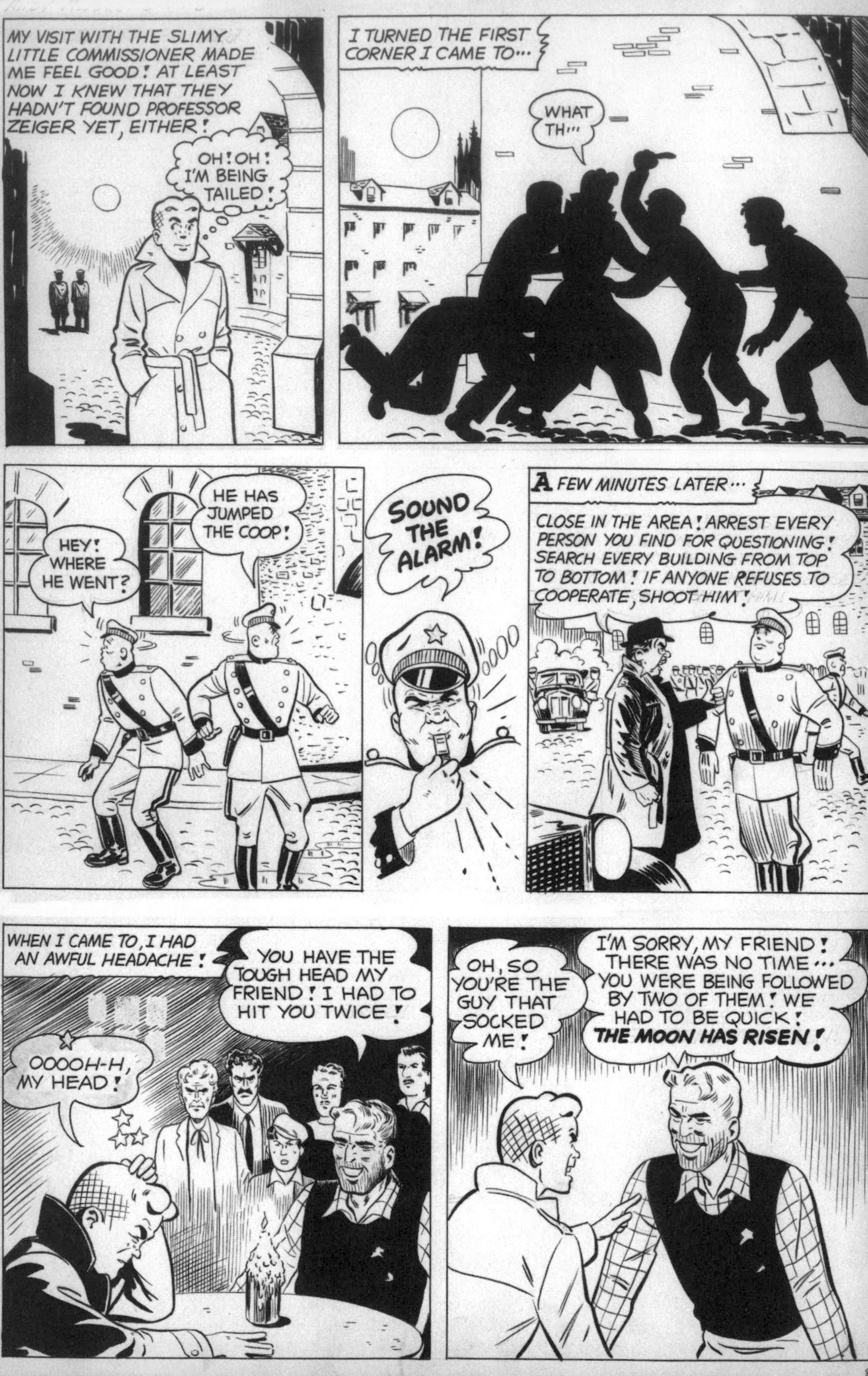
MY VISIT WITH THE SLIMY LITTLE COMMISSIONER MADE ME FEEL GOOD! AT LEAST NOW I KNEW THAT THEY HADN'T FOUND PROFESSOR ZEIGER YET, EITHER!
OH! OH! I'M BEING TAILED!
I TURNED THE FIRST CORNER I CAME TO...
WHAT TH...
HEY! WHERE HE WENT?
HE HAS JUMPED THE COOP!
SOUND THE ALARM!
A FEW MINUTES LATER...
CLOSE IN THE AREA! ARREST EVERY PERSON YOU FIND FOR QUESTIONING! SEARCH EVERY BUILDING FROM TOP TO BOTTOM! IF ANYONE REFUSES TO COOPERATE, SHOOT HIM!
WHEN I CAME TO, I HAD AN AWFUL HEADACHE!
YOU HAVE THE TOUGH HEAD MY FRIEND! I HAD TO HIT YOU TWICE!
OOOOH-H, MY HEAD!
OH, SO YOU'RE THE GUY THAT SOCKED ME!
I'M SORRY, MY FRIEND! THERE WAS NO TIME... YOU WERE BEING FOLLOWED BY TWO OF THEM! WE HAD TO BE QUICK! THE MOON HAS RISEN!

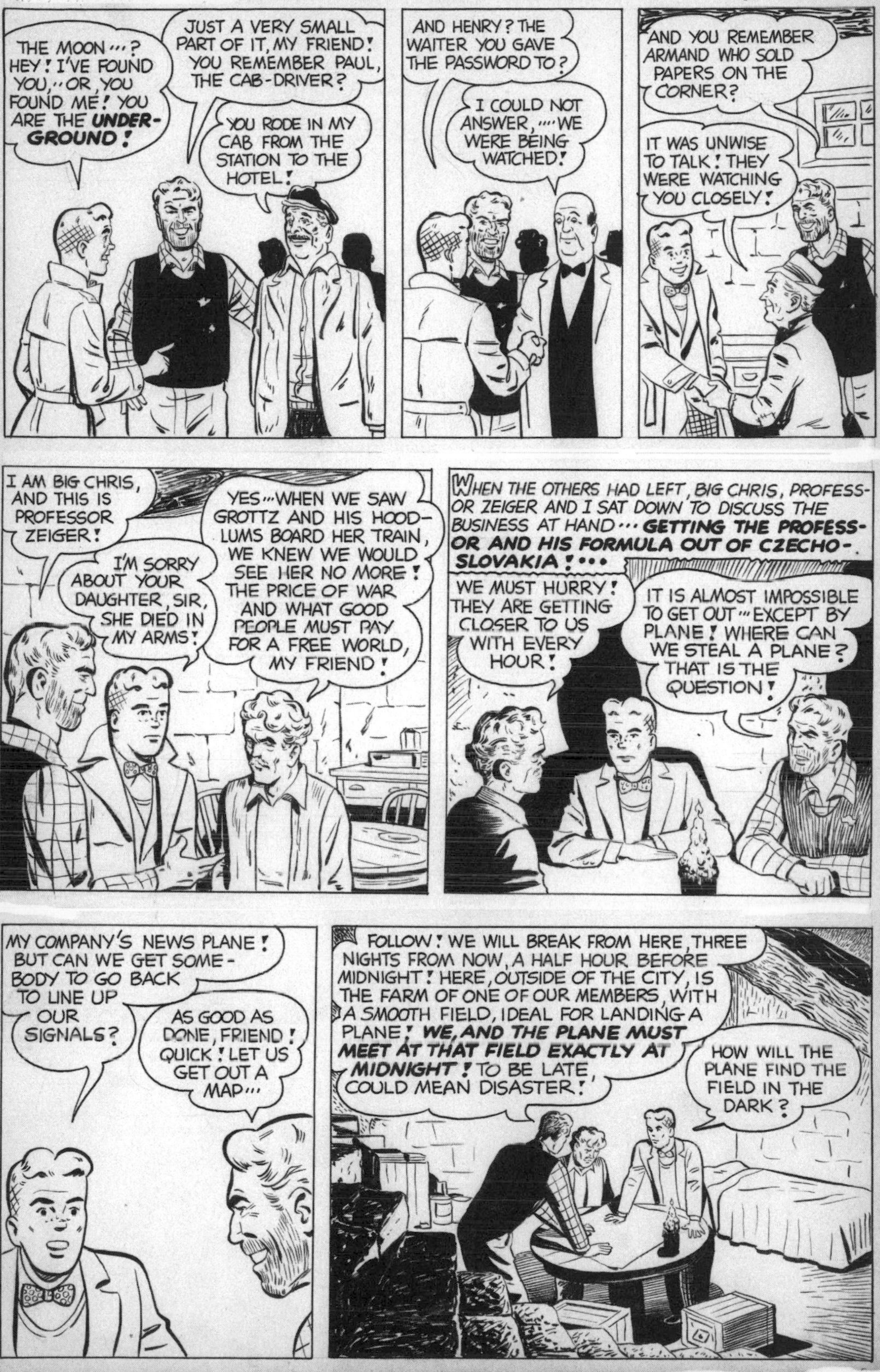
THE MOON ... ? HEY! I'VE FOUND YOU, .. OR, YOU FOUND ME! YOU ARE THE **UNDERGROUND**!
JUST A VERY SMALL PART OF IT, MY FRIEND! YOU REMEMBER PAUL, THE CAB-DRIVER?
YOU RODE IN MY CAB FROM THE STATION TO THE HOTEL!
AND HENRY? THE WAITER YOU GAVE THE PASSWORD TO?
I COULD NOT ANSWER, ... WE WERE BEING WATCHED!
AND YOU REMEMBER ARMAND WHO SOLD PAPERS ON THE CORNER?
IT WAS UNWISE TO TALK! THEY WERE WATCHING YOU CLOSELY!
I AM BIG CHRIS, AND THIS IS PROFESSOR ZEIGER!
I'M SORRY ABOUT YOUR DAUGHTER, SIR, SHE DIED IN MY ARMS!
YES ... WHEN WE SAW GROTTZ AND HIS HOODLUMS BOARD HER TRAIN, WE KNEW WE WOULD SEE HER NO MORE! THE PRICE OF WAR AND WHAT GOOD PEOPLE MUST PAY FOR A FREE WORLD, MY FRIEND!
WHEN THE OTHERS HAD LEFT, BIG CHRIS, PROFESSOR ZEIGER AND I SAT DOWN TO DISCUSS THE BUSINESS AT HAND ... **GETTING THE PROFESSOR AND HIS FORMULA OUT OF CZECHOSLOVAKIA! ...**
WE MUST HURRY! THEY ARE GETTING CLOSER TO US WITH EVERY HOUR!
IT IS ALMOST IMPOSSIBLE TO GET OUT ... EXCEPT BY PLANE! WHERE CAN WE STEAL A PLANE? THAT IS THE QUESTION!
MY COMPANY'S NEWS PLANE! BUT CAN WE GET SOMEBODY TO GO BACK TO LINE UP OUR SIGNALS?
AS GOOD AS DONE, FRIEND! QUICK! LET US GET OUT A MAP ...
FOLLOW! WE WILL BREAK FROM HERE, THREE NIGHTS FROM NOW, A HALF HOUR BEFORE MIDNIGHT! HERE, OUTSIDE OF THE CITY, IS THE FARM OF ONE OF OUR MEMBERS, WITH A SMOOTH FIELD, IDEAL FOR LANDING A PLANE! **WE, AND THE PLANE MUST MEET AT THAT FIELD EXACTLY AT MIDNIGHT!** TO BE LATE, COULD MEAN DISASTER!
HOW WILL THE PLANE FIND THE FIELD IN THE DARK?

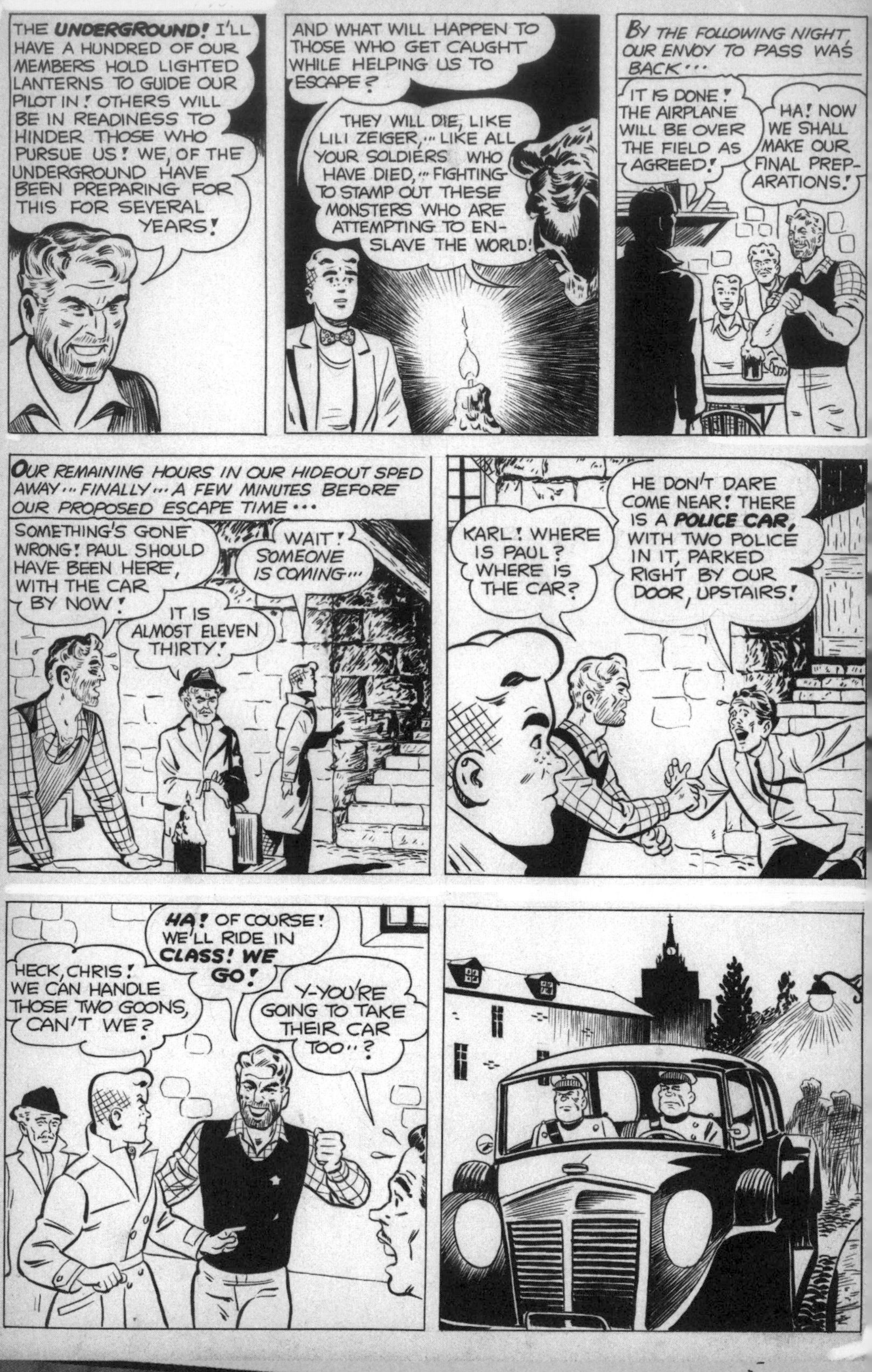
THE UNDERGROUND! I'LL HAVE A HUNDRED OF OUR MEMBERS HOLD LIGHTED LANTERNS TO GUIDE OUR PILOT IN! OTHERS WILL BE IN READINESS TO HINDER THOSE WHO PURSUE US! WE, OF THE UNDERGROUND HAVE BEEN PREPARING FOR THIS FOR SEVERAL YEARS!
AND WHAT WILL HAPPEN TO THOSE WHO GET CAUGHT WHILE HELPING US TO ESCAPE?
THEY WILL DIE, LIKE LILI ZEIGER,... LIKE ALL YOUR SOLDIERS WHO HAVE DIED,... FIGHTING TO STAMP OUT THESE MONSTERS WHO ARE ATTEMPTING TO EN-SLAVE THE WORLD!
BY THE FOLLOWING NIGHT, OUR ENVOY TO PASS WAS BACK...
IT IS DONE! THE AIRPLANE WILL BE OVER THE FIELD AS AGREED!
HA! NOW WE SHALL MAKE OUR FINAL PREP-ARATIONS!
OUR REMAINING HOURS IN OUR HIDEOUT SPED AWAY... FINALLY... A FEW MINUTES BEFORE OUR PROPOSED ESCAPE TIME...
SOMETHING'S GONE WRONG! PAUL SHOULD HAVE BEEN HERE, WITH THE CAR BY NOW!
IT IS ALMOST ELEVEN THIRTY!
WAIT! SOMEONE IS COMING...
KARL! WHERE IS PAUL? WHERE IS THE CAR?
HE DON'T DARE COME NEAR! THERE IS A POLICE CAR, WITH TWO POLICE IN IT, PARKED RIGHT BY OUR DOOR, UPSTAIRS!
HECK, CHRIS! WE CAN HANDLE THOSE TWO GOONS, CAN'T WE?
HA! OF COURSE! WE'LL RIDE IN CLASS! WE GO!
Y-YOU'RE GOING TO TAKE THEIR CAR TOO..?

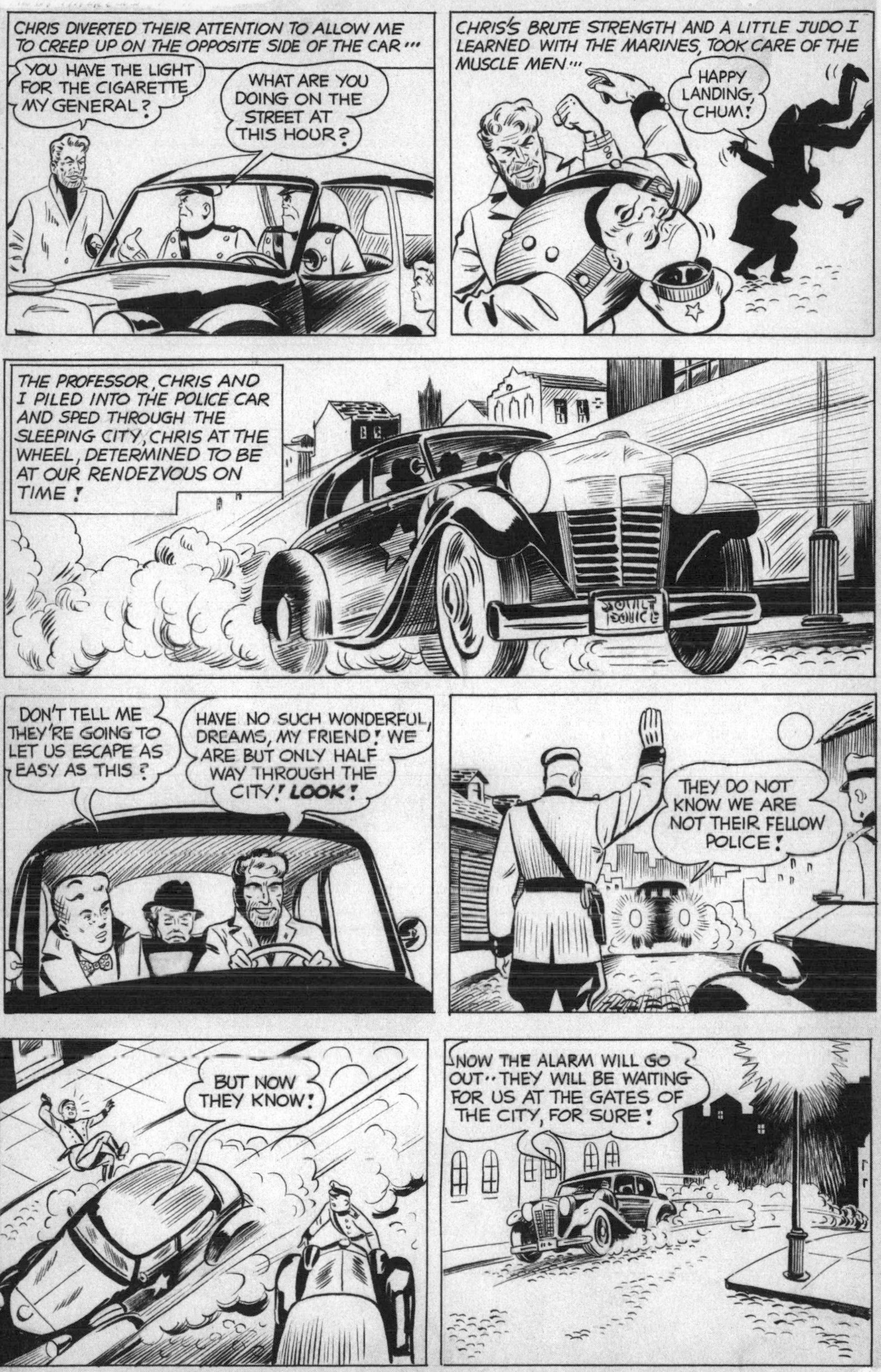
CHRIS DIVERTED THEIR ATTENTION TO ALLOW ME TO CREEP UP ON THE OPPOSITE SIDE OF THE CAR...
YOU HAVE THE LIGHT FOR THE CIGARETTE MY GENERAL?
WHAT ARE YOU DOING ON THE STREET AT THIS HOUR?
CHRIS'S BRUTE STRENGTH AND A LITTLE JUDO I LEARNED WITH THE MARINES, TOOK CARE OF THE MUSCLE MEN...
HAPPY LANDING, CHUM!
THE PROFESSOR, CHRIS AND I PILED INTO THE POLICE CAR AND SPED THROUGH THE SLEEPING CITY, CHRIS AT THE WHEEL, DETERMINED TO BE AT OUR RENDEZVOUS ON TIME!
DON'T TELL ME THEY'RE GOING TO LET US ESCAPE AS EASY AS THIS?
HAVE NO SUCH WONDERFUL DREAMS, MY FRIEND! WE ARE BUT ONLY HALF WAY THROUGH THE CITY! LOOK!
THEY DO NOT KNOW WE ARE NOT THEIR FELLOW POLICE!
BUT NOW THEY KNOW!
NOW THE ALARM WILL GO OUT.. THEY WILL BE WAITING FOR US AT THE GATES OF THE CITY, FOR SURE!

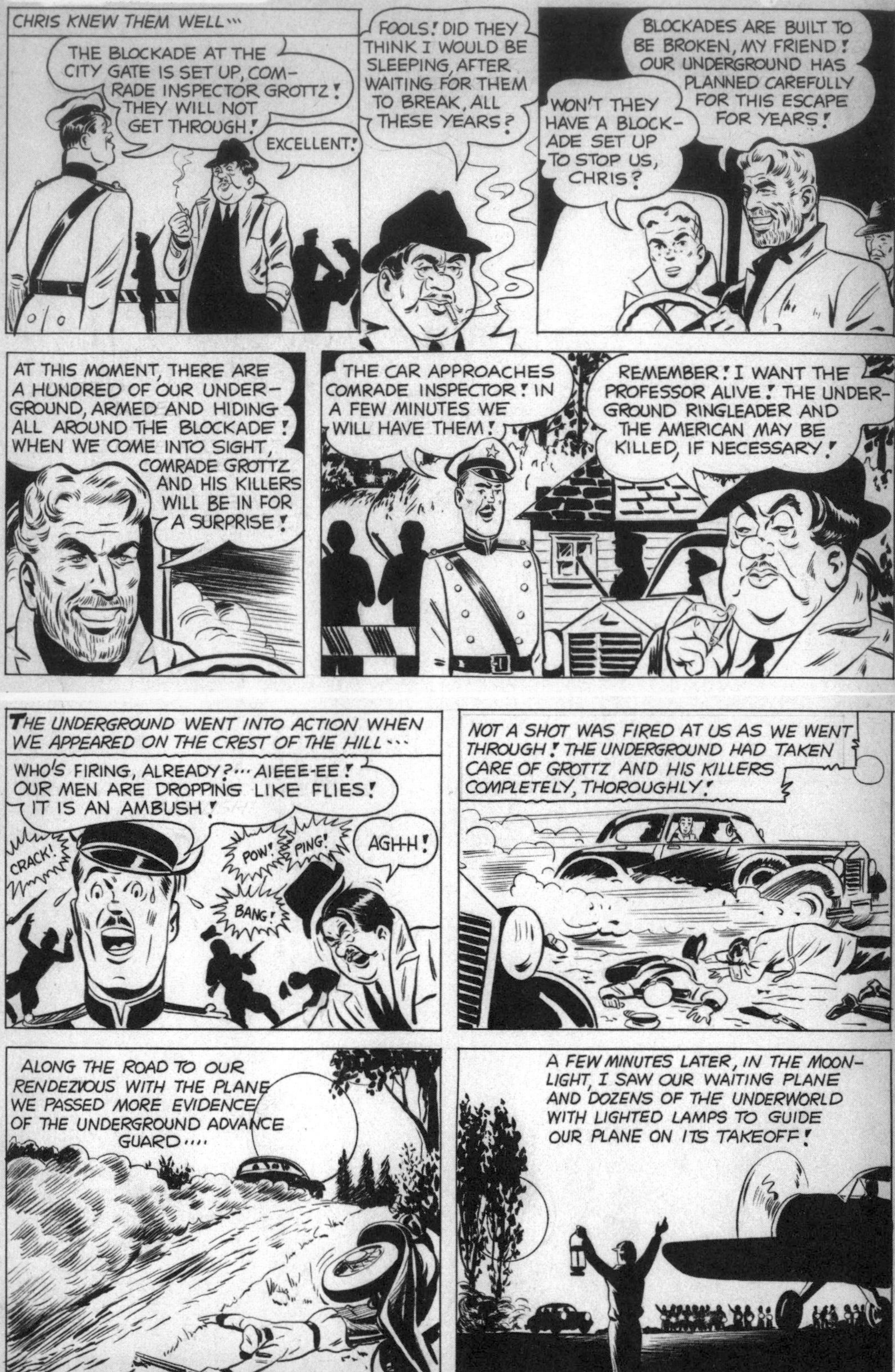

CHRIS KNEW THEM WELL...
THE BLOCKADE AT THE CITY GATE IS SET UP, COMRADE INSPECTOR GROTTZ! THEY WILL NOT GET THROUGH!
EXCELLENT!
FOOLS! DID THEY THINK I WOULD BE SLEEPING, AFTER WAITING FOR THEM TO BREAK, ALL THESE YEARS?
WON'T THEY HAVE A BLOCKADE SET UP TO STOP US, CHRIS?
BLOCKADES ARE BUILT TO BE BROKEN, MY FRIEND! OUR UNDERGROUND HAS PLANNED CAREFULLY FOR THIS ESCAPE FOR YEARS!
AT THIS MOMENT, THERE ARE A HUNDRED OF OUR UNDERGROUND, ARMED AND HIDING ALL AROUND THE BLOCKADE! WHEN WE COME INTO SIGHT, COMRADE GROTTZ AND HIS KILLERS WILL BE IN FOR A SURPRISE!
THE CAR APPROACHES COMRADE INSPECTOR! IN A FEW MINUTES WE WILL HAVE THEM!
REMEMBER! I WANT THE PROFESSOR ALIVE! THE UNDERGROUND RINGLEADER AND THE AMERICAN MAY BE KILLED, IF NECESSARY!
THE UNDERGROUND WENT INTO ACTION WHEN WE APPEARED ON THE CREST OF THE HILL...
WHO'S FIRING, ALREADY?... AIEEE-EE! OUR MEN ARE DROPPING LIKE FLIES! IT IS AN AMBUSH!
CRACK!
POW!
PING!
AGH-H!
BANG!
NOT A SHOT WAS FIRED AT US AS WE WENT THROUGH! THE UNDERGROUND HAD TAKEN CARE OF GROTTZ AND HIS KILLERS COMPLETELY, THOROUGHLY!
ALONG THE ROAD TO OUR RENDEZVOUS WITH THE PLANE WE PASSED MORE EVIDENCE OF THE UNDERGROUND ADVANCE GUARD....
A FEW MINUTES LATER, IN THE MOONLIGHT, I SAW OUR WAITING PLANE AND DOZENS OF THE UNDERWORLD WITH LIGHTED LAMPS TO GUIDE OUR PLANE ON ITS TAKEOFF!

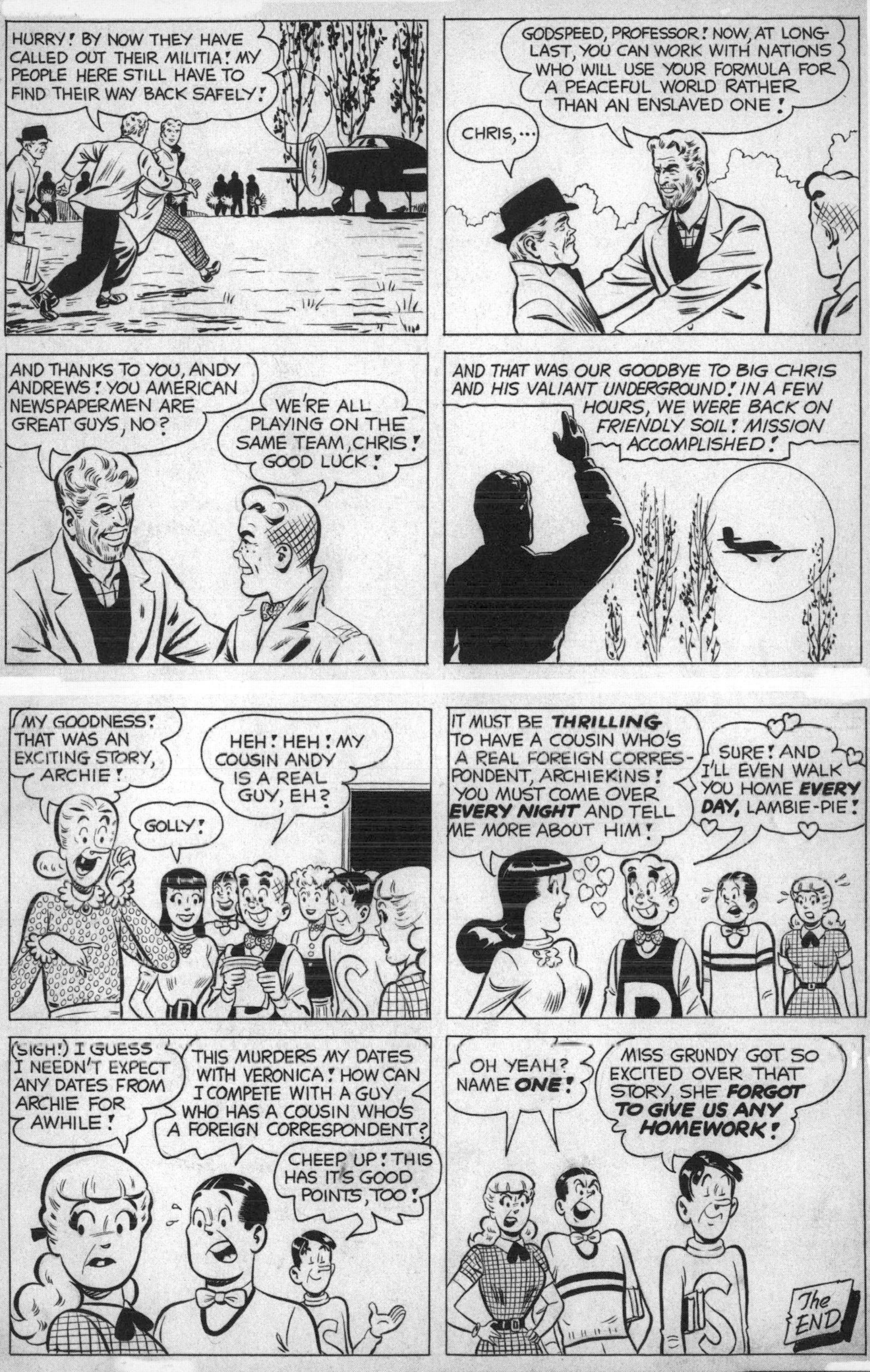
HURRY! BY NOW THEY HAVE CALLED OUT THEIR MILITIA! MY PEOPLE HERE STILL HAVE TO FIND THEIR WAY BACK SAFELY!
GODSPEED, PROFESSOR! NOW, AT LONG-LAST, YOU CAN WORK WITH NATIONS WHO WILL USE YOUR FORMULA FOR A PEACEFUL WORLD RATHER THAN AN ENSLAVED ONE!
CHRIS, ...
AND THANKS TO YOU, ANDY ANDREWS! YOU AMERICAN NEWSPAPERMEN ARE GREAT GUYS, NO?
WE'RE ALL PLAYING ON THE SAME TEAM, CHRIS! GOOD LUCK!
AND THAT WAS OUR GOODBYE TO BIG CHRIS AND HIS VALIANT UNDERGROUND! IN A FEW HOURS, WE WERE BACK ON FRIENDLY SOIL! MISSION ACCOMPLISHED!
MY GOODNESS! THAT WAS AN EXCITING STORY, ARCHIE!
HEH! HEH! MY COUSIN ANDY IS A REAL GUY, EH?
GOLLY!
IT MUST BE **THRILLING** TO HAVE A COUSIN WHO'S A REAL FOREIGN CORRESPONDENT, ARCHIEKINS! YOU MUST COME OVER **EVERY NIGHT** AND TELL ME MORE ABOUT HIM!
SURE! AND I'LL EVEN WALK YOU HOME **EVERY DAY**, LAMBIE-PIE!
(SIGH!) I GUESS I NEEDN'T EXPECT ANY DATES FROM ARCHIE FOR AWHILE!
THIS MURDERS MY DATES WITH VERONICA! HOW CAN I COMPETE WITH A GUY WHO HAS A COUSIN WHO'S A FOREIGN CORRESPONDENT?
CHEEP UP! THIS HAS IT'S GOOD POINTS, TOO!
OH YEAH? NAME **ONE**!
MISS GRUNDY GOT SO EXCITED OVER THAT STORY, SHE **FORGOT TO GIVE US ANY HOMEWORK**!
The END

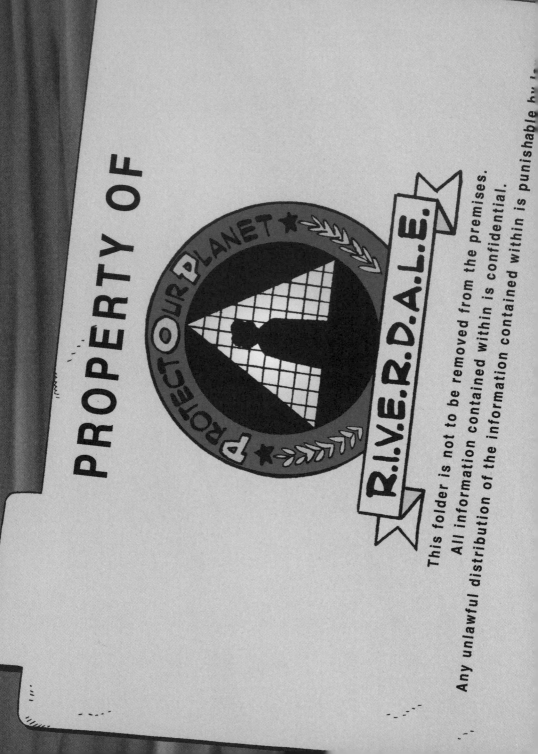

PROPERTY OF

PROTECT OUR PLANET

R.I.V.E.R.D.A.L.E.

This folder is not to be removed from the premises.
All information contained within is confidential.
Any unlawful distribution of the information contained within is punishable by law.

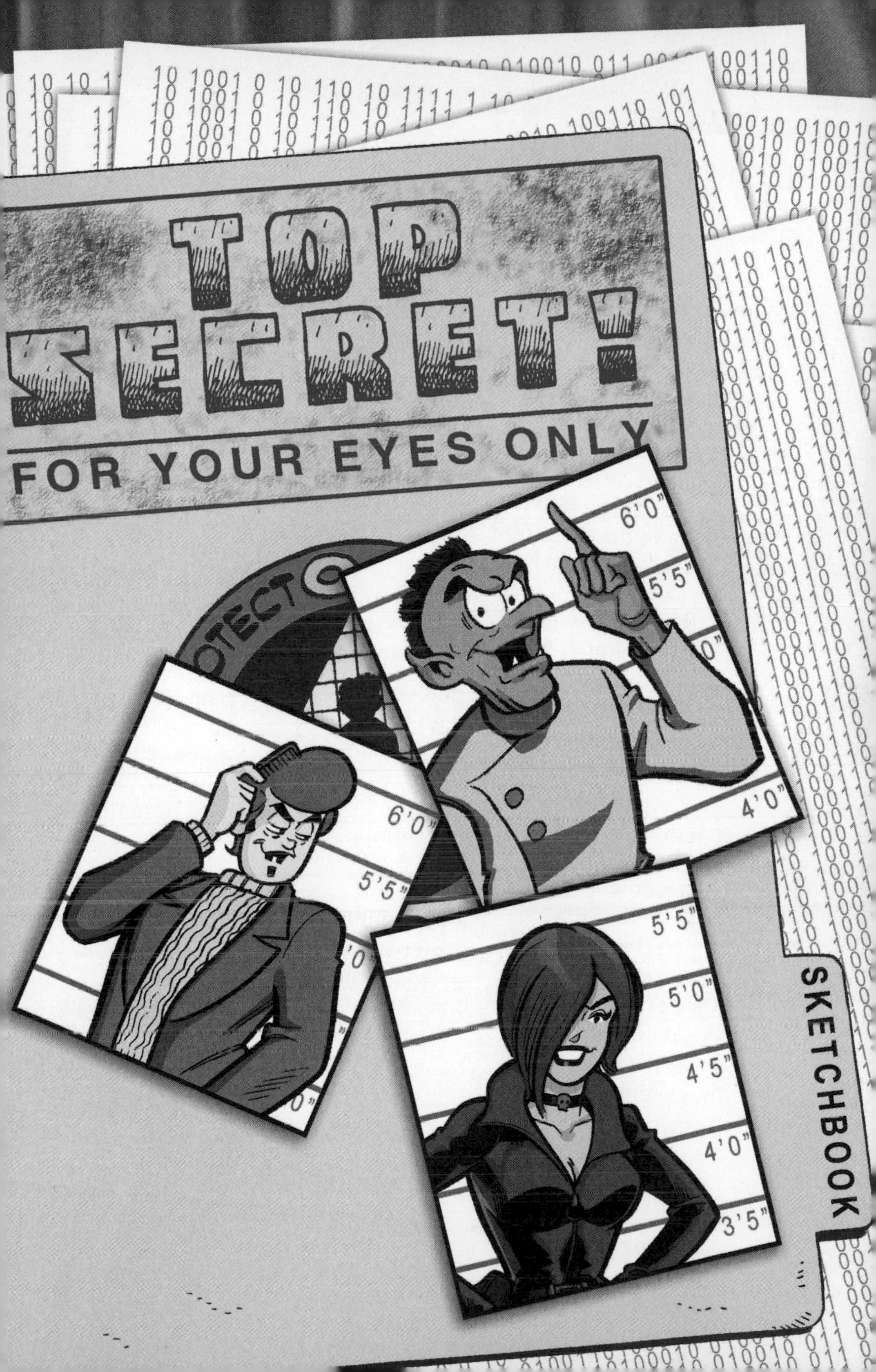
TOP SECRET!
FOR YOUR EYES ONLY
PROTECTO
6'0"
5'5"
4'0"
6'0"
5'5"
5'5"
5'0"
4'5"
4'0"
3'5"
SKETCHBOOK

TO: DIRECTOR OF P.O.P.
FROM: FERNANDO RUIZ
SUBJECT: PROJECT R.I.V.E.R.D.A.L.E.

Most of the time we see Archie, he's driving Mr. Weatherbee crazy at Riverdale High or hanging out at the Chok'lit Shoppe, sharing a soda with Betty & Veronica. Sometimes we find our freckled friend where we least expect him! Like duelling with dinosaurs in "Archie 1," evading extraterrestrials in the future as in "Archie 3000," or battling giant lobsters and teaming up with the Shield and the Mighty Crusaders in "Archie's Weird Mysteries." I never know what I'm going to be drawing next, so when editor-in-chief Victor Gorelick asked me to draw a brand new Man from R.I.V.E.R.D.A.L.E. story, I knew I was in for a treat!

I'd read Archie's early adventures as a super-spy when they first appeared in the original "Life With Archie" series. You had the fun humor of Archie with all the expected excitement, adventure, and vile villains of a great spy epic. Now I was going to draw Archie's NEW adventures as **The Man from R.I.V.E.R.D.A.L.E.** Best of all, I got the opportunity to work with one of my heroes, Tom DeFalco, who wrote a brilliant script that gave me a lot of room to go crazy. I got to draw Mad Doctor Doom, his lackey Chester, super spy Andy Andrews, and my new favorite character, Sharry the Spy Girl!

This was an exciting adventure story and I wanted the art to jump from the page. Archie wasn't just strolling down the halls of Riverdale High, he was running from the Walking Dazed, chasing enemy spies and fighting mad scientists. Over the next few pages, you'll get a look behind the scenes to see what went into making this very special story.

FERNANDO RUIZ

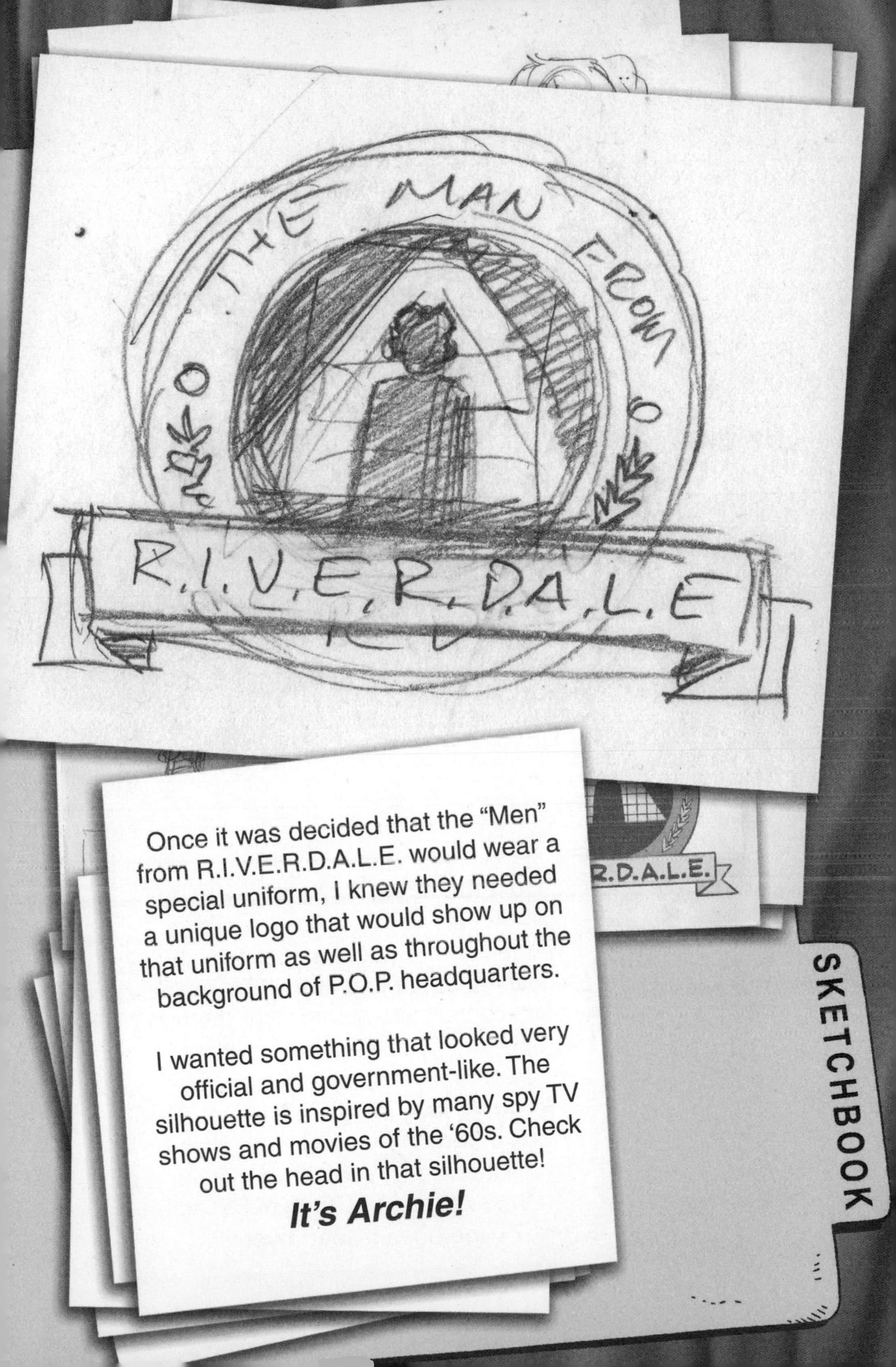
THE MAN FROM
R.I.V.E.R.D.A.L.E

Once it was decided that the "Men" from R.I.V.E.R.D.A.L.E. would wear a special uniform, I knew they needed a unique logo that would show up on that uniform as well as throughout the background of P.O.P. headquarters.

I wanted something that looked very official and government-like. The silhouette is inspired by many spy TV shows and movies of the '60s. Check out the head in that silhouette!

It's Archie!

SKETCHBOOK

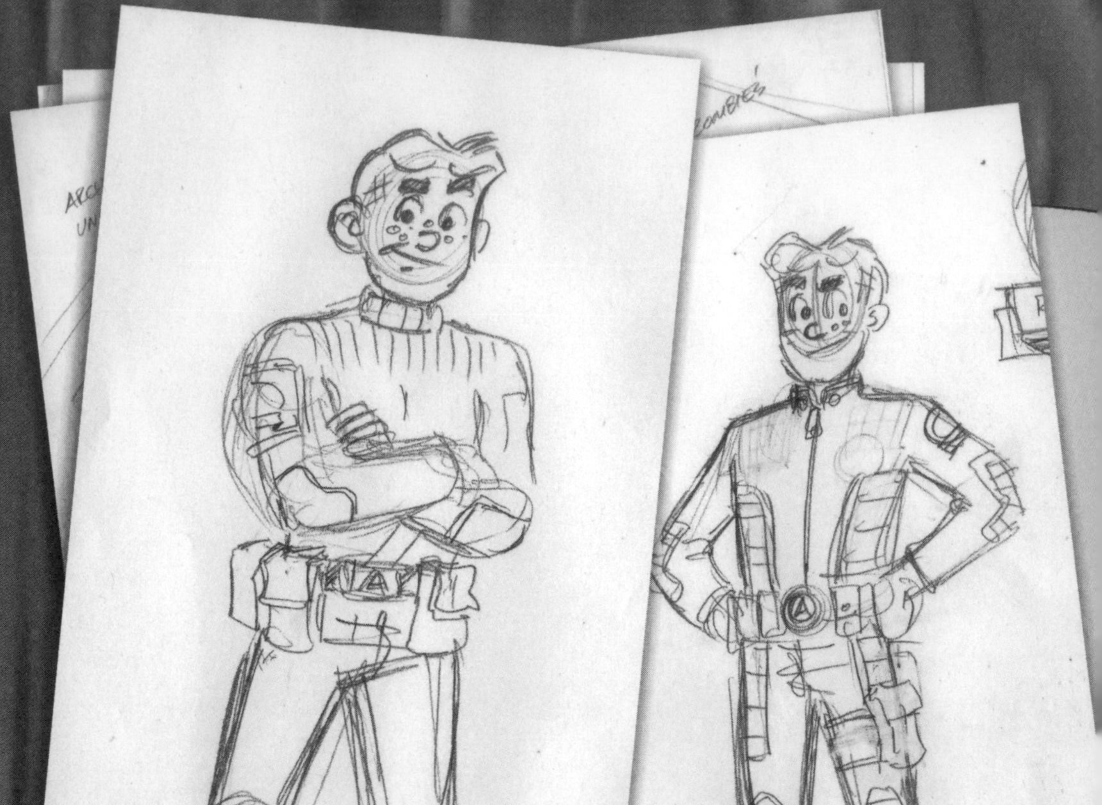

Here are a few very early sketches for the R.I.V.E.R.D.A.L.E. uniform. I wanted something that looked vaguely military but not so much that Archie would look like a soldier. In the first one, Archie is wearing a turtleneck sweater (eventually, this became Reggie's look in the final issue). The idea of the one-piece jumpsuit came later. Check out Archie's cool sneakers in the second one! They're based on the ones I wear myself!

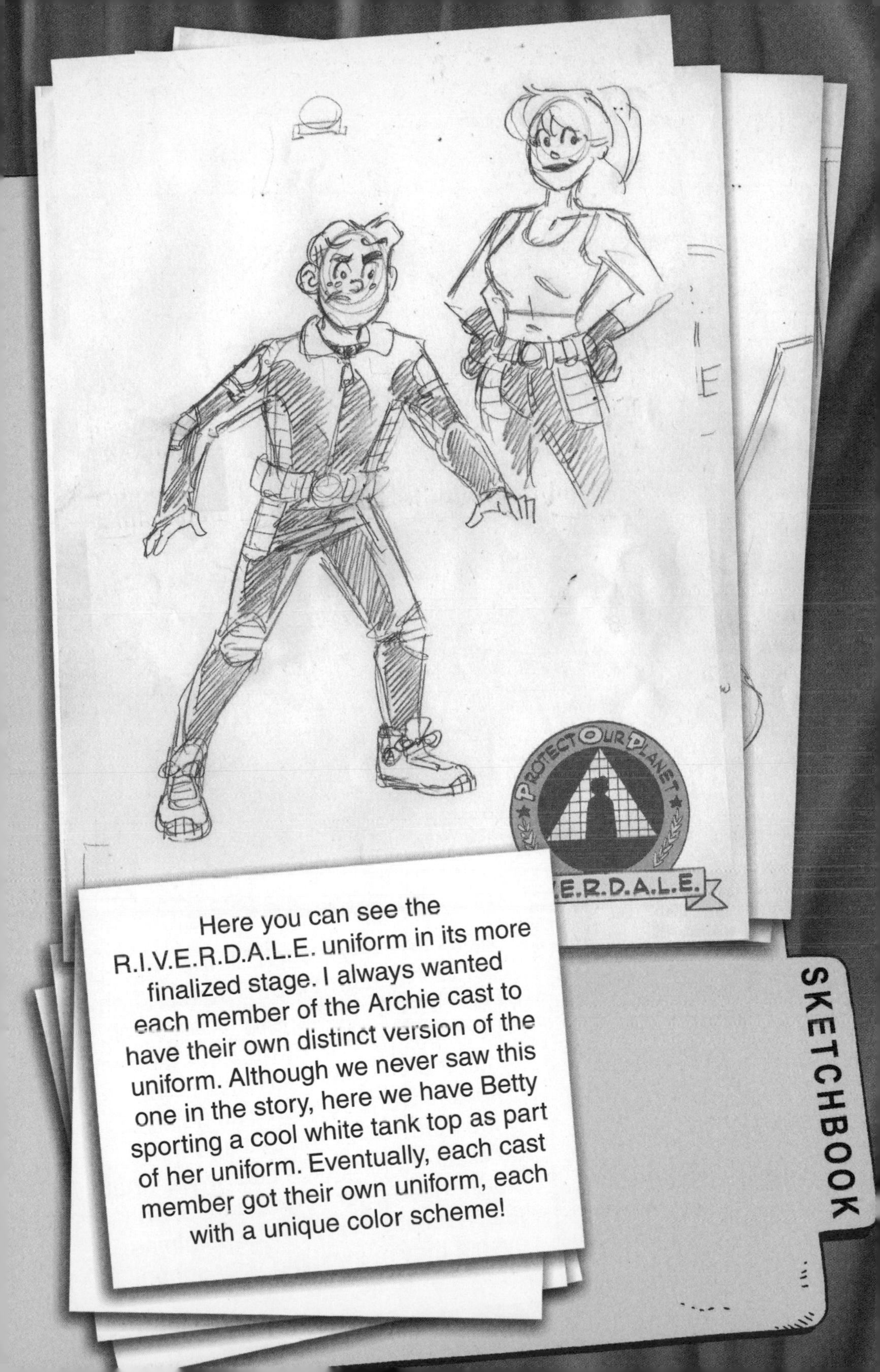
PROTECT OUR PLANET

Here you can see the R.I.V.E.R.D.A.L.E. uniform in its more finalized stage. I always wanted each member of the Archie cast to have their own distinct version of the uniform. Although we never saw this one in the story, here we have Betty sporting a cool white tank top as part of her uniform. Eventually, each cast member got their own uniform, each with a unique color scheme!

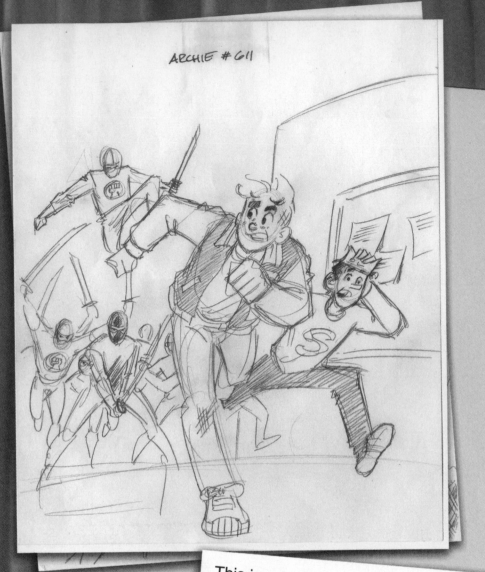

ARCHIE #611

This is an early sketch for the cover of Archie #611, part 2 of "The Man from R.I.V.E.R.D.A.L.E." Very often comic book covers are drawn even before the story is written. At this point, I knew Riverdale High was going to be stormed by the evil agents of C.R.U.S.H., but I didn't know yet what form those agents would take. So I said, "Ninjas! Everyone loves ninjas... even if they're invading your school!"

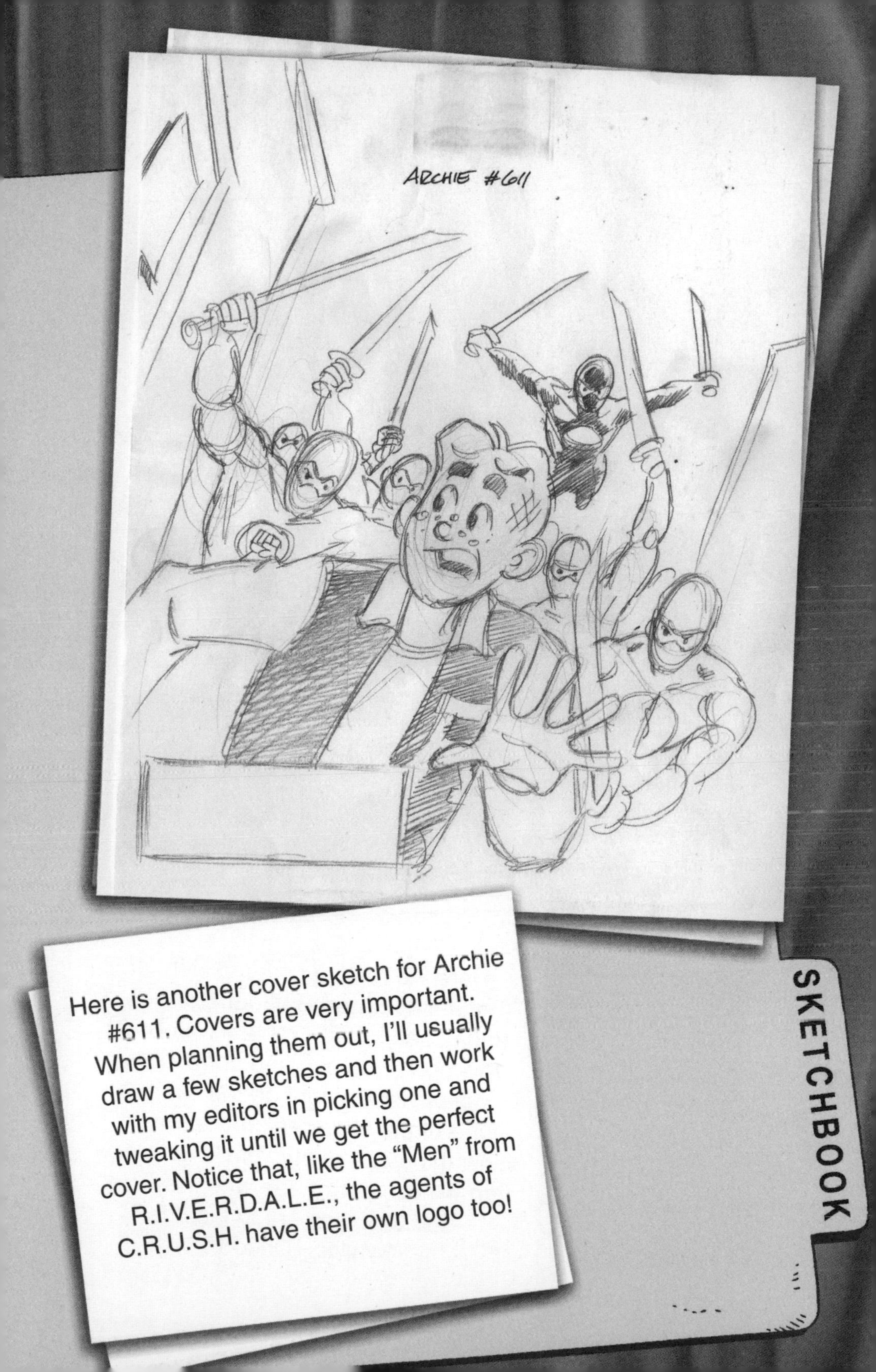
ARCHIE #611

Here is another cover sketch for Archie #611. Covers are very important. When planning them out, I'll usually draw a few sketches and then work with my editors in picking one and tweaking it until we get the perfect cover. Notice that, like the "Men" from R.I.V.E.R.D.A.L.E., the agents of C.R.U.S.H. have their own logo too!

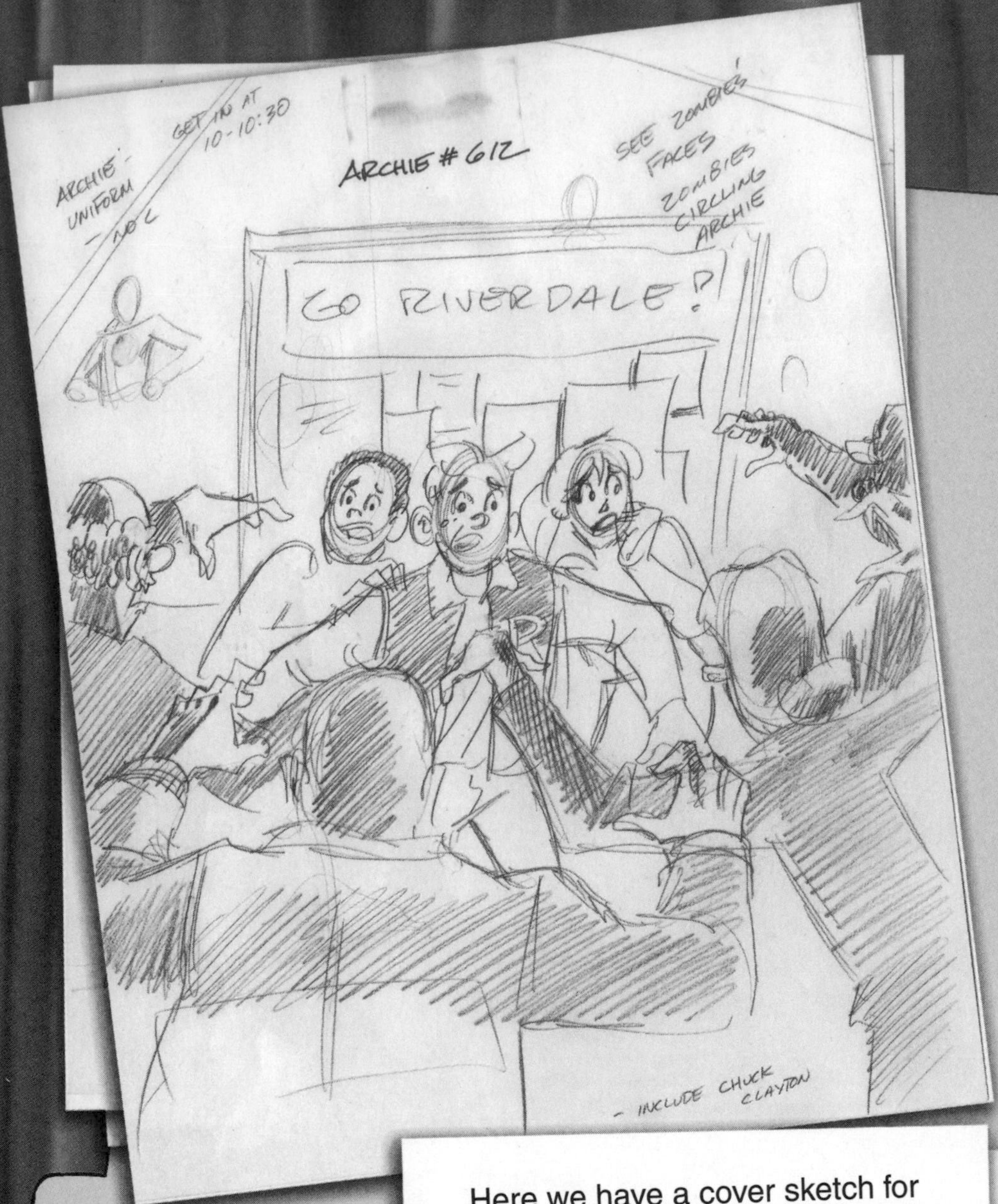
ARCHIE - UNIFORM - NO C
GET IN AT 10-10:30
ARCHIE # 612
SEE ZOMBIES' FACES
ZOMBIES CIRCLING ARCHIE
GO RIVERDALE!
- INCLUDE CHUCK CLAYTON

Here we have a cover sketch for Archie #612, part 3 of our story. I still hadn't settled on Archie's uniform at this point. You can see some of my notes written right on the sketch. One of the changes I made was to show the faces of our "Walking Dazed" so we can better see who they are and that they are in fact the "Walking Dazed"!

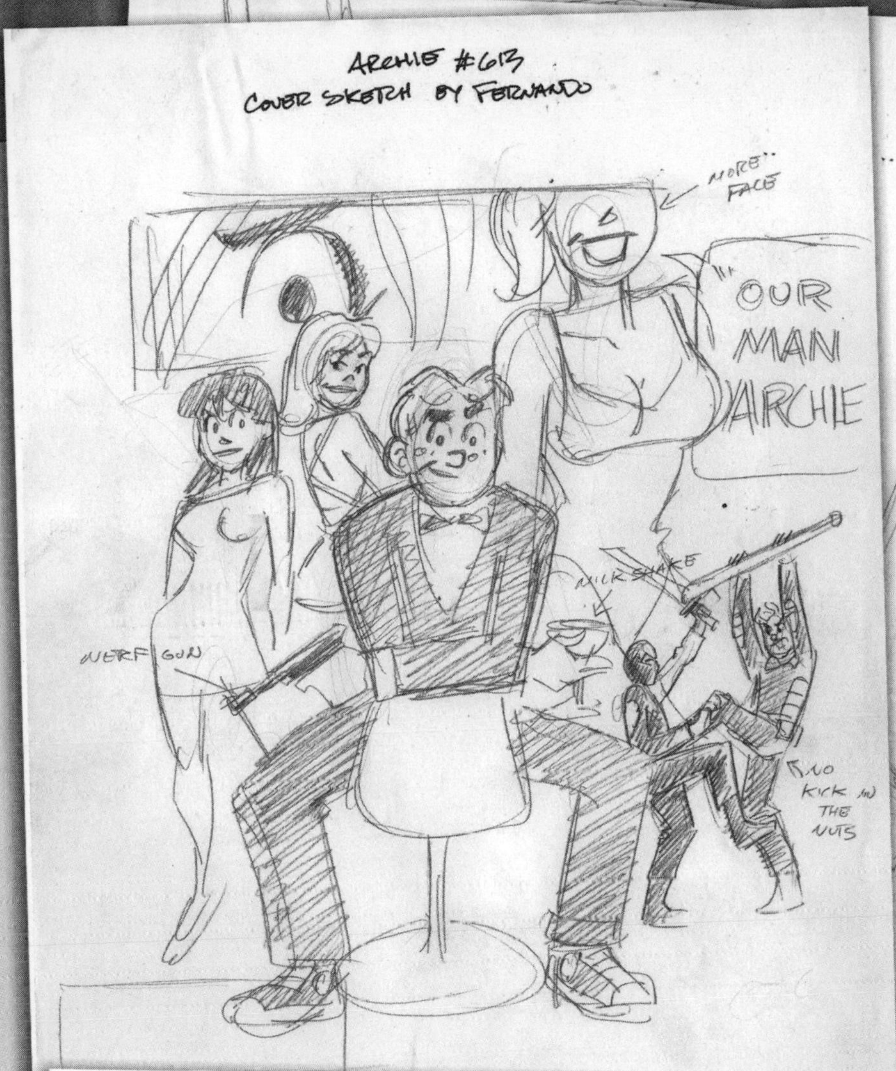
ARCHIE #613
COVER SKETCH BY FERNANDO
MORE FACE
"OUR MAN ARCHIE
MILK SHAKE
NERF GUN
NO KICK IN THE NUTS

This one was a fun idea! Suggested by Archie Project Coordinator Joe Morciglio, a fan of the 1960s spy film "Our Man Flint," this one was inspired by the poster for that classic movie. I drew it as a possible cover sketch but we never knew exactly where we were going to use it. This was one of my favorite sketches and I'm glad we got the chance to use it here.

SKETCHBOOK

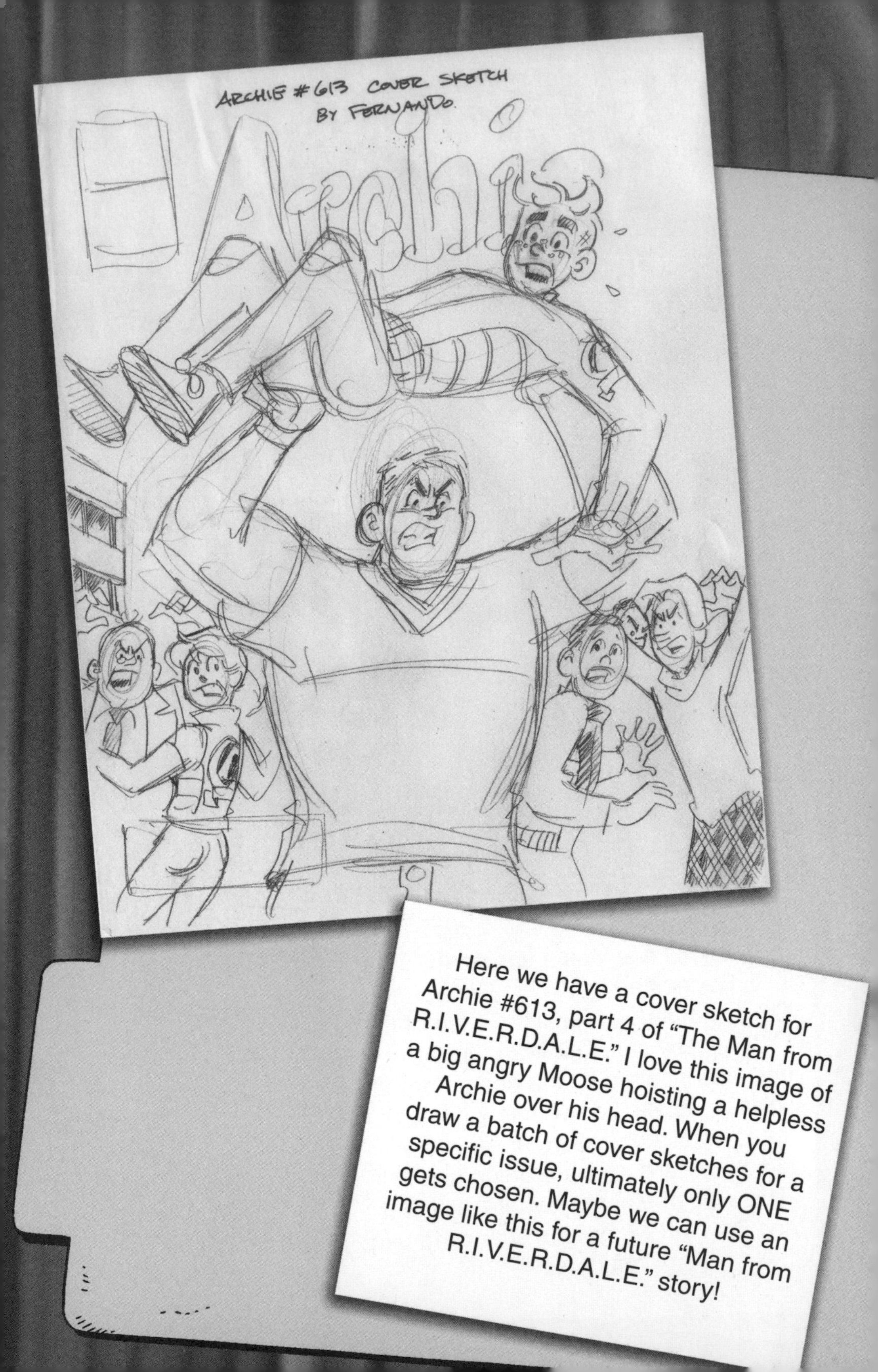
ARCHIE #613 COVER SKETCH
BY FERNANDO.

Here we have a cover sketch for Archie #613, part 4 of "The Man from R.I.V.E.R.D.A.L.E." I love this image of a big angry Moose hoisting a helpless Archie over his head. When you draw a batch of cover sketches for a specific issue, ultimately only ONE gets chosen. Maybe we can use an image like this for a future "Man from R.I.V.E.R.D.A.L.E." story!

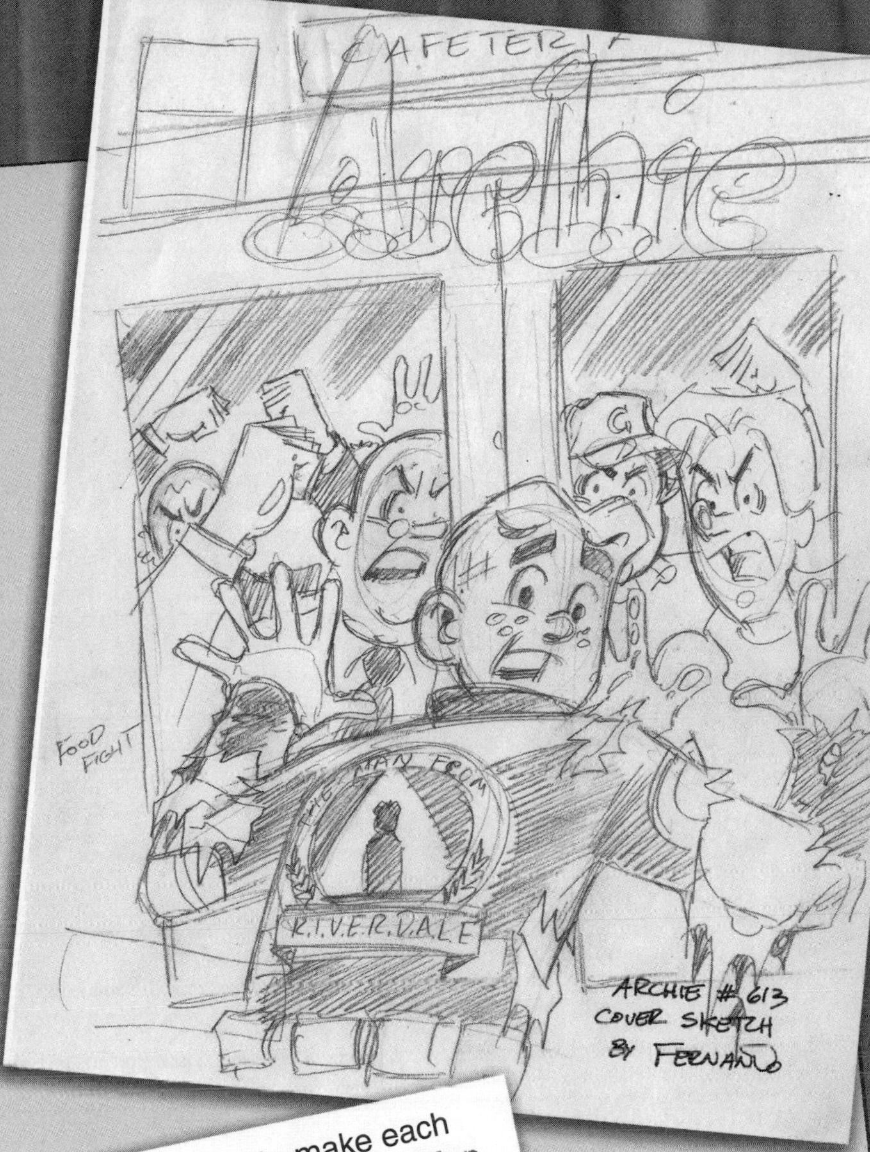
CAFETERIA
FOOD FIGHT
THE MAN FROM
R.I.V.E.R.D.A.L.E
ARCHIE #613
COVER SKETCH
BY FERNANDO

We tried very hard to make each cover for the four issues of our "Man from R.I.V.E.R.D.A.L.E." story very distinct from one another. This sketch, another one for Archie #613, came close, but ultimately it was too similar to the cover we'd chosen for Archie #612. We went instead with the big image of Archie and a pair of Walking Dazed hands crashing through a door towards him!

SKETCHBOOK